SLICE

Mrs. Whitman walked into the kindergarten classroom and tidied up the desks. She erased the letter *D* from the blackboard, written in pink chalk in both capital and small formations. She was about to gather up her books from her desk when she heard the sound of the door opening. She looked around.

"Yes?" she asked the new arrival. "May I help you?"

When she didn't get an answer right away, she asked, just the slightest trace of concern in her voice, "How did you get into the school?"

They were the last coherent words Theresa Whitman ever said.

Suddenly she felt a sharp pain in her abdomen. She looked down to see the long metal blade that had just sliced into her flesh. She watched, in a kind of gauzy, slow-motion awareness, as the blood began to stain her white blouse after the blade was withdrawn.

Mrs. Whitman's knees crumpled and she fell to the floor.

Her eyes looked up into the face of her killer as the razor blade swung down again across her neck. Theresa Whitman tried to scream, but her throat was filled with blood. . . .

SLICE

WILLIAM PATTERSON

PINNACLE BOOKS
Kensington Publishing Corp.
www.kensingtonbooks.com

PINNACLE BOOKS are published by

Kensington Publishing Corp.
119 West 40th Street
New York, NY 10018

All Kensington titles, imprints, and distributed lines are available at special quantity discounts for bulk purchases for sales promotions, premiums, fund-raising, educational, or institutional use.

Special book excerpts or customized printings can also be created to fit specific needs. For details, write or phone the office of the Kensington special sales manager: Kensington Publishing Corp., 119 West 40th Street, New York, NY 10018, attn: Special Sales Department; phone 1-800-221-2647.

ISBN-13: 978-0-7860-2764-4
ISBN-10: 0-7860-2764-9

First printing: March 2013

10 9 8 7 6 5 4 3 2 1

Printed in the United States of America

PROLOGUE

Carrying her infant daughter up the stairs of her new apartment building, Jessie Clarkson tried not to think about the other baby, the one she had wished away, the one who had ended up in a puddle of blood.

Keep your mind on the present, she counseled herself. *You are starting a whole new life.*

Her nose crinkled against the smell of cabbage boiling on someone's stove in an apartment down the hall.

"Okay, so it's not the Taj Mahal," Monica was saying as she unlocked the door to Jessie's new home. "But I think you'll be comfortable here."

Jessie stepped inside. The place was small, painted a dull, flat beige throughout. It consisted of a kitchen that opened onto a tiny living room that overlooked an alley, and past that, a windowless bedroom. Jessie couldn't suppress a small smile. After all that had happened to her, this was where she had ended up. A tiny box, four flights up, in Manhattan's East Village. Comfortable she might not be. But safe—she'd be safe here.

And that was all that mattered.

"It's clean," Jessie said, looking around.

She was glad of that, and grateful that the apartment

came furnished, with a serviceable couch and a plain square table with four chairs. It had been Monica who'd found the apartment, renting it in her own name so that Jessie could live here with Abby in secret and no one would be able to find them. That's all that was really important—not the size of the place, or its furniture or even its cleanliness. All that Jessie really cared about was that no one would know where she and Abby were.

"And here," Monica was saying, "is a little house-warming present for you. I had it sent up this morning."

A crib made of light wood stood in front of the two windows that looked down on Second Avenue, adorned with a big red bow.

"Thank you, Monica," Jessie said. "For everything."

She and her sister had never really been friends. Not since Monica had stolen Todd from her in high school. After that, they'd seemed always to be on opposite sides of things, especially when Mom died. And Monica had been very judgmental when Jessie found herself in all the trouble. But that was all ancient history now. Monica had come through for her, and found her this place to live. Jessie was truly grateful.

"No need for thanks," Monica was saying, a small smile tightening her face. "That's what sisters are for, isn't it?"

Jessie lay Abby down in the crib. She was such a good baby. Hardly ever cried. Abby just cooed as Jessie laid her down, her tiny blue button eyes popping open briefly to look up at her mother. Jessie smiled.

She was grateful every day that Abby looked like her side of the family.

"I had the fridge stocked with food to get you started," Monica said, her voice as efficient and direct as always. "But there's a market right downstairs if you need anything else. Would you want me to make a run now?"

"I'll be fine," Jessie told her.

Monica gave her the small, tight smile again. "And you know Todd and I are less than an hour away. Well, except at rush hour."

"I'll be fine," Jessie repeated. She glanced down at her sleeping daughter. "I should say, *we'll* be fine."

Monica didn't look into the crib. "I'm sorry that I have to run, but I have to get back—"

"Of course," Jessie said. She knew her sister had work to do, that Monica, unlike Jessie, had a job, and responsibilities. "You should get back to Sayer's Brook before the rush-hour traffic. I'm fine here. I'll unpack and settle in."

Her bags had been brought up earlier. Jessie didn't have much. Unpacking wouldn't take very long.

"All right then," Monica said, looking over her shoulder as she headed toward the door. "I think you're all set here."

"I am," Jessie assured her.

Jessie wanted to embrace her sister for all she'd done, but Monica moved quickly to the door. It was probably just as well. They'd never been all that affectionate a family. A hug now would feel awkward. Jessie suppressed the urge, and just thanked her sister again for probably the hundredth time. Monica waved her hand at her, and then was off, down the stairs and out onto the street, where her car was double parked.

Jessie glanced out the window, but she couldn't see the street. Just a Dumpster and the windows of the building next door. She let out a long sigh.

Now she and Abby were really alone.

Alone in a city of more than eight million.

That's why she had decided to live in the city. The little Connecticut hometown of Sayer's Brook where she and Monica had grown up would never do anymore, not now, not with everyone knowing her business. Here in Manhattan she could be anonymous, just one more face among countless others, just one more young woman with a baby in her arms. In the throngs of people that passed through the streets of New York, Jessie could blend in, drop out, disappear, become lost to those who would find her.

And there was one person who wanted very much to find her.

A shudder rippled through Jessie's thin body.

After taking a deep breath and checking that Abby was still asleep, she headed into the bedroom and snapped open the first of her suitcases. Methodically, she removed blouses and socks and panty hose, carefully placing them in the drawers of her new bureau. The place was small enough that she could easily hear Abby if she woke up. Still, Jessie kept peeking around the corner of the bedroom to glance back in at her daughter, still sound asleep in her crib.

She hoped eventually she wouldn't be so jittery. But she supposed it would take a while. It wasn't easy, her doctors and therapists had told her, to live with a memory as horrible as the one Jessie carried with her.

A memory of pain, and violation, and betrayal.

Jessie had loved Emil. At least, she had thought she

had. He had provided fun and escape after her breakup from Bryan. Yet another man she had loved who had been stolen by a woman she had trusted. Heather had once been Jessie's best friend and, like Monica, had zeroed in on Jessie's boyfriend and whisked him away. Jessie had long ago stopped blaming either Monica or Heather. It had to be something in her, some deep-seated failure in herself, that had caused both Todd and Bryan to dump her for someone else.

She stole a glimpse of herself in the mirror. Mom had always said that Jessie was pretty—"prettier than Monica," she would whisper to Jessie. But Jessie wasn't sure. Her eyes used to be a vivid blue, but now they seemed colorless. Her hair used to be thick and blond, but now it was too wispy, she thought. She wore it long, parted in the middle. And if only she could lose a few pounds. . . . Everyone told Jessie she was too thin, but looking into the mirror, Jessie saw a girl who had lost the slim, pretty shape she'd had in high school. No wonder no man wanted to stick around.

Except Emil. He'd been right there waiting for her after the heartbreak of Bryan's rejection, straddling his big black Harley Davidson. Together they'd roared out of town, leaving all cares behind. For a few months Jessie had really believed she loved the big lug. Emil Deetz was the exact opposite of Bryan Pierce and Todd Bennett, whose button-down oxford shirts and carefully ironed khakis perfectly delineated their stiff personalities. Emil, by contrast, laughed loud and often, tossing back long black hair and flashing big black eyes. Jessie had never seen him wear anything other than dirty dungarees and a crackled leather jacket. He smelled of cigarettes and beer.

Monica had, of course, accused Jessie of acting out. It was out of character for her, Monica had scolded. Until that point, Jessie had been a girl who never got into any trouble. She'd always gotten good grades. She'd graduated from college at the top of her class. So the association with Emil had been shocking. Monica said that Mom and Dad, rest their souls, would have been heartbroken at Jessie's choice of a boyfriend.

Jessie hadn't argued with her. She'd known Monica was right. She had indeed been acting out. And after the terrible heartache she'd felt over losing two men—one to her best friend and one to the sister who now sat in judgment of her—Jessie had loved every minute of her acting out.

Until the night she'd seen Emil slit a man's throat without so much as a blink of his bloodshot eyes.

Hanging a blouse in her new closet, Jessie suddenly shuddered. Would she always find herself remembering such things when she least expected it? Would she never be able to forget that night?

Her therapist had taught her exercises to block out bad memories, or at least to dilute their power over her. Jessie tried one of them now, fixing her thoughts on something else, something that made her happy. *Abby*. Jessie peered out again at her sleeping daughter and smiled. Abby did indeed make her happy.

And Emil had given her Abby. As horrible as her time with him had been—as much of a mistake as it no doubt had been—she wouldn't have Abby if not for Emil. Yet, to her eternal relief, she saw nothing of Emil's darkness in Abby. She joked to her therapist that it was like a virgin birth. Abby was *her* daughter, not his.

Thankfully there seemed to be not one drop of Deetz blood in Jessie's little girl.

It wouldn't have been the same for the boy.

Again, Jessie tried to push away a thought that caused her too much distress. Worse than remembering Emil was remembering the baby in the pool of blood.

Jessie finished unpacking, slamming her suitcases shut. She headed back into the living room, confirmed that Abby was still sound asleep, then checked the refrigerator. Monica had been very kind to fill it up with food. There was bread and cold meats and cheese, cans of soda, bottles of milk and orange juice. Plus jars of baby food for Abby. Jessie withdrew a Diet Coke and popped open the top. She took a sip, heading across the room to stare down into the alley. The sounds of traffic from Second Avenue rose to her ears. Car horns and skidding brakes and the sheer rush of humanity, four floors down. But up here, Jessie was alone.

Alone and safe.

She had to believe that.

Emil, wherever he was, couldn't find her here.

But Emil wasn't the only one she feared.

"Oh, stop it," Jessie whispered to herself, just as Abby gurgled in her sleep and turned her little head on her pillow.

Jessie left the window to stand over her daughter's crib.

There should have been two babies.

"It wasn't my fault," she whispered again.

That's what her therapist had told her, over and over. She hadn't caused the miscarriage. She had done nothing out of the ordinary that day. She had been in bed, almost asleep, when she'd noticed the blood. She'd called 911 and the ambulance had taken forever to get there. Jessie been terribly distraught. She had been in tears when the paramedics finally arrived. She had been desperate not to lose the baby. . . .

That wasn't entirely true.

She had been desperate not to lose the girl.

Jessie didn't like admitting it, but it was true.

"Don't let me lose the girl," she'd kept praying, over and over to herself, in the ambulance on the way to the hospital, though she wasn't sure if God listened to her anymore. "If I have to lose one baby, let it be the boy! Don't let me lose the girl!"

Jessie had been told she was carrying twins a few months before. She'd asked her doctor if he could determine the gender. Not quite yet, he'd told her. But soon. A few weeks later, after an ultrasound, Jessie was told she had one of each: a girl and a boy.

Her pregnancy had been quite the surprise. At first, Jessie had been overjoyed when her doctor had told her, and she couldn't wait to tell Emil. But that night, as she waited to give him the news, Emil didn't come home. Jessie sat in front of the television, texting him repeatedly, but getting no answer. Finally she went to bed. It had been happening more frequently—Jessie waiting at home for Emil, who didn't show up for a day or two, and when he finally came straggling in, he was hungover, or worse. What made his behavior even more unusual was that he was hanging out with a new set of friends, and Emil seemed to be the one always picking up the tab. Jessie wondered how he was suddenly so flush with cash, how he'd managed to buy a brand new Harley for himself. His job at Jiffy Lube sure wasn't bringing in that kind of money. So that night—the night she was going to tell him she was pregnant—Jessie let her doubts get the better of her. Instead of just waiting meekly at home for Emil, tossing and turning all night, she'd gotten out of bed and gone searching.

When one goes searching, however, one should be prepared for what one might find.

Jessie had spotted Emil's bike in the parking lot of the Black Wolf tavern. She wandered around back. Emil and some other guy were standing next to the back entrance. Jessie couldn't see the other man clearly, but he had long reddish hair, and was wearing a leather jacket. She could tell that he and Emil were arguing, in low, ominous voices, as if they didn't want anyone hearing them. Harsh whispers cut through the night.

Jessie was about to call out to Emil, but something stopped her. Her voice dried up in her throat. That was because she'd suddenly spotted the glint of a blade in the moonlight. She watched in horror as Emil nonchalantly slit the man's throat. He just reached over and swung the blade as if he'd suddenly gotten bored with their argument and decided to end it. Jessie saw a spurt of blood. She suppressed a scream.

But it was what she saw next that terrified her most. Emil's eyes found hers, and the cavalier expression on his face changed. Now fear, confusion, and rage rushed in to fill his black eyes. Jessie turned and ran. She got to her car, fumbled her keys into the ignition, and peeled out of the parking lot.

That was the last time Jessie saw Emil.

And that was why she hadn't wanted to look upon the face of his son.

After witnessing the murder—the man's name, Jessie would learn, had been Screech Solek—she'd wanted to end the pregnancy. As the police interrogated her and she learned all the crimes Emil had been involved in— selling drugs, stolen merchandise, even pornography— she became more and more repulsed. What had she seen in him? Monica had been right. She'd been acting out, and had taken up with someone that despicable, that loathsome, just as a way of getting back at the people who had hurt her. Jessie felt used and foolish. How could she bear that man's child?

But when the ultrasound came back and showed that she carried both a girl and a boy, Jessie couldn't bring herself to have an abortion. She wished to God that she wasn't having twins—that she wasn't having Emil's son. But she couldn't get rid of the boy and not the girl.

She was terrified. Emil had fled. The police were searching for him. But Jessie knew they'd never find him. Emil knew how to hide. He also knew how to get revenge. She had seen him kill a man. Monica and Todd took her in, saying nothing judgmental, though Jessie could see it in their eyes and hear it in their voices. Jessie didn't blame them for judging her. She judged herself just as harshly.

As she lay in bed every night crying, she wished she was carrying only a girl. A girl she might be able to save. But a boy would carry Emil's black heart. She visualized a little Emil growing inside her. She was certain his son would look just like him, with his black eyes and mean, cruel smile. Jessie had even allowed herself to imagine the very scenario that ultimately occurred: that she would miscarry, but only the boy. The girl would remain safe. She had actually lain in bed wishing for such a thing.

And it had happened.

Looking down at Abby now, Jessie surprised herself by crying. A tear rolled down her cheek and plopped softly on her daughter's pink blanket.

She hadn't done anything to cause the miscarriage. It was not her fault. You can't *wish* something like that into occurring.

But she *had* wanted it.

There was no denying that.

She felt as if she had willed it to happen, and sometimes the guilt threatened to overwhelm her.

Jessie stood at the window again watching the sun set over the city. Shadows filled up the alley between the buildings. Lights popped on in windows across the way and the traffic from the street cast a swaying red and yellow glow against the bricks. Abby awoke then, muttering—never crying—and Jessie held her on the couch as she breast-fed her. The baby cooed happily, then went back to sleep.

Jessie supposed she should eat something herself, so she fixed herself a sandwich from the cold cuts Monica had put in the fridge, washing it down with the last of the Diet Coke. There was an Entenmann's coconut custard pie in there, too, but she decided she wasn't hungry enough for dessert. Besides, she needed to watch her weight.

The one thing the apartment didn't have was a television set, which Jessie was glad about. It would only distract her from her work. She had no real job, of course. The money Mom and Dad had left her would carry her along for a bit. But she'd always wanted to write. At school her teachers had all encouraged her, telling her that she had "a way with words." Jessie wasn't sure about that, but after everything she'd been through, she thought maybe she might have a story to tell.

Just what that story was, however, wasn't exactly clear. She flipped open her laptop and sat on the couch staring at the screen, her fingers poised over the keyboard. How did she begin? The night Mom died? The day she learned Monica had stolen Todd? Or Heather had stolen Bryan? Maybe she should start the night she'd met Emil, but Jessie wasn't ready to remember all that quite yet.

Finally she sighed and closed her laptop. It was too soon. She couldn't write about anything that had happened. Not tonight, anyway.

She realized she was sitting in the dark. The sun had made its last drop behind the buildings of the city while she had been sitting there staring at her computer screen. But rather than turning on a light, Jessie decided to go to bed. Tomorrow would be a new day. She should have a good night's sleep before making a fresh start.

In the small bathroom, she washed her face and brushed her teeth. She looked at her eyes. She'd always been told she had pretty eyes. But now the blue seemed duller than it used to be. She'd once been attractive. She wondered if she ever would be again.

She checked on Abby one more time. Her daughter slept soundly.

But her son was dead.

Sleep. She needed sleep.

Jessie undressed and slipped into a short pink nightgown. As tired as she felt, when she lay down she simply stared up at the ceiling, unable to sleep. The images were there, playing out like a movie. Closing her eyes did no good; they went right on playing.

She got out of bed.

Abby was still sleeping peacefully. The city was pulsing below her. All of those people going on with their lives. People were cutting through the alley, bathed in the amber glow of security lamps. Three teenaged boys sauntered through, their pants sagging so far down their legs that their underwear was entirely exposed. A pretty girl hurried past, jabbering on her cell phone. At the far end of the alley, a man was standing under a NO LOITERING sign.

Jessie looked again, harder.

The man under the sign.

It was hard to tell at this distance and angle, but he appeared to be looking up at her apartment.

A terrible chill ran through Jessie's body.

His hair was shorter, but he wore a leather jacket.

"No," she mumbled.

It couldn't be Emil! He couldn't have found her!

Then a woman approached the man. They embraced and walked away. Jessie let out a long breath of relief.

"Stop being so nervous," she scolded herself, and marched straight back to bed.

This time, she fell almost immediately to sleep.

She awoke sometime later. Abby was crying. That was unusual. Abby never cried. Jessie threw the sheet off of her and hurried into the living room.

But Abby was sleeping peacefully.

Jessie cleared her mind from the fog of sleep to make sure. Yes, Abby was fine. Her soft breathing calmed her

mother. Jessie smoothed out her baby's little pink blanket. She must have only dreamed that Abby was crying.

Making her way back to bed, Jessie felt as if every
step had become an enormous effort. She hadn't been
this tired in a very long time. Once her head hit the pillow, sleep came back quickly, greedily.

"Mommy," came a voice.

She was dreaming.

"Mommy!"

And suddenly Abby was crying again. Jessie forced
her eyes open, shaking off the heaviness of the dream.
She listened again. Yes, there was definitely crying coming from the living room. This time it was no dream. She
was awake, and Abby was crying. More intensely this
time. The sound of frustration.

Why aren't you coming for me, Mommy?

Jessie hurried out of bed once again and rushed to
the baby's crib.

"No," she murmured softly to herself, looking
down.

Abby slept. There were no tears. The little blanket
showed no signs of being disturbed.

So what had she heard?

Jessie reached down into the crib and lifted Abby in
her arms. The baby cooed against her chest. Carefully
she carried Abby back with her into the bedroom, placing her down beside her on the bed. She stroked Abby's
head as the baby, waking only briefly, drifted back to
sleep. "There, there, sweetie, Mommy's here," Jessie
said.

Soon her own heavy eyelids dropped and she fell
back to sleep.

The clock read 3:15 when her eyes opened again.

Once more, the sound of crying drifted in from the living room.

Jessie looked at Abby, slumbering in peace beside her.

She listened to the frantic sounds from the other room.

She didn't move. Cold terror gripped every muscle in her body.

The crying continued, becoming ever louder, even more frantic. It was more than just frustrated now. It was angry. Filled with rage.

How dare you not come for me, Mommy?

Jessie sat up. What was happening?

She pushed herself off the bed and back into the living room. From here she could see that something was in the crib. *Something.* She could see it thrashing about.

Jessie forced herself to look down into the crib.

She screamed.

There, looking up at her, was a naked, screaming baby boy.

He had Emil's black eyes.

And he was covered in blood.

FIVE YEARS LATER

ONE

It was one of those perfect late-summer Saturdays in Sayer's Brook, Connecticut, just over the New York line, when the dragonflies hovered lazily atop black-eyed Susans and the itchy fragrance of goldenrod powdered the air. Monica Bennett stood on the back deck of her house, watching her husband, Todd, swim laps in their pool, his strong tanned arms breaking the water in a rhythmic motion. In the trees, blue jays screeched.

"Todd, honey?" Monica called.

Her husband paused in his swim and looked up at her, the sun catching the beads of water in his russet hair.

"You will help her with her bags when she gets here, won't you?"

"How much stuff can she possibly have?" he called back.

"Not much. But she'll need help regardless."

"She always needs help," Todd grumbled, and returned to his laps.

Monica sighed, and went back into the house.

Aunt Paulette sat at the dining table, laying out her tarot cards in front of her. "Well," she said, placing one card down in the middle of all the rest. "The Lovers. What an interesting way for this reading to turn out."

"Maybe it means you're finally going to find a man," Monica said, pouring herself a glass of red wine from the bottle they'd opened last night. It was only eleven in the morning, but she had a feeling she was going to need some help in getting through this day.

"Oh, no, silly goose, that's not what the card means," Aunt Paulette was saying. She held it up so that Monica could see the image on its face from across the room. An angel hovered over a naked man and naked woman. "Now, it's true that The Lovers *can* mean romantic love, but as a point of fact, it's much, much more than just that. It's about *duality*." The chubby woman with the shoulder-length gray hair replaced the card on the table, then turned around in her seat to flash a broad, red-painted smile at Monica. "It's associated with the star sign Gemini, and in some decks, it's known as The Twins."

"Aunt Paulette," Monica said, leveling her eyes at her. "You know I don't believe in any of that crap."

The older woman looked offended. "I just think it's an interesting card to turn up on the day we're celebrating your sister coming home."

"Jessie and I aren't twins," Monica said, taking another sip of wine. "There's eleven months between us. And four days."

She wanted to add that "celebrating" was hardly the word she would have chosen to describe Jessie's homecoming, but she held her tongue. At least for now.

It had been five years since her sister had scandalized them all by taking up with that filthy thieving murderer. Monica would never forget the spectacle of police cars all along Hickory Dell, their quiet little cul-de-sac. That obnoxious Gert Gorin from next door had had her long nose pressed up against Monica's windows for days trying to learn what was going on. When the news hit the papers that Emil had killed a man, everyone whispered that Jessie must have known about it, or possibly been in on it. The police tore through Monica's house and Mom's old house for any evidence of Jessie being involved in Emil's drug and porn trade. They found nothing to link her to Emil's crimes, but Monica was never entirely convinced of her sister's innocence.

"She's done nothing wrong," Aunt Paulette had insisted, claiming she had read Jessie's mind and seen no villainy there. "She's merely an innocent victim in all this."

Monica wondered why she had been cursed with such a bizarre family. Jessie was a rebel, and Aunt Paulette was a loon. She read tarot cards and told fortunes, and honestly seemed to believe in all that malarkey. Mom had been similar. She didn't go so far as Aunt Paulette, her younger sister, and claim to be clairvoyant, but she was always taking about fate and karma and was always burning incense in front of little green jade Buddhas. Monica was definitely her father's daughter: sensible, rational, business-minded.

Daddy would be proud of me, Monica thought, sipping her wine.

Todd might be the real moneymaker in the house, establishing a name for himself on Wall Street as a young up-and-comer for one of the largest multinational bulge bracket investment banking and securities firms, but Monica had shown she could make a penny or two all on her own. Soon after they were married, Monica had dropped out of college and started her own home business, Baskets by Monica. At first she'd just held classes in basketmaking in the room over their garage, teaching the ladies of Hickory Dell—Gert Gorin, Heather Pierce, Millie Manning—how to weave and cut and the difference between wicker and twine. But as word spread among the ladies of Sayer's Brook— most of whom didn't work outside the home—one class had led to two and then three and four. Over the last six years, Monica had expanded the business so far that she now had assistants teaching classes in Greenwich and Stamford, and Baskets by Monica® were now sold in shops throughout Connecticut and spreading nationwide—not to mention their catalog sales. In the latest sign of her success, Monica had just gotten a mention in *Better Homes and Gardens* magazine. Homemakers who knew what was "in" would never think of decorating their houses without a few Baskets by Monica®—New England swamp ash or Southwestern limberbush—strategically placed for all to see.

Knocking back the last of her wine, Monica dreaded the question that the ladies of her basket classes were sure to ask this coming week: "Who's that living in your mother's old house? That isn't your *sister*, is it?"

Monica had thought Jessie was safely hidden away in New York. She still remembered the day she had driven Jessie and Abby into the city, five years ago now, setting them up in their apartment—all paid for by Todd, of course, and Jessie had yet to pay them one thin dime of it back. Monica had thought that Jessie, with her bohemian ways, would have made Manhattan her home. But something had happened to Jessie in

that apartment. Monica remembered the sobbing tele-
phone call she'd gotten the morning after her sister's
first night in the city. She'd been blubbering about her
miscarriage, about the baby she'd lost. Monica had had
no patience and no sympathy. Jessie might have lost
one of the babies she'd been carrying, but she'd delivered Abby, hadn't she? She'd given birth to a fine and
healthy girl. Meanwhile, ever since her marriage to
Todd seven years earlier, Monica had been trying without success to get pregnant. She didn't envy Jessie
much—why should she, given her sister's miserable
life?—but she did envy her Abby.

"How is she getting here from the city, by the way?"
Aunt Paulette asked, shaking Monica out of her reverie.

"Todd had one of the drivers from the office bring
her up in a company car," Monica replied, pouring herself a little more wine—not much, just a splash.

"Well, she should be here soon, shouldn't she?"

Monica glanced at her phone sitting on the counter.
She had three text messages. She typed in her pass
code and read them. They were all from Jessie. One
had come in an hour ago, telling her they were leaving
the city. Another had come a half hour later, reporting
that they were stuck in traffic. The last text had come
fifteen minutes after that, letting Monica know that the
traffic had dissipated and they were moving again.

"Yes," Monica told her aunt. "I'd say she should be
here any minute now."

And she filled her wineglass right up to the top.

If Monica was honest with herself, and sometimes,
when she drank enough wine, she could be, she'd admit
that she didn't only envy her sister for having produced

a living, breathing, healthy child. She also envied her for something else—something far less tangible. She envied her for her "joie de vivre" —or at least, the exuberance for life she had shown before Emil. Jessie was always the prettier, the more outgoing of the two sisters in high school. She'd been Mom's favorite, too—at least, Monica had felt she was. The two of them had always been laughing and carrying on, taking off on hikes or bike rides or fishing trips; Monica was definitely not the outdoor type. And the boys had always responded to Jessie in ways they never responded to Monica.

That was why Monica had taken such pleasure in stealing Todd away from her. She knew it had broken Jessie's heart—and that did trouble Monica's conscience, especially because of the underhanded trick she'd used to accomplish her task—but in the end, Monica believed, it had all worked out for the best. Jessie would never have been happy with such a button-down Wall Street kind of guy as Todd, and he sure as hell wouldn't have been happy with a hippie-chick wife like Jessie. He needed a business-savvy wife like Monica, someone who strove to be part of the one percent, not someone whose sympathies were always inclined toward the ninety-nine percent. So maybe Monica's means, and her motivation, had been a little shady in stealing Todd away from her sister. But the end really did justify it all. No two people could be happier than Todd and Monica.

At least, Monica wanted to believe that, as she swallowed the last of her second glass of wine.

She heard the tires of a car crunching gravel in her driveway out front.

"She's here!" Aunt Paulette shouted, stumbling out of her chair in excitement. A couple of tarot cards fluttered up from the table, disturbed by the breeze she'd stirred up. One fell to the floor. Monica noticed it was The Lovers.

The Twins.

No, she and Jessie weren't twins.

Far from it.

But Jessie had been carrying twins when she miscarried. . . .

"Oh, she's here, she's here!" Aunt Paulette kept repeating, happily scampering out of the dining room through the sunroom and toward the front door. "And that precious little girl, too! Helloooo! Jessie! Abby! It's Auntie Paulette!"

Monica walked over to the back door and peered out through the screen. Todd was still swimming laps.

"She's here," she called out.

Her husband stopped mid-stroke and looked up at her.

"And now the fun begins," he said.

"Get out and help her with her bags. It's a long hike up to Mom's house."

The driveway ended at Monica's house, and the only way up to Mom's house—now, Jessie's house—was by foot up a rather steep hill. Monica would have to get used to her sister and her niece traipsing past.

She turned away from the door. From where she was standing, Monica could see the driveway through the sunroom and through the large picture windows that fronted the house. A young man was emerging from the driver's door of a black Lincoln town car and going around to open the door in back. Monica took a deep breath. She recalled again the harrowing phone calls she'd gotten from Jessie in those first few weeks after she'd moved to New York, how terrified she had been, how she'd thought she was seeing ghosts and strange apparitions of bloody babies, how convinced she'd been that Emil was lurking somewhere out on the street, watching her, waiting for her. For a while Monica had thought she might have to have Jessie committed. Her sister had seemed to be cracking up. Finding her a place in the city hadn't helped her. In fact, it had seemed to make things worse.

But, then, all at once, everything had changed. A few months after Jessie's move to the city, they'd gotten a call. Emil was dead. He'd been shot by Mexican police in a drug bust in Ciudad, Juarez. U.S. agents had identified his body through fingerprints. Jessie was at first uncertain whether she could believe it, but Aunt Paulette did a psychic reading and announced she could no longer see Emil anywhere on the planet, meaning that he must really be dead. That seemed to convince Jessie.

From that moment on, she'd been like a woman reborn. She'd started writing for magazines and newspapers, and two years later, had had a book published called *You Can Survive Anything*. She'd even been on local radio stations being interviewed about it. Little Abby, meanwhile, was growing up happy and healthy—and smart, too; Monica had been impressed when she was already reading words at the age of three. Now Jessie had been signed to another book contract, and Abby was getting ready to start kindergarten. Monica had believed her sister was doing fine, and that she'd

live out her life in New York. They'd see each other occasionally at holiday times. That would be it.

But then Jessie had announced she wanted to move
back in to their mother's house, which had sat empty
since Mom's death, up on top of the hill at the very end
of the cul-de-sac. Both girls had inherited it, but Todd
had never wanted to live there, not liking its old Victo-
rian floorboards and creaky stairs. That was why they'd
built this modern place of spun glass and marble. Monica had figured eventually they'd sell Mom's house, and
the small parcel of land it stood on. But Jessie wanted
to live there. She said she wanted Abby to grow up and
go to school just like she had in Sayer's Brook.

Monica wasn't happy that her sister would now be
her neighbor. Not that she had to worry anymore about
the kind of criminals and thugs Jessie had once associated with; she had seemed, these last five years, to have
sworn off men entirely. She was a successful author
now, and a happy, devoted mother of a beautiful daughter. If Monica was being honest with herself, and she
was being brutally so right now, she'd acknowledge
that Abby was the real reason she didn't want Jessie
living next door.

That, and the fact that her sister looked damn good
again—and Todd was sure to notice. In her heart of
hearts, Monica worried that, for all his disdain of Jessie's
bohemian lifestyle, Todd might still be hot for the girl
he'd dumped in high school.

"Jessic, honey, welcome home!"

Aunt Paulette's voice came lilting in from outside.

Monica watched as Jessie stepped out of the backseat of the car, the sun catching the gold in her hair.

Right behind her little Abby came scrambling, her golden ringlets a match of her mother's. The little girl ran straight into Aunt Paulette's outstretched arms.

In that moment, Monica hated her sister more than she had ever loved her.

Stretching her lips into a tight smile, she headed outside to welcome Jessie home.

Two

"The neighborhood still looks the same," Jessie was saying, as she, Abby, Monica, Todd, Aunt Paulette, and Abby's nanny, Inga, headed up the hill to Mom's house, each of them carrying a suitcase. Even Abby lugged a little bag, though hers was filled with dolls. "Does Mrs. Gorin still live across the street?"

"Sure does," Todd replied, as he hauled Jessie's heaviest bag. "And she's as nosy a bitch as ever."

"Hush, Todd," Monica scolded. "Voices carry."

"I found her once peering into my back window," Aunt Paulette said, a mountain of Jessie's clothes draped over one arm. "Gert claimed she'd tried ringing the doorbell, but I knew she just wanted to catch me casting spells or stirring my witch's cauldron."

"Are you a witch, Aunt Paulette?" Abby asked, her little pink face looking up at the older woman.

"No, sweetie, but some of the neighbors think I am."

"Why do they think that? You don't wear a black pointy hat like Elphaba."

"Well, I have a pink pointy one that I'll show you one of these days!"

"That's like Glinda's!" Abby exclaimed.

Jessie grinned and looked over at her sister. "I took Abby to see *Wicked* five times. She loved the show."

"You're going to miss being able to do things like that," Monica told her, "now that you're not in the city anymore."

"Oh, we're less than an hour away," Jessie replied. "Besides, I want Abby growing up hiking in the woods and catching fish in the brook, not hiking up Second Avenue and catching subways."

She smiled, looking around at the family property. It was good to be home. The maples glowed with a greenness as vivid as Jessie remembered from her childhood. The tall fir trees still resembled the protective sentinels she'd imagined they were as a kid. The birds hooted in the trees as they always did; the brook that cut through the property still babbled like it had in the days when it lulled her to sleep. The family owned seventeen and a half acres—most of it had come from Mom's family, though when she'd married Dad, they'd bought the lot next door as well, adding to their domain. Aunt Paulette had gotten her share some time ago—as well as the little cottage that had once housed the estate caretaker, back when the Clarksons had employed servants. But, being childless, she was leaving it all to Jessie and Monica, so the land was definitely staying in the family.

Jessie had told Monica that with the money she hoped to make on this new book, she planned to buy her half of the estate, including Mom's house. She also wanted to pay her and Todd back for helping her move to New York five years before.

That seemed like such a long time ago now. Jessie

no longer even thought about Emil or the baby boy she'd miscarried—well, at least she didn't think about them much. She'd found herself again, the girl she'd been in high school, not the angry rebel of college or the madwoman bent on self-destruction, as she'd been during her time with Emil. She looked forward to being back here in Sayer's Brook, reestablishing herself as part of the community, and bringing Abby up in the same place. If some in the neighborhood and the town still remembered her wilder past—the swarms of blue-uniformed policemen that had once swept across these very same green hills, looking for Emil and his stashes of drugs—well, then, Jessie would just have to show them that she had grown up and changed. People had loved Mom in Sayer's Brook. Jessie hoped they'd love her and Abby as well.

"Wait a minute," she suddenly said, pausing in their trek up the hill. Mom's house was still a few yards away, but Jessie had noticed something in the trees to her right. "What is that?" she asked, pointing.

A brick structure loomed over the tops of the maples.

"That's John Manning's house," Monica told her.

Then Jessie remembered. John Manning. The best-selling horror writer. He'd bought a portion of their property the year Jessie had moved to New York. No wonder she didn't remember right away. She'd been dealing with horrors far more real at that moment than Manning's vampires and werewolves. So she'd never met him, just heard about him from Monica. But now she was remembering something else. . . .

"Wasn't there," she asked, "some kind of scandal a couple years ago . . . ?"

"Yeah," Todd was saying, lifting an eyebrow over at the house. "John Manning. The guy who killed his wife."

"Todd," Monica scolded again. "What did I say about voices carrying?"

"He killed his wife?" little Abby asked.

"No, sweetie, that's not what your uncle said," Abby's nanny, Inga, piped in, taking the child's hand and leading her a few feet away, pointing at a flock of geese that had landed near the brook.

Jessie was grateful to Inga. She was a lithe but sturdy German girl of nineteen. With all of Jessie's writing deadlines and interviews over the past year, Inga had been indispensable. Inga had spent more and more time with Jessie and Abby, becoming part of the family. It seemed only natural to invite her to move with them here in Sayer's Brook. Jessie was going to need help not only in taking care of Abby, but also in fixing up the old house. Inga was particularly good with her hands. At the New York apartment, she'd re-wired lighting fixtures for Jessie, and retiled the bathroom. Jessie figured Inga would prove very handy around Mom's house, which was over a hundred years old, and had now sat vacant for more than five years.

"He was cleared after an investigation," Monica was saying, coming to their famous neighbor's defense.

Todd just shrugged.

"John Manning is no murderer," Monica insisted. "He's just a very private man, so everybody jumped to conclusions when they found his wife's body."

Todd made a face. "But she had told friends she feared for her life, that he might try to kill her."

"Millie was paranoid," Monica retorted. "She used to come to my basket classes. She was always thinking that her husband's fans were following her. She was jumpy and nervous and unbalanced. No wonder she fell."

"I don't know," Aunt Paulette said. "When I tune in, I feel very mysterious energy emanating from that house."

"Oh, please, enough with the mumbo jumbo," Monica said. "John *is* a little mysterious. After all, he's a horror writer. But he's not a murderer."

They had resumed walking. Jessie tried to get a better glimpse of the house, but much of her view was obscured by the tall pines. She could make out a tall wooden fence surrounding the house. She was remembering now some of the details she'd read about the case. "The wife fell down the stairs or something, right?" she asked.

"Actually, she fell off the back upstairs deck," Todd corrected her. "Facedown onto the concrete patio." He winked at her. "Splat."

Jessie shuddered. But she wondered if her shudder was from the image of the woman's horrific death or from the fact that Todd had just winked at her.

She had a flash—high school—Todd Bennett, varsity track star, winking at her in chemistry class. He'd winked, he'd smiled, he'd flashed some pearly whites and the deepest dimples Jessie had ever seen. Not long after that, they'd started going out together. Jessie had been head-over-heels in love.

But now Todd was her brother-in-law.

With exactly the same dimples.

They had reached Mom's house. Except, it was no longer Mom's house. It was Jessie's house. Jessie and Abby's house.

The little girl ran up the front stairs. "Can I go inside?" she asked excitedly.

"You sure can, Abs," Jessie told her. "This is home now."

The living room looked as if Mom were still living there. The old checkered sofa was still rumpled and throw pillows were still scattered across it, as if Mom had been stretched out there just this morning, doing her crossword puzzles and watching *Dr. Phil* on the old television set in its wooden cabinet across the room. Little figures of Buddha and Quan Yin still stood on nearly every mahogany table, surrounded by dozens of ancient votive candles in little glass jars, burned down to almost nothing. Framed family snapshots—Mom and Dad on their honeymoon in Aruba, Jessie and Monica in second and first grades—still hung on the walls, their glass shrouded in a thin veneer of dust.

"I came in yesterday and cleaned up a bit," Aunt Paulette said, wiping some of the dust off of Jessie's grade-school face with her fingers. "But there were a lot of cobwebs. Nobody's been in here for some time."

"It just needs a good vacuuming and airing out," Jessie said, throwing open the windows to let in some of that crisp summer day. "What do you think, Inga? Anything that a new coat of paint can't spruce up?"

The German au pair was peering down toward the floor. "These electric sockets could use some updating," she said. "I could try, but I expect you'd need a real electrician to do that."

"All in good time," Jessie said. "We'll just be careful not to overload them right away."

As the adults set their loads down in the living room, little Abby was already running out into the kitchen. Jessie followed. She half expected Mom to be in there, with an apron around her waist, baking her famous cornbread. Or, since it was Saturday, browning some pancakes in the skillet. The kitchen was small and old-fashioned, especially compared to the modern stain-less-steel-and-glass kitchen at Monica's house. But something about the old black stove made Jessie feel happy, as if everything was going to be just fine in their new home.

"You'll need a new fridge," Aunt Paulette was saying. "I tried turning it on yesterday and getting it cold for you, but it's dead."

Jessie placed her hand on the side of the old avocado-green Frigidaire. A couple of magnets still adhered to the door. AN EYE FOR AN EYE LEAVES THE WHOLE WORLD BLIND and LIVE AND LET LIVE. They were two of Mom's favorite sayings.

"For now, you can keep food that will spoil over in our house," Monica was saying.

"Thanks, Monica," Jessie said, and offered her sister a smile. As usual, Monica avoided eye contact. It was just that way between them, Jessie thought a little sadly.

"Plumbing works," Inga announced, coming out of the small bathroom off the kitchen. The sound of tap water rushing into the sink reached their ears, along with the flushing of a toilet.

"I brought over some fresh linens this morning,"

Aunt Paulette said. "What was left of your mother's was pretty dusty and moth-eaten."

"Thank you so much, all of you," Jessie said, looking around at the three of them.

"Of course, honey," Aunt Paulette said, embracing her. "It's just so good to have you and Abby home."

"It's good to be home."

Jessie noticed that Monica busied herself emptying a bag of silverware and canned goods. Todd had drifted off toward the back door, where he stood with his back to them, gazing out into the yard. He was wearing a white T-shirt, and Jessie noticed how fit he'd been keeping himself. His shoulder muscles filled the tee with a solidity and hardness that surprised Jessie, and his horseshoe-shape triceps flexed instinctively as he moved the curtains on the back door aside.

"I'll mow the grass back there," Todd was saying. "We haven't been keeping up with this part of the property, but now that you're back, Abby might want to use the swing set."

"Oh, thanks, Todd," Jessie said, but she was drowned out by Abby's outburst of excitement upon hearing the words "swing set."

Todd smiled down at the little girl. "Yes, Abby, there's a swing set, though it's pretty old and rusty."

"Nothing a little oil and paint can't fix," Inga said, peering out at the decrepit metal swing set through the back window. Jessie and Monica had played on it when they were kids. Against the tall green and yellow grass, the swings looked black, like relics from a burned-out city.

"Well, we should let you and Abby settle in," Mon-

ica said. "You have unpacking to do, and I'm sure
you'll want to run down to the market to do some shopping. Feel free to take my car."

"It'll feel strange to drive again," Jessie said.

"The keys are hanging next to the phone in our
pantry. Just come in and get them when you need
them."

"Thank you again, Monica," Jessie said.

But once more when she tried to find her sister's
eyes, Jessie was unsuccessful. Monica was already
heading out of the kitchen and back toward the front
door.

Todd turned to follow his wife. But before he left he
looked at Jessie and gave her another wink.

"You're looking good," he told her.

Jessie felt her cheeks get hot. "Thanks," she said, in
a tiny voice.

Todd headed out. Jessie heard the screen door close
as he and Monica left the house.

"Now, sweetie, do you need anything else?" Aunt
Paulette was asking.

"Nothing at the moment, darling Auntie. Thank you
for—"

"Stop saying thank you. It's what family is for. And
my baby sister Caroline would want me to make sure I
was taking care of her baby girl."

They embraced again.

"Call me later. Maybe we can barbecue out on the
grill. Would you like that, Abby?"

"Yeah!" the little girl chirped.

Aunt Paulette kissed her on the top of the head, then
headed back out herself.

"Well, should we go check out the bedrooms?" Inga asked.

"You and Abby go," Jessie said. "I just want to sit in Mom's kitchen for a while."

"All right."

The nanny scooped up a couple of small suitcases and headed up the stairs, Abby following close at her heels. Jessie could hear their footsteps across the floorboards above her, and her daughter's voice announcing, "This is my room! I like the pretty wallpaper in here!"

Jessie smiled. She felt close to her mother sitting here, at her old Formica-topped kitchen table. They'd been friends, not just mother and daughter. Jessie was glad that Mom hadn't lived to see the troubles with Emil, or the spectacle of Jessie on the back of a roaring Harley riding down the main street of Sayer's Brook. The cancer had come out of the blue, and Mom had been gone so quickly. Surely, Jessie thought now, her grief over her mother's death had played as much a part as her heartbreak over Bryan's rejection in the way she'd acted out by taking up with Emil.

Bryan. Jessie realized that when they'd spoken of neighbors just now, no one had mentioned Bryan.

She was well aware that in another house on their little cul-de-sac lived another of her old flames. Jessie had taken up with Bryan Pierce while both were juniors at the State University of New York—known as SUNY—in nearby Purchase. During spring break, she'd invited him up here to meet Mom—and her best friend across the street, Heather Wilson. Little did Jessie know that Heather decided from the moment she laid eyes on Bryan that she would snatch him away. Heather connived to see him, slipping him her number when Jessie wasn't looking. Heather proved willing to give Bryan something Jessie had been withholding: herself.

Maybe it was old-fashioned, but Jessie hadn't wanted to have sex with Bryan right away. They'd been dating for eight months, and despite his fervent attempts, Bryan hadn't been able to get Jessie to go all the way. But Heather did, the first night they met, clandestinely, and at that moment, Jessie lost Bryan. The old stories about a guy not respecting a girl who puts out too soon turned out to be false. Mom had predicted that Bryan would come back to Jessie now that he'd had Heather, but that didn't turn out to be the case. Just as had happened with Monica and Todd, now another woman had gotten ahold of Jessie's man—and held on to him. In less than two years' time, Heather had married Bryan; thankfully, they'd eloped, so there had been no wedding invitation in Jessie's mailbox. And now that Heather's parents had moved to Florida, they'd taken up residence in the family home, right down the street. Monica had told her that Heather and Bryan now had two little children, a girl and a boy, Piper and Ashton. "Maybe they can be playmates for Abby," Monica had said.

Jessie sighed. Did her sister ever stop to think how hearing about Bryan's two little kids might make Jessie feel?

Of course not. She'd done the same thing to Jessie as Heather had done.

Jessie stood, scolding herself for feeling like a victim. Even if it was just a fleeting thought, she didn't like feeling that way. That was the whole point of the book she was writing: you can't be made a victim by anyone but yourself. All those soap operas between her and Heather and Monica and Bryan and Todd were years ago. Jessie had been just a kid. She'd never been serious with either boyfriend, even if her feelings had been strong and the rejection devastating. So she could either go through life feeling bitter and resentful—or not. She chose the latter. Jessie didn't like what bitter and resentful did to her. It had made her reckless, and destructive, and unhealthy, and unattractive. So, with the help of a good therapist, she had made the choice to move past it. Both Todd and Bryan were corporate types anyway. She'd probably never have lasted with either of them even if Monica and Heather hadn't intervened.

Jessie had come to the sad conclusion that she had never really been in love. She'd *thought* she'd been, with both Todd and Bryan, and certainly when Emil showed up, she'd convinced herself that he was the real thing, her true soul mate. Jessie wasn't proud of the fact that such a foul thing as Emil had been the first man she'd given herself to. Even Todd or Bryan would have been better choices. But in her acting-out phase, Jessie had been all too glad to let Emil be her first. She remembered the night she lost her virginity, in a boozy haze in the back of Emil's van, to the sharp, shattering soundtrack of rap music. She'd thrown up afterward. The pain had been terrible, and she'd thought she could never do such a thing again. If that was what sex was like, why did so many women say they liked it? But Emil had gotten sex from her whenever he wanted it, even after Jessie got pregnant. Jessie was eternally thankful that part of her life was over.

She was starting a new life. Maybe, somewhere in this new existence, she'd meet a man, a good man who could help her discover the true pleasures and intimacies of sex, things she'd never experienced. The only orgasms she'd ever achieved had been brought about by her own fingers, and she wasn't even really sure about those. Jessie hoped someday she might meet a man and discover whether romance might still play a part in her life. She was only twenty-seven, after all. She still had plenty of time.

But in fact what really motivated her at the moment wasn't the desire to fall in love again. Instead, it was to raise Abby right, the way Mom had raised her, to love nature and to see the goodness in the world around her, and to instill the kind of self-respect and confidence that Jessie herself had forgotten during those few terrible years with Emil, and which she now held so firmly in her hands once again. She was excited to make a life for them here on the green, green lands of Hickory Dell, and to spend her days while Abby was in school writing her book up in her room, overlooking the great fir sentinels that stood protecting her and reassuring her that she was home.

Stepping outside onto the back porch, Jessie inhaled the crisp, clean Connecticut air. Her nose twitched. Sometimes goldenrod made her sneeze. But even that she welcomed—it was far preferable to the exhaust of cars and the steam of subway trains. She glanced around the yard, at the maples and the white birches. A hawk soared above, making a long, sweeping arc through the shockingly blue sky. Her eyes followed the creature as it disappeared into the trees that surrounded the stone peak of John Manning's house next door.

Jessie gasped.

In the topmost window of the house, someone stood looking out. It was impossible to know for sure, because the figure was cloaked in shadow, but it seemed as if the person in the window was staring directly down at her.

THREE

"**I** tell you, Arthur, it was *her*," Gert Gorin was saying, eyes pressed against binoculars that were in turn pressed against the glass of the Gorins' picture window. "It was the same girl who the cops once thought was involved in that drug-and-porn ring."

"Get away from the window, Gert," her husband told her. "Somebody's going to see you."

Gert looked over at her husband, the binoculars having left red rings around her bulging brown eyes. "She arrived in one of Todd Bennett's company cars. I know it was a company car because it had New York plates and I've seen very similar ones pick him up before when he doesn't drive his own car."

"You really should have pursued a career in the FBI, Gert," Arthur said, sitting in his overstuffed armchair and reading the sports pages of the *Daily News*.

"She had a child with her, a little girl." Gert's face was red and splotchy. She stood barely more than five feet, and was almost as wide as she was tall. "That's the baby she had with that guy Deetz. I don't know if they ever got married."

"Isn't that what you spray on to ward off mosquitoes?"

Gert made a face. "What?"

"Deetz."

"You numbskull, that's Deet. This guy's name was Deetz. Emil Deetz. I remember because he killed a guy. Don't you remember, Arthur? He slit a guy's throat behind one of those dives over in Port Chester."

"All I remember is it's past lunchtime, and I'm getting hungry. How about a bologna sandwich on rye?"

Gert had replaced the binoculars to the window and was peering out through them again. "I wish I could see the old Clarkson house better. That damn new monstrosity the Bennetts built is in the way. God, is that an ugly thing. I can only make out the side of the old house, but I think I can see some movement upstairs. There's another woman with the Clarkson girl and her kid—"

Gert suddenly made a sound in her throat and pulled away from the window.

"What is it?" her husband asked. "You see somebody naked?"

"I just thought of something," Gert said, returning her eyes to the binoculars. "Maybe she's gone lesbo or something. You know, after all the problems she had with men. You know Bryan Pierce down the street dumped her, right? That was before she took up with Deetz. So maybe she's gone gay all of a sudden. Because there were definitely two women that got out of the car and went up to the house. And the other one, the one who wasn't the Clarkson girl, seemed kind of mannish to me."

"As opposed to your delicate femininity, I take it."

"Damn," Gert said, adjusting the focus on the binoculars. "I think they've drawn the blinds."

FOUR

"**M**ommy, there's a little girl at the house down the street," Piper Pierce announced as she ran into the kitchen, her pink shorts green with grass stains. "I saw her get out of the car. I want to go up and play with her. Maybe she has toys I don't have."

Heather Pierce looked up from the table where she was planning the seating arrangement for tonight's dinner party. "I doubt she has toys you don't have," she told her daughter. "That would be impossible. You have every toy ever produced."

"I do not!"

Heather just rolled her eyes.

"I want to go up there!"

"No, you are *not* going up there," she told her daughter.

"But Mommy—"

"Please don't throw another tantrum. I don't think I can take another. Just go outside and play with your brother."

The redheaded seven-year-old made a face in frustration, but did as she was told.

"What house down the street?" Heather's husband, Bryan, asked from the refrigerator, where he'd been pouring himself a glass of lemonade. Their housekeeper, a heavyset, gray-haired woman named Consuela, plopped a sprig of fresh mint into it for him as she walked past.

"The Bennetts," Heather told him, not looking up from her table diagram.

"Who's the kid?" Bryan asked, carrying his lemonade over to the table and sitting beside his wife. "They finally adopt since Monica seems to have turned out to be sterile?"

Heather sighed and lifted her eyes to look at him. "Apparently Jessie's moved back into her mother's old house."

Bryan just stared at her.

Heather looked back down at her diagram. "So it must be her kid who Piper saw."

"Wow, Jessie." Bryan took a sip of his drink. "Well, what do you know? The prodigal has returned." He looked over at the maid. "You're right, Consuela. Everything does taste better with a bit of fresh mint."

"That is true, Mr. Bryan."

His eyes returned to Heather and he leaned in close. "Maybe I oughta try putting a sprig between your legs," he whispered.

"You're a pig," she replied.

Bryan laughed, placing his lemonade on the table and sitting opposite his wife. "How does she look?" he asked.

"How does who look?"

"Jessie. Miss Jessica Clarkson, late of SUNY Purchase."

"I don't know," Heather said, still not looking back up at him. "I haven't seen her."

Consuela set a glass of lemonade down beside Heather, topped with a bright green mint leaf.

"Thank you," Heather said. She looked up at Consuela, who gave her a sympathetic gaze. Heather took a sip of the lemonade, feeling as if she might burst into tears.

Bryan got up and sauntered outside, carrying his glass, calling to his kids, who ran toward him. Heather watched through the window. She knew what Bryan was thinking. Jessie Clarkson. The girl from college he'd never gotten into bed. Heather knew Bryan kept track of things like that. For Bryan, it was all about the score—even after being a supposedly "happily married man" for the past six years. Heather knew he'd already had Betsy Blair from the office, and Michele Mariano, the girl who used to help Heather at catering events. Not to mention Clare Dzialo, the kids' nineteen-year-old babysitter, with whom Bryan had convinced Heather to join for a three-way. Heather had only done so because she knew otherwise he'd have done the deed without her, and better that she know about Bryan's trysts than not. She knew her husband well enough to know that his testosterone-fueled brain—located not in his head but in his cock—was already clicking with ideas on how to finally get his old flame Jessie into bed with him. Heather would have to do what she always did. Join in, or look the other way.

God, she hated him.

She watched Bryan playing horsie outside on the

grass, Piper and Ashton crawling over him, their tinkly laughter floating into the house through the windows.

Well, Heather thought, what was good for the gander was good for the goose. She flipped over her cell phone and tapped in a text message to John Manning.

FIVE

"A party? Oh, I don't know, Aunt Paulette."

Jessie sat with her aunt on their back porch as Todd rode a lawn mower back and forth across the yard, the sharp fragrance of cut grass swirling through the air. In an area of the lawn already cut, Inga was painting the swing set a bright neon pink, as Abby danced around her, barely able to contain her excitement over her new toy.

"Yes, a party," Aunt Paulette replied. "I think it would be wonderful for everybody along Hickory Dell to come and see how wonderful you look and how good you're doing."

Jessie admitted to herself that she might not mind that, either. She'd seen the looks Gert Gorin had thrown her as she and Abby had strolled down the street, or the glance Bryan Pierce had given her when she'd driven past in Monica's car. Jessie hadn't stopped to say hello to anyone. She'd been back for four days now, and still she hesitated to reintroduce herself to these people from her old life. They knew too much about her, and what had happened. She couldn't just pull up alongside Bryan and lean out the car window and gush, "Bryan, old pal, old buddy! How've you been?" Too much had happened between them—and to Jessie—for their first interaction after all this time to be so casual.

But a gathering . . . here . . . in her own home . . . on her own turf . . . with Abby . . . and Mom's things all around them. . . .

"We could invite old Mr. Thayer," Aunt Paulette was saying, "and Bryan and Heather and their two little kids to play with Abby. . . ." Her voice trailed off. "Oh, honey, maybe you don't want to see Bryan. . . ."

Jessie smiled. "It was a long time ago, Aunt Paulette." She took a deep breath. "Maybe you're right. Sure, let's have a party. I've got to meet the neighbors again eventually. Might as well do it all at once."

"Wonderful." The older woman clapped her hands together, a wide smile stretching across her leathery face, browned and roughened from years of being outdoors without any sunblock. "How about this Sunday afternoon? We'll make a picnic out of it."

"That sounds good."

"I suppose we'll have to invite the Gorins, too. We can't invite the whole street and leave them out."

Jessie smiled. "Well, maybe coming up here and seeing me and what we've done to the house will sate Mrs. Gorin's curiosity. I've seen her looking over here with binoculars."

"You're being kind when you call her curious. She's plain nosy. Why, once when I saw her snooping around the mailboxes, I read her mind and saw that what she was considering was pilfering everyone's mail, steaming it open, then returning it."

"That's definitely not a good thing," Jessie said, "but, honestly, Aunt Paulette, isn't reading someone's mind without their permission just as bad as reading their mail?"

The older woman's cheeks blushed red. "You're right, sweetie. I try not to. But sometimes . . . it just comes. It just happens."

Jessie reached across the table and patted her aunt's hand. For all Mom's belief in fate and karma and the power of nature, she had never quite believed that her eccentric older sister had "the gift." She used to say that Paulette had to believe she was good at something, because she'd tried going to teacher's college, then nursing school, then cosmetology classes—and each time, she'd been unable to graduate. It wasn't that Aunt Paulette was unintelligent—she was, in fact, quite bright—but she had little patience for protocols and discipline and rules and deadlines. Good thing that her own parents had left her enough money that she'd never really had to work.

For most of the last twenty years, Aunt Paulette had read tarot cards and performed psychic readings for forty-five dollars an hour. She kept an ad running in a local "New Age" journal, which meant that, periodically, a car full of housewives, or college students, would show up on Hickory Dell, and they'd all traipse up to the cottage of "Madame Paulette Drew" to learn from the lady with the bright red lipstick if they were about to come into some money or meet any tall, dark, and handsome strangers. Mom dismissed it as "all in good fun"—a line that Aunt Paulette had to officially maintain herself. She billed her readings as "entertainment," since actual "fortune-telling" was illegal in Connecticut. But there was no doubt, to Mom or to Jessie, that she honestly believed her gift was real.

Jessie wondered if there had ever been a man in Aunt Paulette's life. She always just smiled when they'd ask her. Marriage had never seemed an option for her. There was so much about her beloved aunt that Jessie just did not know.

She raised her eyes to look back out at the yard. Todd was almost done mowing. He'd switched the ride-on for a handheld mower, using it to get in closer to the trees and the side of the house. His taut muscles held Jessie's gaze for a moment, before she looked over at the swing set. Inga was nearly finished with her paint job, but now Abby was nowhere in sight.

"Inga!" Jessie called, standing up. "Where's Abby?"

"She's down at the brook," the nanny called back. "Don't worry, I can see her from here. She's fine."

Jessie tried to see herself, but from where she was sitting on the deck she couldn't see the brook.

"Some little boy wandered up and they started playing together," Inga told her.

"A little boy?" Jessie asked, as she headed down the deck stairs out in the yard.

"Must be Bryan's son," Aunt Paulette ventured.

Jessie was walking quickly across the grass trying to get a better view. But by the time the brook, so blue in the afternoon sun, came into view, Abby was trudging back up toward them through the grass. She was alone.

"That's funny," Inga said. "The boy was just there. . . ."

"Abby, come on back up here!" Jessie called.

"Hi, Mommy!" Abby called, and continued her march through the daisies and wildflowers. When she reached the yard, Jessie hugged her—a little too forcefully, perhaps, because Abby asked, "What's wrong, Mommy?"

"Nothing, baby. Who were you playing with?"

"A little boy."

"Was his name Ashton?" Aunt Paulette was asking, having come down from the deck herself.

"He didn't tell me his name," Abby replied.

"Well, it must have been Ashton," Aunt Paulette reasoned. "He's the only little boy in the neighborhood. Did he have red hair?"

"I don't remember," Abby said.

"It might have been red," Inga said. "It was hard to see, since he was a few yards away and the sun was in my eyes."

Jessie smiled. "Well, anyway, Aunt Paulette, will you take Abby inside and help her get washed up for lunch?"

"Certainly. Come on, sweetie."

Abby took her grandaunt's hand and they headed back up the deck stairs and into the house.

Jessie turned to Inga. "Don't ever let her leave the yard alone again!"

Inga looked at her quizzically, the paintbrush in her hand dripping pink paint. "Jessie, I never took my eyes off her. She never left my sight. The brook is just down the hill. It's practically part of the yard."

"You said the sun was in your eyes and you couldn't see. What if Abby had fallen into the brook?"

Inga stiffened. "I might not have been able to see the color of the boy's hair, but I could see the two of them playing just fine. And you know very well that the water of the brook barely comes up Abby's ankles. If she'd fallen in, I could have been there in thirty seconds and all she would have suffered would have been a wet and muddy bum."

Jessie sighed. "I'm sorry, Inga. I didn't mean to snap."

Inga's defensiveness evaporated and she smiled. "We're not in the city anymore, Jessie. There aren't dangers lurking behind every corner out here in the country."

Jessie nodded. She supposed it was just an old instinct, left over from the days when she'd thought Emil was still alive, that he was out there lurking, waiting for the right moment to make his move. But Emil was dead. And she and Abby were here, starting over in Mom's house. Life was good.

Jessie glanced out toward the brook. Overhead the hawk soared again, looking for prey.

SIX

Monica wasn't happy about this party. Not at all.

"Hurry up, Todd," she said, calling over her shoulder as she sat in front of her vanity, brushing mascara onto her lashes. "And don't wear shorts. Put on a pair of chinos."

Her husband was still in the shower. "Why do I have to go at all?"

"Because she's gone ahead and invited the whole damn neighborhood. Everyone will be there. And if you're not, they'll wonder why. And Gert Gorin will start spreading stories."

"Is that prick Bryan Pierce going to be there?" Todd called, the sound of water splashing against tiles as he moved around in the shower.

"Yes, she's invited Bryan and Heather."

"Fuck."

Just why Jessie had invited the guy who'd broken her heart and the former best friend who'd been the cause of it, Monica wasn't sure. Then again, her sister had gotten pretty used to dealing with exes, with Todd living down the hill from her. Monica was pleased that, so far at least, Todd and Jessie had barely spent any time together. Even the day he'd mowed her lawn, he'd barely lingered to talk. There seemed to be no interest on either part to renew even a modicum of the closeness they'd had in high school. *There's been a lot of water under that bridge*, Monica thought. Surely both of them must be glad they didn't end up together.

So far, too, there had been no real problems with Jessie living in Mom's house. She and Abby and that German nanny respected Monica's privacy. The few times they'd come down to the house, they'd called first, and then their visits were always functional and brief, usually to borrow some tools or retrieve items they'd stored in the icebox. Even the frequency with which Jessie had borrowed Monica's car in the first few days after her arrival had tapered off; two days ago, Monica had noticed her sister pull into the driveway in an old Volvo station wagon. "My own wheels!" Jessie had exclaimed, waving the keys at her. She'd bought the car over in Port Chester for two-and-a-half grand. It had some rust and the doors squeaked when they opened, but it ran, and that was all that a bohemian like Jessie cared about. Monica was relieved that she no longer had to worry about her sister borrowing her powder-blue Beemer.

Jessie had also purchased a new refrigerator. It had been delivered last Wednesday by Home Depot, hauled up the hill by two big, burly black men; Monica hadn't been surprised when she'd discerned Gert Gorin peering out her window with her binoculars, watching their every move.

She sat back and inspected her eyes. Then she puckered up and applied a light coating of pink lipstick. She heard Todd shut the water off and step out of the shower.

"Who else did Jessie invite to this thing?"

Monica sighed. "To be fair, it was Aunt Paulette's idea. She's the one who ran up and down the street with invitations."

"So it's everybody then. The whole freaking neighborhood."

"Yes."

"Even—?" Todd stood behind her stark naked, the hair on his head and legs and arms still alive with static electricity after a fierce towel dry. He was pointing over his shoulder with his thumb toward the north side of the house.

"Yes," Monica said, standing from the vanity. "Even John Manning."

"Well, he never comes to anything."

She shrugged. "All I know is that Aunt Paulette went over there with an invitation."

"Christ."

"I don't like it any more than you do." Monica drew close to her husband, running a sharp pink fingernail down the sexy line that divided his torso, down between his pecs and his abs and coming to an end at his navel, like an exclamation point. "Believe me, I'd much prefer to spend this quiet Sunday afternoon all alone with you, just you and me, a bottle of wine and the Jacuzzi. . . ."

He made no response. He stepped over to the closet and withdrew a pair of chinos. "These okay?" he asked.

Monica gave him a small smile. "Fine."

"Can I at least wear flip-flops?"

"Wear whatever you want." She herself was only in her bra and panties. She took a glance at herself in the full-length mirror. She might be getting close to thirty, but Monica still looked good. Damn good. "Anything special you'd like me to wear, Todd?"

"What do I look like, a fashion coordinator?" He was pulling on a pair of underwear.

"No," his wife said. "Not with chinos and flip-flops, you definitely don't look like a fashion coordinator."

She slipped a yellow-and-white polka-dotted sundress over her head. From the window she could see down to the lawn that stretched between their house and Mom's—or rather, Jessie's—house. The first arrivals were making their way up the hill. Gert Gorin, of course, not wanting to miss anything, charged ahead like a soldier into battle, her husband trudging along listlessly a few feet behind her. Gert carried something in her hands; it looked like a casserole dish. Behind Arthur Gorin walked old Mr. Thayer, stiff and erect like a bishop on a chess set. Mr. Thayer had given Todd his first job on Wall Street. He was very fond of Todd and Monica, and they of him. As usual, even on a warm day like this, Mr. Thayer was dressed in a blue blazer and ascot tie.

Monica took one last glance in the mirror and headed downstairs to join her sister's housewarming party. Todd followed, the sound of his flip-flops in her ears.

SEVEN

Jessie took a deep breath and opened the door, stepping out onto the front porch to greet her new neighbors.

Of course, they weren't really new. She'd known them since she was a little girl, when she and Monica, dressed up as princesses or Spice Girls, would ring their doorbells, trick-or-treating along the cul-de-sac of Hickory Dell at Halloween time. The Wilsons—Heather's parents—had given out the worst treats: a single bite-size Tootsie Roll wrapped in a Bible verse. The Gorins—even if Mrs. Gorin was the nosiest neighbor of all time—had given out the best: homemade red velvet cupcakes with orange buttercream frosting. The problem was, if you didn't eat the cupcakes right away, they tended to get smooshed in your trick-or-treat bag. So Jessie and Monica had usually wolfed them down and then continued on their way, frosting all over their chins and fingers.

But the world had moved on since those innocent days. Now, as the residents of Hickory Dell made their way up Jessie's lawn, they remembered not the little girl dressed as Sleeping Beauty with frosting on her face but instead the young woman on the back of a Harley, her eyes caked in black mascara and eye shadow. They remembered the suspected criminal the police had interrogated, and the searches across the Clarkson property with dogs and flashlights.

I was innocent then and I'm innocent now, Jessie thought as she lifted her hand to wave hello to her arriving guests.

"Jessica!" Mrs. Gorin beamed a smile in her direction. "How lovely to have you back in the neighborhood! And where is that darling little girl I glimpsed from the window?"

"Hello, Mrs. Gorin," Jessie replied, looking down at the round little woman. "Abby is out back with her nanny, firing up the grill."

"I brought a tuna casserole," Gert Gorin told her, handing the ceramic covered dish up to her.

Jessie accepted it and grinned. "Thank you so much. Though I must admit that I was hoping you might bring those red velvet cupcakes I remember so well."

The older woman made a face that looked as if she'd suddenly sucked on a lemon. "I only make those at Halloween time. Can't risk making them more often. You see, Arthur is at risk for diabetes if he doesn't lose some weight."

"I am not at risk for diabetes and I am not overweight," Mr. Gorin said, approaching them now, a little out of breath. "Do I look overweight to you, Jessie?"

He did indeed look a little paunchy, but not any more than most men his age; Jessie estimated both Gorins to be in their mid-sixties. "I think you look just fine, but I guess it's good to have your wife watching out for you," Jessie said diplomatically. "Please, both

of you, head around back and grab a glass of punch.
I'll be around momentarily."

She noticed Gert eying the house through the front
door. "Don't we get a tour of the place?"

"Oh, sure, in a bit. We've only just started the reno-
vations. Inga is starting on the kitchen—"

"Inga?" Gert's penciled eyebrow arched up at Jessie.

"Yes. Abby's nanny. She's really become part of the
family."

"I see . . ." Gert Gorin said, insinuatingly, as she
nudged her husband in the ribs with her elbow. She
didn't think Jessie saw, but she did.

As the Gorins headed around to the backyard, Jessie
greeted the next visitor up the hill. Oswald Thayer was
probably past eighty now, though he was far better pre-
served than Arthur Gorin. Still slim and trim, with a
full head of bright white hair carefully combed and
slicked into place, Mr. Thayer wore his perennial white
twill pants under a blue blazer with gold buttons, finished off with a bright red ascot tie bulging from a
crisply starched, open-collared white shirt. Jessie didn't
think she'd ever seen him dressed any other way, except in the wintertime, when his twill pants were gray.
A broad smile of dazzlingly white dentures bloomed
on his face when his blue eyes met Jessie's.

"Welcome home, my dear," he said, extending his
hand. "Your dear mother and father would be so happy
to know you were back in the family homestead."

"Hello, Mr. Thayer. Thank you so much for coming." Jessie shook his hand warmly, balancing the casserole dish in her other hand. "And thank you for the
lovely flowers. They arrived this morning. They're in
the living room on the mantel."

"I felt flowers were the better alternative, as I don't have Gertrude Gorin's culinary skills in being able to whip up a tuna casserole," he said, dropping his gaze to the dish in Jessie's hands.

Jessie laughed. "I've never been all that good in the kitchen myself. That's why my daughter and her nanny are handling the grill this afternoon."

Mr. Thayer had fixed her with a serious look. "I meant it when I said that your parents would be glad to see you here. You know that your father was a dear friend of mine. Rather like the son I never had."

Jessie smiled. She had never been as close to Dad as she had been to Mom; Monica had tended to be their father's favorite. But she had still loved him, and respected him; they had just been very different sorts of people. Dad had been a banker and a broker, and a Republican; Mom had been a hippie and a poet, and a Democrat. Yet somehow they'd always made their marriage work, right up until the day Dad died, much too young, of a heart attack at age forty-four. Their long, happy, successful marriage had always inspired Jessie, but also intimidated her. She'd never been able to find the kind of relationship her parents had enjoyed.

Monica had, of course.

"I remember," Mr. Thayer was saying, seeming to warm to his purpose for coming over here today, "something your father once said to me. Your sister was the one he understood best, because she was like him. But you . . . you were the one he most admired. Because, after all, you were just like your mother, the woman he loved."

Jessie was touched. "Thank you for telling me that, Mr. Thayer."

"He was a good man, your father. I tried hard to get him to run for mayor of Sayer's Brook. I had the entire Republican Town Committee ready to back him. But then, the heart attack took him from us." A flicker of moisture appeared in the old man's bright eyes. "He would have been a good mayor."

"Yes, he would have, indeed," Jessie said.

Mr. Thayer squeezed her hand. "And now I will make my way around to the back and mingle with the Gorins. I am sure the conversation will be scintillating. That woman knows everything that goes on in this town."

Jessie laughed, and smiled after him as he walked off. She could see Monica and Todd coming out of their house now, heading up the hill, and in the street it looked like Heather and Bryan and their kids were on their way. Jessie took another deep breath and scooted back inside the house to put Mrs. Gorin's casserole on the table.

For a moment, she wanted to hurry upstairs to her bedroom and lock herself in her room. Jessie looked out the window as the guests assembled in the back-yard. Aunt Paulette had walked up from her cottage carrying the big bowl of salad she'd made. The Gorins were greeting Monica and Todd, and Mr. Thayer was kissing Heather on the hand, and clapping Bryan on the back. Everyone had so far been nice to her; Mr. Thayer had even gone out of his way to tell her something nice about Dad. This was going to be easy. No one was going to hold any grudges about the troubles with Emil. That was six years ago now. It was over. Jessie needed to just forget it and move on. No one was blaming her anymore.

But it wasn't so easy to move on.

At least, not from everything.

She'd grown accustomed to seeing Todd in the last week. It wasn't so hard seeing him. After all, their romance had been in high school. They'd just been kids. Sure, at the time, Jessie had been convinced Todd was her true and everlasting love—but she'd been a teenager, and most teenage girls believe their high school boyfriends are their soul mates, even if very few turn out to be so. So Jessie had been able to put some closure on Todd's long-ago rejection of her in favor of her sister. It was Bryan Pierce who still dredged up the raw feelings.

Unlike Todd, who'd become part of Jessie's family, Bryan hadn't been around in the days before Jessie left. He and Heather had been living elsewhere when Jessie had taken up with Emil, and it had only been while Jessie had been away that the happy couple—and their two adorable kids—had moved into the Wilson house on Hickory Dell. So Jessie had maybe seen them just two or three times—and then just fleeting encounters—since college and the heartache of the breakup.

And Bryan held a different place in her heart than Todd. Jessie had really, really fallen for Bryan. She had allowed herself to go so far as to imagine marrying him. She'd been twenty and twenty-one years old when they'd dated, old enough for deeper, more profound feelings than the teenage crush she'd had on Todd. So when Bryan told her he had fallen in love with Heather—the best friend in whom Jessie had confided her hopes and dreams of marriage—it had been a devastating blow. It had left Jessie shattered, and susceptible to the machinations of Emil Deetz.

She looked outside through the window once again. There was Bryan, looking a little older than she remembered him, with his red hair slightly receding at his temples, but really just as handsome as ever. He was flashing that smile of his, and his green eyes still sparkled when he did so. Heather stood by his side, not smiling much, as Bryan spoke with Mr. Thayer, and their two little kids, redheads like Bryan, clung to their father's pants.

Those could have been my kids, Jessie thought.

But she'd her own kid, and Jessie wouldn't trade Abby for anything, for any other life. For all the pain she'd been through with Emil—and the memory of the callous way he'd slit that man's throat would never fully leave her—Jessie wouldn't change what she had been through. If she hadn't met Emil—if she hadn't slept with him—she wouldn't have Abby. And life without Abby was unimaginable.

You didn't feel that way about the boy.

Jessie forced such thoughts out of her head. It had been a while since she thought about the twin she'd miscarried, the little boy fetus in the pool of blood— the little boy who had haunted her dreams for so long. For the last couple of years—and especially since she'd learned Emil had been killed—Jessie had been largely free from such haunting memories. Why was she suddenly thinking about the baby she'd lost this afternoon—when she had a yard full of guests to entertain?

She knew why. Those people out in the yard represented her past. They knew Mom and Dad. They knew her secrets. They knew what she had been through. Not just with Emil either. They knew about her heartbreak with Todd and with Bryan, and they all would watch to see how Jessie reacted when she greeted them, their wives at their sides.

Jessie held her chin high and walked through the dining room toward the back door. As she did so, she passed a photograph of Mom. She'd found it yesterday, and slipped it into a frame and hung it on the wall. It was a picture that her mother had given her when she had gone off to college. Jessie had been nervous, afraid she wouldn't be able to handle the workload and the pressures of living away from home for the first time in her life. Mom had found a photo of herself from when she was Jessie's age—seventeen. In the photo, Mom was smiling wide, sporting her mid-1960s hairdo that flipped up at the ends. She wore a little black choker with a heart in the center. And she'd taken a black felt-tip marker and inscribed the photo for Jessie.

You can do anything, my sweet baby. There is nothing you can't accomplish when you put your mind, heart and spirit into it.

She'd signed it, *Love, Mom.*

Jessie paused and looked at the photo, rereading the inscription. Then she nodded to herself and headed outside.

She walked straight into the foursome of Monica and Todd, and Heather and Bryan.

"Hello, Jessie," Heather said.

There was a brief hug between the two women.

"Welcome home," Bryan told her.

Jessie didn't hug him, but shook his hand.

"Thank you." She paused. "It's good to be home."

"You look great," Bryan said.

His words seemed thick, and pointed, and full of meaning. In that unspoken way Aunt Paulette would have described as psychic, Jessie seemed to sense Heather's discomfort with her husband's observation.

"Jessie always looks great," Todd reiterated, and this time Jessie felt Monica's discomfort.

"Where are your children?" Jessie asked, directing the question to Heather. She found she couldn't look at Bryan fully. "I thought I saw them a moment ago."

It was Bryan who answered her. "They spotted the swing set," he said.

They all looked in that direction. Bryan's two kids were scrambling onto the two swings, leaving Abby just to watch. Inga was with them, supervising it all.

"Piper and Ashton are thrilled to have someone in the neighborhood finally to play with," Heather said.

"I hope they'll be good friends," Jessie said.

There was a moment of awkward silence. "Good friends" was a term with some freighted history among that particular group.

"I was pleased to see how well your son and Abby played together the other day," Jessie said at last, breaking the silence. "Why didn't your daughter come up as well?"

Bryan and Heather were looking at her blankly.

"Your son," Jessie repeated.

"This is the first time Ashton has been here," Heather said.

Jessie smiled. "No, actually, he came up the other day. . . . He and Abby swung on the swings for a bit, then walked down to the brook. Inga was with them."

"That's impossible," Heather insisted. "Ashton never goes anywhere without his sister, and they know better than to leave our yard without asking permission."

Jessie frowned. "Well, it was *some* little boy. . . . Aunt Paulette said it must have been Ashton because there aren't any other little boys in the neighborhood."

"That's right. No other little kids, period. I don't know who it was that played with your daughter, Jessie, but it wasn't Ashton."

Jessie looked off at the boy on the swing set.

"Strange," she said.

"Well," Bryan offered, "I suppose whoever it was, we'll learn next week. Is Abby starting school at Independent Day?"

"Yes," Jessie replied. "She starts kindergarten."

"Ashton's in first grade there, and Piper's in second," Bryan said. "I imagine you'll find Abby's little playmate there. Maybe he comes from one of the new houses they built on the other side of the woods."

"But then he would have had to cross Manning's property," Todd said, "and our esteemed neighbor has 'no trespassing' signs everywhere."

"I don't know about you, Todd," Bryan said, "but a 'no trespassing' sign never stopped me as a kid."

"Well, some of us like to play by the rules," Todd replied icily.

Jessie picked up on the disdain between the two men, and wondered why. Then she remembered that they worked at rival investment brokerages in the city. Both had gotten help early in their careers from Mr. Thayer, but then Bryan had jumped ship, going over to the other side. Now they were like two hostile tomcats, each staking out their territories and trying to assert their claim as the alpha male. Jessie found it all terribly tedious, and oh so terribly just like men.

Another awkward silence had descended.

"You should see the work Jessie has already done inside Mom's house," Monica said, trying to keep the conversation going. "Hardly here a week, and already she's retiling the bathroom and repainting the kitchen. . . ."

"Well," Jessie admitted, "it's mostly Inga, Abby's nanny. She's a terrific help around the house. Really handy."

She watched as Bryan's eyes looked back over at the swings and seemed to take in every detail of Inga's solid, strong, full figure.

"We've been through four nannies in six years," Heather said, sighing. "Our two are rather . . . a handful."

At that moment Ashton was shouting at the top of his lungs, angry at his sister for swinging higher than he could manage. The little girl was laughing derisively at him. Jessie noticed that Abby still stood off to the side, watching the other children monopolize her swing set.

"Kids," Heather said, shaking her head.

"Well, I should mingle," Jessie said, feeling she'd spent more than enough time trying to make conversation. "Please help yourself to some punch."

Everyone smiled as Jessie moved off across the yard.

She headed straight for the swing set.

"Everything going okay?" Inga asked as Jessie approached.

Inga knew the backstories that united the afternoon's guests. Jessie had shared the basic details: the breakups, the rejections, the heartbreak, the scandals. So the nanny understood all too well the difficulties Jessie would face meeting everyone today.

"As well as can be expected," Jessie said, with a small laugh.

She looked at the little redheaded boy with freckles sprinkled across his cheeks and the bridge of his nose. He was attempting to swing as high as his older sister but without much success. His face was flushed and his teeth were gritted.

Inga seemed to intuit Jessie's thoughts.

"Not the same kid," she said. "Not the one who was up here the other day."

Ashton's big green eyes made contact with Jessie's. She looked away.

"Mommy," Abby said, tugging on Jessie's khaki shorts. "When can I have a turn on the swings?"

"These are our guests, sweetie. Let them swing first. I'm sure they'll give you a turn soon."

"No, I won't," said the little girl, Piper. "I am going to swing all day. Ashton can give her his swing, since he keeps losing to me anyhow."

"I'm not getting off, either," Ashton shouted. "I am going to beat you, Piper. You'll see!"

"Five more minutes and one of you is giving Abby a turn," Jessie told them. "These are her swings, after all."

"I'll make sure they do," Inga said, giving Jessie a wink.

Jessie tousled Abby's hair and started back across the yard before Inga stopped her.

"Remember the crap you've been through, Jessie," the nanny told her. "You got through all of that. And you'll get through today, too."

Jessie gave her a smile and a thumbs-up.

Aunt Paulette was passing around a tray of cheese

and crackers among the guests. "Everyone keeps saying how pretty you look," she whispered as Jessie passed.

Dear Aunt Paulette. She made Jessie think of Mom, and that was a good thing.

"When are we going to get the house tour?" Gert Gorin was asking as Jessie approached.

"Well, come along now then," Jessie replied. "There's not a lot to show, but you can see what there is to see."

The Gorins and Mr. Thayer followed her into the house. She took them through the kitchen, instructing them to step over the paint cans and containers of spackle, and then up the stairs, where hours of scrubbing and vacuuming had left the wood floors shining and the windows sparkling in the afternoon sun. Jessie noticed Gert Gorin's eagle eyes taking in everything, her inquisitive mind soaking it all up.

"Where does the nanny sleep?" Gert wanted to know.

"Her room's down the hall," Jessie replied.

"Mmhmm," Gert said, looking away.

Jessie glanced out the window down at the guests. She was glad to see that Abby had finally gotten onto the swing set, but she sat by herself. The other two kids were chasing each other in circles through the grass. Inga had moved over to the grill, where she was lighting the charcoal. It was an old-fashioned grill, no gas, no instant charcoal. It would take a while for the briquettes to get hot enough for cooking. Monica and Todd and Heather and Bryan were still together, the women largely silent as the two men spoke about something—something boring and corporate, Jessie was sure. She had no doubt they were constantly trying to one-up each other. Aunt Paulette still flitted among them all with her platter of cheese.

Jessie was about to look away from the window when she spotted something else. A man was walking through the bushes at the far end of the yard toward the house. From up here Jessie couldn't make out what the man looked like. But he seemed tall and dark. He walked slowly, carefully, deliberately.

It could only be John Manning.

So their famous neighbor had decided to grace them with his presence after all.

Jessie hurriedly finished the tour so she could get back outside and greet her newest guest. She'd never read any of John Manning's books—she didn't like horror stories; she'd lived through enough of her own—but she knew people who did. Her editor at the publishing house was a huge fan of Manning's, and wished she could lure him away from his current contract. After all, John Manning's books had sold millions of copies, and made him and his publishers millions of dollars. A number of movies had been made from his books, and his latest, *The Sound of a Scream,* was being turned into a TV miniseries. Inga had just started reading it, curious about the man who lived just beyond their pine trees—and whose wife had died in a mysterious fall just a few feet from where they lived.

"What a dark imagination," Inga had said after reading the first few pages. "He sure enjoys slaughtering people."

It was hard for Jessie to imagine writing about such things. In her own work she wrote about transformation and survival and joy—not death and destruction. And she'd come to believe that what one wrote reflected the core of who one was. So she was more than a little apprehensive about meeting this neighbor of theirs.

When they returned outside, they found that the sun, so bright just moments before, had slipped behind a cloud. The shadows had abruptly disappeared from the yard, leaving the day shrouded in a bluish haze. Jessie noticed that John Manning had approached none of the adults, but rather had paused at the grill, where the three little children were now watching Inga lay the hamburger patties over the smoldering coals. He was saying something to the kids, though Jessie couldn't hear what he said. He seemed so enormous standing next to the children. Well over six feet, he was dressed all in black: a black T-shirt over black jeans, and on his feet he wore black sneakers. Jessie felt a sudden chill and forced herself to shrug it off.

"Hello," she said, approaching, her hand held out in greeting, a smile on her face.

John Manning's deep-set dark eyes looked up from the children and found her gaze. Jessie took a small, involuntary step backward, as if knocked off stride by the man's extraordinary, movie-star good looks. He reached out and took Jessie's hand.

"Ms. Clarkson, I take it," he said.

"Yes," Jessie replied, and realized her voice unexpectedly trembled a bit. She was being foolish. She wasn't usually impressed by celebrities. Even handsome celebrities. "Thanks for coming."

John Manning gave her a small, tentative smile. "I thought I should, given that we live next to each other.

I've gotten used to seeing this house always dark. Now I'll need to accustom myself to seeing lights over here."

Jessie remembered the day she'd seen him stranding in his window, staring over at her house. For some silly reason, she trembled again. Her hand was still in Manning's, and he must have felt the tremor pass through her body.

"You seem cold," he observed, "and on such a beautiful, warm day."

There was something about his eyes. So dark, so magnetic. It was as if Jessie was being drawn into his mind against her will. Suddenly she saw an image: Manning's wife, Millie, lying facedown in a pool of blood on their concrete patio. She trembled again.

"I guess I'll feel better once the sun comes back out from behind the cloud," Jessie said, and extricated her hand from Manning's grip.

He smiled a little wider. "We won't have to wait long for that, I don't think." He looked up. "Except for that one big cumulus straight above, the sky is otherwise a solid sheet of blue."

Even as he spoke the sun emerged from behind the cloud, filling the yard up once again with golden light.

"Happier now?" Manning said, his smile turning cheeky.

Jessie laughed. "Thanks for arranging it."

"Anything to be a good neighbor," he told her.

In the direct sunlight, Manning seemed even more handsome. His dark eyes were flecked with gold. Jessie didn't know what it was, but she found herself entranced by this man, and she felt as if she could stand there all day looking into his eyes.

"I understand you're a writer," Manning was saying.

"Yes," Jessie said, although her voice seemed a world away. "I . . . am."

He smiled. "Perhaps we can share trade secrets sometime."

Jessie felt her whole body blush.

But then Inga was at her side, breaking the spell.

"Excuse me, Mr. Manning," the nanny was saying, "but I wanted to tell you I'm a third of the way through *The Sound of a Scream* and you have me absolutely hooked."

Jessie noticed the small smile that had been playing with Manning's lips suddenly broaden across his face. "Well, thank you very much," he said, turning his attention away from Jessie and toward Inga. "It's especially rewarding to have such a pretty fan."

"This is Abby's nanny, Inga," Jessie said, as introduction. She noticed Inga was blushing a bit.

"And such an exquisite accent," the author was saying, taking Inga's hand in his and kissing it. He hadn't done that to Jessie. "I'd say it's Bayerisch, if I hear correctly."

Jessie was surprised. She thought Inga barely had an accent at all. She spoke perfect English to Jessie's ears.

It was Inga's turn to smile broadly. "Yes, indeed it is. I am impressed. I was born in the south of Germany. You must have traveled quite a bit in my country."

"I have indeed."

Suddenly Manning began speaking in thick, guttural German to Inga's obvious delight. It wasn't often she got to converse with someone in her native tongue.

Jessie stood by awkwardly as the two carried on in a lively conversation completely oblivious to her. It was as if neither even remembered she was standing there. She felt oddly left out—even jealous.

She told herself she was being ridiculous.

"Help yourself to some punch," Jessie whispered, leaning in toward Manning, who barely acknowledged her comment. He was too busy speaking fluent German, telling Inga something about his book, since the phrase "sound of a scream" kept popping out from the indistinguishable foreign words. Jessie gave them both a little smile and slunk away.

Of course John Manning would pay greater attention to Inga than to Jessie. Inga was nineteen years old, shapely and sexy, with the biggest, brightest blue eyes Jessie had ever seen. She had some experience with men preferring other women to her. Why should she have been surprised by Manning's sudden diversion of interest? Moreover, why should she be bothered by it?

But she was. She couldn't deny that what had just happened did bother her.

Once again, she scolded herself for being ridiculous.

"Mommy."

Abby was tugging on her hand.

Jessie looked down at her daughter. "What is it, sweetie?"

"Those kids are back on the swings and won't let me swing again."

"Come on, baby," she said, taking Abby's hand. "Let's go over and talk with them."

"No!" shouted Piper, when Jessie asked her to give Abby a turn, as she swung higher and higher into the sky.

"No!" echoed her brother Ashton, desperately trying to keep up with her.

"Well, they are Abby's swings, after all," Jessie said.

"But we're your guests," Piper shrieked, as she whizzed past Jessie and Abby, flying higher with each rotation. "My mother says guests come first."

"That's right," came a voice behind Jessie.

It was Heather. She had wandered over to the swing set, attracted by her children's voices.

"But we must be good guests, too," she told Piper. "Five more minutes, then let Abby have a turn."

Jessie was about to tell Heather "five minutes my ass" and order the little brat off the swing pronto. But she held her tongue. She didn't want to cause friction with the neighbors on their first day of contact. Besides, she thought part of her anger was still, absurdly, rooted in the little scene back by the grill between she, Manning, and Inga.

It seemed Heather had observed that interaction as well. "Tell me, Jessie," she said, her voice reminiscent of a cat's purr. "Does that girl you have working for you always pounce so quickly on available men?"

Jessie laughed a little. "Oh, I wouldn't say that Inga pounced. . . ."

"No? John walked into the yard and suddenly she was all over him."

Jessie looked at her old friend. Heather seemed upset, even jealous. This was getting crazier. What kind of effect did this John Manning have on women?

"You called him John," Jessie said. "Do you know him well?"

Heather averted her eyes. "We're friendly. We're neighbors, after all."

"Monica said he keeps to himself. I was surprised he came by today."

Heather was watching the conversation between Manning and Inga, still proceeding intensely beside the grill.

"He's a lonely man," Heather said. "His wife's death really affected him. I'd hate to see some gold-digging teenager take advantage of him."

Jessie's momentary pique at Inga dissipated and she came to her defense. "Inga is no gold digger, Heather. She's a hardworking girl. All she did was tell Mr. Manning she was enjoying his book, and then was delighted to find he could speak German."

"I assume she's in this country legally?" Heather asked, her eyes finally returning to Jessie.

For a moment Jessie was flabbergasted. "Of course, she is," she finally managed to respond.

Heather just shrugged and walked away.

"Wheeee!" came the voice of little Piper, behind them on the swings.

Jessie turned and made a beeline over to the kid.

"Off," she ordered.

"But my mommy said five minutes."

"Yeah, and those five minutes are up. Off!"

Piper let her feet touch the earth and then sprung off the swing. Jessie caught it in midair and motioned for Abby to get on.

As Piper ran crying over to her mother, Ashton giggled. "Wanta race?" he asked Abby, who nodded, and soon they were off.

Even as she kept up her running conversation in German with John Manning, Inga managed to grill the burgers, and soon everyone had one in their hands, except for Abby and Ashton, who kept up their swinging. A pouty Piper refused to eat, her big lower lip protruding, her little freckled face scrunched up like an old lady. Jessie noticed how Heather managed to get a seat next to John Manning at the picnic table, and how she whispered something in his ear. The handsome author seemed to pay no notice to what she said, keeping his attention on Inga. Heather seemed furious.

What the hell was going on here?

Jessie took a seat beside Aunt Paulette, who was applying relish to her burger—a veggie patty, since the older woman didn't eat meat.

"You notice anything weird between Heather and Mr. Manning?" Jessie whispered.

Her aunt lifted an eyebrow. "Gert Gorin was just telling me she's seen Heather leaving Manning's house several times late at night."

"Gosh," Jessie said, grinning despite herself. "The things those binoculars have seen."

"Remember to keep your blinds closed," Aunt Paulette cautioned.

Jessie was suddenly aware of Bryan sitting down beside her. With his wife trying—in vain—to get the attention of Mr. Manning, Bryan was apparently left free to make his own moves. And Jessie was startled to realize he was moving in on her.

"I have to tell you, Jessaloo, you look amazing," he breathed in her ear as he sat down.

Jessaloo was the name he'd called her in college. Jessie blushed despite herself.

"Really, really amazing," he said, keeping his eyes on her as he took a bite of his hamburger, juice running down over his chin.

"Thanks," Jessie said, stiffening.

"Look," Bryan said, smiling at her, "it can either be comfortable or uncomfortable living down the street from each other." He paused. "I vote for comfortable."

"Of course," Jessie said, keeping her shoulder from touching his and her eyes from returning his gaze. "That's why I had this picnic. I want us all to be good neighbors."

"You know I'm sorry for how everything happened. . . ."

"It's ancient history, Bryan," Jessie said. She turned to Aunt Paulette and asked how she liked her veggie burger, but before her aunt could reply, Bryan was touching her shoulder, indicating he had more to say.

"I made the wrong choice, you know," he whispered. "I never should have married Heather. I should have—"

"Don't say any more," Jessie said harshly, spinning around to look at him. "Don't you dare say another word."

Gathering her plate and napkin, she stood up from the picnic table and stalked off. Aunt Paulette followed.

"You okay, honey?"

"Yes," Jessie said. "Just need to use the little girl's room."

She hurried back inside the house, letting the screen door slam behind her.

She took a deep breath. Then another, and another.

She couldn't eat any more of her burger, so she tossed her plate into the trash.

How dare Bryan say such a thing, after all this time,

and with Heather sitting just a few feet away at the other table?

Was it even true?

Jessie felt certain that something was going on between Heather and John Manning. If his wife was having an affair, Bryan would naturally want to lash out. And who better to make Heather jealous than Bryan's former girlfriend, the woman he'd left on her account?

That was all it was. Bryan was trying to use her in a ploy against his wife, to get back at Heather, to have a little revenge.

But what if what he'd said was true?

Jessaloo, you look amazing.

Jessie looked at herself in the hallway mirror. She *did* look good. She was finally starting to see that about herself again. She was pretty. She could admit that now.

Maybe Bryan really did feel he'd been wrong to choose Heather over her.

What if seeing Jessie again had rekindled his feelings for her? What if he really did regret hurting her the way he had, and wanted to see if he still had a chance?

"All the more reason to spit in his face," Jessie whispered again.

What a lout for saying such a thing—*now*, in front of everyone.

Jessie couldn't believe how furious she was. Maybe this whole housewarming party was a mistake. What had she accomplished? She knew Monica and Todd weren't happy about the idea. They guarded their privacy closely; they never liked socializing with the neighbors. And Jessie had gone and invited that snoop,

Gert Gorin, right into their yard. Moreover, she'd brought Todd into contact with Bryan, a man he loathed, and she'd forced Abby to endure the brattiness of Bryan's two spoiled, selfish kids. She'd dredged up all sorts of emotions she'd thought she'd banished forever: insecurity, rejection, jealousy, heartbreak. Jessie just wanted all these people to go home, right now.

But she couldn't exactly head back out there and order them all off her property. She looked again at the photo of Mom and the words she'd written. Jessie could get through this. She'd gotten through far worse.

She returned to the party.

The first thing she noticed was that John Manning was gone. When she inquired of Aunt Paulette, she was told the author had asked her to give Jessie his thanks, but he really had to get back to his writing. He was on a deadline. Jessie felt it was rude for him to leave without saying good-bye to her in person. She'd only been inside for a few minutes, after all. But then she noticed Heather and Bryan off to the side of the yard in the midst of a rather intense conversation themselves, and she suspected something had happened that had caused John Manning to make a quick getaway.

Within a few minutes, the dueling couple were gathering their kids and making their own farewells.

"It was wonderful to see you again, Jessie, it truly was," Heather said, taking her by the shoulders and kissing the air beside her face. "Sorry we can't stay, but I have a ton of work to do. Catering a big party tomorrow."

"I'm glad you could come," Jessie said, reflecting on the irony of her words.

"Good-bye, Jessie," Bryan said, "and thanks."

His eyes barely made contact with hers. Jessie noticed she wasn't "Jessaloo" anymore.

Bryan and Heather hurried back down the hill, their kids screaming after them.

Mr. Thayer was the next to leave, thanking them far more authentically and telling Jessie once again how pleased he was that she had returned to the neighborhood. Monica and Todd took that as their cue to leave as well. Monica asked her sister—halfheartedly, Jessie thought—if she needed any help cleaning up, but Aunt Paulette piped in that she'd take care of everything. Monica didn't object, and she and Todd headed back to their house. That left the Gorins, who didn't leave until Inga had wrapped the last of the uneaten burgers in cellophane and Jessie had begun peeling the plastic covers off the picnic tables.

"Well," Aunt Paulette said with a sigh when they were finally alone, "was it so bad?"

"I guess it was good as a way to break the ice," Jessie acknowledged, "but I'm glad it's over."

"Do I have to play with those kids again?" Abby asked.

"Not if you don't want to," Jessie told her.

"They weren't very nice."

"I know, baby." She smiled sadly. "But apples don't tend to fall too far from the tree."

She saw something suddenly, out by the brook.

It was a child.

A little boy . . .

Had Ashton returned?

No, it wasn't Ashton. The boy was standing down at the brook, staring up at them. Jessie couldn't make out his face, but she could see he wasn't a redhead like Ashton.

"Abby," she called. "Look down there. Is that your little friend—?"

But in the moment Jessie had moved her eyes over to look at her daughter, the little boy had disappeared. When Jessie looked back at the brook, there was no one standing there anymore.

"Where, Mommy?" Abby asked.

"Never mind, honey. I guess I made a mistake."

The sun was dropping lower in the sky and the yard was filling up with shadows.

"Jessie," came Inga's voice. "Everything's cleaned up here. Do you mind if I run over to Mr. Manning's house for a moment?"

Jessie looked at her. "Whatever for?"

"He told me he'd give me a couple more of his books, and an autographed copy I could send home to my mother."

Jessie approached her. "You sure were in quite the conversation with him."

"I know." Inga blushed. "He was very charming, a very nice man. He knew the town where I was born. He's been all over the world."

Jessie tried to push away the ridiculous feelings of jealousy she felt. "Of course, Inga," she said. "Go on over. Everything's under control here."

"Thanks. I won't be gone long. I'll be back to help get Abby ready for bed."

Jessie watched the nanny scurry across the lawn toward the line of fir trees that divided their property with John Manning's. She hadn't noticed how skimpy

Inga's shorts were before, or how perfectly they showed off her long, shapely legs.

She sighed.

"Abby," she called to her daughter, who was heading back over to the swing set. "Let's go inside and watch television okay?"

For some reason, she wanted Abby close to her tonight, and inside the house. A smile stretched across Jessie's face as the child hurried over to her and took her hand.

EIGHT

"**D**id you see what happened over there?" Gert Gorin gushed to her husband as they returned to their own house. "Did you see the way Bryan grabbed Heather and practically yanked her away from that wife-killer?"

"You know, Gert, you really ought to be a headline writer for the *National Enquirer*."

Arthur was about to settle into his favorite, frayed, worn-down armchair. Pointing the remote control at the television set, he pressed his thumb and the Yankees game appeared like magic on the screen. He settled back into his chair.

"I'm telling you, Arthur, something very peculiar is going on in this neighborhood. I've seen Heather Pierce go in and out of John Manning's dark, gloomy castle more times than I can count. And today, I saw the way she was looking at him, her eyes all filled with jealousy and rage, while he carried on with that German teenager." Gert was taking down her binoculars, which she kept hanging on the wall from a hook. "But the joke was on him! He didn't know that girl is actually Jessie's lover." She placed the binoculars against the glass of the picture window and pressed her eyes into them to peer outside. "I don't really blame Jessie for going lesbionic after all the crap she's been through with men."

"Maybe you oughta try it, Gert," Arthur said, not really paying attention to her, keeping his eyes on the ball game.

"But I wasn't the only one to notice Heather's raging eyes. Her husband saw it all too well. And you saw what he did, didn't you, Arthur?"

Her husband didn't reply. The bases were loaded. He leaned forward in his chair, watching the television.

Gert pulled away from the binoculars and looked over at him. "You saw what Bryan did, didn't you, Arthur?"

"Not really," he said, watching the guy at bat strike out and cursing under his breath. "But I'm sure you're going to tell me."

"He decided two could play that game so he started hitting on Jessie. You know they used to date in college. I remember the day she brought him up here to meet her mother. And I also remember that fast-and-loose Heather swinging her butt up the road in her short shorts and stealing Bryan right away from innocent little Jessie." Gert shook her head and returned her eyes to the binoculars. "Back in those days Jessie was still innocent. My, how times change."

"Except for one thing."

"What's that?"

"You, poking your nose into other people's business."

Gert spun around at him. "I don't get involved! I just watch! Because it's better to know what's going on in the neighborhood than be surprised. Remember, I was fully aware of how dangerous that Emil Deetz was months before he killed that man. I'd been watching him and Jessie fly up and down the road on that ungodly loud motorbike of his. I knew something bad was going to happen, so I was prepared. When everyone else was shocked to see the police cars across the street, I wasn't. I had expected something like that all along."

The guy up at bat got a hit, and the guy on third base slid home. Arthur let out a whoop.

"Oh, Arthur, stop yelling! It scares me!" Gert gave up on the binoculars. It was getting too dark to see anything. "But I tell you, seeing Bryan try to hit on Jessie was something else entirely. Really, the man has no shame. I understand that his wife was embarrassing him, plopping herself down next to John Manning and making goo-goo eyes at him. But after how Bryan dumped Jessie, for him to start whispering to her . . ." Gert shuddered. "I mean, did you see the way she stood up so quickly and stormed off? I can only imagine what he said to her."

For the next hour, as the last of the sun disappeared behind the trees, Gert kept up her watch of the neighborhood, peering out the window, hoping to see something, anything. Finally, just as she was about ready to call it a night, something caught Gert's eye. She quickly grabbed the binoculars again.

"Somebody's coming out of John Manning's house," she announced. "I can't see who, though. Too many trees."

"I'm sure Mr. Manning will be glad to dig them up to give you a better view."

"Whoever it was didn't walk out into the street," Gert said, straining her eyes to make something out in the darkness. "He—or she—must have cut through the trees toward Jessie's house."

A flash of movement, a hint of color, suddenly appeared among the shadows. Then it was gone.

But it was quickly followed by what sounded like a scream.

"Arthur!" Gert shrieked. "Did you hear that?"

But he didn't reply, All he could hear were the horns and chants coming from the bleachers at Yankee Stadium.

"Arthur!" Gert said, waving at him to get his attention. "I just heard a scream."

"Of course you did, Gert. You *live* to hear screams."

"No, I did! Seriously! Please come here! Put the ball game on mute and come over to the window. Please, Arthur!"

He groaned, but he did as his wife asked. He knew if he resisted, she'd keep caterwauling until he followed her instructions. So he turned off the volume on the television and pushed himself up and out of his chair. His back was aching him, so he walked extra slowly over to the picture window.

"Hurry up, Arthur!"

"I don't hear anything."

"I'm telling you, I heard a—"

The sound came again. It was high-pitched and shrill.

A strange sort of sound. Maybe a scream . . . but maybe laughter.

"That's what you heard, Gert," Arthur said, shaking

his head. "The little girl is over there playing. Sorry to tell you, but the show's over for tonight."

He shuffled back over to his chair. Within moments the sounds of Yankee Stadium were once again filling their living room.

Gert peered outside. She tried to see something. Anything. But finally she gave up. Arthur was right. The show was over.

But she'd be back at the window the next morning. Who knew what she might see then?

NINE

It was pitch dark, and getting close to nine o'clock. But still Inga hadn't returned from John Manning's house.

"Well, that's just crossing the line," Jessie said to herself, as she turned down her sheets, surprised by how annoyed she felt. She'd finished cleaning up, gotten Abby ready for bed, tucked her in and turned off her light, and then taken her shower—and throughout that whole process, she kept expecting Inga to come in at any moment. But here it was, nearly an hour and a half after the nanny had gone next door, and she still wasn't home. That was definitely crossing the line.

It's her life, Jessie tried telling herself. *She's not on the clock twenty-four-seven. Besides, I told her to go.*

But still. An hour and a half.

What were they *doing* over there?

"It's none of my business," Jessie tried reasoning with herself.

The problem was, Jessie had a pretty good *idea* of what they were doing, and it pissed her off. Absurdly.

Why should she care what Abby's nanny did during her time off?

It was John Manning's eyes.

He had been so compelling. He had looked at Jessie and she'd practically melted. And then Inga had walked up and he'd forgotten Jessie even existed.

Just like every man in her life.

She looked at herself in the mirror. How had she allowed herself to believe she was getting prettier? She was just as plain as ever. . . .

"Okay," she told her reflection, transferring her annoyance with Inga to herself. "Now you are playing victim. What would all your readers think of that?"

She realized this little episode would make a great anecdote for her new book. She would write that even when we think we've stopped playing the victim card, we can still fall back. She'd describe this event—changing the names, of course—to illustrate how old patterns of self-destructive thinking can recur at any moment. Old jealousies and insecurities can resurface, and we have to recognize them for what they are, gently pushing them away before letting them take hold.

But in fact she couldn't stop thinking of John Manning's eyes.

If Heather's behavior was any indication, the celebrated author had a certain effect on women. Jessie resolved not to become one more smitten female mooning around the dark and handsome Manning. She should be glad, in fact, that Inga was over there, possibly in a passionate embrace with Manning, because that would mean Heather's affair with him—if there was, in fact, an affair—was over, or at least not very serious. And *that* would suggest that Heather and Bryan would stay together—and *that* would make Jessie's life easier.

Applying moisturizer to her face in front of Mom's old vanity mirror, Jessie recalled how upsetting Bryan's come-on had been. It had exposed the wound that she had thought had fully healed. Again, she told herself, it was all fodder for the new book. She'd write about how some wounds never really heal. The best we can do is keep them protected from greater infection. Jessie had been surprised by the surge of old feelings for Bryan— the anger, certainly, but also, deeper down, the hope. *Might he still love me? Might he come back to me, even now?*

She didn't like that part of herself, the weak little woman who still lived down deep inside her. But now that she had revealed herself, Jessie had to treat her gently, and tenderly. "You don't want Bryan," she spoke into the mirror. "He's not the kind of man you want. He's greedy and manipulative and selfish, and disrespectful of women." What she didn't say out loud, but thought, was: *Just like Heather. So they're perfect for each other.*

"Mommy!"

Abby's voice from the next room startled her.

"What is it, honey?" Jessie called, hurrying away from the vanity and out into the hallway. The moonlight was coming through the window in her daughter's room, and Jessie could see the little girl's silhouette as she sat up in bed.

"I heard something scary," Abby said as Jessie reached her and switched on the light.

"What did you hear, honey?"

"I heard a scream," she said.

"A scream?"

Abby nodded. "I think it was Inga."

There was fear in Abby's eyes, but not terror. Certainly not panic. Abby was the calmest little kid Jessie had ever known. She never threw tantrums, rarely complained of pain or discomfort, and even accepted other kids' bullying—like Piper Pierce's—with a minimum of protest. Abby wasn't easy to rattle. She was also almost impossible to fool, and never indulged in childish fantasies. If she said she'd heard Inga scream, she was being serious.

"When did you hear this, sweetie?" Jessie asked.

"A little while ago. I didn't call you right away, because I was trying not to be a crybaby."

"Oh, honey, you can always call me. . . ." She stroked her daughter's hair. "Maybe it wasn't a scream. Laughter can sound like screaming sometime. Maybe it's just somebody in the neighborhood having fun. The night is so still, and everybody's windows are open. . . . Maybe, if it *was* Inga, Mr. Manning had just told her a joke."

The little girl shook her head. "It wasn't laughter."

Jessie sighed. "Okay, sweetie. You get back down under the covers and I'll go take a look. I'm sure it's nothing. Inga will be home soon from Mr. Manning's."

"Okay, Mommy."

Jessie pulled the sheet up and kissed Abby on the forehead. "Do you want me to leave the light on for you?"

"No, that's okay. Now that I've told you about it, it doesn't seem scary anymore."

Jessie smiled. What a brave kid she had. "Okay, sweetie, pleasant dreams."

"Good night, Mommy."

Jessie switched the light back off and stepped out of Abby's room.

She was in her nightgown, a sheer, filmy pink thing, so she pulled a terrycloth robe from a hook in the bathroom and wrapped it around herself.

She hadn't heard a thing. She'd been too wrapped up in her own thoughts, Jessie supposed as she headed down the stairs. She had her own idea about what Abby might have heard. She suspected it had been neither a scream nor laughter—or rather, she suspected it had been a combination of both. What Abby had likely heard was Inga and John Manning carrying on, their crescendo of passion floating out from the open windows through the still night and reaching the ears of the five-year-old girl.

Jessie was back to thinking that the nanny had crossed the line as she pushed open the screen door and stepped out into the dark night.

TEN

"**D**id you hear something a little while ago?" Monica asked Todd as she got into bed.

"No," he mumbled, reading the stocks on his Black-Berry.

"It sounded like a scream."

"Probably a bird."

"It was no bird." Monica shuddered, pulling the sheet up around her. "It was creepy. I was brushing my teeth in the bathroom and I heard it from the window."

"Then maybe a cat. You know how cats in heat sound."

Monica pouted. She knew very well how a cat in heat sounded, but she wasn't sure Todd did, with the way he'd been utterly clueless to her attempts to get him to make love to her lately. "It wasn't a cat either," she said. Todd just grunted.

Monica was still stewing about the party, about all the little dynamics of tension she'd spotted bubbling under the surface. She knew Todd still resented Bryan for jumping ship and leaving their company and heading over to one of their biggest rivals. She knew that Bryan and Heather were unhappy—that was plainly obvious in the way they looked at and spoke to each other—and she suspected Bryan had made a pass at Jessie, because her sister had bolted up from the picnic table at one point and stalked inside. Monica was very grateful that her own marriage was as solid as it was, and that her sister's return would not cause the same kind of temptation for Todd.

Of course, Todd's lack of interest in sex lately did trouble her. Mostly Monica tried not to think about it, but sometimes it became unavoidable, as it had just now with Todd's comment about a cat in heat. That had made Monica think about the lack of heat in her own relationship. But still, she didn't think there was a problem in their marriage. It was just that Todd was consumed with work. The economic downtown had meant the banks were recalculating everything. Todd was constantly figuring and refiguring and sometimes sat up late at night on the computer, telling her to go on to bed without him. Monica often found him slumped over in his chair in the morning.

"Honey," Aunt Paulette had said to her, "maybe he's . . . maybe he's avoiding something."

"Avoiding something?" Monica had asked.

"Sounds to me like he's losing interest in intimacy."

"That's crazy!"

"Don't be angry, honey. I'm just getting a vibe that he's using work to avoid being close. . . . Maybe you ought to see a counselor."

That had really enraged Monica. Her nutty old aunt's "vibe" was wrong. Todd was trying to make sure he didn't lose his job. He was trying to guarantee their income stayed high because soon, very soon, Monica wanted to have a baby—

She thought the hardest part of today hadn't been Bryan or Heather or anything else. It had been watching Jessie and Abby together. How badly Monica wanted a child. Bearing Todd a son or a daughter would really bond them together. But they'd been trying for more than six years now. They'd seen all sorts of specialists and Monica had tried all sorts of fertility drugs, but nothing had helped. Doctors had determined the problem was with her, not Todd; it wasn't that she was completely infertile, just that it was very, very difficult for her to get pregnant. For a while, to increase their odds, they had been having sex all of the time, practically nonstop, in fact—on the kitchen table, outside in the yard—hoping one of those times would be the charm. But in last few years all that frantic sexual activity had dwindled off, and by now they'd stopped talking about having a baby altogether. Adoption was out of the picture; Todd insisted he wanted a kid who carried on his genes. And Monica wanted so desperately to give it to him.

She was being punished.

There were times she truly felt that way. If she believed in fate and karma and all that craziness Mom used to talk about, she might even be convinced of the fact. Monica lived with a secret, something she'd never confided to anyone, something she kept down deep in the darkness of her mind and tried not to remember. In her junior year of high school, she'd deliberately gotten Todd—her sister's boyfriend—drunk, and then had sex with him in the back of his car. Jessie had been home with the flu; Monica and Todd had gone out with a bunch of other friends, one of whom had snuck out a couple of bottles of Jack Daniel's from his father's liquor cabinet. Monica kept pushing Todd to take another swig of the whisky, daring him to drink it all.

She'd had a crush on him for months; she'd hated the fact that Jessie had won him and she hadn't. Monica was very bitter that Jessie always seemed to get whatever she wanted. The teachers at school all thought Jessie was so smart and so clever; their friends all preferred Jessie to her, since Jessie was funny and warm and always offered such good advice to problems. Mom certainly favored Jessie—they were like two peas in a pod—and even though Dad always said Monica was "just like" him, Monica suspected that even Dad, deep down, had a respect for Jessie that he didn't have for her. So, for as long as Monica could remember, she'd envied her sister.

Stealing her boyfriend, she'd reasoned, would balance things out.

Monica had hoped that having sex with Todd— something she knew Jessie refused him—would win him over. But it hadn't. The morning after, he'd told her it had been a mistake, that he still cared about Jessie. That was when the plot hatched in Monica's mind. A couple of weeks later, she informed Todd that she had missed her period. It was a lie. But the fear that she might be pregnant with his child brought them into conspiracy together. Todd accompanied her to Planned Parenthood, where she had the pregnancy test. She insisted he wait for her outside. When she came out, Monica lied again and told him that the test had shown that she was indeed pregnant. Todd vowed to stick by her. He broke up with Jessie, though until he and Mon-

ica could decide what to do, he didn't give her the full
reason. He just said he wanted to be with Monica.

Jessie, of course, was devastated. Monica even found
herself feeling a little bad for her sister. But not too
much.

Meanwhile, Monica and Todd discussed their op-
tions. An abortion? Monica wasn't sure she could go
through with it. Todd, who'd been brought up Catholic,
said he thought it would be murdering his child. Giving
the baby up for adoption? Then they'd still have to deal
with the scandal, while losing their child forever. How
convincingly Monica had cried in Todd's arms. How
tenderly he had consoled her. And in the course of it,
they'd fallen deeply in love.

Or at least, Monica liked to believe that they had.

Most of the time, she had no trouble believing that
Todd loved her. But occasionally those pesky little
doubts crept up in her mind. She'd gotten quite profi-
cient at shooing them away.

She knew that Todd's feelings for Jessie had been
strong. Although he'd vowed to stay by Monica's side,
Todd kept hoping Jessie would forgive him, and Monica feared they'd get back together. So she had quickly
lied again, telling Todd that she'd already broken the
news to Jessie and that Jessie had insisted they stay together for the sake of the baby. The only request Jessie
had made—or so Monica had lied—was that Todd
never, *ever* bring up the subject with her. It would break
her heart all over again—or so Monica insisted Jessie
had told her. So Todd reluctantly agreed never to bring
up the issue with Jessie. After that, the two of them pretty
much ceased all communication, and Monica breathed
a sigh of relief.

Then, just at the moment when Monica should have started showing her pregnancy—the moment she and Todd planned to break the news to their families—Monica suddenly had a "miscarriage." At least, that was what she informed Todd. It generated a new round of tears and intense emotion, further bonding him to her. With Jessie avoiding him and Todd afraid to approach her, there was no chance of a reconciliation. Monica had won. Todd was hers.

Many times during the ensuing years Todd had commented on the fact that Monica had gotten pregnant so easily when she was sixteen years old, on their very first try. But after that, every time they would try for real, her body failed to respond. Todd wondered if the "miscarriage" had left her unable to conceive. Doctors thought that unlikely. And all the while, Monica stayed mum about the deception that had brought them together, sometimes even swearing her doctors to silence when they discovered there had never, in fact, been a pregnancy all those years ago.

Yes, indeed, if she believed in karma, Monica might have reckoned that her teenage treachery against Todd and Jessie was catching up with her. But she didn't believe in karma. And she hadn't given up hope that one day she'd truly be pregnant with Todd's child.

If only he still wanted to make love to her . . .

"Monica!"

She was startled out of her reverie from a voice, coming from outside.

It was Jessie.

"What the fuck?" Monica said, swinging her legs out of bed. "What is Jessie doing outside?"

She flew to the window, looking down into the dark.

Jessie stood below on the grass, wrapped in a white terrycloth robe, looking up toward her sister's bedroom.

"What's going on?" Monica called down.

"Did you hear anything? Something that sounded like a scream?"

Monica hesitated. "Actually I did," she admitted. "A little while ago."

"Yeah, Abby heard it, too. And Inga isn't home."

"Where is she?"

"She went over to John Manning's house to get some books."

Monica smirked. "They seemed rather tight at the party earlier."

"It's been two hours since Inga went over there," Jessie said. "She said she'd be right back. I'm going over to check."

Suddenly Monica felt Todd behind her. "Jessie," he said, calling over Monica's shoulder. "I don't want you going over to Manning's house alone."

"It's okay," Jessie called back. "It's just through the trees."

"No," Todd said firmly. "I'll be right down. I'll go over with you."

Monica spun around to watch him as he pulled on his jeans and slipped a sweatshirt over his head. "What's with the Sir Galahad routine?" she asked him snidely. "You're always saying Jessie is a pain in the ass—"

"I'm not letting her go over in the pitch darkness to the house of a man who may have killed his wife."

"Oh, please, you don't really believe he killed—"

Todd snapped his head up to look at her. "Lots of

people think he pushed Millie off that deck. There was no reason for her to fall. There was a nearly shoulder-high railing. You don't fall off a deck with a shoulder-high railing."

"The police declared him innocent."

"No. They just said there was no evidence. There's a difference."

Monica frowned. "Well, I just think you're over-reacting. Even if he killed his wife, I doubt Jessie's in any danger just walking over there and ringing his bell. He's probably in there fucking that German girl. You could see he wanted to at the party."

But then again, Monica thought, maybe Todd didn't notice such things anymore.

"I'll be right down," he called through the window to Jessie. "Wait for me."

Monica watched as he hurried out of the room. She snorted in annoyance and got back into bed.

ELEVEN

"**R**eally," Jessie said, as Todd hurried to join her, "you don't need to come."

"I don't trust Manning," her brother-in-law said. "Never have."

Crickets kept up their constant song in the bushes all around them. The moon rode high in the sky, providing the only illumination in the dark night.

"Is Abby okay by herself?" Todd asked.

"Aunt Paulette's with her," Jessie said. "I stopped by her cottage on the way over here and asked her to stay with Abby while I went next door."

"Okay, then let's go," Todd said.

Jessie made a face. "I thought about just calling, but I don't know Mr. Manning's number. And Inga didn't take her cell phone." She smiled weakly. "We might be very embarrassed if we interrupt something."

"I guess we'll just take that chance."

They headed into the row of fir trees between the properties. The air was fragrant with pine needles. The woods were a little deeper here, adjacent to Todd and Monica's house, than they were farther back, closer to Jessie's house, where Inga had crossed through. Here, for a moment, the trees blotted out the moonlight, and Jessie instinctively gripped Todd's hand. She realized it had been thirteen years since she had held his hand. She felt a tingle, despite herself.

On the other side of the trees, a stone gate surrounded John Manning's stone mansion. There was an intercom with a buzzer. Todd pressed the red button, producing a short, sharp electronic hiss. In a moment a man's voice crackled over the intercom. "Yes?"

"Manning? It's Todd Bennett."

"This is Mr. Manning's assistant. I'm sorry, but he's gone to bed."

"We're looking for Inga," Todd said. "Is she still there?"

There was silence from the intercom.

"Hello?" Todd called after several moments had passed.

"Good evening, Todd," came the voice of John Manning. "How can I help you?"

"I'm here with my sister-in-law, Jessie. We're looking for Inga."

"Why don't you come inside?" Manning asked, and suddenly a buzzer sounded, long and deep, like the call of a train. The gate in front of them swung open slowly. Todd and Jessie looked at each other.

"I'm hardly dressed for a visit," Jessie complained, indicating her terrycloth robe and the flip-flops on her feet.

"Looks like you just came from the pool," Todd said, smiling a little.

They walked up the length of John Manning's black-top driveway, the sound of Jessie's flip-flops echoing in the still night. They passed a silver Porsche 911 Carrera, and in the open garage they could make out several other cars in the moonlight, including a shiny, restored black Corvette from the 1970s and a newer white Bentley. Suddenly the front porch light popped on in front of them, and Jessie and Todd were bathed in an amber glow. They hurried up the stone steps and rang the bell.

The door was immediately opened by a young man with shoulder-length blond hair and wire-rimmed glasses, wearing a green Izod shirt and khaki shorts. "Hello," he said cheerfully. "I'm Caleb. Please come in. Mr. Manning is waiting." He held the glass outer door open as Todd and Jessie stepped inside.

The house was enormous. Great vaulted ceilings with exposed dark mahogany wood beams. In many places the stone of the exterior was visible throughout the foyer and the cavernous parlor beyond. Bookshelves skyrocketed from the floor with a library ladder attached to a slider. In the center of the parlor stood an enormous marble abstract sculpture, fronted by three huge vases filled with calla lilies.

"Please," Caleb said, "have a seat. Mr. Manning will be with you momentarily."

"Really, we don't mean to intrude," Jessie said. "We were just concerned that Inga hadn't come home yet. We don't want to bother—"

"No bother at all." This was the voice of John Manning, who emerged from the dark corridor leading off the foyer. He wore a dark blue satin smoking jacket, tied at the waist, and what looked like black silk pajamas underneath. He was barefoot. Once again those deep-set eyes caught Jessie's, and for a moment she felt dizzy. She had to look away.

"Look, Manning," Todd said, "we're not here on a social call. Is Inga still here?"

"Why, no, she isn't." Manning looked from Todd to Jessie. "She left here some time ago, with the books I gave her."

"Well, she hasn't come back," Jessie said. "And my daughter thought she heard someone scream."

"Scream?" John Manning looked skeptical. "I heard nothing of the sort."

"Inga is a very responsible girl, Manning," Todd said. "If she left here some time ago, she would have gone right home. If the two of you are having a little fling, no one is passing any judgments. We just want to make sure she's okay." He narrowed his eyes. "So are you sure she's not still here?"

Manning's dark eyes narrowed in return. "Are you accusing me of lying, Mr. Bennett?"

"No, no, he's not," Jessie interjected. "We're just concerned about Inga. Especially after my daughter said she heard something."

"My wife heard it, too," Todd said, and his voice was accusatory.

Manning was silent for a moment. "Caleb," he said finally. "What time would you say that the young lady left here?"

"About thirty-five minutes ago, sir."

Manning was nodding. "Indeed. Inga and I sat right in here, in the parlor, talking about literature, both American and German, and sharing stories of her homeland, to which I have traveled often, and for which I have considerable affection. I suppose the time did get away from us. We had so much to occupy ourselves with." He smiled enigmatically. "Perhaps she stayed longer than she intended. But I can assure you that she *did* leave here. I walked her to the door, kissed her hand, and bid her good night." Manning looked deliberately at Jessie. "Would you like to look around the house, Ms. Clarkson, to convince yourself that I haven't kidnapped her, tied her up perhaps, and hid her in a closet somewhere?"

"No," Jessie said uncomfortably. "That won't be necessary."

"But maybe we ought to take a walk around the property a bit," Todd suggested. "After all, it's no more than a five-minute walk from here to Jessie's house, and if Inga left here half an hour ago, and people heard a scream right around that time, maybe she fell. Maybe she's hurt."

Jessie noticed a change in Manning's expression. His eyes became less defensive and more concerned. "Yes," he said. "Of course." He looked down at his feet. "In fact, I'll put on some shoes and come help you."

"I'll get some flashlights," Caleb offered.

"If you'll excuse me," Manning said, and he disappeared back down the dark corridor.

Caleb had opened a cabinet in the hallway, producing two small flashlights. "We have some bigger ones in the supply room," he said.

"These will do for us," Todd said, accepting one and handing the other to Jessie. "We'll head outside now."

"Mr. Manning and I will join you in a moment," Caleb promised.

Jessie thanked him and followed Todd back out the front door. They hurried down the steps and through the front gate, and then into the thicket of pine trees, their flashlights swinging from right to left. The twin beams of light sliced through the darkness, sometimes intersecting with each other, illuminating nothing more than tree limbs and brush.

"She would have gone up this way," Jessie said. "It would be a quicker route back to our house." She told Todd she'd check up that way; he should look around the denser woods closer to Manning's house.

Inga might have fallen. It would be easy to trip among these tangled roots and the thick blanket of old pine needles. If she'd fallen, twisted her ankle, she would have cried out—the scream that Abby and Monica heard.

"Inga!" Jessie called.

Until this point she had been concerned, but not really alarmed. Until this point she really had believed Inga had been with Mr. Manning, maybe getting it on with him. Now . . . now she was scared.

Up ahead of her she spotted something in the moonlight. The vague outline of a shape—a shape that suddenly moved. Jessie heard the crunch of leaves and pine needles. She swung her flashlight toward the sound, but there was nothing.

Through the trees she could now see her house. The lights were all lit downstairs, and she could discern Aunt Paulette walking from the kitchen into the living room. Upstairs Abby's lights were still off. That was good. The little girl had fallen back to sleep.

"Inga!" Jessie called out again, not so loud that she might wake Abby, but loud enough, hopefully, for the nanny to hear her if she was nearby.

There was no response.

"Inga!" Jessie tried again, her flashlight swinging madly.

Movement again, the scuffle of needles, this time behind her. Jessie swirled around, searching with the beam of her flashlight. Nothing.

Was someone—something—in the woods with her? Watching her? Following her?

Jessie turned back around. She was just a few feet from the end of the row of trees now, practically in her own backyard. She was about ready to give up when she turned her flashlight once more onto the carpet of pine needles ahead of her.

And in its glow she suddenly saw a face.

A face that was covered in blood.

Jessie screamed.

TWELVE

"Jessie!" came Todd's voice behind her. "What is it?"

"Inga!" she screamed. "Oh, God, Inga!"

The young woman was sprawled at Jessie's feet. Her throat had been slit. Her eyes were open, staring like glass into the beam of the flashlight. Blood covered her face and her neck, and was seeped into her blouse.

Todd ran up alongside Jessie, breathing heavily.

"Jesus!" he shouted upon seeing Inga. He frantically slapped the pockets of his jeans. "My cell phone is in the house! We've got to call an ambulance."

Jessie had stooped down and was feeling for a pulse. "It's too late for that," she said, the words drying up in her throat.

"Jessie!" came Aunt Paulette's voice. She was standing at the back door of the house. "What's wrong?"

"Call the police!" Todd shouted over to her. "Inga's been attacked!"

"She's dead," Jessie said quietly, as she let go of the

young woman's wrist and stood back up. The tears came. "Oh, dear God, who could have done this?"

It was at that moment that John Manning, followed by Caleb, joined them, each bearing a flashlight. Manning was now dressed in the black jeans, T-shirt, and sneakers he'd worn earlier that day.

"Oh, God," Caleb uttered upon seeing the body.

Jessie noticed the look the young man gave to his employer.

"The poor girl," Manning said, staring down at Inga's body.

Caleb seemed as if he might retch, and he turned away, shaking terribly. But Manning stood there calmly, saying nothing, not even asking any questions, just looking down at the dead girl on the ground.

"The police are on their way," Aunt Paulette called. "Is Inga . . . all right?"

"She's dead," Todd told her.

"Shh," Jessie said. "I don't want Abby to hear."

She glanced up at her daughter's bedroom. The light was still off.

"Who could have done such a thing?" Jessie asked again.

She felt terribly guilty for the anger she'd felt toward Inga earlier. Inga had been her friend. One of Jessie's first friends after she had emerged from the fog of depression and fear that had cloaked her early days in New York. The tears rolled down Jessie's cheeks, falling from her face. How could she possibly relay such terrible news to Inga's parents back in Germany? How could she tell them they'd never see their beautiful daughter again—that someone had slit her throat in a quiet, pristine Connecticut backyard?

"Who could do this?" Jessie asked again. Louder now, more distraught.

She dropped to her knees and lifted Inga's lifeless hand to her lips, kissing her friend good-bye.

THIRTEEN

"**A**rthur! Sirens!"

Gert Gorin jumped out of bed as if she'd just heard she'd won the lottery. Her husband just groaned as she scurried out of the bedroom and into the living room. Outside the picture window, the night had turned red and gold. Police lights flashed from across the street, much as they had years ago, when the hunt was on for Emil Deetz. Now the cops had returned to the Clarkson residence—for who only knew *what* this time.

"There's an ambulance!" Gert shouted.

Arthur shuffled out of the bedroom, wearing his rumpled New York Yankees pajamas, rubbing his eyes like a little kid.

"That scream I heard!" Gert announced triumphantly. "It must be that scream I heard!"

She considered the binoculars, then decided instead to get an even closer look. She headed toward the front door.

"Gert, you can't go outside like that. You're just wearing your nightie."

She looked down at herself. Her sleeping attire was an old pink silk negligee that Arthur had given her probably fifteen years ago. It was ragged with age, and threadbare. But she cherished it. They had been happy then. Young. She wouldn't throw it away until it literally fell to pieces.

But she had no time to change. She wanted to see what was going on. So she grabbed Arthur's old flannel coat that was hanging in a nearby closet and slipped it on. It hung on her like a sack, but she didn't care.

Gert Gorin rushed outside.

FOURTEEN

"**S**o let's get this straight," Sergeant Mike Wolfo-witz was saying to Jessie. "Your daughter heard a scream about what time?"

"I don't know. I guess a little over an hour ago now."

"May we speak with her?"

Jessie wrapped her arms around herself. "I really don't want to wake her. She's going to be very upset when she finds out about this, and I'd rather break it to her when there aren't police and flashing lights around."

"But we need to determine when she heard that scream," the cop said.

"I can tell you." The voice was Monica's, coming up behind them. "I heard it too. It was exactly an hour and fifteen minutes ago. I remember looking at the clock."

"And you are . . . ?" Wolfowitz asked.

Monica gave her name and explained the circumstances of being in the bathroom and hearing a scream.

"Did you see anyone around the property at all?" Wolfowitz asked, looking at the entire group. In addition to Monica and Jessie, Todd was there, standing behind his wife, as well as Caleb and John Manning.

Aunt Paulette watched from the back door, and out in the street, Gert Gorin was angling to hear what was going on, though she was prevented from coming into the yard by a couple of policemen.

"We saw no one," John Manning told the sergeant.

"I didn't see anyone either," Todd said.

Jessie hesitated. "I . . . may have." She swallowed. Off to her left, the coroner had arrived and was standing with an assistant over Inga's body. A huge light was switched on, practically turning night into day. "I may have seen . . . something," Jessie said.

"What did you see?" Wolfowitz asked.

"A figure. Something in the darkness. Right before I found the body. Something moved."

"A person?"

"I can't say for sure. It was so dark, and whatever it was, it moved before I could land my flashlight on it."

"Could it have been a person?"

"I don't know. . . ." Jessie tried to remember. She hadn't really seen anything, just a shape in the darkness, and the sense of movement. "To be honest, it didn't seem big enough to be a person."

"An animal, then?"

Jessie nodded. "Yes, probably."

"Whoever took this girl down was very strong," Wolfowitz said.

Jessie saw who he was looking at.

John Manning.

"I'm going to have to ask all of you to come down to the station with me," the cop said. "We need statements from all of you. What you saw, what you heard . . ." He returned his eyes to John Manning. "And where precisely you all were exactly one hour and fifteen minutes ago tonight."

The five nodded. Jessie asked if she could go into the house and put on some clothes. Wolfowitz agreed, but told her to hurry. She scurried inside, filled a tearful Aunt Paulette in on the details, and pulled on a pair of jeans and a light sweater. She wanted to run into Abby's room and give her a quick kiss, but she didn't want to risk waking her up. She told Aunt Paulette not to tell the girl anything yet if she woke up. Jessie hoped she wouldn't be gone long. Then she rejoined the group outside.

In the back of Wolfowitz's car, she cried all the way to the station. The image of Inga's throat—sliced open, gushing blood—was burned into Jessie's mind.

Whoever had killed Inga had done so in exactly the same way Emil had murdered his victim six years earlier.

FIFTEEN

Oswald Thayer didn't sleep well anymore. Not since Antonio had died. He doubted he'd had one solid night of more than three hours of sleep since the day dear Antonio, who was supposed to have lived long enough to take care of Oswald, had passed away, quite peacefully, in his sleep. Ever since that time, the old man had always awakened an hour or so after nodding off, a pattern that was repeated several more times each night. So it was no surprise to him when his eyes popped open this evening as well. What *did* startle old Mr. Thayer was the flashing red light that circled in his room.

With difficulty, because his joints were failing and the walk up to the Clarkson place this afternoon had left him exhausted, Oswald got out of bed and shuffled across the room to the window. The source of the lights wasn't clear, but they came from somewhere down toward the end of the cul-de-sac. Squinting his eyes, he thought he detected an ambulance. He wondered if there had been sirens, and if it had been the sirens, and not his usual insomnia, that had roused him from his slumber.

He hoped no one was ill.

Oswald turned away from the window. An ambulance had come to this house, too, when he'd discovered Antonio lying cold and motionless beside him. Oswald had never understood how a heart attack could take a man as young as Antonio—he had been just forty-three!—in the middle of the night. He had been absolutely fine, chipper, and cheerful when they'd gone to bed. Yes, Antonio had just taken up running, and he was maybe fifteen pounds overweight, and when he'd come in that evening after his run, he'd seemed particularly short of breath. But a heart attack? No one had suspected it. Antonio had been as healthy as a horse. He was supposed to be here now, taking care of Oswald in his dotage, as they used to jokingly call old age. That was the benefit of these May–September romances. Oswald had taken care of Antonio, who'd been a poor Mexican immigrant when they met. And then Antonio would take care of Oswald.

It hadn't quite worked out that way.

Of course, Oswald had servants to do the job. Drivers and assistants and housemaids and part-time nurses. But it wasn't the same.

It wasn't the way it was supposed to have been.

Old Mr. Thayer sat back down on the edge of his bed. He lifted the photograph of his deceased partner from the bedside table, where he kept it so he could roll over and see Antonio's face, just as he could when Antonio was alive. He gazed down into the soft brown eyes. Not a day, not an hour, went by that Oswald didn't miss him.

He replaced the photo on the table and lay back down. The flashing red lights continued to circle the room as Oswald fell back to sleep.

SIXTEEN

"**S**omething's going on down there," Heather said, peering out of her window toward the end of Hickory Dell.

"You're acting like Gert Gorin," Bryan said from bed.

"Jesus Christ," Heather said, unable to look away. "It looks like they're carrying somebody out on a stretcher."

"A stretcher?" This piqued Bryan's interest, and he threw off the sheet and hopped out of bed to join Heather at the window. "Are you sure?"

"They definitely carried something out to the ambulance," Heather reported.

Bryan leaned up close, his nose almost pressing against the glass. "Is it Jessie's house, or Monica's, or the Gorins'?"

"Hard to say," Heather replied. "But it looks like they're all congregating on the Clarkson side of the street."

"Damn, that's a lot of police cars," Bryan said. "There's got to be at least five."

"Just like all those years ago, when Jessie was mixed up in that drug ring." Heather pulled away from the window. "I wouldn't be surprised if she's still involved in all of that business."

"Now you're taking crazy, Heather. Jessie was never mixed up with that shit. She just got involved with a creep who—"

"Who killed a guy." Heather sighed and got back into bed. "You don't get involved with a bastard like that and not know something about what he's like."

Bryan was still peering out of the window, trying to figure out what all the commotion was about. "I just think you're jealous of her, that's all," he said quietly.

Heather nearly exploded out of bed. She lurched forward, her face twisted, her mouth open in large O. "Jealous? Of Jessie Clarkson? I hardly think so."

Bryan turned to her and smirked. "Come on, baby. I haven't said anything about it, but this afternoon, at the picnic at her house, the way you suddenly grabbed me and announced we were leaving after I simply shared an innocent joke with her . . ."

"An innocent joke?" Heather had been keeping her rage bottled up ever since they'd gotten home. She and Bryan had barely spoken for the rest of the day, and certainly no words had been exchanged about what had happened at Jessie's house. "I hardly think Jessie would have bolted out of her seat the way she did and stormed into the house if all you'd made was an innocent joke."

Bryan laughed and turned to look out the window again.

"Admit it!" Heather shouted, moving down the bed on her hands and knees like a tigress. "You hit on her! I saw how cozy you were trying to get with her. You said something that pissed her off—"

"Cozy?" He turned back to her and leveled her with one of his evil grins, the kind that made him look like a villain on a Saturday morning kids' cartoon. "You mean cozy like you were trying to get with John Manning?"

Heather sat back on her haunches. "I wasn't trying to get cozy with John."

Her husband barked out a laugh and came around to sit on the edge of the bed, going eye to eye with her, seeming to find this battle with her suddenly far more enjoyable than the view of the police cars outside. "Oh, yes, you were, my darling, and it was you who was the jealous one, absolutely furious that your dashing famous author was paying attention to that sexy—and very young—German au pair."

Heather laughed unconvincingly. "Why would I care if John pays attention to some kid?"

"Because she's way younger than you are, and her breasts are far perkier, and there's not a trace of cellulite in her legs."

Heather glared at him. "You are a pig."

"See, what I don't understand," Bryan said, crossing his arms over his chest and lifting his eyebrows, "is why you refuse to admit to me that you've been having an affair with John Manning. After all, I tell you about the girls I fuck. I even invite you to join in sometimes. It's what makes our marriage work, darling." He grinned again, his eyes dancing. "You know, I wouldn't mind joining in for a three-way with you and Manning, if he's open to it. I haven't done two guys on one girl in a long time."

"You truly make me sick, you know that?"

Bryan just threw his head back and laughed.

Heather got out of bed, her heart beating hard in her ears. Her husband infuriated her. But she was glad that he knew about her affair with John. It kind of balanced things out in a way. Still, she'd never admit it to him. It was her private little world, one that she intended to keep as separate from Bryan as possible.

Heather returned to the window. A few police cars were now leaving the scene, driving slowly down the street, their lights no longer flashing and their sirens muted.

Bryan was right about one thing, however—though once again, Heather would never admit it in a million years. She *had* been jealous of John's attentions to that German girl. Why did every man she fell for have such a wandering eye? Was she not enough for anyone? She'd been frantic watching the flirtation between John and Inga, and when she confronted him about it, asked him what the hell was going on, John had gotten defensive. Heather had left the picnic angry with both John *and* Bryan, and she was sure that busybody Gert Gorin had picked up on it. Well, let the neighbors gossip. Heather didn't care.

She just wanted to make sure that John never saw that German bitch again.

Another police car slowly passed under Heather's window. She couldn't be sure, but Heather thought she saw Jessie sitting in the backseat. A small smile stretched across Heather's face. She was right. Her former best friend was mixed up in something. And Heather couldn't be more pleased about that fact.

SEVENTEEN

It was nearly two o'clock in the morning when Jessie got back home. Aunt Paulette was waiting for her. Thankfully, Abby had never woken up.

Jessie flopped down in Mom's old chair and started to cry. It seemed impossible to imagine. . . . Just this morning, Inga had been bustling around the house, helping Jessie get set for the party. And now she was gone. Everywhere Jessie looked she was reminded of her friend. The tiles were still piled in neat rows waiting for Inga to finish installing them in the bathroom. The paint cans she was using to spruce up the kitchen were still under the cabinet. Her tool belt dangled from a hook in the pantry.

And now she was dead.

Murdered.

Outside, a few policemen were still combing the yard. Orange tape had been stretched from pole to pole surrounding the property, marking off the area as a crime scene. News crews had descended, and a couple of intrepid reporters had tried thrusting microphones at Jessie when a police cruiser dropped her and Monica and Todd off. But they'd all stayed mum, rushing past the reporters and barricading themselves in their houses. In the morning, Jessie knew, MURDER IN SAYER'S BROOK would be bannered across the local paper, and the local television and radio shows would lead off their newscasts with the story of Inga's death. The whole neighborhood, the whole town, would learn that a murder had taken place on Hickory Dell.

And once more, in the center of the storm, would be Jessie Clarkson.

"Oh, Aunt Paulette, why? Why Inga?"

Jessie cried harder, as her aunt, kneeling in front of her, wrapped her arms around her. She had no answer. If she saw anything in her psychic visions, she offered none of it to Jessie. For the moment, she just held her.

The police station had been a nightmare. They'd all been interviewed separately. Two officers, a man and a woman, had taken Jessie into a room and had her repeat her story three times. They looked at her with stone-cold eyes, as if they suspected her of killing Inga. The female cop was worse. She was a small, beady-eyed woman, who admitted at one point that she remembered Jessie from the whole mess with Emil. The implication, Jessie felt, was that the cops still believed she'd had something to do with Emil's drug and porn ring, and that she may have known more about the murder of Screech Solek than she'd ever let on. And so now they suspected she knew more about Inga's death than she was saying, too.

But the cops' suspicion of Jessie had been understated compared to the grilling they gave John Manning. When Jessie emerged from her hour behind closed doors, she could hear the heated, raised voices from the room down the hall. Other cops were forcing

Manning to repeat his story, over and over, clearly trying to find an inconsistency. Although an investigation had found no evidence to link Manning to his wife's death, it was clear that police still believed him to have been involved. As Jessie sat on a hard plastic chair beside Todd and Monica, none of them saying a word, Manning's voice, loud and hostile, echoed down the corridor.

"I'll tell you this for the last time, and then, if you detain me here any longer, I will demand my lawyer be present," Manning had boomed. "I want to help in any way that I can to find the person who killed that poor girl, but I will not sit here any longer and have you insinuate that I—"

"No one's insinuating anything, Mr. Manning," came the quieter voice of a police detective. "We would just like you to tell us one more time about what happened tonight when the girl visited you."

"As I've told you now three times," Manning growled, "she came over, we sat in my parlor, I gave her some books, we flirted, we laughed, we made vague plans to get together again, and then she left."

"With the books?"

"Yes, with the books."

"But no books were found anywhere near the body. Or anywhere, so far, on the property."

"I am aware of that," Manning said. "You've told me that repeatedly."

Finally, they let him go. He stormed out of the room and looked straight past Jessie and the others. Jessie noticed the way Todd's eyes had followed him, accusatively.

They were all driven back to Hickory Dell, Manning

and Caleb in a separate cruiser from Jessie, Monica, and Todd. They were told that their properties would remain crime scenes for the time being, and that investigators would be in and out of their homes for the next several days. They'd get search warrants if necessary, but everyone involved—except for Manning—agreed that the police would have all the access they needed.

"I just can't believe she's gone," Jessie said now, a fresh cascade of tears falling down her cheeks. "She's been my rock, my best friend, for so long."

Aunt Paulette held her by the shoulders and looked into her eyes. "My poor baby," the older woman said, near tears herself.

"How fast life can change. This morning all I worried about was whether the neighbors would accept me returning here. Now I all can think about is who killed Inga, and why, and if whoever did it is still around, and if we're safe."

"While you were gone, honey, several policemen came through and checked the house from top to bottom," Aunt Paulette said. "They even went into Abby's room, and the little angel slept peacefully right through it. They found nothing to be concerned about. And now there are cops all over the place outside. We're safe here." She smiled. "I sense no danger myself."

Jessie shivered. "Have the police notified the neighbors?"

"They told me as soon as the sun starts to come up, they will begin knocking on doors. Gert Gorin was over here, however. No surprise. So I'm sure she'll be letting everyone know what happened herself."

So much for starting over with the neighbors.

"Oh Aunt Paulette," Jessie cried, running her hands

through her hair in a sudden burst of fear and despair. "It makes me feel . . . oh God . . . it makes me feel like Emil has come back."

"Oh, baby, you know that's not possible. Emil was shot to death in Mexico in that big drug bust. Police identified his body."

"I know," Jessie said. "But the way Inga died . . . her throat slit. It was the way Emil killed that man. It just feels so . . . so . . . terribly familiar."

"Baby." Aunt Paulette wrapped her arms around Jessie again. "You've got to stop thinking that way. It's a horrible, horrible coincidence." She stroked Jessie's blond hair. "There was a policeman here while you were gone, a very nice man," Aunt Paulette told her. "He said it looked like it was a random act. Somebody who was prowling around, maybe looking to rob a house, and who came upon Inga in the woods. Maybe he tried to assault her, and she fought him off. So he killed her. And now, this policeman believed, the killer is miles and miles away. He was sure to hightail it out of here, because he didn't want to get caught."

"Still," Jessie said, "it doesn't make any sense. We are far, far away from any crime areas. . . ." She shuddered. "Five years in New York City and never once did I encounter any major crime."

"It can happen anywhere," her aunt told her. "I think we should have security systems installed. Monica and Todd have one. We should get them for our houses as well."

"Yes," Jessie said. Her eyes drifted over toward the staircase. "And Abby never stirred?"

"Not once. I stood beside her bed as the detectives searched her room. She slept like an angel."

"Oh, God, Aunt Paulette, what am I going to tell Abby? She adored Inga."

"We'll know better what to say in the morning, baby." The older woman took Jessie by the hands and encouraged her to stand. "I know it's going to be hard, but you need to get some sleep."

Jessie stood. She felt more tired than she had ever felt before in her entire life, but she knew she wouldn't be able to sleep. Still, she allowed Aunt Paulette to accompany her upstairs, where Jessie made a deliberate effort to avoid looking at Inga's room. The door was closed, for which she was thankful. She couldn't have managed looking at Inga's things tonight. With Aunt Paulette following behind, Jessie tiptoed into Abby's room, where the little girl slept soundly. The thin sheet covering her rose and fell with each gentle breath she took. Jessie bent down and kissed her daughter on the forehead.

Dear God, she thought, as the tears started again. *How am I ever going to tell her?*

Eighteen

"That's right," Gert Gorin was saying into the phone even before the sun was fully up. "Dead. Her throat was slit practically from ear to ear. No, they don't know who did it. But I'm sure it must be a revenge killing, or somehow connected to all that nastiness Jessie Clarkson was involved with six years ago. How can it not be?"

She was speaking to Rose O'Connell, who lived across town, and who kept Gert apprised of all the goings-on over there as fully as Gert kept her up on Hickory Dell. Gert had known Rose wouldn't mind in the least being awakened at the crack of dawn with such juicy news.

"I mean, imagine!" Gert exclaimed. "Right across the street from me! A girl murdered in cold blood!"

Rose opined that Gert must be terrified.

"Well, Arthur has a gun," Gert said. "I just hope he remembers how to use it. With my luck, he'd shoot himself in the foot instead of aiming at an intruder."

In fact, Gert was less frightened than she was exhilarated. This latest development was even more exciting than the drug search of six years ago, which, of course, had turned up nothing. A real, actual murder meant that Gert could be on the phone all day, telling everyone all the salacious details.

"The sheet they covered her with when they carried her body to the ambulance was just sopping with blood," Gert informed Rose. "I mean absolutely drenched. It didn't look white. It looked red. Oh, and you should have seen how angry John Manning was when the cop car dropped him back off at two in the morning. He looked like a snarling bull. He was—"

Rose interrupted her to suggest that Manning could've killed the girl.

"That's also a possibility," Gert admitted. "Don't think I didn't consider that. I remember very well all the cops who were here the day poor Millie was found dead face-first on her concrete patio. Can you imagine all the broken bones she must have suffered falling three floors smack down onto concrete? But of course, they never found proof that Manning had pushed her."

Rose volunteered that she had never been convinced of his innocence.

"Well, neither was I, Rosie. Come on, you can't put anything over on Gertrude Gorin. And I think the police must have felt the same way. Not finding any evidence to convict him isn't the same as finding evidence that exonerates him." She snorted. "And given how rip-roaring angry he was when he got back from police questioning last night, I'd say Manning was once again given a thorough grilling down at the station."

Rose asked her why, then, did she think it was more

likely that drug gangsters involved with Emil Deetz, instead of John Manning, had killed the poor girl?

"It was the *way* she was killed," Gert said. "Slitting her throat like that. Remember, that was the way Deetz killed his victim. I think it was a warning to Jessie that they weren't through with her."

Rose argued that Deetz was dead.

"But I'm sure he still has cronies out there. And who knows? I've always thought Jessie knew more than she was saying. Maybe in fact there are drugs still stashed over there—or money. She may have stolen drug money from them, and this is their way of pressuring her to give it up."

Arthur had walked into the room then, still in his pajamas. He hadn't slept well after the commotion last night, and now his wife's blabbering on the phone so early in the morning had woken him up again.

"Enough with all your cockamamie speculation," he grumbled. "Why isn't coffee on?"

"I've got to go, Rose," Gert said. "The Kraken wakes."

She hung up the phone.

"Forty years of marriage and still you don't know how to make coffee."

Gert placed a filter into the bowl of the coffeemaker and then scooped in the ground coffee. She could use a cup herself. The adrenaline from the night before was starting to wear off, and she'd need a burst of caffeine to finish all her calls. She had to call Sylvia Rush, and Randi Phillips, and Darla Hood, and Samantha Stevens. . . .

As the coffee began to drip into the pot, Gert lifted

her eyes and looked out the window into her backyard. Three decades ago, Arthur had erected a little gazebo out there. That was before he'd retired from the post office, when he'd spend his weekends doing little projects like that around the house. Nowadays, he spent every day—every hour, practically—in front of the television set. But Gert remembered a time when, during the period when they'd still hoped to have children, she and Artie would sit out in the gazebo with a bottle of wine, a romantic little interlude before coming inside to make love. The gazebo might have been prefab—with imitation brick and an aluminum weather vane on top—but it had been their little cozy hideaway. Gert couldn't remember the last time she'd sat out there.

But now, looking out the window as the sun's first pink rays filled up her backyard, Gert saw someone else was using the gazebo.

A little boy sat there, all by himself.

Gert poured a cup of coffee for Arthur, who sat groggy-eyed at the table. "Here's your coffee," she said. "I'll be right back."

For some reason she didn't tell Arthur about the boy. She pulled her robe tighter around her and stepped out the back door. The birds were chattering in the trees, excited by sun. But the boy just sat there, staring straight ahead, unmoving. He was wearing just a white T-shirt and blue shorts. Gert noticed he was barefoot.

"Hello," Gert called, approaching the gazebo.

The boy didn't turn to look at her.

As Gert neared, she saw that his shirt and face and feet were dirty. Finally he lifted his eyes to look at her.

"Hello," Gert said again.

"Hello," the boy replied.

His voice was friendly, but rather disinterested, as if Gert had just interrupted him in deep thought. He couldn't have been more than four or five or six. . . . Gert wasn't good at determining kids' ages, but he wasn't very old.

"Can I help you with something?" Gert asked the boy.

He looked at her oddly, as if he didn't understand the question. Then he shook his head no.

"Well, where do you live?" Gert inquired.

He pointed toward the woods. Gert nodded. They had built a whole section of new housing on the other side of the woods. She didn't know any of the families there, but had heard there were a lot of kids. She sometimes heard them playing through the trees.

"I think you should run along home," Gert told him. "This old gazebo isn't safe anymore."

She glanced at the old structure. The wood was rotted, the imitation brick colorless from thirty years of winters, the weathervane bent and broken and rusted.

But the boy didn't budge.

"Really, sonny, move along," Gert repeated. "Go home. It's not safe out here today. There's a bad man on the loose."

That caused the boy to turn his eyes sharply to her. It seemed to wake him up, frighten him. Gert was glad. Better the boy be scared than out by himself where the maniac who'd slit poor Inga's throat might get him. Suddenly the child bolted from where he was sitting and ran past Gert into the woods. She could hear the leaves and branches crunching under his feet. A flurry of crows flew out of the trees.

Really, Gert thought as she headed back into the house. *What kind of mother lets her kid run around without any shoes?*

NINETEEN

"**H**ave a good first day in school, baby," Jessie called to Abby as the little girl, her pink backpack strapped over her shoulders, toddled off with the other children into the classroom. Jessie could feel the tears wanting to pop out of her eyes.

But Abby was smiling and waving happily. She had already made friends on the playground with another little girl, and together they walked hand in hand behind their teacher, excited to be starting their first day of kindergarten.

"I remember your first day of school," Aunt Paulette told Jessie as they walked back to the car. "I went with your mother to bring you."

"But I had Monica a grade ahead of me, and she was always there to help me find my way," Jessie lamented. The tears finally came as she slid behind the wheel of the car. "Abby's all alone in that big school."

"Abby is a very resilient little girl," Aunt Paulette said.

Starting the ignition and backing out of the parking space, Jessie had to agree. Abby had received the news of Inga's death with a certain calmness. She had cried a little, and said how much she'd miss her, but she'd also said that now she had a guardian angel to watch over her, and that she'd see Inga in her dreams. Of course, Jessie hadn't told Abby *how* Inga had died—she said she'd merely had an accident on her way back to the house—and Abby hadn't asked for more details. If she made the connection with the scream she'd heard the night before, Abby didn't mention it.

The school psychologist had counseled Jessie that eventually she might have to provide Abby with more of the truth. Now that she was at school, she might hear details of the murder from other kids. At that point, Jessie had to be ready to help guide her gently through all the questions she would have.

The crime-scene tape had come down, and although police cars still cruised up and down Hickory Dell a few times a day, there was no longer the around-the-clock watch. News crews had traipsed all through the neighborhood for a few days. Now they, too, had disappeared, as Inga's murder faded off the front pages. Police announced they were pursuing several leads, but Jessie knew they had nothing specific. They'd been back to question her a couple of times, and she'd seen police cars over at John Manning's, too. But it was coming to seem as if Inga's killer had gotten away scot-free.

They'd had a little memorial service for their beloved nanny in the backyard. Jessie, Abby, Aunt Paulette, and Todd had all picked daisies and lit candles and said a prayer. It had seemed to provide Abby with the kind of closure she needed, at least for the time being. Monica had been invited to their little ritual, but she'd had a basket class to run. It was just as well; the murder had made Monica edgy toward Jessie. The sisters had barely spoken since that terrible night. Jessie felt Monica was upset that, just as Jessie had returned home, terrible things had started happening all over again. She'd tried talking to Monica about it, but Monica was always too busy. She was clearly keeping Jessie at arm's length.

Todd, however, had understood. "You can't blame yourself," he'd told Jessie. "This was a random act. A terrible coincidence. All we can do is move forward."

Jessie was grateful for Todd's words. But she had to admit, sometimes she didn't blame Monica for her reaction. Inga's death didn't feel like a coincidence to Jessie. As she pulled into their driveway, Jessie averted her eyes from the spot where Inga's body had been found. She hadn't been able to bear looking in that direction since she'd found her body there. She got out of the car and, after thanking Aunt Paulette for going with her to drop Abby off at school, walked quickly into the house, looking straight ahead.

Inside, she poured herself a cup of coffee and settled into Mom's chair to think. In the immediate aftermath of Inga's death, Jessie's impulse had been to leave Sayer's Brook and go back to Manhattan. She had felt safe and anonymous there. But here . . . it was as if coming back here she had somehow awoken Emil's ghost. She knew it sounded crazy, and her rational mind rejected the idea. But deep down in her heart, she was convinced that Emil had come back from the dead to kill Inga as a way of having revenge on Jessie. The police might not have any leads, but Jessie felt she knew who the killer was.

What convinced her had been the return of the dreams.

The dreams of the baby—Emil's son—that she had wished dead.

The son she had killed.

She'd be sleeping, only to be awakened by the sound of a baby crying. And Jessie would get out of bed and hurry to Abby's room, only to see, instead of her daughter, a baby boy covered in blood.

Only then would Jessie realize she'd dreamed the entire thing.

She'd had this same dream five times now. Aunt Paulette said it was normal. Of course the trauma of Inga's death would bring back the trauma Jessie had experienced with Emil. To appease Jessie, her aunt had done a tarot reading, saying all she could see was the need for continued perseverance, and the promise of eventual liberation from fear. She insisted that if Emil's ghost had returned—Aunt Paulette didn't discount the possibility of ghosts—she would have sensed it.

Jessie wasn't sure how much she believed in the tarot or Aunt Paulette's psychic abilities. She didn't disbelieve, but, like Mom, she was never entirely convinced either. Still, it did give her some consolation that her aunt saw no ghosts and no looming threats when she worked her magic. It was better than the alternative.

Jessie took a deep breath and stood from Mom's chair. She had decided the best way to move forward, as Todd had described it, was to finish what she and Inga had started. She would get back to painting and tiling the kitchen and the bathroom. And after that, she'd paint the upstairs. It was what Inga would have wanted her to do. Jessie glanced up at the photo of Mom on the wall and the inscription she'd left there:

There is nothing you can't accomplish when you put your mind, heart, and spirit into it.

Jessie took another deep breath and got down to work.

TWENTY

Heather made her way up John Manning's driveway, past his Porsche and his Bentley. She knew the security code to the front gate; she didn't have to wait to be buzzed in. Still, John insisted that she always let him know whenever she was coming; if he was writing, he hated to be disturbed. But lately whenever Heather had texted him, suggesting a rendezvous, he'd always claimed to be too busy. This time she was coming unannounced.

If she rang the front bell, or even just barged in, she'd have to deal with that annoying Caleb. John's young, protective assistant would surely play interference, insisting that his boss was writing and couldn't be disturbed. So Heather wouldn't go through the front door. She knew John usually wrote in his little, mostly glass casita out in back, where he had a view of the woods. The wooden fence that ringed the property protected him from overzealous fans—but his fans didn't have the security code for the front gate. Now that she was inside the compound, it would be easy for Heather to slip around the side of the house and surprise John in his writer's lair.

Hidden by bushes, Heather stealthily made her way toward the backyard, hoping Caleb wouldn't spot her from a window.

She knew she was being foolish and rash, and that John deplored foolishness and rashness. She should be home at this very moment, baking bread and pies, because she was catering the Sayer's Brook Historical Society's quarterly meeting tonight. But Consuela—who was housekeeper and catering assistant as well as nanny until they could find one who'd put up with Piper and Ashton—had things under control. And the kids were at school and Bryan was at work, so Heather finally had the opportunity she'd been waiting for. She would spring up on John unannounced and demand to know why he was avoiding her.

She was Heather Wilson Pierce—head cheerleader of Sayer's Brook High, don't forget—and she would *not* be ignored.

It had all started the day of Jessie's fucking picnic, the day that German girl got murdered. Heather had texted John earlier, hoping to see him that night, when Bryan left to play basketball with friends. John had agreed tentatively, telling her it depended on how much work he got done. He was working on a new book and had a deadline to meet. So Heather had been very surprised to see him saunter over to Jessie's yard, and even more surprised to see the attention he'd paid to that girl. How Heather had hated her, right from the start. Now that she was closer to thirty than to twenty, Heather hated just about any female who was younger than she was, especially when they were as pretty as Inga had been.

But Inga wasn't pretty anymore. She was dead—her throat cut from ear to ear.

Bryan had been certain that John Manning was the killer. But Heather had coyly suggested another suspect. "Maybe Jessie did it," she offered. "After all, she seemed mighty put off by John's attention to the girl, and then when you made your ridiculous pass, you just pushed her over the edge."

Bryan told her she was crazy.

Maybe she was. Heather knew sneaking around someone's backyard wasn't exactly sane behavior. But she didn't care. At the moment, all she cared about was confronting John. Ever since they'd begun their affair about a year earlier, John had been all Heather could think about. She was obsessed with him. With the way he smelled, the way he spoke, the way he felt, the way his eyes seemed to bore into her. She'd divorce Bryan in an instant if John only gave the word. Heather had thought she meant something to him, too. She had thought those passionate nights up in his tower bedroom, the moonlight streaming in from the window, had been more than just sex. She had thought John was in love with her the way she was in love with him,

Apparently she'd thought wrong. And the realization enraged her.

Coming around the side of the house, she spied John in his little glass house, staring down intently at his titanium MacBook.

She glanced over her shoulder at the row of pine trees on the other side of the security fence. That was where Inga had died.

She couldn't help the small, satisfied smile that turned up the corners of her lips.

With that smile on her face, Heather walked boldly out of the trees and across the yard. It was too late for Caleb to stop her now.

She noticed John look up and spot her as she approached. He grimaced.

"Good morning, darling," Heather said, opening the door to the casita and walking in. "Or is it afternoon yet? Are you hungry? Can I fix you some lunch? I'm known for my culinary skills, remember. As well as other talents." She giggled aggressively. "But I do think you've forgotten all of my good attributes."

Heather smiled wider and sat down on the small leather couch opposite John's desk. She crossed her legs.

John glared at her. "You know I don't like being disturbed when I'm writing."

Heather's smile grew even wider. "You know I don't like not having my texts and phone calls returned."

"I've been very busy. I have this deadline I must meet. I'm writing every day—"

"And entertaining visitors from the Sayer's Brook Police Department, I see."

John glowered at her. "More interruptions I don't need."

"Do they really think you killed that girl?"

He averted his eyes from her, looking once again at his computer screen. John was wearing a plain black, short-sleeved oxford shirt, with several buttons undone, over a pair of cut-off black denim shorts. He was barefoot.

"I don't know what they think," he said.

"Well, they must think *something*, because they've been back here so many times."

"Asking the same questions, for which they get the same answers."

Heather leaned forward on the couch. "You can tell me the truth, John."

His eyes flashed over to her.

"What do you mean by that?"

"Did you do it?"

His expression grew stern. "Did I do what?"

"Did you kill her?"

"And if I did," he asked, a smile now blooming on his own face, "do you think I'd confide in you?"

Heather sat back on the couch, her lower lip protruding. "When did you suddenly tire of me, John? I don't recall a quarrel. The last time we were together, in fact, it was quite nice, as I remember." Her eyes narrowed at him. "I did that thing with my tongue that you like so much."

John stood from his desk with a sigh. "Look, Heather, I've just been very busy."

"Bullshit."

"And yes, this past week has been particularly difficult, with the girl's death and the police making such nuisances of themselves."

Heather stood as well, approaching him. John faced away from her, looking out of the large glass window that dominated the casita's eastern wall. She touched his shoulders with her long pink fingernails.

"What did you do with her that night?"

He sighed again. "What night?"

"The night you killed her."

He spun around to look at her.

"I'm just joking, John," Heather said. "Lighten up."

He moved away from her.

"I didn't do anything with her," he said.

"All the papers said that she came over here, that you were last to see her alive."

John regarded her carefully. "Yes, I was the last to see her alive . . . except for her killer."

Heather laughed, "Oh, of course. Excuse my error."

"Yes, she came over here," John said, looking through some papers on his desk. Heather had the sense he wasn't looking for anything in particular; he just needed something to do with his hands. He was actually nervous. Talking about the girl's death actually got John Manning anxious. How very interesting. "She came over here and I gave her some books."

"But Jessie and Todd had to come over looking for her, since she was here so long," Heather countered.

"We talked for a while."

Heather made a dismissive laugh. "I know you, John. You don't just talk to a pretty girl when you get her alone in the house."

"Believe what you want then." He looked over at her sharply. "Really, Heather, I need to get back to work."

"And I need to see you!" She suddenly lunged at him, gripping the sides of his shirt in her hands. "I love you, John! Don't you understand?"

He said nothing, just glared at her with those dark, hypnotic eyes.

"Please don't," he said. "You sound like a character in a bad romance novel."

"I don't care how I sound. It's been *hell* not seeing you."

She tried to kiss him. At first he resisted. Then he succumbed. He kissed her back.

But almost as soon as Heather was ready to melt in his arms, Jon thrust her away again.

"I can't, Heather. I just can't."

"Why?"

"You need to leave now," he said, and his voice was throaty with a jumble of emotions Heather couldn't easily recognize. "If you don't, I'll have to phone the police."

Her eyes widened in shock. "You'd actually call the cops on me?"

"I wouldn't want to, but if I have to, I will."

Heather was at a loss for words. She just stood there, her mouth open, staring at the man she used to meet two or three times a week for some of the best sex she'd ever had in her life. The man who'd given her an escape from the nightmare of her own marriage, the man she'd contemplated leaving Bryan for.

"I'm sorry if I've hurt you," John was saying, although his words only partially reached her ears, seeming to come from many, many miles away. "You're a fun girl, Heather. And very sexy. But it's over. Please accept the fact that it's over."

Still Heather stood there, dumbstruck.

"I'm going to have to ask you to leave again," John said.

That was when Heather noticed Caleb standing outside, watching them through the large picture windows. It dawned on Heather that when John had been fiddling with the papers on his desk he hadn't been just idly anxious. He'd been pressing the call button he kept there, summoning Caleb. Now the efficient assistant stood waiting on the other side of the glass to escort Heather off the property.

She found her voice.

"I'll leave, John," she said. "I don't stay where I'm not wanted."

"Thank you, Heather." He paused. "I hope we can still be friends."

"Of course," she said, smiling brightly. "I'll be the very best friend you ever had in your entire fucking life."

She meant it as a threat, and it was clear that John heard it that way.

Heather hurried out of the casita, brushing past Caleb. "I know my way out," she snarled at the assistant. She made her way, walking as fast as her legs would carry her, around the house and out through the front gate. She felt certain that this very afternoon they would change the security code to keep her from pulling another stunt like this one.

But that wouldn't stop Heather. She'd find a way back into that house.

That much she vowed.

TWENTY-ONE

Just a few yards away, Jessie sat at her own Mac-Book trying to coax the words out of her head and onto her computer screen. She'd been doing her best over the last few days to get back to her book. But writing wasn't easy when at any moment she might suddenly, without warning, find herself in tears, remembering Inga. She had decided to try using that raw emotion to write—since, after all, her book was about finding the strength and power within one's self to survive anything. She had made some progress, but it was hard. It was very, *very* hard.

"Jessie?"

She looked up. It was Monica, tapping lightly at the screen door. It had been a while since Monica had walked up the hill to see her. Jessie jumped from her seat and hurried to the door.

"Monica! Come on in!"

"I just have a package for you," her sister replied. "It was left down at my house by mistake. I don't need to come in. I can just give it to you. . . ."

"No, please, come in. I'd like to speak with you for a moment."

She could see the reluctance in her sister's face as she opened the screen door. "I have a basket class later this afternoon, and I need to get a shipment over to the general store. . . ."

"It'll just take a moment. Please, Monica. Just come in for a moment."

Monica sighed and stepped inside. She handed Jessie the package from UPS. It was from Jessie's publisher. Jessie put the package aside and gestured to Monica to sit. But her sister shook her head.

"Really, Jessie, I can only stay a second," she said.

"Okay." Jessie let out a breath, trying to find the right words. "Look, Monica, it's felt a little weird between us this past week. . . ."

"Weird? What are you talking about?"

"Well, I hardly ever see you. Todd comes up all the time. . . ."

She noticed the tightening of her sister's lips at that point and the way she looked away from her. "Yes," Monica said. "Todd sure has been coming up here a lot."

Jessie realized her sister wasn't happy about that.

"I haven't asked him to, Monica. He's just been very sweet, coming up and helping me finish the painting and the tiling." Her voice cracked a little. "You know, all the stuff Inga was doing before she . . . before she died."

"I'm glad he's been a help to you, Jessie," Monica said.

"But I sense that ever since Inga's death, you've . . . I don't know. I sense you've wanted to avoid me."

Monica leveled her eyes at her. "It's been a difficult time for everybody."

"But why—?"

"Look, Jessie, it was not good for my business that all the people who buy my baskets, either wholesale or retail, had to pick up the newspaper and read that I was called down to police headquarters to be questioned about a murder!"

"The papers were clear that you—all of us—were just being questioned as witnesses. There's been no suggestion any of us were guilty."

Monica sighed. "That doesn't matter. Our names were in the paper. A girl was killed on the border of our property. I've had a number of people cancel out on basket classes because they don't feel comfortable coming here."

Jessie was looking at her. "I'm sorry about that, Monica. Really I am. But you speak as if I'm somehow at fault. That somehow I caused Inga's death and all this inconvenience to you."

Monica closed her eyes and seemed to count to ten. When she reopened her eyes, she was already speaking. "It just brought back bad memories," she said, "of when you lived here before."

"Monica," Jessie said, reaching out and trying to take her sister's hand. But Monica avoided her, walking over to the window. "Monica, this has been a horrible experience for everyone. I've been getting phone calls from Germany in the middle of the night from Inga's grief-stricken parents. They keep wanting to know if their daughter's killer has been found. We're not the only ones impacted by this."

Monica just stared out the window, not saying anything.

"Monica," Jessie said, approaching her but not attempting to touch her. "I want us to be close again, like we used to be."

Her sister spun around to look at her. "We were never close, Jessie."

"Yes, we were," Jessie insisted. "When we were girls . . ."

"No." Monica's voice was calm and steady. "You were Mom's favorite, and I always felt that. I always felt left out by the two of you."

"We never meant to make you feel that way," Jessie said. "Mom loved you! She called you her beautiful porcelain doll!"

"But you were the one she took with her everywhere."

"That's because you didn't like going to those New Age shops. You complained you couldn't abide the smell of Nag Champa. Besides, for every outing Mom took me on, Dad took you on your own adventures."

Monica snarled. "Going into the office with him while he went over his accounts hardly counts as an adventure. He only took me because otherwise I'd have been left home alone, since you and Mom were out mushroom picking someplace, or fording some goddamn river."

"You could always have come with us," Jessie replied. "We always asked you. And you always said no, because you didn't want to get dirty."

Monica said nothing.

"Monica, I never knew this troubled you so deeply. I always thought you were okay being Dad's girl and I was Mom's girl."

"You know, let's put to rest right here the fallacy that I was Dad's girl." Monica took a couple of steps toward

Jessie so that she was only a few inches from her sister's face. Jessie could see years of rage and resentment shining in her eyes. "Sure, Dad liked to talk about business with me. But I was always keenly aware that he wished he were talking with you instead."

"That's your own imagination," Jessie said quietly.

"You were the one Dad really admired! You were the one who he wanted to impress. Because you were like Mom."

Jessie looked away, Mr. Thayer's words came back to her.

You were the one he most admired. Because, after all, you were just like your mother, the woman he loved.

"I'm sorry you've felt this way," Jessie whispered. "I never knew."

"Well, now you do. So please stop with the nonsense about us being close. We weren't even close in school, the way the teachers all favored you, and the boys . . ."

Jessie's eyes darted over to her sister. "I recall one boy who didn't favor me," she said, sharper than she expected.

Todd.

Sooner or later, all their problems returned to Todd.

Monica actually smiled. "Todd was the one person who ever preferred me to you," she said. But Jessie thought her sister's words sounded hollow somehow, as if she didn't really believe what she was saying. Jessie remembered Monica's pique at how much time Todd had been spending up here lately, helping fix up the house.

"Look, Jessie," Monica said, her hand on the door-

knob as she prepared to leave, "I've tried to be support-
ive of you. I really have. But it seems every time I do,
something terrible happens. And I just need a little
space."

"Fine," her sister said, not looking at her.

"Helloooo!"

The sudden interruption of Aunt Paulette's voice,
lilting through the windows, startled both of them.
They heard car doors slam, and footsteps crunching on
the gravel driveway. Through the window Jessie could
see their aunt heading up the hill, holding Abby's hand.
Jessie had lost track of the time. She'd asked Aunt
Paulette to pick Abby up from school today.

"Monica?" Aunt Paulette was calling in her sing-
song voice. "Are you up there, too? We can see you!
And we have something to show you!"

Jessie saw Monica resist rolling her eyes.

Aunt Paulette and Abby were coming up the stairs
into the house now. Abby was carrying a big sheet of
white paper.

"Wait until you girls see this!" Aunt Paulette sang
out as they came through the door. "Show them, Abby!"

The child held up the sheet of paper. In shaky printing she had written MY FAMILY across the top. The "F"
was printed backwards. Below this there was a rough
drawing of a house with a lot of green scribbles for
grass and trees, and in front of the house were six stick
figures, one smaller than the rest.

"Tell them who everybody is, sweetheart," Aunt
Paulette instructed.

Abby pointed to the first of the stick figures, which
had yellow hair atop its head. "This is Mommy," the little girl declared. Next she pointed to a nearly identical

stick figure, although this one had brown hair. "This is Aunt Monica." A stick figure with no hair at all was Uncle Todd, and one with a bright red smile was Aunt Paulette. The last figure, standing alongside the rest, was Inga. "And the little one is me," Abby said.

Jessie could see that Monica was touched. She bent down and kissed Abby on the head, then pleaded she was late and rushed off, the screen door banging behind her.

"I'm going to hang this beautiful family portrait up right away," Jessie announced. With magnets, she carefully affixed the drawing to the front of the refrigerator, and they all stood back to admire it.

"I think we have a budding artist in our family," said Aunt Paulette.

"Mommy, can I go play on the swings?" Abby asked.

"Okay, honey," Jessie told her, and the little girl scurried out the door into the backyard.

"Did her teachers say how things went today?" Jessie asked Aunt Paulette as she returned to sit in front of her computer.

"The same."

The two women exchanged looks. Once word of the murder had gotten around the Independent Day School, teachers noted that many of the children seemed leery of playing with Abby. They were apparently acting on orders from their parents. Even the little girl who had befriended Abby on the first day of school had drifted away from her on the second day. It was as if parents believed that associating with a child whose nanny had been murdered might place their children in a similar kind of danger. Or maybe, Jessie speculated, there was still some reserve hostility toward Abby's mother—

who, after all, had been witness to another murder not that long ago. Whatever the reasons, Abby's teachers had noticed that the little girl ate her snacks alone and was often the last chosen by her classmates in games and other events. They were doing their best to disrupt this pattern and to fully integrate Abby into classroom activities, but they had put Jessie on alert to what was happening.

"Breaks my heart to think of her sitting all by herself in class," Jessie said, shutting her computer. She realized she'd get no more work done today.

"But she hasn't complained," Aunt Paulette said. "She's never mentioned anything. When you ask her how school was, she always says it was good."

"That's Abby," Jessie said. "She never complains. She rarely even cried as a baby."

Jessie glanced out the window at her daughter, swinging on the swings. Abby was talking to herself. She'd seen the little girl do that yesterday as well when she came home from school.

"An imaginary playmate," Aunt Paulette said, observing the same thing.

"Because she has no friends in school," Jessie said, and she felt as if she'd cry.

"Maybe we ought to ask Bryan and Heather's little ones back up to play with Abby," Aunt Paulette suggested.

"Those two brats?" Jessie sighed. She was still peeved at Bryan for what he'd said to her at the picnic, but if his kids could give Abby some company, she shouldn't stand in the way. "Maybe. I don't know. Abby didn't really enjoy their company. But I'll ask her."

Abby had gotten off the swings now and was engaged in an animated conversation with her invisible playmate. She was talking intensely, and moving her hands, and pointing across the yard, and then laughing uproariously to herself.

Both Jessie and Aunt Paulette watched.

"Gosh," Jessie said. "She's really into this. . . ."

"I know. Isn't she cute?"

"But is it okay? I mean, it's not a . . . a problem, is it?"

Aunt Paulette looked over at her. "To have an imaginary friend? Oh, no! All kids have imaginary friends. You did."

"I did?"

"Oh, yes. His name was Billy. It was so cute!"

Jessie smiled.

Outside, Abby was moving around behind the swing, still talking to herself. Jessie watched as she began to push the swing, as if she were giving her imaginary friend a ride.

"Okay, sweetie," Aunt Paulette announced, "I'm going back to my cottage. Call me if you need anything."

"I will," said Jessie. "Thank you for picking Abby up today."

"Anytime!"

Her aunt left, humming as she crossed the yard back to her little cottage.

Jessie kept her eyes on Abby. The little girl was still pushing the swing out in front of her, carrying on a conversation with the imaginary playmate. Jessie couldn't hear what she was saying, but it was clear she was enjoying herself. Over and over again she pushed the swing. It would fly outward then drift gently back to her, and then she'd push it again.

But as she watched, Jessie saw something very peculiar.

Each time Abby pushed, the swing sailed higher and higher into the air, and each time it did so, it came back toward Abby a little more swiftly, a little more dangerously. Abby had to move back a few steps each time to avoid being hit. Jessie was perplexed. Either her daughter was far stronger than she imagined—being able to send that swing farther and farther into the sky—or there really *was* an invisible playmate on that seat.

TWENTY-TWO

Detective Wolfowitz, whose friends called him Wolfie, didn't relish another confrontation with John Manning, but that was what he and his partner, Harry Knotts, were heading toward. The search warrant sat on the seat of the cruiser between them. Manning was sure to be very displeased when Wolfowitz flaunted that in his face. There would probably be another scene, more of his big booming voice raised in anger.

Let him rant, Wolfie thought. *I just want to see inside that house*.

The police detectives were coming under increasing pressure from the mayor, from the local media, and from people in the street to find the German girl's killer. No one felt safe in their homes, especially not the folks on Hickory Dell. Wolfie kept getting calls from Gert Gorin every time she saw a strange car turn around in the cul-de-sac or spied what she thought was someone lurking in the bushes. The girl's murder had really got the town riled up. People were just beginning to recover from Sayer's Brook's last murder six years ago—when Sammy "Screech" Solek had had his throat sliced by Emil Deetz, Jessie Clarkson's crazy ex-boy-friend.

But that had been a drug deal gone bad. This latest murder, by contrast, seemed to be random and motive-less. The German girl had just moved to town. She had known no one here. Except Jessie Clarkson, of course, and her neighbors.

And Jessie Clarkson was what the two murders had in common.

As Wolfie turned the police cruiser onto Ridge Road, the long stretch that led from the town center out to Hickory Dell, he knew that there were quite a few people who suspected Jessie knew more than she was saying about both killings, and Wolfie had his own sus-picions. How could she have lived with Emil Deetz, been pregnant with his kid, and not known what he was doing? How could she have not known where his money came from?

There were some in the department who couldn't accept as mere coincidence Jessie being associated with the last killing in town and then, as soon as she re-turned to Sayer's Brook, being associated with another.

Wolfie was definitely keeping his eye on Jessie, but his line of reasoning led him elsewhere. Jessie had seemed utterly believable in all of her statements to po-lice, both six years earlier and more recently. Some of the cops didn't think so, but Wolfie did. Maybe that was because, unlike those same cops, he didn't view Screech Solek as the last murder in town. He believed another murder had taken place a couple of years ago.

That of Millie Manning.

Three years ago, he and Harry had been the first on

the scene when they'd gotten a call of death out at John
Manning's house. Wolfie's ex-wife, Pam, had been a
voracious reader of everything Manning had ever written. How many nights had Pam lain beside Wolfie in
bed with the light on until two in the morning, her nose
in between the pages of a turgid John Manning horror
novel? How many times had Wolfie tried to get cozy
with her and Pam had brushed him away, caught up in
Manning's vampires or witches or ghosts? The bloom
might have already been off Wolfie's marriage—he and
Pam had been married for eighteen years at that point,
and their two daughters had been in high school—but
Wolfie still harbored some resentment at Manning for
coming between him and his wife. Irrational, maybe.
But it was there.

So when he and Harry had arrived at Manning's
house to find Mrs. Manning facedown on the concrete,
Wolfie had had quite a few questions to ask, and he
hadn't always asked them kindly. Where had Mr. Manning been when his wife had supposedly fallen off the
back deck? How did he explain that fall? The railing
around the deck was very high. One couldn't just stumble and fall off it. It nearly came to Mrs. Manning's
shoulders. She would have had to climb up onto it for
some reason. Had she been trying to fix something?
Get something? See something? Or had she climbed
up there in order to jump and kill herself?

Manning had had no answers to any of the questions, except for where he'd been when it had happened. He'd been in his glass casita, writing. So absorbed
had he been in his work that he hadn't emerged for several hours, and when he had, he'd found his wife dead
on the ground. But when Wolfie had checked out the

casita, he'd realized its big windows would have enabled the author to see the back deck of the house quite clearly. Wouldn't his wife plummeting to earth from the third floor of the house be something that might catch his attention?

Manning claimed to have seen or heard nothing. "When I write," he said with an eerie calm to his voice, "I block out the entire world."

Wolfie hadn't bought it. But other detectives had concluded that it was possible to sit in the casita, facing a certain way, and not see a woman tumble down onto the deck. And with the music playing that Manning said he listened to as he wrote—that day it was Rachmaninov—he might not have heard anything either.

But how had Millie Manning gotten up onto that railing to fall? Suicide, some detectives had determined. But she'd been in the middle of making a basket. The materials had all been carefully arranged on the deck, and she had completed about half of the basket. Manning's assistant, Caleb, had stated that he'd last seen Mrs. Manning around noon that day, before he'd left to head into the city on errands for his employer. At last glimpse, Mrs. Manning had seemed in a pleasant mood, eager to finish her basket before her class with Monica Bennett that night. She wanted to show all the ladies that she could make a basket on her own.

Wolfie didn't believe she'd stop halfway through to commit suicide.

Unless something had happened. Unless there had been some argument with her husband. But Manning claimed he'd been in his casita all day writing. He hadn't seen Millie since breakfast that morning.

Except, Wolfie suspected, when he'd gone up to that third-floor deck, soon after Caleb had left for the day, and tossed his wife over the railing.

There were no fingerprints on the corpse to prove such a thing. There was not the tiniest scrap of evidence to indicate that Manning had done the deed.

But Wolfie had thought the man far too composed, far too careful in his words and his emotions, to make a convincing grieving spouse. In fact, he'd seemed utterly indifferent to his wife's death. The stories of his affairs with other women, both prior and subsequent to the tragedy, just added fuel to Wolfie's suspicions.

He steered the cruiser onto Hickory Dell.

The death of Millie Manning had been ruled accidental. A few bands of wicker had been found on the ground and in the gutters of the house. It had been a fairly windy day, and some detectives speculated that some of her basket-making material may have blown up onto the railing. Millie may have attempted to climb up and grab a piece that had blown onto an eave of the house and, in doing so, lost her balance and fallen.

But Wolfie didn't believe it.

They passed Mr. Thayer's house on the left, and several yards past that, the home of Bryan and Heather Pierce. Deep green woods filled the spaces between the houses of Hickory Dell. Some of the guys in the department speculated the killer of the German girl could have very easily hidden in the woods after the murder. Even with the moon that night, it got very dark along the cul-de-sac.

But Wolfie suspected the killer had just gone back into his house, washed his hands, disposed of the knife, and waited for the body to be found.

Just as he had three years earlier with his wife.

Sadly, there had been no DNA evidence on the corpse to link anyone to the girl's death. No blood or skin under her nails, suggesting there had been no struggle. There had been no sexual assault. The body had been free of bruises except those minor ones sustained from when she'd fallen to the ground. Her throat had been sliced open with a very specific kind of long razor; if they could find the weapon, the forensics department thought they could easily match it.

Other than the throat, the only other wounds on the body were on the legs. These had puzzled the coroner and the detectives. The same razor that had been used to slit the girl's throat had also been slashed a couple of times across the back of her thighs. She had been wearing shorts, and the blade had sliced her skin cleanly, if not very deeply. The wounds were just superficial, nothing that would have caused too much bleeding. But they would have been painful. Since they had been made before the girl's throat had been slit, the coroner speculated that the attack on her thighs had been used to bring her down. Her throat had been cut while she was lying on the ground, looking up at her killer.

The detectives passed the Gorins' house on the left and turned into the gravel driveway across the street. At the bottom of the hill was the sleek glass-and-metal Bennett house. Farther back on the property, up the verdant hill adorned with daisies and goldenrod, stood the old Clarkson house. Wolfie switched off the cruiser's ignition. They'd park here because there was little room next door. John Manning had an imposing privacy wall surrounding his estate, and the lack of publicly accessible space in front of his house was designed to keep his fans away. So Wolfie figured on parking in the Clarkson driveway and walking over through the small patch of trees that divided the two properties. Besides, he liked the element of surprising Manning.

"Bring the warrant," Wolfie instructed Knotts as they got out of the car.

Manning had said he'd bid the girl good night and walked her to the gate. She'd only had a few yards to walk through the trees to return home. Afterward, he'd heard no scream, as nearly all of the other neighbors had. He'd had music playing again, Manning explained—this time Chopin, and in his study, not his casita. And he had a corroborating witness this time, his assistant, Caleb. But Wolfie didn't trust Caleb. The young man seemed much too obsequious toward Manning, as if his employer could murder Caleb's own mother and Caleb would lie to cover it up.

Walking through the trees toward Manning's home, Wolfie rued the fact that it had taken so long to get this search warrant. How much evidence had Manning destroyed in the meantime? Wolfie didn't expect to find the murder weapon just sitting out on a counter. But it was crucial to see if there was any blood or DNA in Manning's house. Maybe on his clothes, if he hadn't burned them all. But evidence of burned clothes might be good to discover as well. As soon as they gained access to Manning's house, Wolfie would phone headquarters and a whole team of forensic investigators would descend on the place. Manning would be powerless to refuse.

"Well," Wolfie said to Knotts as they stood outside Manning's gate. "Here goes. Get ready for a lot of screaming and hollering."

Knotts just shrugged.

Wolfie reached up and pushed the buzzer.

TWENTY-THREE

"**A**rthur!" Gert Gorin shrieked, her binoculars pressed up against the window. "Two policemen just pulled up into the Clarkson driveway and are walking into the woods."

"Gert, for the last time, get away from the window."

She looked back at him impatiently. "Don't you care if they ever find that girl's killer? I can't sleep at night thinking that beast might be still out there, lurking in the woods."

"You'll hate when they find the killer because you won't have anything to keep looking for out that goddamn window."

He didn't even remove the newspaper he was reading from in front of his face as he spoke to her.

Gert returned her eyes to the binoculars. "I think they're going over to John Manning's house. You know, Arthur, I find it very peculiar that he was the last one to see that poor sweet girl alive."

"You thought she was a lesbian hussy when you met her at the party."

"I wonder why he killed her," Gert mused, still searching for any sign of movement across the street, although the policemen had disappeared into the trees. "I mean, I know why he might have killed Millie. She was such a pest to him, always complaining about his book tours, or the pretty fans who threw themselves at him." She paused, trying to calculate dates in her mind. "Had Manning started his affair with Heather Pierce yet when Millie died? I don't think so. But maybe."

"Why don't you just call up Heather and ask her?"

"Oh, look!" Gert shouted. "Now Jessie's coming out of her house. And Paulette is there, too. They must be wondering why a police cruiser is in their driveway, but no one came up to talk to them!"

This is getting exciting, Gert thought.

TWENTY-FOUR

"They must have gone next door," Aunt Paulette surmised about the police car. "Guess they had a few more questions to ask Mr. Manning."

Jessie and her aunt walked back up the driveway. "I just wish they'd find who did it so we could put all of this in the past," Jessie said, shivering suddenly.

Aunt Paulette stopped walking. "You know, Jessie," she said, reaching out and taking her niece's arm. "I think . . . I think I see an end to this."

"What do you mean?"

"The killer . . ." Aunt Paulette gazed over toward the trees that surrounded John Manning's stone mansion. "They're about to find him."

"You mean . . . Manning?" Jessie asked. "Are you getting some kind of vision or something?"

"I can't be sure," Aunt Paulette said. "It's just a feeling or a sense I have. They're close to him. They're closing in."

At that very moment a whole squad of police cars suddenly arrived out front, parking in the street. At least a dozen of detectives, most of them in plainclothes, got out of the cars and swarmed up to John Manning's front gate. Jessie couldn't resist a small laugh.

"Well, Aunt Paulette," she said, "maybe you're on to something."

It was her aunt's turn to shiver. "Well, let's hope so," she said.

They resumed walking up the driveway.

"Do you think Mr. Manning could have had anything to do with it?" Jessie asked. "I mean, all those police cars . . ."

"It's probably just a search of his house," Aunt Paulette replied. "I understand he refused to let police in—whereas we let them come and go, look anywhere they wanted."

"I hope he didn't do it," Jessie said. "I'd hate to think that I let Inga go over there and then he killed her."

"You couldn't have known, sweetie."

Jessie bit back the tears. She had cried so often since Inga's death. She didn't want to let loose another waterfall.

Back in the house, she started dinner, trying to put whatever was going on in the house next door out of her mind. She'd make baked macaroni and cheese. Mom's recipe.

"Stay and eat with us?" she asked Aunt Paulette.

"Sure, baby."

Abby came through the back door.

"Have fun on the swings, Ab?" her mother asked her.

"Yes," the little girl replied, noticing the block of cheddar Jessie was slicing on the chopping board. "Are you making mac and cheese?"

"I sure am. Your favorite."

"Gramma's recipe?" Abby asked.

"That it is," her mother replied.

"I wish you had known your grandmother, Abby," Aunt Paulette said. "How she would have loved you."

"I wish I had known her, too," the little girl mused, snitching a piece of cheese and placing it in her mouth.

"Abby," Jessie said. "I notice when you play on the swings you talk to somebody."

Abby nodded.

"Is it a friend of yours?" Jessie asked.

Again Abby nodded.

"What's her name?"

"It's not a girl."

"Oh?" Jessie asked, cutting the block of cheese into small cubes that she planned to melt in a pan with some seasoned milk. "Then what's *his* name?"

"I don't know."

Jessie smiled over at Aunt Paulette. "He's just your friend, I guess."

"Well, actually," Abby said, seeming to consider her mother's statement, "he's more than a friend."

Jessie smiled wider. "Oh, really? How is he more than a friend?"

Abby looked up at her with her big round eyes. "He's my brother."

The knife in Jessie's hand suddenly sliced down into her finger, drawing blood, and she gasped out loud. Not from any pain, or from the blood that now dripped onto the chopping board.

But from Abby's words.

He's my brother.

"Jessie!" Aunt Paulette cried, jumping up and running over with a dishtowel. "Are you all right?"

The older woman immediately used the dishtowel to wrap Jessie's finger in an attempt to stanch the flow of blood.

"It's okay," Jessie managed to say in a small, shaky voice. "It wasn't very deep."

"Mommy, are you okay?" Abby asked.

Jessie gave her a smile. "Yes, sweetie, I'm fine. Just cut my finger a tiny, little bit."

She walked over to the sink and, removing the dishtowel, ran water over her finger. The wound was really just superficial.

"Are you sure you're okay?" Abby asked.

"Yes, baby. It's all better now." She smiled over her shoulder. "Go wash up for supper, okay, Abs?"

"Yes, Mommy," the little girl said, and hurried upstairs.

"Jessie," Aunt Paulette said, suddenly at her side.

"Did you hear what she said?" Jessie asked her aunt. "She said she was playing with . . . *her brother*."

Aunt Paulette knew all about the dreams she'd had, the visions, the terrible guilt she carried with her about her lost twin son.

"Sweetie," Aunt Paulette said, "little children often play with imaginary siblings. It's nothing to be alarmed about."

"It was just the way she said it." Jessie was wrapping a Band-Aid around her finger. "So matter-of-factly."

"Right now, Abby's going through a difficult time at school. She feels she doesn't have any friends. She sees the Pierce kids, little Piper and Ashton, and she wishes she had a brother, too, someone who would always be with her, and play with her."

"I suppose you're right," Jessie said. "Oh, my poor baby."

"It's just a simple child's game," Aunt Paulette said.

Jessie nodded. But she couldn't get the image of that swing out of her mind—the way it had seemed to move, entirely on its own.

TWENTY-FIVE

What surprised Wolfie most was how cooperative, even pleasant, John Manning had been to them. When Wolfie had shown him the search warrant, the author had given him a gracious smile, stepped aside so that the policemen could enter, and said, "Please, come in. Search whatever and wherever you need. Be my guest."

What surprised him less was that they found nothing.

No blood, no burned clothes, nothing.

The forensics team had descended as soon as Wolfie had called them, and they'd swept through the house, opening drawers and closets, looking in safes and locked compartments, sifting through the ashes in the fireplace, dusting for fingerprints, using X-ray technology and a bloodhound to search for even minuscule droplets of blood.

Nothing.

They found the girl's fingerprints, but that didn't mean anything. Everyone acknowledged that she had been there. But nothing was found to shed any light on how or why she had been killed.

As they searched, Manning kept up his smiling pretense, having Caleb make coffee for some of the detectives, though Wolfie declined a cup. Manning led them out into the back courtyard and let them poke through his writing casita as well. Wolfie noticed how extra charming Manning was to one of the female investigators, smiling at her, often directing his comments to her. The guy was really a womanizer, Wolfie thought.

The police detective stood off to the side, watching the forensics team work. He guessed he shouldn't have been that surprised that they'd found nothing. It had been more than a week since the murder, after all. The goddamn judge had waited far too long in giving them the warrant; that had given Manning plenty of time to clean the place of any last scrap of evidence. Wolfie wondered if Manning's millions had spoken; had he pulled strings somehow in the courts to delay the release of the warrant? Wolfie wouldn't put it past him.

He didn't trust John Manning. He believed he'd killed his wife. And now he believed he killed the German girl as well.

Wolfie watched how the esteemed author was doing his best to dazzle the policewoman. Diane Ballard was a hard-edged, tough-as-nails detective. Her head wasn't easily turned. And yet, Wolfie noticed the small smile she gave Manning when he made some little witticism. He had to give it to Manning: he did have a way with women.

A way of *killing* women.

"Wolfie?"

The police detective was pulled out of his thoughts by Harry Knotts, coming up behind him. "What is it, Knotts?" Wolfie asked.

"I think you ought to come out to the casita," Knotts whispered.

"You find something?"

Knotts held his gaze. "Just come take a look."

The two men walked outside. They didn't hurry. Wolfie was careful not to draw attention to their movements. He didn't want Manning following them. At the moment, Manning was busy trying to make Detective Ballard smile again, but she was proving a hard sell. *Keep him occupied, Diane*, Wolfie sent out in a telepathic request.

There were several investigators going through drawers in the casita. Another was seated in front of Manning's computer, his fingers on the keyboard, going through the author's files. Manning had joked they could read anything they wanted, as long as they didn't reveal the ending to his latest novel-in-progress.

"What do you have for me?" Wolfie asked as he entered the casita.

"Not sure, sir," said Davidson, a young detective. "But Detective Knotts says this might be relevant in some way."

Davidson was flipping through a spiral-bound notebook. There were about twenty leaves in the notebook, cellophane holders with newspaper articles, printed out from a computer, slipped inside each one. Wolfie bent down to read them, but realized he needed his glasses. He fumbled them from his front pocket and slipped them onto his face.

"Seems Manning is interested in another case we investigated out here six years ago," Knotts said, coming up beside Wolfie.

Wolfie looked down at the notebook. The headline on the first sheet read:

MAN FOUND WITH THROAT SLIT IN PARKING LOT.

Wolfie flipped to the second page.

LOCAL WOMAN QUESTIONED ABOUT SLAYING.

The third page had two photographs: Screech Solek and Emil Deetz.

"Well, bust my buttons," Wolfie murmured. "This is about Jessie Clarkson's ex-boyfriend. Who, coincidentally enough, also sliced open someone's throat."

"Hardly seems a coincidence to me that Manning would have a notebook all about that case, when he hadn't even been living in Sayer's Brook at that time," Knotts said.

Wolfie looked over at his partner. Knotts was a good detective but sometimes a little slow on the uptake when it came to irony or sarcasm. "I was speaking facetiously, Knotts," Wolfie told him.

"Oh, right."

In fact, it *couldn't* be a coincidence. John Manning downloads all these newspaper articles about his next-door neighbor—and then, in his own backyard, a girl gets murdered in the exact way described in the articles? A razor swung nearly from ear to ear across the throat. But what connection could there be?

The rest of the notebook contained all the rest of the newspaper coverage. There were the reports about Jessie's eyewitness testimony about the murder, and the revelation of Deetz's drug and porn ring, and the search of the Clarkson property, and then the manhunt for Deetz that moved out from Sayer's Brook and extended all across the country. Finally, the last pages of the notebook included the report that Deetz had been found in Mexico after his fatal shoot-out with police.

"When did he compile this?" Wolfie wanted to know. "If he did it *after* the killing of the German girl, it could just be morbid curiosity."

"Nope," Davidson said. "There are dates on the printouts. They're from more than two years ago."

"Ah, yes, I see." He kept flipping through the notebook. At the very end was a short article that quoted Wolfie himself, saying that, with Deetz's death in Mexico, he now considered the Solek case "closed."

Maybe he'd been too hasty.

"Find anything interesting?"

The detectives turned around. Manning had walked into the casita.

Wolfie discreetly closed the notebook before turning around to face Manning.

"Just reading your novel on the computer, Mr. Manning," Wolfie said, a smile playing on his face. "Have to admit it takes a lot of twists and turns."

Manning smiled back at him. Neither smile was genuine, but that was the game they'd been playing all day.

"Well, you do know if you breathe a word of it," the author said, "you'll have to face the wrath of John Manning fans all around the world."

"Believe me," Wolfie said, "we wouldn't want that."

Manning held his eyes for several seconds He didn't trust Wolfie, and Wolfie knew it. Manning wasn't worried about police spoiling the ending of his novel. He was worried about something else, and Wolfie knew that, too.

The author gave a final little smile and left the casita.

"Why didn't you ask him anything about the notebook?" Davidson wanted to know.

"Instinct," Knotts answered for Wolfie. "We'll ask him about it when we know more of why we're asking."

Wolfie smiled. "Indeed you are correct, Knotts. We need to first find out if Manning had any kind of relationship with Deetz. And we need to look into what kind of relationship, if any, he has with Jessie Clarkson."

"Yes, sir," Davidson said. "Shall I confiscate the notebook?"

"Just take photos of it, high resolution, every page, and dust it for fingerprints. I don't want him to know yet that we're interested in it." Wolfie had moved to stand in the doorway of the casita. From there, he could see the upper deck where Millie Manning took that one last flying leap to her death.

But Wolfie was certain she had been pushed.

TWENTY-SIX

A few days after the detectives had been to Manning's house, igniting a frenzy of talk and wild
speculation among the neighbors, Todd Bennett placed
a ladder against the side of his sister-in-law's house and
lugged a can of paint with him up to the top step. He
was helping Jessie spruce up the house, giving the
weathered old shingles a fresh coat of yellow paint.

Like most everyone else, Todd had some very deep
suspicions about their famous neighbor. He'd always
though Manning had had something to do with his
wife's death. Now he felt the bestselling author definitely knew more about Inga's murder than he was saying. Todd had thought Manning had looked awfully
shifty that night. He wasn't sure if Manning was the
murderer, or if the actual culprit was that obnoxious
Caleb, and Manning was just covering up for him. But
he hoped that detective had found something in his
search of Manning's house to implicate one of those
two creeps in Inga's death.

From up here, Todd had a good view of the backyard. As he gently layered fresh paint onto the shingles, his eyes kept wandering over to watch Jessie as

she cleared away a thicket of brush that had grown over her mother's garden. Next spring, Jessie said, she planned to plant tomatoes and beans and squash and peas and peppers. Todd watched as Jessie ripped out tall bunches of crabgrass and yanked up the tangled orange roots of bittersweet vine. Her blond hair was tied back in a ponytail.

She looked beautiful.

Todd sighed and returned his eyes to his painting.

He wasn't sure when he'd fallen out of love with Monica. In fact, if he was honest with himself, he wasn't sure he ever *had been* in love with Monica. He would never have dumped Jessie for her if Monica hadn't been pregnant. He knew that for sure now. Todd had been a scared kid, terrified of what his deeply religious parents would say if they knew their son had gotten a girl "with child," as they called it. He knew they'd have ordered him to "do the right thing" and marry her.

But then Monica had lost the baby. By then, she'd convinced Todd that he *was* in love with her. She'd been so fragile after the miscarriage, too, crying all the time, that Todd couldn't have left her, even if he had wanted to.

He *had* wanted to.

At the time, Todd hadn't allowed himself to believe so. But now, looking back, Todd knew that he *had* wanted to leave Monica and go back to Jessie. He had wanted to do so very much. But he had simply been unable to do so.

When he'd married Monica, Todd had believed he loved her. But as the years passed, things changed. They bickered. They fought. And Monica could never get pregnant. Todd remembered the doctor saying it was unusual for a woman to get pregnant so easily the first time, and then never again. It had left a little nagging question in the back of Todd's mind, one that he had never allowed himself to articulate out loud.

Had Monica really been pregnant?

Or had she used the claim as a ruse to get him away from Jessie?

That was crazy. Monica wouldn't have done that to her own sister.

But Todd saw how jealous Monica always was when it came to Jessie. Todd admitted that he hadn't wanted Jessie to come back to Sayer's Brook. After all the problems Jessie had caused with her dalliance with Emil Deetz, Todd had been very glad when she'd moved away to New York. There had just been too much unpleasantness. Even after she'd moved away, Jessie had still been so distraught, at least in the beginning, always calling Monica about nightmares and hallucinations she was having. That eventually stopped, after Emil was shot to death in Mexico. But still Todd had worried that if Jessie ever came back, the drama would return, and Todd was a man who could not abide drama.

Taking a step down the ladder so he could paint the next row of shingles, Todd supposed that the drama *had* returned. Everything had been quiet and uneventful here on Hickory Dell before Jessie's homecoming. Todd and Monica had had their routine. They bickered now and then, but no real arguments tore up their marriage anymore. They had settled into a kind of numbness. They hardly made love anymore. Todd just didn't have it in him; she didn't excite him the way she used to. His work kept him preoccupied, especially as the banks struggled to stay afloat during this economic downturn. It wasn't an exciting life, but at least there was no drama.

Then Jessie came back and within a week there was a murder practically in Todd's backyard.

But Todd found himself wanting to protect Jessie from the stress of it, not blame her. He'd told Monica that they couldn't blame Jessie for this. If they should cast blame, it was at John Manning, in Todd's opinion. Jessie had had absolutely nothing to do with this, Todd believed. She was as devastated as any of them—actually far more devastated. Inga had been her friend. Abby had been devoted to her. Todd told Monica that Jessie and Abby needed their help and support during this time, not their resentment.

Monica didn't quite see it that way. But Todd made sure that Jessie knew he was there for her if she needed him.

The Jessie Clarkson who had come back to Sayer's Brook wasn't the Jessie who had left it. This new woman was strong and determined, and funny and warm and human. She was rather like the girl Todd had fallen in love with in high school. The girl he might have married had Monica not gotten in the way. He couldn't deny that he'd rather be over here helping his sister-in-law than sitting home with his wife.

"Looking good, Todd!"

He glanced down. Jessie stood at the foot of the ladder, looking up.

"The house really needed a new paint job," he said. "Especially before winter sets in."

"I really appreciate your help, Todd," Jessie called up to him.

He smiled. "No problem, Jessie, Glad to do it."

"You're very sweet." She placed her hands on her hips. "Can I ask why you're not at work today?"

"I'm a big shot, haven't you heard?" he called down, laughing. "I can set my own hours."

"Well, you are Mr. Successful, aren't you?" Jessie teased.

Todd smiled again.

No, he thought. *I'm not successful. I have a great job and I make a lot of money. I live in a gorgeous home I designed myself. I drive a fancy car and am financially set for the rest of my life.*

But I'm not successful. I don't love my wife and I have no kids.

It would have been different, Todd thought, as he started painting the next row of shingles, if only he hadn't gotten Monica pregnant that one drunken night in high school, a night that had set his life on a course he'd never have chosen otherwise.

A night he couldn't remember and would forever have his doubts about.

"Todd," Jessie called up again. "I'm driving over to the school to pick up Abby. Will you still be here when I get back?"

"I will indeed," he told her.

"Good," Jessie said. "I'll make us all some lunch."

Todd smiled.

TWENTY-SEVEN

Jessie waited with a group of other mothers at the Independent Day School for the morning kindergarten class to come running through the doors. By now, she'd gotten used to the ladies of Sayer's Brook keeping their distance from her. They stood aside, in little groups, offering barely a nod of acknowledgment in Jessie's direction. Some of these women she'd known all her life. There was Terry Carmichael, who'd been her best friend in first and second grades, and Georgina Paxton, with whom Jessie had shared pancake and rouge in their high school musicals. There was Yvette Osborn, who came from the town's very first black family, and whom Jessie had befriended right away in tenth grade even as the other girls viewed her as a kind of exotic oddity. But now all of them, driving up in their Mercedes and BMWs and wearing their Manolo Blahnik shoes, kept their distance from Jessie. Two weeks ago, they might have been willing to forgive and forget Emil Deetz. But Inga's death had made them suspicious of Jessie all over again.

Jessie leaned against a pole, looking at her watch. She didn't care that they cold-shouldered her. But it was unforgivable that they'd told their kids to steer clear of Abby.

From inside the building came the muffled sound of a bell ringing. Suddenly the school seemed to shudder with activity, and within moments the doors flew open. A couple of teachers' assistants guided the flock of kindergartners out to their parents. Jessie searched the throng for Abby.

"Mommy!"

Her little girl came running to her, her backpack flopping. Abby was clutching a large piece of construction paper.

"Look, Mommy!" Abby exclaimed.

Jessie examined the paper. It was another drawing, two stick figures, one drawn in red crayon, with yellow hair, and the other drawn in black crayon, with no hair at all.

"Oh, this is beautiful, Abs!"

Abby beamed and hurried ahead of her mother to the car.

Jessie buckled her into the passenger seat of the Volvo. "So you had a good day at school?" she asked.

"It was the best day ever!"

Jessie smiled. "Why is that, sweetie?"

"Because my friend and I colored together."

Jessie's heart soared. "You and a friend? Oh, that's wonderful, Abs."

She gently closed the passenger-side door and hurried around to slide in behind the wheel. Other mothers were behind her. Yvette Osborn had tooted from her Mercedes SL 550 to get Jessie moving.

Jessie started up the ignition and steered the Volvo

out of the lot. Abby was still gazing at the picture she'd drawn.

"This is me and my friend," she told Jessie. "I mean, my friend and I."

"How come she doesn't have any hair?" her mother wanted to know.

Abby looked at her. "Because it's not a girl, Mommy. It's a boy. Can't you see?" She held the drawing up so Jessie could see it again.

"Oh, sorry, honey."

"Today was his first day in school," Abby said.

"Really? Why did he start late?"

Abby was silent for a moment, as if considering the question. "I don't know," she said finally.

They had stopped at a red light. "So," Jessie asked, "what's your friend's name?"

"Aaron," Abby said.

A kind of red flash seemed to obscure Jessie's vision for a moment.

Red.

Blood.

Blood everywhere.

Her hands were covered in it. Blood was running down her legs.

Jessie couldn't speak. She just kept staring at Abby.

"What—?" she finally managed to say.

"Aaron," Abby said again.

Jessie took a deep breath.

There are lots of little boys named Aaron, she told herself.

Of course there were.

But it was also a fact that when Jessie had first

learned she was pregnant with twins, she'd decided the girl Abigail—and the boy Aaron.

She couldn't stop staring at Abby.

From behind her, Yvette Osborn tooted again. The light had turned green.

Jessie refocused her eyes on the road and drove on.

TWENTY-EIGHT

"**W**ell, this isn't working."

Bryan Pierce got out of bed. Behind him Heather and Clare Dzialo were still in a halfhearted lip lock, naked. Bryan lit up a cigarette. He hardly ever smoked, but he needed some kind of stimulating satisfaction now that his erection had withered to a little stub.

"What's wrong, Bry-Bry?" Clare asked.

"Heather's not into it," Bryan said with a sulk.

His wife sighed and got out of bed herself. "I'm sorry, Bryan, but I'm not a lesbian. I don't get into kissing other girls."

"I wasn't asking you to eat her out," Bryan spit.

"I'm a bisexual," the teenaged Clare said. "I like both guys and girls the same."

Bryan patted her head. "You're a good girl, Clare."

Heather snorted, pulling on her robe. "Fuck you, Bryan."

He snarled at her, "If you can't do such a simple thing as kiss this pretty little girl for me, then I guess I can't ask you to do anything." Bryan stalked over to the window, where he puffed on his cigarette as he looked out into the night. It had started to rain.

"Why don't you two just finish up on your own?" Heather suggested, seemingly utterly disgusted by the whole scene. "I'll be downstairs."

"Okay," Clare said cheerfully, casting adoring eyes over at Bryan.

"You know what your problem is, Heather?" Bryan asked. "You have no imagination. None at all."

"Fuck you again, Bryan. I have plenty of imagination." She looked away. "I just don't waste it on you."

He laughed. "Oh, really, now? I'll bet you'd be more than happy to make out with a girl if John Manning asked you to." He laughed again, louder. "Maybe he has!"

Heather's lips tightened.

"Why don't you just fucking admit that you're sleeping with him?" Bryan shouted. "Why this big goddamn secret?"

Heather glared at him, then stormed out of the room.

"Come on, baby," Clare said, holding out her thin little arms toward him.

"Get dressed, Clare, and run along home," Bryan grumbled. "I'm not in the mood anymore."

"Oh . . ."

The girl was clearly disappointed. Bryan knew she'd developed a crush on him. She harbored dreams of splitting him and Heather apart, and taking Heather's place as Mrs. Bryan Pierce. Bryan couldn't blame the kid for such wishful thinking. After all, he knew how handsome he was, what a great body he had. He was a very successful man. A nineteen-year-old kid would definitely see him as quite the catch.

He watched as Clare reached around and snapped her bra back into place. She stood and slid her panties back up her legs, and then buttoned her blouse, and wriggled into her jeans. Bryan was getting aroused again.

But not by Clare.

When he was finally alone, Bryan opened his closet and found his metal lockbox, hidden under a pile of sweaters. Only he knew the combination. Heather had once asked him what he kept in there. He'd told her stocks and bonds and certificates. In fact, the box's contents were even more valuable than that.

Bryan turned the combination and the lid popped open.

Inside were photographs. Hundreds of them.

Of nearly every woman he'd ever slept with.

He'd take pictures of them when they were sleeping, or drunk. He'd spread their legs open, or stick his cock into their mouths, and set his camera to go off. Some of the photos were taken with the women's consent: nasty girls who didn't mind posing with cucumbers up their butts or pinching their nipples. But those photos didn't excite Bryan nearly as much as the ones where he'd managed to sneak a lewd shot without the woman ever knowing it. It was seeing so-called "nice girls" looking like whores that turned him on. It was the very secrecy of it—the unknowing violation—that got Bryan off. He had some of Heather like that in here, but photos of Heather no longer excited him. Bryan dug down to the bottom of the box.

A toothy grin stretched across his face.

Here were the photos he was looking for.

The first ones he'd ever taken, in fact.

Three Polaroids of Jessie Clarkson.

His sweet little Jessaloo.

Bryan had taken them one night during their sopho-more year at SUNY Purchase. They'd been up late studying for midterms in Bryan's dorm room. His room-mate was gone for the weekend. When three o'clock rolled around, Jessie's head began nodding over her book. Bryan told her that it was so late no one would know that she slept over. He assured her that she could sleep in his bed and he'd sleep in his roommate's bed. Jessie had been too tired to resist. She had zonked out within moments. Bryan had fantasies of fucking her while she slept, but he knew it would wake her up. So he came up with another idea. His cock raging hard and driving his thoughts, he began to fondle Jessie's breasts through her T-shirt. She was kind of a hippie chick, and didn't always wear a bra. He was terribly afraid she'd wake up, but when she started to lightly snore, he became more daring. He lifted her T-shirt to expose her breasts. He wanted so badly to touch them, but was too frightened she'd awaken. So he'd gotten out his Polaroid and snapped two pictures, one from far-ther away, so he could see her face, and then a close-up, so he could see the nipples clearly later when he jacked off.

But by then he couldn't stop. He had to get one more photo. But what?

Setting his Polaroid up on the desk, he'd aimed it at the bed. Pulling his pants down he got up on the bed, and crouched over Jessie. If she woke up now, he was dead meat. But he was driven. His heart was thudding madly. He couldn't stop.

He pulled his underwear down, and dropped his cock and balls into his little Jessaloo's face. The Polaroid snapped the picture.

Jessie had never woken up.

She had no idea such photographs existed. But they were Bryan's most treasured possessions.

He took them out of the lockbox and placed them carefully on the floor. After so many years, the edges were brown with smudgy fingerprints. Bryan jacked off looking at them, remembering how sweet Jessie's hair smelled. Even as he shot big ropes of semen across the room, he knew that, with Jessie so close by, he wasn't going to be satisfied with photographs anymore.

Bryan had to have her. Sooner or later, he would fuck Jessie Clarkson.

Whether she agreed or not.

TWENTY-NINE

"It's not that uncommon a name," Aunt Paulette was telling her.

"I know," Jessie said.

She was sitting in Mom's chair, holding a cup of tea in her palms, as the rain tapped against the windowpanes. Her aunt sat opposite her on the couch. Abby was upstairs asleep.

"It was just . . . unnerving, you know, to hear the name Aaron, especially with the whole imaginary playmate thing," Jessie said. "And Abby's insistence she'd been playing with her brother."

"Let's just be happy she's made a friend," Aunt Paulette told her. "A real friend. Not an imaginary one."

Jessie nodded. "Her mood was so improved when I picked her up today. She was positively glowing. You know Abs. She never complains. But in the past, she'd be kind of flat when I asked her about school. Today she was exuberant."

Aunt Paulette looked as if she might cry. "I am so happy to hear that."

"Let's hope things get better from here on," Jessie said.

The older woman nodded. "Oh, I'm certain they will. I did a tarot reading today. And what came up was the Justice card. I am certain that means Inga's killer will soon be caught, and we can all sleep better at night."

Jessie shuddered. "I wonder if that means the police found something from their search of John Manning's house."

"That I can't say. I've tried focusing in on Mr. Manning, but I can't get anything."

Jessie smiled. "Your powers are failing you, Auntie."

She shrugged. "Either that or Mr. Manning is an incredibly defensive, defended, guarded, private man. People can throw up all sorts of psychic walls around themselves that become very difficult to penetrate."

"I'd say that describes John Manning."

Aunt Paulette nodded.

From upstairs, there came a bang. They both glanced up at the ceiling.

Then came the sound of footsteps.

"Abby?" Jessie called.

Now there was laughter.

Abby's laughter.

But not just hers.

There was someone else up there, laughing with her.

And the footsteps . . .

Jessie stood bolt upright from her chair, dropping her cup and spilling tea all over the wooden floor.

There was more than one child running around upstairs!

"Abby!" Jessie shrieked.

Aunt Paulette followed her as Jessie took the stairs

two at a time. She skidded down the hallway, stumbling a little as a throw rug got tangled around her bare feet. She grabbed ahold of Abby's doorknob and threw the door open.

Abby's room was dark. But Jessie could make out her daughter sitting on the bed.

Behind her, Aunt Paulette switched on the light.

Abby was sitting up in bed, smiling at them.

"What was going on up here?" Jessie demanded.

"I was just playing," Abby said.

"Who was up here with you?"

"Nobody," Abby said. "I was just playing by myself."

Jessie noticed the window was open. The cool night air blew in. She hurried over to slam it shut.

"Why is this window open?" she demanded to know. "I never open that window because there's no screen. Why did you open it?"

"I don't know, Mommy," Abby said. Her little blue eyes looked up at her as if Jessie was making much more out of this than she should.

"I heard two sets of feet up here!" Jessie said. "And it wasn't just your laughter I heard, Abby!"

"It was just me," the little girl repeated.

Jessie spun around at Aunt Paulette. "You heard it, too, didn't you? You heard two sets of footsteps? Two kids laughing?"

"Oh, dear," Aunt Paulette said, her hand to her face. "I'm not sure, Jessie. It could have just been Abby."

"It was just me, Mommy. I couldn't sleep so I got up and started to play. I'm sorry, Mommy."

Jessie didn't know what to say. Suddenly she felt ridiculous. Could she have been wrong? Could her anxiety over Abby's new friend's name have made her hear things that weren't there?

"Try to go to sleep now, baby," Aunt Paulette was telling Abby, pulling the sheet up around her.

"Yeah, Abs, go to sleep," Jessie said in a small voice, looking away from her daughter.

"I'm sorry, Mommy."

"It's okay," Jessie said. She looked over at the window, and walked decisively over to lock it. "Don't open this anymore, understand? You'll let mosquitoes and moths in. Okay, Abs? Promise?"

"Yes, Mommy."

"Come on, honey," Aunt Paulette said, gently guiding Jessie out of the room, switching off the light behind her and shutting the door.

THIRTY

Detective Wolfowitz plopped himself down in the chair in front of Chief Belinda Walters's desk.

"You know, Wolfie, John Manning is perhaps the most admired author in the country," the chief said, leaning back in her chair, her strong jaw clenched firm. "And he donates huge portions of his profits to hundreds of charities. Cancer, AIDS, scholarship programs for underprivileged kids." She paused. "The Policemen's Benevolent Association."

"I don't care if he's Jesus, I still think he had something to do with that girl's death."

Wolfie folded his arms across his chest. He missed the days when Joe Martin had sat in the chief's chair. He never felt right reporting to a woman. How Belinda Walters had gotten the promotion and not Wolfie, he'd never understand.

"I'm not telling you to call off your investigation," Walters said, sitting back in her chair. She was a tall, broad-shouldered woman, with a square face and iron-gray hair cut in a pageboy style. "I'm just telling you that you're going to have to find some indisputable evidence before going public with any kind of accusation, because the man has a lot of friends in high places."

"Come on, B'lin. You were just as skeptical as I was when he claimed not to see his wife take that tumble off the deck."

"Skepticism needs to be matched up with hard evidence. We never found any."

Wolfie unfolded his arms and reached across Walters's desk, slapping the stapled papers he had placed there. "How do you explain this?" he barked.

"I can't," she said, glancing down at the sheets of paper. "But neither do these hold any proof that Manning murdered the German girl."

Wolfie snatched up the papers and read from them. "Confidential report, Federal Bureau of Investigation, Ciudad Juarez, Mexico. Suspect Emil Deetz cornered in house with [names redacted] by Mexican drug police at intersection of Vial Juan Gabriel and Niños Heroes. Massive shoot-out, six dead, including suspect."

Walters nodded. "You didn't need the FBI report for that, Wolfie. That much was reported in the *Sayer's Brook Crier*."

He turned over a page of the report. "Large crowds gathered around the building prior to, during, and following the shoot-out. Identified was bestselling American author [name redacted.]" Wolfie threw the papers back onto Walters's desk. "I can fill in the blank."

"Oh, really? Let's see. Bestselling American author? That could be John Grisham, or Stephen King, or Anne Rice, or Stephenie Meyer, or Dan Brown, or Patricia Cornwell, or—"

"None of those people also keep a dossier on Emil Deetz in their private files."

"How do you know?"

Wolfie could feel himself getting hot under his collar. "None of them subsequently then went and bought property right next door to Emil Deetz's former girlfriend."

Walters just sighed.

"He was there when Deetz was killed! Why was he in Mexico?"

"Lots of people go to Mexico."

"Ciudad Juarez isn't Puerto Vallarta or Acapulco. It's the most violent place in Mexico, riddled with drug violence."

"Manning's a writer. Maybe he was gathering information."

"He writes about vampires and werewolves and sexy male witches." Wolfie grunted, remembering the nights when his ex-wife stayed up so late at night reading that trash, keeping him from falling asleep.

"Look, Wolfie," the chief said, leaning toward him. "I agreed to let you pursue this because I, too, want to know why Manning kept a dossier on the Deetz case. He wasn't even living in Sayer's Brook then. But you're a better detective than to sit there and start making all sorts of presumptions without gathering all the information first." She leaned back in her chair. "At least, you used to be a better detective than that."

He frowned. "I'm not making presumptions. I'm asking questions. And don't worry, I've requested the FBI review its classified information and consider revealing the names it redacted in the report, for law enforcement purposes."

"Well, that's a first step."

"But come on, B'lin. You know what this smells

like. You were a good detective, too, once. Sometimes puzzles just suddenly fit into place even before you find all the pieces."

"I'm just telling you to dot your i's and cross your t's, Wolfie."

"I mean, don't you just have to wonder why, after seeing Deetz get shot to death in Mexico, Manning comes to Sayer's Brook and makes Monica Bennett an offer on a piece of family property that wasn't even for sale?"

"He's said in interviews that he liked the town."

"But there were other properties that *were* for sale. Why buy a chunk of the old Clarkson estate?"

"He liked the brook. He liked Hickory Dell."

"Or maybe he knew where Emil Deetz had stashed his cash, or his drugs, or whatever it was that he stashed out there before he fled."

Chief Walters sighed again. "Wolfie, we went all over that property for *weeks*. Metal detectors, bloodhounds. We found nothing."

"Doesn't mean something wasn't there, hidden really deep down."

She made a sound of dismissal through pursed lips. "I think you're reaching now."

"But I can keep looking into it?"

The chief nodded. "Yes. Just don't write your final report until you've done all your homework ahead of time." She lifted the papers from her desk and slipped them into a drawer. "Have you asked Manning yet why he had the dossier on Deetz?"

"Not yet. I don't want him to know quite so soon that I've discovered that little factoid about him. I want to ask him about it when I have more information to throw at him, like confirmation from the FBI that he was indeed in Mexico when Deetz was killed."

"Now, that's spoken like a good detective." The chief stood. "Thanks for the update, Wolfie."

He stood and gave her a little salute in jest.

Wolfie left the chief's office. He'd show her. He'd prove that not only had John Manning been involved in Deetz's crimes, but that he had killed the German girl as well. Maybe she'd stumbled onto something that connected him to Jessie's ex-boyfriend while she was at the house.

Wolfie had believed Manning should have gone to jail a long time ago. Maybe he'd never pay for killing his wife.

But Wolfie would make sure he paid for something else.

THIRTY-ONE

Jessie tugged and tugged and finally the stubborn bittersweet root gave way, ripping through the soil and sending her backwards onto her butt. She laughed out loud, then got back on her haunches to attack the next invasive vine.

She was cleaning out the patch of land on the side of the house, where her property adjoined John Manning's. It was all overgrown with weeds and vines. In the spring, she thought she might put in a little pond here, where she could maybe have some koi in the summer—with a protective scrim on top to keep the raccoons out—and a couple of benches. It was the perfect place to sit in the afternoons, shaded by the tall fir trees. She could even write out here.

She'd forced herself to return to the spot where Inga had died so that she could exorcise those particular demons from her head. Building a garden on the spot would make her feel better. Indeed, being outside these last few days had restored much of Jessie's equilibrium. She was still unable to write, so this was definitely better than just watching television all day. She knew that when she *did* start writing again, she'd be better able to describe dealing with such trauma. She'd explain that you don't force yourself to do what you think you *should* be doing. You confront your fears, but you're gentle with yourself, and you give yourself the time you need to heal. For right now, getting her hands dirty with soil and earth was more soothing than sitting at her computer.

And it was working. As Jessie cleared out vines and weeds and pruned back perennials in the hopes of a second bloom, her spirits were rising. She had been worried that her old jitters and fears were returning. Abby's imaginary playmate and her use of the word "brother"—and the coincidence of her new friend Aaron's name—had threatened to send her spiraling back down into the anxieties she'd lived with in New York. The nightmares had returned—but thankfully only briefly. Jessie realized she was stronger now than she'd been when she'd first moved to New York. She had written a book about survival and was starting on another. She had to remember who she was, not who she had been.

True, she wished Abby's friend at school wasn't named Aaron. But she was just glad that her daughter had a friend. It was so wonderful to see how happy Abby was when she came home from school these days.

"Mommy!"

The sound caused Jessie's ears to perk up.

It was a child's voice, but it wasn't Abby. Abby was with Aunt Paulette in town, shopping for new shoes.

"Mommy!"

Jessie felt a strange trickle of fear.

It was a little boy's voice.

And then she saw him through the trees.

It was little Ashton Pierce. Bryan and Heather's kid. He was running up John Manning's driveway. Following behind were Heather and the little girl, Piper.

Jessie could make them out through the thicket of pine trees. If she stayed quite still, she didn't think they'd notice her. She wasn't sure why she wanted to remain unnoticed and watch them, but she did. She stopped moving around and settled in to see what she could see.

"Mommy, hurry up!" Ashton was demanding. "I want to see the brontosaurus."

"Well, press the buzzer," Heather was telling him.

"I can't reach it! Come on, Mommy! Why do girls have to walk so *slow*?"

Heather had reached the front gate of Manning's house by now.

"I don't care about any stupid brontosaurus," Piper was telling her brother. "I want him to take us into the greenhouse so I can see the orchids."

"Orchids are stupid!" Ashton shouted.

"Mommy! Ashton said orchids are stupid!"

"Be quiet, both of you," Heather said, as she pressed the buzzer on Manning's gate. "He won't be able to hear me with you two squawking."

Jessie noticed that Heather was wearing extremely short denim cutoffs, and a sleeveless white midriff blouse, revealing her belly button. Her hair was tied in a ponytail with a big pink bow. Jessie thought Heather was too old, at twenty-seven, to be dressing like Miley Cyrus, especially in front of her kids.

"Caleb," Heather said into the intercom. "It's Heather. You meanies changed the code on me so I can't come in. I'm with the kids, Ashton and Piper. Say hi, kids!"

"Hi!" shouted Piper.

"I want to see the brontosaurus," demanded Ashton at the top of his voice.

Caleb said something back to Heather that Jessie couldn't quite make out. But she did hear Heather grumble, "Jesus Fucking H. Christ."

Jessie wasn't terribly religious, but she always cringed when she heard someone using Jesus's name like that. What did Jesus ever do to deserve such disrespect except tell people to love one another?

"How come he's not buzzing us in?" Piper asked.

"Because he's a prick," Heather said with a long sigh.

"I. Want. To. See. The. Bronto. Saurus," Ashton insisted, enunciating his syllables for emphasis. Jessie could see this was one a very impatient kid. She could never imagine Abby acting like that.

"Just hold on," Heather told her son. "He's coming down."

Jessie waited and watched. She heard a clang, and then the gate opened from the inside. John Manning appeared.

He didn't look pleased.

"I told you not to come by unannounced," Manning snapped at Heather.

"The kids wanted to see you," she replied. "Didn't you, kids?"

"I want to see the brontosaurus!" Ashton whined.

"And I want to see the orchids in the greenhouse," Piper sang.

Manning looked at them and then back at Heather.

"This is low," he growled at her. "Using your kids to get to me . . ."

"Please, Unca John!" Ashton yelled. "I want to see the brontosaurus!"

"I'm sorry," Manning told him. "I'm in the middle of writing. I told your mom I can't be disturbed."

"That's not fair!" Ashton shrieked, and he kicked the gate. The action set off a security alarm. A long, high-pitched wail suddenly soared out through the neighborhood. Startled, Jessie stood up, and as she did so, she was afraid she might have been spotted. But no one looked in her direction. Manning was hurrying back inside the gate, where he evidently tapped in a code on a keypad and switched the alarm off.

Ashton and Piper were still covering their ears when the angry author came back outside.

"You really have to go now!" he ordered. "Heather, I'm telling you for the last time. Do not show up here unannounced!"

"You're a meanie!" Piper spit.

"I should have kicked *you*!" Ashton shouted.

John Manning just glowered down at them.

"Come on, kids," Heather said, shooing her children back toward the road. "We don't stay anyplace we're not wanted!"

Jessie watched her wiggle her ass down the driveway. The two brats ran ahead of their mother, Ashton's squeaky little voice was echoing through the trees. "But I wanted to see the brontosaurus. . . ."

What a pathetic display, Jessie thought, her eyes following them as they made their way back down the road to their house.

When she returned her gaze to John Manning's front

gate, it was still open. But Manning was nowhere to be seen.

Jessie turned, intending to resume pulling up the bittersweet.

But as she did so, she nearly collided with someone standing right beside her.

John Manning had snuck through the trees while she had been watching Heather and the kids make their retreat.

"Oh!" Jessie shouted, startled.

"I thought Gert Gorin was the only snoop in the neighborhood," Manning said, looking intensely at her with those deep dark eyes of his. He stood only inches from her.

Jessie's heart started thumping wildly. She felt an absurd jolt of fear.

But John Manning was smiling.

And not a mean smile, she realized.

"I'm sorry if I startled you," he said.

"Well, I—I—" Jessie struggled to catch her breath and find her words. "I didn't mean to snoop. I wasn't eavesdropping. I was just clearing out this patch of all the weeds and vines and then I looked up and saw . . ."

"It's fine, Jessie," Manning told her. "I was just joking." His smile faded. "I'm sorry you had to witness that."

Jessie wanted to get away from him. She didn't trust this man. He might have killed Inga. . . .

"Look, I've been meaning to come by and speak with you," Manning said. "Might I have just five minutes of your time?"

Jessie just looked up at him. She had the same sense

of being somehow mesmerized when she looked into those mysterious, reflective eyes as she had on the day of the picnic. She found she couldn't speak.

"I just want you to know how sorry I am about Inga. I've stayed away because of all the harassment from the police. I figured it was best. But I know how close the two of you were. She was a lovely girl. And you have my deepest condolences."

Was he being sincere? Jessie studied his eyes, but she could see nothing there but reflections of herself.

"You know," Manning said, "I was hoping you and I could be friends. We have a great deal in common."

"We do?" Jessie asked.

"Yes, we're both writers." And he smiled, sadly this time. "And one half of the town thinks you had something to do with Inga's death, the other half thinks I did."

"Did you?" Jessie found herself asking, even before she was aware that the words were on her lips.

Manning's smile faded. "The police went over every square inch of my house. They found nothing."

Jessie stiffened. "That's not answering my question."

"I didn't kill Inga," Manning told her.

For some reason, Jessie believed him.

"If I can be of any help to you, Jessie," Manning said, "I'd like to be. Whether that's as a writer, or as a neighbor, or as a friend. I know what it's like to be looked at and whispered about. This town has been saying all sorts of things about me ever since Millie died. So if you need a friend ever, I'm here."

"Thank you," Jessie said. "But I'm doing okay."

"You seem very strong," Manning said. "Bittersweet roots can be tough to get out. And if you don't get it all, it'll just keep growing."

He bent down and grabbed hold of one gnarly root and gave it a good yank. It resisted, but under his strength it finally gave way, cracking through the soil and mulch and pine needles to reveal its long orange tail.

"Thank you," Jessie said, smiling.

"No problem," Manning said, and he started back toward his house.

"Hey," Jessie called after him.

He looked back around.

"Do you really have a brontosaurus in there?" she asked.

Manning smiled. "I have the partial skull and jaw of one. I picked it up on one of my travels. Maybe Abby would like to see it sometime."

"I think she'd prefer the orchids in the greenhouse," Jessie told him.

"I'd be happy to give her a guided tour," Manning replied.

Jessie smiled.

Manning smiled back, then disappeared through the trees.

THIRTY-TWO

The night was quiet. Not even the crickets were chirping. A sliver of moonlight striped the floor. Abby lay awake in her bed, staring at the ceiling and waiting.

Then she heard it.

The whistle.

Just a low sound, hardly anything more than the stray call of a bird. Abby could hear it through her window, even though the window was closed. The little girl didn't move at first. She waited to hear the whistle again, which she did. Then she threw off her sheet and stepped out of her bed.

Moving over to the window, she looked down into the yard. There, in the moonlight, stood her friend.

Her only friend.

No one else at school talked to her but Aaron.

The little boy lifted his hand and gestured for her to come down and join him. It was better that way. Mommy would hear them if they played up here again.

Abby pulled on a hoodie that was hanging on the post of her bed, and stuck her bare feet into a pair of sneakers. She didn't bother trying to tie the pink laces, since she wasn't that good at it yet, and she certainly wasn't going to ask Mommy.

She opened the door of her room and peeked out into the hall. There was no one in sight. She tiptoed toward the steps, pausing at the top to listen. She could hear Mommy in the kitchen, the soft tap-tap-tap of her computer keyboard reaching the little girl's ears. When Abby had gone to bed, Mommy had been sitting at the kitchen table, trying to write. Abby was glad that her mother seemed to be writing now. She knew Mommy was always happiest when she was writing.

She took the first few steps down the stairs.

Abby knew sneaking out of the house was bad, and she didn't like to be bad. But Aaron was outside waiting for her. She couldn't say no to Aaron. She would just have to be very, very quiet so Mommy didn't hear.

Abby reached the bottom of the stairs. She peered around to look into the kitchen. Mommy was at the table, with her back facing Abby. But the moment Abby made a move toward the front door, Mommy stopped typing and got up out of her chair. Abby froze, taking a step back on the staircase, ready to scramble back up to her room. But Mommy moved out of the little girl's view. Abby heard the refrigerator open, and then the pop of a lid on a can of Diet Coke.

In that instant, Abby made a mad dash for the door.

In the kitchen, Jessie thought she heard a sound.

Taking a sip of her Diet Coke, she strolled out into the living room. She looked around and saw nothing. Then she noticed the front screen door wasn't closed tightly. That must have been what she'd heard—the

door rattling. She thought she had shut it securely earlier—and locked it, too. She'd been very careful about
keeping the doors locked ever since Inga's death. She
pulled the door shut, pressing the lock into place. It
was an old lock, and could easily come loose. That
must have been what had happened. Even a breeze
could rattle the door and unlock it. She needed to fix it.
Jessie looked outside. It was such a quiet night. Even
the crickets were silent. The trees stood utterly still.
There was no breeze, none at all.

So how had this door come unlocked?

THIRTY-THREE

"**B**ut I don't *wanna* go to bed!" Ashton was shrieking.

"Our mother never makes us go to bed this early!" Piper wailed.

Consuela was having none of their guff. "It's past nine o'clock," the housekeeper-cook-assistant told the children. "And nine o'clock is your bedtime on Sunday nights."

Heather was still at the Radisson Hotel downtown, overseeing a catering job. Consuela was standing at the bottom of the stairs, pointing her finger up at Ashton and Piper and telling them to stop yelling and screaming and throwing things and get to bed. Bryan, meanwhile, sat within earshot in the living room, pouring himself another Manhattan. He preferred not to get involved in such squabbles.

"You're just a *servant*!" Ashton shouted at Consuela. "You work for *us*! You can't tell us what to do."

"Your mother left me in charge," Consuela replied, hands on hips now. "And she said you should be in bed by nine."

"I wonder if you're even in this country legally,"

Piper charged, tossing a tennis ball down at Consuela. In the living room, Bryan heard it hit the marble floor and bounce several times.

"If my father wants us to go to bed, he'd tell us himself," Ashton whined.

Bryan paused, his drink to his lips. Sure enough, Consuela poked her head in the room. "Mr. Pierce?" she asked, her face tired.

"Get to bed, you goddamn brats!" Bryan shouted at the top of his lungs.

He heard muttering and grumbling and maybe even a curse word or two. First and second graders using "fucks" and "shits." What kind of kids were they raising?

But there was no more whining. He could hear the kids scuttling overhead into their respective bedrooms.

"Thank you, Mr. Pierce," Consuela said.

"Don't mention it," Bryan said, taking another sip of his Manhattan. "By the way, Consuela, you'll be here for a while longer, won't you?"

"I told Heather I'd wait for her to get back so I could help her put away the dishes from the catering job," she replied.

Bryan smiled. "Good. Because I'm going for a walk. Just out to the brook and back."

"Oh, do be careful, Mr. Pierce," Consuela pleaded. "They still haven't caught that madman who killed that poor German girl."

Bryan laughed. "My money's on Todd Bennett as the killer. Probably killed the chick because she rebuffed his advances."

"Oh, no, I don't think Mr. Bennett—"

Bryan stood up. "One never knows what a man is

capable of, Consuela," he told her with a wink. "Or what lurks down deep in his soul."

Consuela shivered and hurried off to the kitchen.

The whisky was making Bryan feel agitated. He couldn't just sit there anymore. Since the other night, he'd been completely unable to get his sweet Jessaloo off his mind. He had to see her. He suspected strongly she was still in love with him. Otherwise she wouldn't have reacted so intensely that day of the picnic when he'd come on to her.

He figured she'd be alone tonight. Her kid would be asleep.

He'd just pop by and say hello.

Maybe he'd even stop and pick her one of Heather's pink roses that were growing on the side of the house. He'd even pluck off all the thorns.

Bryan smiled.

Yes, he'd do just that.

A rose without any thorns.

That would win her over.

THIRTY-FOUR

Gert Gorin was feeling restless. Arthur was snoozing in his chair, having fallen asleep in the middle of the baseball game on television. Gert had switched the channel, watching some of Bill O'Reilly and then a little of an old melodrama starring Ava Gardner on Turner Classic Movies. But she had a sense that something was happening tonight. And Gert had learned a long time ago to trust her senses.

They'd never failed her. She had known that Millie Manning had taken that swan dive off her back deck even before any cops had arrived. Gert had heard something, a strange kind of thud. It had come from across the street, from the direction of the Manning house. Granted, the Manning house was several yards down the road, and surrounded by the big security wall and all those tall pine trees. But still Gert had heard something. She figured she had supersonic ears. She'd gotten out her binoculars, hidden behind a bush and tried to see what she could find out, aiming the specs at the Manning mansion. She had seen nothing unusual, but it hadn't been long before she'd heard the sirens.

Gert had been right. Something had indeed happened over there.

Millie Manning was dead. And her husband may well have pushed her off that deck.

Tonight Gert felt the same sort of tingling. It started at the base of her neck, at the top of her spine, and crept down her arms and into her fingers. She switched off the TV and got up off the couch.

"Hey!" Arthur croaked, immediately awake. "Why'd you turn off my game?"

"Here," she said, tossing him the remote control. It landed in his lap. "I'm taking a walk."

"At this hour?"

"Something's up," she told him. "I can feel it."

"You'll never learn, Gert," her husband said.

Gert pulled on a sweater and headed outside.

The night was chilly. Summer really was ending, she realized, and fall was around the corner, and then winter not long after that. Gert hugged herself for warmth and hurried across the grass toward the road. She looked around. Not a soul to be seen. Not a sound. The lights were on in Jessie's house, but dark in Monica's. Gert thought she could detect a light through the trees over at the Manning mansion, but she couldn't be certain. The other houses of Hickory Dell—where the Pierces and old Mr. Thayer dwelled—were farther down the road, hidden by the woods, and Gert couldn't see them.

So where did this tingle in her arms come from?

Then she heard the snap of a twig.

Gert snapped her head in that direction. She spied a

flash of color across the street, down toward the end of the cul-de-sac.

She was frightened. Maybe she was being foolish wandering outside in the dark. After all, a few weeks ago, a girl had been brutally murdered out here, on a dark, still night much like this one. Gert thought she should just scurry back into the house now. But instead she ducked behind a tall blue spruce tree in her front yard and peered across the street toward the place where she'd seen the flash of color. There. She saw it again.

Children.

Two children were walking through the woods down to the brook. For the slightest of seconds, the kids emerged from the shadows and walked through a column of moonlight, and Gert thought she recognized one of them as Abby Clarkson. The other child was a boy. . . .

No, Gert thought, not Ashton Pierce. Even from this distance and in the dim light of the moon, Gert could tell the child didn't have red hair.

The boy with Abby looked more like the one who'd been sitting in her gazebo a few weeks earlier.

Now why would Jessie let her daughter wander down to the brook this late at night—and with the killer of her nanny still not caught?

The children disappeared into the trees. Gert lost sight of them.

But then, still peering through the branches of her blue spruce, she spotted something else.

Bryan Pierce, crossing the street, and slinking

through the shadows toward Jessie's house. And Gert was certain that he was carrying a rose.

Her fear finally getting the best of her, Gert scrambled back inside.

"Well, how do you like these apples?" she announced to Arthur as she strode into the kitchen. "Bryan Pierce is carrying on an affair with Jessie Clarkson!"

"I thought it was his wife who was carrying on an affair with John Manning," Arthur grumbled, his eyes on the television set.

"I don't know where that affair stands," Gert said, "but I just saw Bryan sneaking up Jessie's driveway carrying a rose."

Arthur shook his head. "Don't think that's the kind of proof that would stand up in a court of law."

"I knew that girl was trouble ever since she first hooked up with that Emil Deetz!" Gert declared. "And do you know, she lets her five-year-old daughter traipse through the woods after dark. . . ."

A thought occurred to her at that moment. Maybe Jessie didn't know Abby was outside. Maybe she'd appreciate Gert giving her a call to tell her that she'd just seen her daughter wandering down by the brook. And even if Jessie *did* know Abby was outside, getting her on the phone right about now could give Gert a clue about what was going on with Bryan. . . . Maybe she'd even hear Bryan in the background.

She quickly punched in Jessie's number on her wall phone.

"Who you calling?" Arthur wanted to know.

"Hush," his wife commanded.

The phone rang and rang, finally switching over to

voice mail. Gert frowned. She decided not to leave a message. Instead, she headed back outside to see if she could spot the children again.

Maybe she ought to walk them back up to Jessie's house. . . .

THIRTY-FIVE

Jessie was halfway up the stairs when her phone rang. She considered going back downstairs and answering it, but then decided against it.

She was worried all of a sudden.

Worried about Abby.

Maybe it was just residual jitters after Inga's death. But ever since she'd found the front door unlocked, Jessie hadn't been able to concentrate on her writing.

Maybe it wasn't jitters.

Maybe it was a mother's sixth sense.

So she let the phone ring as she continued up the stairs toward Abby's room.

THIRTY-SIX

"**W**here are we going?" Abby asked Aaron.

They had stepped over the brook and continued deeper into the woods.

"A special place," Aaron replied, easily making his way across the sticks and twigs and stones despite his bare feet.

Abby was glad she'd worn her sneakers, even if she did keep stumbling on the untied laces.

Up ahead a dark shape loomed among the trees. Abby had never been this far in the woods before.

"I'm scared," she said.

Aaron turned around and took her hand. "Come on, Abby. You'll like this place."

The dark shape in the trees, as they drew closer, revealed itself to be an old, dilapidated barn. Aaron held Abby's hand tightly as they passed through the big open door. The roof of the structure had collapsed in several places, allowing moonlight to fill much of the interior. Aaron led Abby over several piles of wood and rusted old piping. With Aaron leading the way, the little girl felt less frightened.

"This is a very special place," Aaron told her.

The barn smelled of old hay and mold. Abby sneezed. At one end, an old tractor rusted in the dark. Empty horse stalls lined another wall. Above, in a section where the roof still held firm, a series of beams ran the width of the barn.

"Let's go up there," Aaron suggested.

Abby looked up. The beams were very high, but not so high that they scared her. After all, she'd lived her first five years in New York City, and she'd often been in buildings much higher than those beams.

"Okay," she said to Aaron.

"We'll climb this ladder here," he told her, pointing to a ladder that rose up from the floor to the first of the beams, "and then walk across the beam and jump into that pile of hay over there." Abby followed the direction of the little boy's finger. At the far end of the barn, under the broken roof, was a mound of hay that looked soft and inviting from here. Aaron's idea sounded like fun.

But the ladder seemed weak and rickety when Abby touched it. She instinctively pulled back.

"I'll go first," Aaron told her, "so you'll see that it's safe."

Abby stood back and let him climb.

Aaron quickly scrambled up the ladder. It barely bent under his weight. Hopping easily from the top rung onto the beam, the boy moved like a cat across its length. He didn't even look down. He just walked along the beam in his bare feet as if he'd done it many times before. Maybe he had, Abby thought.

At the end of the beam, he stood over the haystack.

"Watch me, Abby!" he called.

Aaron leapt into the air. He tumbled down gracefully, turning a somersault in the air. He landed on his butt into the hay, which acted like a soft cushion, breaking his fall. His laughter echoed through the old barn.

"Now you do it, Abby!" he sang out.

Abby thought it looked like a lot of fun. So she grabbed hold of the ladder with both hands and put her right foot onto the first rung. The ladder trembled in her hands and made a long, low creaking sound. She took another step up the ladder and it shook some more. She paused, worried that the ladder might break.

"Come on, Abby!" Aaron called.

Abby took a deep breath, and then another step.

THIRTY-SEVEN

Bryan stood outside Jessie's house watching from behind a wall of lilac bushes, their blooms all dried and brown from last spring. He could see Jessie through the lit windows as she headed up the stairs. She'd turned back once, when the phone rang, but paused only for a moment. The phone had rung several times, then stopped, apparently sending the caller to voice mail. Bryan watched as Jessie disappeared upstairs.

He stood back. In a couple of moments he saw the light go on in a room upstairs. Then he heard Jessie's muffled scream.

Bryan pulled back deeper into the shadows behind the bushes, still clutching the rose in his hands. He was glad he'd removed every thorn on his way over here, because otherwise he'd surely have cut his hand holding the damn thing in the dark. He heard Jessie's footsteps running back down the stairs.

"Abby!" she was calling. "Dear God, Abby!"

Suddenly the back door flew open and the motion-detector light flooded the yard with a bright golden glow. Bryan moved farther into the bushes so he wouldn't be noticed. Jessie was in the backyard now, calling for her daughter. The lights in Paulette's cottage came on, and within seconds the older woman was at her door, asking Jessie what was wrong.

"Abby's missing!" Jessie screamed. "She's not in her room!"

THIRTY-EIGHT

Jessie was in an utter panic. "My baby!" she kept shrieking. "My baby is gone!"

"We'll find her, honey," Aunt Paulette assured her, rushing about the yard.

They heard a voice calling to them.

"I saw her!" It was Gert Gorin, huffing and puffing as she made her way up the hill. "I tried calling you, but there was no answer. I saw her walking into the woods!"

"The woods!" Jessie echoed.

"Yes," Gert told her. "With a little boy. They were heading toward the old barn. That's when I figured I should come get you, because that place is just too dangerous for me to go in after them."

Jessie was already barreling down the hill toward the brook and the woods beyond. She wished Monica and Todd were home. They'd gone into the city for the night for some event hosted by Todd's firm, and they wouldn't be back until very, very late. Jessie knew that Todd had been in that old barn many times. He knew his way around it, since he'd been considering restoring it. Decades ago, when Jessie's family had actually run a farm on the property, the barn had been in use. But ever since she could remember, the barn had stood there rotting, the trees growing thicker around it.

The moon slipped behind some clouds, plunging the night into total darkness.

Still, Jessie managed to leap over the brook in a single bound and head into the woods. Ahead of her, the beam of a flashlight kept bobbing from place to place. Aunt Paulette was following her, Jessie realized, and had wisely thought to grab some light for them. The older woman was aiming it ahead of Jessie so that they could at least make out where they were. Jessie sensed Gert Gorin was somewhere behind them as well.

"Abby!" Jessie yelled.

There was no response except for the flutter of wings in the trees above.

She reached the barn. "Abby!" she shouted again.

"Mommy?" came a little voice from the dark.

Aunt Paulette staggered up behind her, out of breath, trying to steady the beam of the flashlight inside the barn. They stood at the entrance facing nothing but utter darkness. The flashlight picked out the remnants of a rusted old tractor, then some decomposing crates, then a ladder leading up to one of the overhead beams.

"Abby?" Jessie said into the dark, more quietly now.

"Mommy." Abby's voice floated out from the darkness. She sounded frightened.

"Where are you, baby?" Jessie asked.

"Up here."

Jessie took the flashlight from Aunt Paulette and aimed it toward the sound of Abby's voice. At first she saw nothing. But then the light found the little girl's face. Jessie saw that her daughter was crouched on a beam. Below her was a drop of some thirty feet to the hard earthen floor of the barn.

Jessie suppressed a scream. "Baby, don't move," she whispered. "I'm going to come get you."

"I was going to jump into the hay pile, Mommy," Abby said. "Aaron already did, and it's safe."

The moon slithered out from behind the clouds at that moment. Through the broken roof it revealed the mound of hay in the far corner of the barn. Gert Gorin had arrived by now, and, breathing heavily, moved stealthily across the floor toward the hay, one eye looking up at Abby at all times.

"No, honey," Jessie said. "Just stay right there. You're not far from the ladder. I'm going to come up and help you come down."

"Okay, Mommy."

Jessie handed the flashlight to Aunt Paulette, who kept it trained on the ladder.

"Be careful, Jessie," her aunt implored.

Jessie gripped the sides of the ladder and placed her foot on the first rung. The ladder was flimsy, as if made of balsa wood. It shook under Jessie's weight. Still, she went up several steps, all the while talking calmly to Abby.

"Sit down on the beam and hold on tight, sweetie," she instructed her daughter. "Then move back toward the ladder on your butt. Don't try to walk."

"Okay, Mommy," Abby replied, and did as she was told.

Jessie was now halfway up the ladder. Aunt Paulette stood below, aiming the flashlight at Abby and holding one side of the ladder to steady it. Gert, having checked out the haystack, hurried over to grip the other side.

Abby had worked her way across the beam so that she was now near the top of the ladder. Her little feet dangled over the side. Suddenly one of her untied sneakers fell off, spiraling down through the air and whizzing past Jessie's face, landing with a thud on the barn floor. Gert Gorin gasped.

"It's okay," Jessie said, her voice steady. "I've almost got you, baby."

She took another step up the ladder, and the rung broke under her foot.

"Jessie!" Aunt Paulette shouted.

"It's okay," she said again, taking a large step to reach the next rung.

Abby was now within arm's length.

"Come on, sweet baby, come to Mommy," Jessie purred. "Shake off your other sneaker. It will be too hard to climb down otherwise."

Abby did as she was instructed. Her second sneaker plunged to the ground, reminding Jessie of just how far the fall would be.

"Come on, Abs."

The little girl moved her feet down onto the top rung of the ladder. Jessie reached up and grabbed her by the waist, guiding her down to the next step. When they came to the broken rung, she held Abby tighter and moved her past the space.

"You're almost down, Jessie!" Aunt Paulette called up to them.

Beneath Jessie's foot, another rung snapped in two. Gert Gorin shouted out in horror.

But Jessie kept going. She was down the ladder far enough now, with Abby securely in her grip, that even if they fell, the worst they might incur was a broken arm.

"Almost home, my babies!" Aunt Paulette sang out.

And then Jessie was down, Abby safely with her. Once she got her off the ladder, Jessie wrapped her arms around her daughter and began to sob.

"It's okay, Mommy," Abby said. "Aaron said it was perfectly safe."

"Where is this Aaron?" Aunt Paulette asked.

"He's in the haystack," Abby said, pointing.

"There's nobody in that haystack," Gert Gorin said. "But come here and see what *is* in there!"

They followed her across the barn, the flashlight illuminating their way.

"Look!" Gert said, pointing down.

There, just under the top layer of moldy stray and hay, protruded the rusted blades of an old lawn mower.

"I don't have to spell out what would have happened to the child if she had jumped into this hay," Gert said, shivering dramatically.

Jessie gripped Abby tightly. "Oh, no!"

"But Aaron jumped in and he wasn't hurt!" Abby insisted.

"Where is Aaron?" Jessie asked, crouching down so she could look Abby straight in the eyes. "Did he bring you here?"

Abby nodded.

"Then where is he now?"

"I don't know."

Jessie looked up at Aunt Paulette, then back at Abby. "Sweetie, could Aaron be an imaginary friend . . . ?"

"No," the little girl insisted. "He's real."

"I'll say he's real," Gert said, folding her arms across

her chest. "I saw the two of them walking together. And I've seen him before, too. He's a very real boy."

Jessie looked up at her.

"A very real, and a very disturbed, boy, I'd say," Gert told her. "If he was trying to coax your daughter into jumping into this hay, then I suspect he wanted to kill her."

Jessie looked back at Abby. Suddenly she pulled her close in an embrace, and began to cry.

THIRTY-NINE

"**A**re you sure you're okay?" Aunt Paulette asked. "Want me to spend the night?"

"No, I'll be fine," Jessie assured her. "Abby's sound asleep now."

She embraced her aunt, then gave her a little wave as she left through the back door and headed across the yard to her cottage. Jessie sighed and shut the door tight, double-locking it. Not for the first time, she wished the security alarm they'd ordered would arrive soon. Because the house was so old, they needed something custom-made. Until then, just a few extra locks from the hardware store would have to do.

What a night. She was still shaking. If Abby had fallen from that beam . . .

She wouldn't think about it. Abby was safe. She was upstairs, sleeping peacefully.

Still, Jessie planned to sleep in Abby's room tonight. She couldn't bear to have her daughter out of her sight for long.

She'd contemplated calling the police, but then decided against it. If Aaron was a real kid, as Mrs. Gorin had convinced them all he was, then surely he had skedaddled as soon as he'd heard Jessie's voice in the barn, knowing he'd get in major trouble for bringing Abby out there. What would calling the police accomplish? Rather, Jessie decided, she'd speak with Abby's teacher tomorrow. Aaron was in Abby's class, after all. They'd figure out exactly what had happened—and what to do about it—then.

Suddenly feeling utterly exhausted, Jessie was about to head up the stairs when she heard a soft rapping on the front door. She peered through the window and saw Bryan standing on the steps, his hands behind his back.

She opened the door a crack.

"Jessie," Bryan said, looking concerned. "Did you find Abby?"

She looked at him strangely. "Abby's asleep," she replied. "How did you know we were looking for her?"

"I was taking a walk earlier, and heard you shouting, so I've been out looking for her myself. Oh, thank God she's okay."

"Yes, we found her. She was out at the barn. . . ."

"I'm so glad you found her. That old barn is dangerous."

Jessie nodded. "I appreciate you going looking for her."

"Of course." Bryan smiled awkwardly. "Jessie, could I come in for just a second? I . . . I want to apologize."

"Apologize for what?"

"For what I said at the picnic. Please? Just for a moment?"

"Okay, but just for a moment. I'm very tired."

Jessie stepped aside to let Bryan in.

"Here," he said, once he was inside, handing her a rose. "A peace offering."

Jessie took it, holding it in her left hand, but said nothing.

"I removed all the thorns," Bryan told her. "Because that's what you've always been to me . . . a rose without any thorns."

"Bryan, please."

He drew close to her, and Jessie could smell the whiskey on his breath. "Ever since you've moved back here, Jessie," he said, his words slightly slurred, "you've been all that I can think about. . . ."

"I thought you came here to apologize," she said.

He took her by the shoulders. "We're meant to be together, Jessie. Can't you see?"

He leaned in to kiss her. Jessie slapped him with her right hand.

"Get out!" she screamed.

He wouldn't let go of her shoulders. He gripped her tighter, and tried to force her down onto the couch.

Jessie kneed him in the groin. Bryan yelled out and let her go.

"Get out of here, you filthy pig," Jessie seethed. "What did I ever see in you?"

"That's what I always wondered."

She looked up. This was a new voice.

Todd stood in the doorway. He had witnessed what had just happened. He let himself into the house and walked over to Bryan, grabbing him by the throat.

"It's okay, Todd," Jessie said. "Just get him out of here."

"Let me hit him just once," Todd said. "I'll say I was defending you."

"I defended myself just fine," Jessie said.

Bryan wriggled out of Todd's grip. "Fuck you both. I just came up because I was concerned about Abby."

"Don't you dare try to frame this as concern for Abby," Jessie told him. "Just get out of my house and never come up here again. Never speak to me again!"

Bryan grumbled and headed out the front door, cursing and swearing as he staggered down the hill.

"Did he hurt you?" Todd asked.

"No." Jessie covered her face with her hands. "What made you come up here?"

"Monica and I had just gotten home, and I saw that weasel walking up to the house. I figured I should find out what he was up to."

"Oh. Todd . . ." Jessie fell into his arms.

He held her tight.

"Why did he say he was concerned about Abby?" Todd asked.

"She wandered off tonight. . . . We were all looking for her . . . but she's okay now. Oh, Todd, it's been a long, long night."

She looked up at him. Their eyes held.

Then Jessie pulled away.

"Please," she said. "Go home."

"But . . ."

"Please, Todd, go home to Monica."

He said nothing. Then he turned and left.

Jessie locked the door and turned out the light. She was walking across the floor when she spotted the rose Bryan had brought. It had fallen to the ground and gotten trampled underfoot. Jessie bent down and picked it up.

Opening the back door, she tossed it outside onto the ground.

FORTY

Paulette saw the man stagger through the dark toward Jessie's house. He moved as if he were Frankenstein's monster, lumbering among the shadows, arms stretched out in front of him. Paulette knew the man would kill Jessie if he reached her, and Abby too.

She had to save them.

But she couldn't move. Her legs seemed made of lead. She couldn't lift them. They seemed cemented to the floor. All Paulette could do was stand at the window of her cottage and watch the man get closer and closer to Jessie's house. It was a dark night, but she could see that he was tall, and dark, and very, very evil.

She tried banging on her window, hoping to make enough noise that the man might get scared away. He stopped his approach for a moment, and turned to look in Paulette's direction. But then he seemed to realize there was nothing she could do to stop him, so he continued on his way, his arms outstretched, his mouth frothing.

Oh, why can't I move? Paulette thought. *Why can't I rush out and save them?*

Because you're dreaming, she answered herself.

And with that thought, Paulette's eyes popped open.

She sat up in bed. Her clock told it was 9:05. The sun was streaming in through her windows and the birds were chattering. She had slept later than usual. All that traipsing through the woods and the barn last night had tired her out.

That dream . . .

Paulette got out of bed and shook a couple of herbal remedies from a bottle into her hand. That dream had been so upsetting it had left her with a headache. Swallowing the remedies with water, Paulette realized it wasn't just a dream.

It was a vision.

She'd had dreams like that before. Psychic dreams. The night her sister died, in fact. She'd dreamed that Caroline had been calling to Paulette, but Paulette couldn't find her. She'd woken up and run over to her house, to find that Caroline had just passed.

And two nights before Millie Manning died, Paulette had dreamed of a woman falling from a cliff. . . . She hadn't known who. If she had, she might have been able to warn poor Millie to stay away from heights.

She hoped she wouldn't be so late in getting to Jessie.

Paulette dressed quickly. There had been another psychic dream, too, once. She had dreamed that Howard, the only man she had ever loved, had taken her to see the Fourth of July fireworks. It hadn't been Fourth of July; it had been November, but such details didn't matter in dreams. Howard had also been far, far away from Paulette at the time. He'd been in Vietnam. He'd left just the week before, and asked Paulette if she'd wait for him. Paulette had promised she would. Then she'd had the dream about the Fourth of July fireworks, and nothing had been the same after that.

In her dream, Paulette and Howard were sitting on a blanket watching the pyrotechnics explode in the sky. They were so beautiful. If Paulette had ever wondered if she dreamed in color or not, this dream proved she certainly did. Reds and greens and golds and purples all shooting through the night sky. How she and Howard had cheered in her dream. But then a stray spark had floated down from the sky and landed on Howard. As Paulette watched, the man she loved—the man she planned to marry—suddenly blew up into a million sparks of light, as beautiful and as colorful as the fireworks in the sky.

In the morning, Paulette had waited. She had sensed bad news was coming. Indeed, less than twenty-four hours later, Howard's father called her to tell her that the helicopter Howard had been riding in had been shot down over a rice field. It had exploded into a raging fireball. Paulette knew that the blaze, while horrific, had nonetheless possessed a certain terrible beauty. She had seen it in her dream.

There would never be another man for Paulette. She had told Howard she would wait for him, and so wait she would.

But she had no time to wait if she wanted to save Jessie and Abby.

Paulette threw on an old house dress and a pair of slippers and rushed out across the grass to Jessie's house. She expected she'd find her niece hunched over her laptop computer at the kitchen table.

"Jessie!" she called, hurrying up the walk to the back door.

But there was no sign of life in the house. Paulette's heart skipped a beat. Was she too late? Had the tall, dark man have gotten here already?

"Jessie!" Paulette shouted through the screen of the kitchen window.

Still no sound, no movement from the house. The curtains just swayed gently in the morning breeze.

Then she noticed Jessie's car wasn't in the driveway.

Of course, Paulette remembered. *She was going in to speak with Abby's teacher this morning. That's where she is.*

She breathed a long sigh of relief. But she knew the danger was still out there. That dream had been a warning. Someone was coming, someone dangerous, and he threatened both Jessie and Abby.

Paulette had learned to trust her dreams.

Turning to head back to her cottage, Paulette dropped her eyes to the ground. There, at her feet, was a smashed, broken rose, its petals splayed and browned. She picked it up. For some reason the rose terrified her.

It was, Paulette decided, an omen.

FORTY-ONE

Mrs. Theresa Whitman was a woman of indeterminate age. She might have been as young as forty or as old as sixty. She greeted Jessie at the door of her office with a smile and a firm handshake, her small brown eyes peering out from behind narrow frameless glasses.

"Hello, Ms. Clarkson. It's nice to see you again," the teacher said.

"Thank you for taking the time to meet with me," Jessie replied.

"No problem at all. The children are coloring at the moment, watched over by my able assistant. Your message sounded urgent, so of course I'd make the time." She gestured for Jessie to come in and sit down. "May I get you a cup of coffee?"

"No, thank you." Jessie sat in one of the two chairs positioned in front of Mrs. Whitman's desk. The teacher poured herself some coffee, then settled down to look over at Jessie kindly.

"I'm aware that this has not been an easy few weeks for Abby," Mrs. Whitman said. "She's a delightful girl, well-behaved, and obviously very bright."

"I'm glad to hear that," Jessie said. "Is she ever trouble in class?"

"Never. Always cooperative, always pleasant."

Jessie smiled. "She's that way at home, too," she told the teacher.

"Then what's the problem, my dear?"

"I wanted to make you aware of something that happened last night. Abby went to bed at her usual time, and I was downstairs working in the kitchen. At one point, I heard something . . . and when I checked, I saw the front door was ajar. Naturally, given everything that has happened, I was concerned."

"Of course you were."

"So I went upstairs to check on Abby. She wasn't in her bed. I looked all over for her and she wasn't in the house. I became hysterical."

"Oh, my dear, where had she gone?"

"Her little friend, Aaron, had come by. She told me later that he'd called to her through the window, and that she snuck downstairs to meet him outside. She told me he encouraged her to do this. I'm not blaming him for my daughter's misbehavior, but Abby has never acted out like this before."

The teacher had set her mug of coffee down on the desk and was cupping it with her hands as she listened intently. "Where did the children go?"

"To an old, dilapidated barn in the middle of the woods on our property. Abby said Aaron called it his secret place. Clearly he's been playing there on his own. Well, he enticed her to climb a ladder and walk across a beam with the purpose of jumping into a haystack. That's where I found her, up on the beam. I had to gently coax her down."

"Oh, my!"

Jessie could feel the terror of last night returning as she told the story. "Even worse than that, if Abby had made the jump, there were old lawn mower blades under the hay. She could have been impaled!"

Mrs. Whitman's face had turned white.

"I don't know how Aaron escaped harm, but miraculously, he did so. Abby said he had jumped first, and he wasn't hurt."

"Do you think he was . . . intentionally trying to hurt her?"

Jessie sighed. "I can't imagine a five-year-old boy wanting to do such a thing. I think he just managed, by sheer luck, to avoid the blades. But who knows if Abby would have been as lucky?"

"Thank God you got to her in time," Mrs. Whitman said.

"Yes. Thank God."

"Did you speak with the boy's parents?"

"No." Jessie leaned forward across the teacher's desk "That's why I'm here. Abby didn't know Aaron's last name, or where he lived, so I thought I should come to you."

"Me?" Mrs. Whitman looked perplexed. "Why me?"

"Because you can tell me that information. Has he been a problem for you in any way in class?"

Mrs. Whitman's brow furrowed. "I'm sorry, Ms. Clarkson, but there's no boy named Aaron in the kindergarten class."

"But . . ." Jessie was at a loss for words for a couple of seconds. "But Abby says she sits with him every day. That he's her friend. She's been so much happier coming home from school since making friends with Aaron."

Behind her glasses, Mrs. Whitman's eyes looked as if they might cry. "Oh, dear, Ms. Clarkson, I'm so sorry to have to tell you that, despite my best efforts to encourage greater fraternization among the students, Abby still tends to be a loner. Unless I deliberately sit her with others, she usually ends up sitting by herself."

Jessie blinked, unable to respond.

Mrs. Whitman hesitated, then continued. "But I must say . . . I often see her laughing and chatting . . . with an imaginary friend."

Jessie's blood suddenly ran cold.

"Did you see the little boy Abby said took her to the barn?" Mrs. Whitman asked.

"No," Jessie said, her mind reeling. But suddenly she looked across at the teacher intently. "But Mrs. Gorin did! She said she saw Abby and a little boy earlier that night, walking toward the barn. She said she'd seen the little boy before, too. She figured he lived in the new houses on the other side of the woods at the end of Hickory Dell."

Mrs. Whitman made a face. "Do you mean Gert Gorin?"

"Yes."

"Oh, Ms. Clarkson, I've known Gert all my life. I wouldn't put an awful lot of stock in what she says she sees. She's always showing up at town council meetings claiming to have spotted bears or bobcats, and arguing for the town to bring in hunters. Or she's thinking someone is having an affair with someone else. She's really a . . . well, as my mother used to say, a busybody."

"I know that," Jessie said. "But why would she make something like this up?"

"Maybe she doesn't make it up. Maybe she's just a bit . . . overimaginative."

Jessie sighed. "But Abby was so clear about Aaron sitting with her at snack time, and helping her carry her books. . . ."

Mrs. Whitman smiled. "I'll tell you what. Come with me. We'll go into class, and ask Abby to point out her friend to us."

"Good idea."

They both stood.

"Maybe she's gotten his name wrong," Jessie suggested as they left Mrs. Whitman's office and headed down the hall to the classroom. "Maybe it's a boy with a different name."

"Maybe," Mrs. Whitman said, though she didn't sound convinced.

The classroom, when they entered, smelled of chalk and crayons. The walls were covered with photos of flowers, kittens, puppies, and waterfalls. At the front of the room, above the blackboard, the alphabet was inscribed in big, red letters. About twenty children sat at tiny desks, coloring a line drawing of a robin on a tree branch. A few of them looked up when Jessie and Mrs. Whitman entered, but most remained intent on their work. The young teacher's assistant, an Asian girl with long black hair, gave Mrs. Whitman a smile.

Jessie spotted Abby off to the side, at a desk beneath the photo of a kitten. She looked up and spotted her mother. "Hi, Mommy," she said, a broad smile filling her face.

"Hi, Abs," Jessie said.

She stooped down so that she was eye-level with her daughter.

"Abs," Jessie whispered, "would you show me which one is Aaron?"

Abby looked at her.

"He's not here today," she said after a short pause, and went back to her coloring.

Jessie stood. "Are there any students absent today, Mrs. Whitman?" she asked.

The teacher shook her head. "All present and accounted for."

That was when the fear really took hold of Jessie's throat. She was barely able to speak for the rest of the day.

FORTY-TWO

Paulette was picking daisies on the side of her cottage when something drew her eye over to Jessie's house. Had she seen movement in an upstairs window? Or had she just sensed it?

All morning long, she'd been on edge. Her dream had really rattled her. She kept an eye on Jessie's driveway, waiting to spot her car rattling back up the hill. Could she have missed Jessie's return? Could that have been Jessie she'd just seen —or sensed—upstairs? She set the daisies down on a table and made her way across the yard back toward her niece's house.

She heard the slam of a door.

"Jessie?" she called out.

But by now she was close enough to see that Jessie was still not home.

The fear bubbled up again, the dread caused by her dream. The slam she'd heard was the front door. Paulette was sure of it. So she *had* seen someone upstairs in the house!

She hurried around to the front but saw no one there.

Her attention was drawn back to the driveway, where she heard the sudden crunch of gravel. Jessie was home.

"Hello, sweetheart!" Paulette sang out.

She didn't want to panic her right away. She knew Jessie was still upset about last night, so first she asked how it had gone with Abby's teacher. When she learned that there was no Aaron in the girl's class—that her companion last night, despite Gert Gorin's insistence to the contrary, might have been imaginary—Paulette's terror only deepened. They were dealing with things here, she realized, that they couldn't explain.

Walking with Jessie up the front walk, Paulette finally told her about her dream. About the dark man who threatened her.

"Look, Aunt Paulette," Jessie said, "I'm already freaked out enough. I respect that you believe your dream was some kind of sign . . . but I just can't take that in right now."

"But it's a real danger, Jessie. I feel it!"

"Aunt Paulette, stop!" Jessie put her hands to her ears. "I can't! No more!"

She hurried up the front steps. Paulette watched as she unlocked the door. *So it was locked*, she realized. Then how could anyone have come out of it?

Maybe she had been wrong. . . . Maybe she hadn't seen or heard anything.

Or maybe locked doors were immaterial to the dark man she feared. . . .

Paulette followed Jessie into the house. "I'm sorry, honey," she said. "I didn't mean to upset you."

"It's okay, Aunt Paulette. I know you meant well."

"I'll make you a cup of tea."

Jessie smiled. "Thanks. That would be nice. I'm just going to run upstairs and change into shorts." The day was getting warmer, and she'd worn wool pants to Abby's school.

Paulette smiled and turned to the stove. Lifting the teapot, she carried it over to the sink and filled it with water. She still believed in heating water over a flame. None of this microwaving for her. She set the teapot back on the stove and turned the burner to high. Yes, a nice cup of tea. That would make them both feel better.

That was when she heard Jessie scream.

Dear God, Paulette thought. *The man is still upstairs! The dark man got her!*

"Jessie!" she shouted, bounding up the stairs after her.

Paulette found her niece standing in the doorway of her room, her mouth in a frozen O. Clothes were strewn everywhere. Every drawer of Jessie's bureau had been pulled open and overturned onto the floor. Bras, panties, and slips were tossed all over the place. Her closet was wide open, with skirts and blouses pulled off their hangers, lying in scattered clumps and piles. Jessie was too stunned to speak.

"Dear God," Paulette gasped.

So she *had* seen someone up here!

The tall, dark man.

What had he been looking for?

And had he found it?

FORTY-THREE

That night, Jessie sat at the kitchen table and sipped her tea, trying to steady her nerves. She'd finally had to ask Aunt Paulette to leave her alone for a bit. The older woman had just kept going on about her dream and how the tall, dark man was a threat to Jessie and Abby. With everything that had happened in the last twenty-four hours, Jessie just couldn't abide her aunt's psychic babble anymore. Normally she tried to keep an open mind and not pass judgment, the way Mom used to do. But this evening Jessie just had just snapped. She was frightened. And Aunt Paulette was making it worse.

For now, there was just one thing on Jessie's mind.

Who had been in her house? And why had they gone through her drawers and closets?

She hadn't found anything missing. Of course, she couldn't be exactly sure. Was all her underwear accounted for? A few pairs seemed to be missing—but who kept track of how many pairs of panties and nylons they had? And surely some intruder wasn't going to break into the house just to steal her underwear. Rather, Jessie thought the motive had been to scare her.

If so, the intruder had been successful.

Was it the same person who'd killed Inga? Was he trying to scare her now into leaving? Or to send a message that she was next?

Emil. In her mind's eye, she kept seeing Emil.

But Emil was dead. The police of two countries, Mexico and the United States, had confirmed it.

She thought about calling the cops, but decided against it for the moment. She couldn't bear having any more policemen traipsing through the house.

But there was another reason she didn't call. Deep down, Jessie worried that she was losing her mind. She had almost done so before, during those first months in New York, when she'd hallucinated all sorts of things. She had seen Emil every time she'd looked out the window. She had seen her bloodied miscarried son screaming in Abby's crib. Might she be losing it again now, stressed out by Inga's murder and Abby's imaginary playmate? Might these things have sent her down crazy lane again?

Might she herself have overturned her drawers and emptied her closet—and not remembered it?

"No," she whispered to herself, rubbing her temples. "I didn't do it. I'm not imagining things."

It was Abby who was imagining things. After meeting with Mrs. Whitman, Jessie had spoken with the school psychologist, Dr. Ed Bauer. He'd told Jessie that it sounded as if Jessie's exploits the night before had been a form of sleepwalking. She may have technically been awake and aware of what she was doing, but her mind was responding to dream-like stimuli—her imaginary friend, the one she called Aaron.

But *was* he imaginary? Jessie couldn't forget Gert

Gorin's absolute insistence that she had seen the boy—
not once, but twice. Mrs. Whitman had said Gert wasn't
to be trusted. She was a hysteric. Maybe so. But Jessie
knew that Inga had seen the boy, too, on one of the first
days after they'd moved here. Inga had watched Jessie
and the boy wander down to the brook. Inga wasn't a
hysteric. She was a sensible, very level-headed young
woman. Inga had seen the boy, so Jessie had to believe
he was real.

Then why did Mrs. Whitman describe Abby as talking to herself—to an imaginary friend—in class?

"Maybe it's both," Jessie said out loud, running her
fingers over the sleek titanium of her laptop, which she
knew wouldn't be opened again today. "Maybe there's
a real boy that Abby has met sometimes, and liked—
and when he's not around, she talks to him, imagining
he's there."

Yes, that had to be the answer, Jessie thought. *Aaron
must be a real kid. He just doesn't go to Independent
Day. Abby imagines he does because she wishes he
did. She wishes her friend could be with her in school.*

Jessie's heart lifted. That had to be the answer.

So the next step was to find where this little boy
lived in town.

A thought occurred to Jessie. Might Aaron have
been the culprit who messed up her room? Just why a
little boy would do such a thing, Jessie had no idea. But
right now she was trying to force all the pieces of the
puzzle together, even if they didn't fit.

A couple of hours ago, when she'd picked Abby up
after school, Jessie had made no further inquiries about
Aaron. She was glad that Abby didn't ask why she'd
been by to talk to her teacher. But the little girl under-

stood that there were repercussions for her behavior the night before. Jessie had explained that her punishment for leaving the house and going to the barn was that she had to stay in her room the whole weekend. She couldn't go outside and play. No swinging on the swings, no walking to the brook. Abby had accepted her punishment without protest. So right after dinner, she'd gone back up to her room, where Jessie had given her a pile of books to read.

A sudden rapping on the door startled Jessie, and she looked up quickly.

In the orange backlight of the setting sun she recognized John Manning through the window, standing on her doorstep. The fading sunlight rendered him mostly a silhouette, and suddenly fear crept back up Jessie's throat.

Aunt Paulette's warning about a tall, dark man.

That described John Manning quite aptly.

Jessie stood and went to the door.

"Hello," she said through the screen.

"Good evening," her neighbor said. "I hope I'm not disturbing you."

"I was just having a cup of tea."

Manning smiled. "I just wanted to make sure everything was okay. I had a visitor earlier today in the person of Mrs. Gertrude Gorin. Apparently she's going around the neighborhood trying to locate a little boy." He paused. "She told me all about Abby's experience in the old barn last night."

Jessie sighed. "Yes. It was a long night. And I think that means I'm turning in early tonight."

"Is there anything I can do? Anything at all?"

Jessie regarded him. Even in the shadows, his eyes

still burned. His voice sounded sincere, but could she trust him? "A tall, dark man is coming," Aunt Paulette had told her, "and he is dangerous to you and Abby." Had this tall, dark man been upstairs earlier today—going through Jessie's lingerie?

She shuddered. "I'm fine, thank you, Mr. Manning."

"Please call me John," he said.

"I'm fine, John. I appreciate your concern. But right now . . . all I want to do is go to bed."

"Of course. I just wanted to come by and offer my services. Good night, Jessie."

Jessie closed the door. She watched until she was certain that Manning had returned to his own yard. Then she double-bolted both her back and front doors, and made sure every window was locked. Damn that security firm for being so slow.

Then she went upstairs and, even before the sun had fully set, thankfully fell into a dreamless sleep.

FORTY-FOUR

At just about five minutes past seven, Theresa Whitman finally finished up the last of her paperwork in her office. She was glad to be done with it all—the grading and the evaluations and the forms—very pleased that she didn't have to carry it home with her to work on over the weekend. She'd been teaching kindergarten now for almost twenty years, and never could she remember having to fill in so much paperwork. The bureaucracy of the school committee was getting ridiculous. It used to be just a matter of grading a child's drawings and evaluating their first halting attempts at printing. Now she had to fill out form after form about what they had learned each day, and how each child had responded to every lesson.

Mrs. Whitman slipped the forms into a large manila envelope and sealed it. Across the front she wrote *Whitman, Morning Kindergarten* in her large, perfect penmanship. She stood up from her desk and carried the envelope out into the hall, where she dropped it through the slot on the door of the administrator's office. The school was utterly quiet. She realized everyone had gone home by now. Mrs. Whitman suspected she was the only person still at the school.

Walking down the hall to her classroom, Theresa Whitman sighed. Staying late hadn't really been an inconvenience. What else did she have to do on a Friday night? Ever since her husband, Lester, had died three years ago, Theresa had spent her nights and weekends mostly alone. Her one daughter had moved to Wisconsin. They had never been close. Theresa's whole life was her students. She fussed over all of them. At the moment, the child who concerned her most was little Abby Clarkson. Such a dear child. And yet such a loner. She'd done her best to get the other kids to warm up to Abby, but they seemed swayed by their parents against getting too close. It was so unfair. And now the poor child was sleepwalking, following imaginary friends. It simply broke Mrs. Whitman's heart.

She walked into the kindergarten classroom and tidied up the desks. She erased the letter D from the blackboard, written in pink chalk in both capital and small formations. She was about to gather up her books from her desk when she heard the sound of the door opening. She looked around.

"Yes?" she asked the new arrival. "May I help you?"

When she didn't get an answer right away, she asked, just the slightest trace of concern in her voice, "How did you get into the school?"

They were the last coherent words Theresa Whitman ever said.

Suddenly she felt a sharp pain in her abdomen. She looked down to see the long metal blade that had just sliced into her flesh. She watched, in a kind of gauzy, slow-motion awareness, as the blood began to stain her white blouse after the blade was withdrawn.

Mrs. Whitman's knees crumpled and she fell to the floor.

Her eyes looked up into the face of her killer as the razor blade swung down again across her neck. Theresa Whitman tried to scream, but her throat was filled with blood.

FORTY-FIVE

Sitting at her dining table, reading the tarot, Paulette suddenly felt the sting of a blade against her throat. She called out in terror. Her hand flew to her throat, but nothing was there.

Rising quickly, she hurried over to the window to look out at Jessie's house. Everything seemed peaceful over there. The lights were all out. Jessie had called to say that she was exhausted and she was going to sleep early.

Let her sleep. She needed it. But Paulette would stay awake, She planned to keep a vigil all night, watching Jessie's house.

The dark man was coming.

Maybe not tonight.

But he was coming.

FORTY-SIX

"**S**ame modus operandi," Wolfie told Knotts, standing over the body of the dead teacher. "Exactly the same as the German girl."

"Well, not exactly, Wolfie," his partner pointed out. "No wounds on the thighs."

"But there's a wound in the abdomen." He bent down, pointing to the hardened purple blood coagulating on the Mrs. Whitman's blouse. "This is what brought her down. Just as the wounds on the German girl's thighs brought *her* down. Then, in both cases, the killer moved in to slice open the throat."

Wolfie stood up and let the coroner's department move in.

A janitor had found Mrs. Whitman's body around eleven-thirty. It was now almost one o'clock. Wolfie had gotten the call at home. He'd been awake, unable to sleep, watching an old Henry Fonda movie on Turner Classics. The one about the jury. Wolfie had known right away that the two murders were connected, as soon as he'd learned the teacher's throat had been cut.

"I wonder if John Manning will have a better alibi this time," he mused to Knotts.

"You know, Wolfie, I think you might have developed a bit of an obsession with that guy," Knotts said. "I mean, what kind of connection does Manning have to some kindergarten teacher? He doesn't have any kids. Isn't it kind of a stretch to suspect that he has something to do with this?"

"Listen to me, Knotts. I got the report back from the FBI. For whatever reason, they couldn't confirm to me that it was Manning their agents had identified in Mexico on the day Emil Deetz was killed in that police ambush. They made a lot of noise about national security classified information, and I argued back that this was a murder investigation! They got very silent, and I asked them if they could at least eliminate Manning as a suspect, by telling me he was *not* the person identified in that report. And they said they couldn't eliminate him for me."

"That's not saying much," Knotts argued. "That's just Bureau bureaucracy doublespeak."

"Come on, Knotts! Manning has a dossier about Deetz and the Screech Solek murder in his house! He buys the property next door to Deetz's ex-girlfriend, and then the ex-girlfriend's nanny gets murdered with the same MO as Solek, and now the ex-girlfriend's kid's teacher gets the same treatment!"

"But what would Manning have against an old lady like Theresa Whitman?"

Wolfie gave his partner a patient smile. "That's what we're supposed to find out. That's why we're the detectives."

Honestly, sometimes Knotts could be so dim.

"But aren't we supposed to follow the leads wherever they take us," Knotts asked, "even if they take us off a path we thought was the right one?"

"Manning is the right path. Trust me, Knotts!"

Knotts just shrugged. "The chief isn't so sure. . . ."

"The chief has her head so far up her ass she can't see straight."

"So when are you going to ask Manning about that collection of articles he has on Deetz? Don't you think we really ought to question him on that before he slips town or something? I mean, I know we had to wait until we got more information, but it seems we've hit a brick wall on more information. So don't you think we ought to nail him down about that as soon as possible?"

Jesus Christ, Knotts could be a nag sometimes. "Yeah, yeah, I've got that planned," Wolfie said. "We're going out there in the morning. It's time to get some answers." He smiled. "From both Mr. Manning and his pretty next-door neighbor."

FORTY-SEVEN

"**N**o," Jessie mumbled into the phone. "It can't be true."

But it *was*, Gert Gorin assured her. She'd just gotten a call from a lady she knew who worked at the school. Mrs. Whitman had been murdered in her classroom last night. Her throat had been slit from ear to ear.

Jessie hung up the phone and began shaking all over. She was glad that Abby was upstairs in her room, unable to see her. How could she possibly give her this news? The shock of Inga's death had only just begun to wear off. Now Jessie had to tell Abby that her teacher was dead, too.

She wouldn't tell her the grisly details, of course. Nor would she share what she and surely the police were fearing: that the same person who killed Inga had also killed Mrs. Whitman.

But why? In God's name, why?

Suddenly Jessie felt cooped up, like a tigress pacing in a cage. She had to get outside. Pushing open the screen door and letting it bang behind her, she strode across the grass toward Abby's swing set. She plopped herself down on one of the swings, holding the chains in both hands. She began to cry.

What was happening? She had come back to Sayer's Brook to start over. She had returned feeling strong and capable, and within a month everything had unraveled. She couldn't help but feel both deaths had something to do with her return to town. It was as if Emil was still out there, stalking her, trying to terrify her. Aunt Paulette had dreamed of a tall, dark man who was coming for her. . . . Emil had been tall and dark. But Emil was dead! This was crazy! She had to keep reminding herself that Emil was dead! Gunned down by federal drug agents. Emil was dead!

But he had had friends. . . .

Emil may have been the leader, but there had been many lieutenants in their drug-and-porn business. The cops had caught some of them; they sat in jails at this very moment. But others were still at large.

Yet why would any of them want to terrify her?

Jessie wiped her eyes. Perhaps she was feeling sorry for herself. Perhaps she was personalizing this in a way that wasn't accurate. If the same killer had struck both times, maybe it had nothing to do with Jessie or Emil. Maybe it really was random—a terrible coincidence. Or maybe, with the news of Inga's death, a copycat killer had decided to leave his own mark on the town.

Or maybe, some old associate of Emil's was trying to get even . . . to take revenge on Jessie for providing evidence about the murder of Screech Solek and, in the process, disrupting their very profitable drug-and-porn trade.

She shivered. As a theory, it seemed far more possible than just some random copycat killer.

And maybe she shouldn't be so quick to dismiss Aunt Paulette's vision of a tall, dark man. . . .

"Is there anything I can do, Jessie?"

She jumped at the voice, coming from behind her. Looking around, Jessie saw John Manning, standing there in his black T-shirt and black jeans.

"I saw you from my window," he said. "I could not in all conscience allow you to just sit here without coming by to offer my help. My offer last night to be of assistance was sincere."

She looked up into his deep, dark eyes. "So then you know?"

He nodded. "Once again, Gert Gorin has been ringing the neighborhood with the latest news."

"It's devastating," Jessie said.

Manning sat down on the second swing beside her. "I'm sure Abby will be crushed."

"I have to be very careful how I tell her."

"Of course. Especially after . . ." The author's voice trailed off.

"I can't deny that I'm freaked out," Jessie said. "I mean, the two deaths . . . so similar. And both connected to Abby and me."

"I expect we'll both be questioned again."

Jessie looked over at him. "I can understand the police questioning me, but why would they question you?"

Manning sighed. "Because they seem to want to believe the worst about me. Even Mrs. Gorin asked me where I was last night."

"She's too nosy for her own good." Jessie looked at Manning intently. "What did you tell her?"

"I told her it was none of her business and hung up on her." He gave Jessie a rueful smile. "I have a bit of a temper, I'm afraid."

Jessie stiffened on the swing. Just how much of a temper did John Manning have? Should she be frightened sitting next to him? He was a tall, dark man, after all. . . .

"In fact," Manning continued, "I was home alone all night. Caleb was off, visiting friends in the city. It was just me, so I'm afraid I won't have much of an alibi."

"There's no reason to suspect you had anything against Mrs. Whitman. On the other hand, I saw Mrs. Whitman yesterday. I'm sure the police are going to want to know why I was in her office."

Jessie remembered the kindness Mrs. Whitman had shown her, and started to cry again.

"She tried to be good to Abby," Jessie said, her voice breaking. "And now, just like that, she's gone . . . her life just snuffed out, like a candle."

Manning reached over and placed his hand on Jessie's shoulder.

"You know, when my wife died," he said, "I thought a great deal about life and death. How quickly, and unexpectedly, death can creep up on us. The line between the living and the dead is really very thin and tenuous."

Jessie nodded, composing herself. "That's for sure. It's still hard to accept that Inga is gone."

Manning sighed. "I've come to believe that when someone close to us dies, a part of ourselves dies, too. After all, we're connected in so many ways. . . . Their energy has blended with our energy. I think that's why grief is so hard. It's a physical thing, a physical loss—like losing an arm or a leg—as well as an emotional one."

Jessie nodded. "Inga had become my best friend."

He smiled sadly. "I can't claim that I was still madly in love with Millie when she died. We had our problems and our differences. But, nonetheless, she was still a part of me. We had been married for eight years, courted for two before that. There were things about me only Millie knew, and vice versa. Did I lose my great love, my life's soul mate when she died? No. But I still lost something. I lost a part of myself."

Jessie was watching him as he spoke. She saw real feeling in his eyes as he talked of his wife's death. Real compassion. Real grief.

"I'm sorry," Jessie said quietly.

"I suppose you've heard the rumors that I had something to do with Millie's death."

Jessie looked away. "I know all too well how people talk."

"People thought I didn't show enough emotion when she died. They had no idea what I was feeling. All the guilt . . ."

"Guilt?" Jessie asked.

"I knew Millie wasn't happy," Manning told her. "She had never taken very well to my success. She was uncomfortable by all the attention we received—well, that I received. And I admit . . . in our unhappiness, I wasn't always faithful to her." His eyes shone for a moment with suppressed tears. "I'm not proud of that. I'm not happy that I caused Millie any additional pain."

"Do you think . . ." Jessie stopped, unsure whether she should continue her thought. But then she decided to finish the question. "Do you think, in her unhappiness, she took her own life?"

"I thought so at first. And I felt tremendously guilty." Manning looked off toward the sky. "But she had never given any indication of it. She was unhappy, but she wasn't depressed." He smiled sadly. "I think it was just a tragic, freak accident. She was making baskets that day out on the deck, you know. She was taking your sister's class, and wanted to prove she could make a basket on her own to show everyone that evening."

"Yes," Jessie said gently. "I know."

"The wind had blown several bands of wicker onto the roof. I think she climbed up over the railing so she could reach them . . . and then she fell."

Manning covered his face with his hands. It was Jessie's turn to reach over and place a hand on his shoulder.

"But you know," Manning said, looking up at her, "for all the problems Millie and I had, I still feel her presence. You see, when someone matters to you, when someone comes into your life in a significant way, you never really lose them. That's the corollary to the idea I expressed earlier—that a part of us dies when someone we love dies. While that's true, I think a part of them lives on in us—a real, physical, energetic part of them. I'm sure you still feel Inga with you."

Jessie smiled. "I do. Especially sitting here, on the swings she painted and restored."

Manning nodded. "At the risk of sounding a bit like some cut-rate Buddha, I do believe we are all connected, and not just in a theoretical way." He looked intently over at Jessie. "Have you ever watched fish swim in schools? In an aquarium, perhaps, or on a television nature program?"

"Yes," Jessie replied.

"Well, then, you've seen how they all move together, in the same exact movements, instinctively. There might be a few here and there that occasionally fall out of line, but generally their movements are all the same, as if they were one single organism."

"I know what you mean. Birds, too, flying in V formations."

"Precisely. And I think that, from a great distance somewhere in the cosmos, that is how we humans must look. We are all moving together, connected, one organism."

Jessie smiled. Somehow the image of a school of fish swimming together, all in formation, comforted her.

"Forgive me if I sound a bit too metaphysical," Manning said. "I'm an amateur philosopher, it's true. But I've been reading quite a bit. Preparing for a new book, where my vampires and monsters reflect a bit on existential themes." He smiled. "Even they occasionally need to give some thought to life and death and love and hope."

"I suppose they do," Jessie said.

They shared a smile that seemed to chase away all the despair Jessie had been feeling just minutes earlier.

But then they heard the slam of a car door.

They looked up. A police cruiser was parked in the driveway. And Detectives Wolfowitz and Knotts were trudging up the hill toward them.

"Well, they get points for predictability," Manning quipped.

"Good morning," Wolfowitz called as he got close enough.

"Good morning," Jessie replied.

"Except that it isn't," the police detective said, breathing a little heavier from his walk up the hill, a few beads of sweat popping on his age-spotted forehead. "Not a good morning, I mean."

"You're speaking of Mrs. Whitman's death," Jessie said.

"I am."

"I got a call a short while ago. I was devastated."

"I understand you were at the school yesterday to speak with her," the detective said.

"I was."

"May I ask what you spoke about?"

"My daughter. I was worried about how she was doing in class."

"Why were you worried?"

Jessie sighed. "The night before, Abby had left the house with a friend to play in the old barn in the woods. I wasn't able to identify the friend and asked Mrs. Whitman if she knew a boy by the name of Aaron."

"Did she?"

"No. But she was very helpful and very kind."

"Did she indicate she was worried or upset or fearful in any way?"

Jessie shook her head. "No. Not at all."

Wolfowitz moved his attention to the other swing. "How about you, Mr. Manning?"

"I never met the woman."

"Where were you last night?" the policeman asked.

"Are you asking where I was when Mrs. Whitman was killed?"

A small smile played with Wolfowitz's lips. "Let's say, between seven and ten last night."

"He was here," Jessie volunteered, before Manning had a chance to reply.

She wasn't sure why she said it. The words just came out of her mouth, without her even thinking about them.

She could feel Manning looking at her, but she kept her eyes on the policeman.

"He was here?" Wolfowitz asked. "With you?"

Jessie nodded. "He came by my house asking if Abby was all right. He'd heard about her adventure in the barn the night before from Mrs. Gorin."

"Why would Mrs. Gorin tell Mr. Manning such a thing?"

"Why does Mrs. Gorin tell anybody anything?" Jessie replied.

The detective narrowed his eyes at Manning. "Is this true? Did you come by here last night asking about her daughter?"

"Yes," Manning said. "I came by."

"What time was that?"

"About seven-thirty, maybe a little earlier." Jessie decided to elaborate on the alibi she was providing Manning. "He came in, and we talked for quite a while."

"What did you talk about?"

Jessie looked over at Manning. "Oh, lots of things. Life and death and love and hope."

"How long did he stay?" Wolfowitz wanted to know.

"For a couple of hours, at least." Jessie knew that by saying this, she was giving Manning an alibi that precluded him from having the time to get into town during the hours of seven and ten.

Detective Knotts was taking all of this down.

"Well, that's all for now," Wolfowitz said. "But I may have more questions." He looked at Manning. "For both of you."

"Anytime, Detective," Manning replied.

The two policemen turned and headed back down the hill. Neither Jessie nor Manning said a word until they were both in the cruiser and backing out of the driveway.

"I was only here for a matter of moments," Manning said. "You wouldn't even let me inside."

"I know."

"So I had plenty of time to leave here, get in my car, drive into town, and murder Mrs. Whitman in cold blood."

"I know." She looked at him. "But you didn't."

He smiled. "Why did you say what you did? I appreciate the alibi, given the vendetta Wolfowitz seems to have against me. But . . . you just gave a false statement. I can't allow you to do that."

"What will you do? Go down to the station and get me in trouble?"

Manning sighed. "Why, Jessie? Why would you want to help me?"

"You came over here wanting to help me, didn't you?"

"Yes . . ."

"And aren't we all connected? Moving in the same formation like one single organism?"

"Still, if it's discovered that I wasn't here during those hours . . ."

"There's no one who can dispute it."

Manning sighed.

"I have a feeling we're in this together, John," Jessie said, placing her hand on his shoulder once again.

He reached up and placed his hand over hers.

FORTY-EIGHT

Three days later, Monica was still ripping mad at her sister. She had seen Jessie that day out in her backyard, sitting on the swings with John Manning, and she'd watched the policemen traipsing up the hill to speak with them. When the phone had rung a moment later, Monica hadn't really been all that surprised to learn from Gert Gorin that Mrs. Whitman, Abby's teacher, was dead and murdered. She'd suspected yet another calamity was heading their way as she'd watched Jessie sit there with Manning, being confronted yet again by the police.

I knew her return to Sayer's Brook would bring nothing but misery for me.

So when Todd had suggested they invite Jessie to join them this evening, Monica had quickly vetoed the idea. Instead, Mr. Thayer had joined them for dinner.

"The lamb was excellent, my dear Monica," the old man said, placing his napkin on his plate as Monica began clearing the table.

"I'm glad you liked it," she replied.

Todd was refilling their wineglasses. "I'm glad you

could come over tonight," he told Thayer. "I've been wanting to ask your opinion about some bonds. . . ."

"No work talk tonight," Monica scolded. "Can't we talk about pleasant things?"

"Well, I'm not sure how pleasant it is," Mr. Thayer said, "but I am highly intrigued by the idea that we have a serial killer loose in town."

Todd sipped his wine. "Well, two killings isn't necessarily a serial killer."

"But in both cases, the throats were slit," Mr. Thayer said.

"Okay," Monica said, rejoining them at the table. "Maybe I'll let you go back to talking about work. It's better than talking about the killings."

Mr. Thayer leaned in toward them, his gray eyebrows furrowed. "I've seen police cars over to John Manning's house twice in the past few days."

"With reason, I imagine," Todd said.

"Stop it, Todd," Monica replied. "There is no connection between John Manning and Mrs. Whitman. If there's any connection between the two killings it's—"

She stopped short, but they knew what she was about to say.

"Poor Jessie," Todd said softly.

"Yes, indeed," agreed Mr. Thayer. "So soon after she comes home to have to deal with two such horrific events . . ."

Monica said nothing. She stood, resuming her efforts to clear away the dishes. She piled the last of the dinner plates on top of one another and carried them out into the kitchen. She could hear the men talking—stocks and bonds. Good. She'd rather them talk about

Wall Street than sit there and voice misplaced sympathy for Jessie.

It's all her own fault, Monica thought as she set the dishes into the sink. *If she hadn't been so damn headstrong, taking up with that horrible Emil Deetz, none of us would be facing these suspicions now. . . .*

But then came another voice. . . .

But she only took up with Emil Deetz because you had destroyed her life.

It was Monica's little conscience, which she didn't listen to very often, nagging deep inside her.

You took Todd away from her on the basis of a lie . . . which sent her off in despair to do stupid things.

"That's crazy," Monica whispered, arguing with herself as she ran the dishes under water before placing them in the dishwasher. "She was well over Todd before she took up with Emil."

If anything, Monica assured herself, it was *Heather* who'd ruined Jessie's life by stealing Bryan away from her.

Bryan.

Monica squinted her eyes as she looked out of the window over the sink. Was that Bryan she'd just seen lurking outside in the dark?

She tried to get a better look, but the glimpse she'd spotted just moments before was gone now. It must have been an illusion. She'd been thinking about Bryan and then she'd thought she'd seen him outside the window.

But in that split second she could have sworn she'd seen Bryan Pierce moving stealthily through the yard, past Monica's house and toward Jessie's.

Wouldn't that be just like her? Monica thought.

It wouldn't surprise Monica in the least to find out her sister was carrying on with Bryan. Jessie brought scandal with her wherever she went.

FORTY-NINE

"**W**hat I want to know," Chief Walters was demanding of Detective Wolfowitz, "is why you haven't yet asked John Manning to explain his reasons for keeping a dossier on Emil Deetz, as well as whether he was in Mexico on the day Deetz was gunned down by police?"

Wolfie sat back in his chair, crossed his arms against his chest, and grinned. "Oh, so now you think I'm not so crazy for suspecting that our esteemed author might be involved in these killings?"

"I'm just expecting you to follow proper police procedure, that's all." Walters eyed him with her sharp blue eyes. "When you find evidence, you question a suspect."

"I'm planning on questioning him. But this new information has led me to postpone it a little while longer. And B'lin, you've gotta admit that if Manning had known I'd seen that dossier, he'd have quickly gotten on the horn to warn these other guys not to speak with me."

"These other guys" were four associates of Emil Deetz, three in prison and one living in Hartford whom the cops had never been able to pin anything on. After speaking with dozens of Deetz's old cronies, Wolfie had found these four guys who admitted yes, they had been contacted by a man named Manning—and paid a considerable amount of money to tell what they knew. They weren't aware that he was a bestselling author; they'd figured "Manning" to be his first name. But the description of the guy was identical in every case, and matched Sayers' Brook's illustrious and enigmatic resident.

"So he told them he was writing a book?" the chief said. "So far, I see nothing suspicious about that. He's an author, remember?"

"Come on, B'lin. You know something smells fishy. Why was he in Mexico at the same time as Deetz's killing? Why did he buy the property from the Clarkson estate? And what is the FBI not telling us? Why won't they confirm or deny that Manning is the guy mentioned in their agent's report?"

Walters shook her head, her short gray pageboy moving like an iron helmet. "That is indeed strange. They usually cooperate in local investigations."

"I suspect they're watching him, too, and don't want to tip their hand." Wolfie was certain that was the case. It made him even more determined to find out the goods on Manning. He resented the feds for not sharing information and for moving in on a case that should fall under local jurisdiction. He'd show them.

"So what did these pals of Deetz tell you?" Walters asked. "What kind of information was Manning looking for when he questioned them?"

"Everything. He wanted every detail of their drug-and-porn ring. Where they got the drugs. What they paid for them. What kind of profit they made. Where the porn was made." Wolfie leaned forward in his chair. "Eastern Europe, if you want to know. And it's the kind of stuff that could land you in jail for a very long time."

"Well, it did indeed land three of those guys in jail," Walters said. "The porn charges against them, for distributing and aiding in producing, landed them longer sentences than the drug charges."

"Yes, they sure did. Only one guy fell through the net. A guy named Ernie."

"Tell me about him."

"He lives up in Hartford. Very cagey. Obviously scared that he'll say something that will finally pin some of the charges to him. But I kept assuring him that by cooperating, he won't be arrested."

"What did he tell you about Manning?"

"That one day he picks up his phone and it's Manning, identifying himself as a reporter and asking for an interview. How Manning got his number, Ernie had no idea. It's unpublished, and even then, listed under his girlfriend's name."

"So how do you think Manning got the number?"

"The man apparently has connections."

"Okay, go on."

Wolfie leaned even farther forward in his chair. "The first time Manning called, Ernie hung up on him. So Manning called again. And again and again, each time getting a thud in his ear. Finally Manning shows up at the guy's house, and flashed a wad of cash when Ernie opened the door. Ernie lives in pretty squalid conditions, so he gave in and let Manning inside."

"Did he tell him everything he wanted to know?"

"I suppose. After three hours, Manning seemed satisfied. Ernie wouldn't let him tape-record anything, so Manning scribbled everything down in a notebook. He wanted every detail of their illegal activities, but he seemed particularly interested in where they'd stashed their cash. The FBI report does mention a large amount of money that was never recovered. Looks like it could be in the millions. Deetz was just one operator in a very large scam, but he was moving his way up the ladder, and apparently was holding on to a big stash. After he got gunned down in Mexico, the rest of the ring was either arrested or scattered. And it's suspected that they're competing with the FBI to find that money."

"So which side is Manning working for?"

"Your guess is as good as mine at this point." Wolfie smirked. "But the fact that he bought the property next to Jessie Clarkson suggests to me he's working with the bad guys. I think that money was stashed on the estate, and Manning bought the chunk that he needed. And when his wife found out what he was involved in, he killed her."

Chief Walters frowned. "And what evidence do you have to support *that*?"

"That part's just a hunch." Wolfie smiled. "For now."

"Where did Ernie tell Manning they'd hidden the money?"

"He didn't know. Only Deetz knew that. All Ernie knew was that it had been buried somewhere."

"And you think it had been buried on the Clarkson property."

Wolfie nodded. "The part that is now the Manning property."

Walters leaned back in her chair. "I still think you've got to confront Manning with this information soon."

"I hear you, B'lin. And I think I'm finally at that point where a confrontation can take place without messing up any other sources." A grin slipped across his face. "And to be honest, I'm relishing the idea of seeing the look on his face when I tell him that I know he's been digging around into Emil Deetz's past." His smile faded as quickly as it appeared. "And I did tell you, didn't I, that last I saw our esteemed author, he was sitting on a swing set with none other than Jessie Clarkson?"

"Yes, you told me that. As well as the fact that she provided him with an alibi for the night of Theresa Whitman's murder."

"Things add up, don't they?"

The chief raised her eyebrows. "Show me your math, Wolfie."

"Don't you think it's curious that Jessie returned to Sayer's Brook when she did? I always suspected she knew more about Deetz's drug deals and shady connections than she let on. Maybe she knew where the money was hidden, and she's in cahoots with Manning. They sure looked awfully cozy that day. And she admitted they spent several hours together the night before talking about 'love.' "

"This is all speculation."

"But there's reason to speculate. Two people are dead soon after Jessie returns to town. Both are connected to her. And she's sitting there making goo-goo eyes at Manning."

Chief Walters stood. She seemed to have heard enough. "Your next step is to question Manning about everything you've found out. What I don't want you doing is drawing conclusions before you have any evidence to support them."

She walked out from around her desk and called to a couple of sergeants passing down the corridor, asking them about another case. Wolfie stewed. Chief Belinda Walters placed too little stock in gut feelings. That was why she'd never be a great police chief. That was why Wolfie should've gotten the job. Sometimes the best police work was done not by relying on hard-and-fast evidence, but that little nagging voice in the back of your head.

And that voice was telling Wolfie that John Manning and Jessie Clarkson were involved in both murders. He'd find the hard-and-fast evidence eventually.

But for now what kept him moving forward was his gut.

FIFTY

Outside Bryan's window, the trees looked as if they were on fire. It seemed that overnight all the deciduous trees along Hickory Dell—the maples and the oaks and, of course, the hickories—had turned bright red, orange, and gold. Autumn was upon them. There was a cold bite to the mornings now when Bryan threw off his covers, and the nights sometimes meant frost on the grass.

Maybe that was why he'd been drinking more than usual. He was trying to ward off the cold fingers of winter, which he felt were just waiting to grab hold of him. Heather had started sleeping in the guest room, unable, she said, to bear his tossing and turning. Bryan figured she just wanted to be away from him, which he didn't mind in the least—except that meant he wasn't getting any tail from anyone. Clare had announced she'd found a boyfriend and so she couldn't see him anymore. And when Bryan wasn't getting sex, he drank more. And when he drank more, he wanted more sex. It was a vicious cycle.

Plus, it had been a bad period at work. His firm was

losing money; this economy was dragging everybody down. There was talk they might have to sell out to another company—possibly the very one Bryan had left, the place where that loathsome Todd Bennett ruled the roost. If so, Bryan felt certain his job would be axed. More than ever, he rued his decision to leave the old firm—and Mr. Thayer's mentorship. He wasn't sure what he'd do if he lost his job. They had quite a mortgage on this house—plus there were the kids. Independent Day wasn't cheap. And Heather expected them to go to the same expensive prep schools she and her brothers had attended. After that, there was college.

Bryan wished they'd never had those two brats.

He could hear them squawking in the other room. Ashton was yelling at Piper to give him back his toys, or maybe it was the other way around. If it weren't for the red hair, Bryan would swear those brats weren't his. Here he was, trying to unwind after a long day at the office—okay, not really so long, he'd left early—and this is what he had to put up with. Something banged against the wall. One of the kids throwing something, in the midst of a temper tantrum.

Bryan flung open the door. "Heather!" he shouted out into the hallway. "Keep those street urchins quiet! I've got a headache and I'm trying to sleep!"

"I'm sorry, Mr. Pierce," came the voice of Consuela, poking her head out from the doorway of the kids' playroom. "Heather isn't home yet. I'm trying to break up an argument between—"

At the moment a stuffed teddy bear came flying out of the door and hit Consuela in the head.

"Between the two children," the long-suffering house-keeper said.

"Well, tell them I said to shut up," Bryan growled. "And don't disturb me. I'm napping."

"Yes, Mr. Pierce."

Bryan slammed the door.

He poured himself another glass of whisky. He was pleased that Heather wasn't home. That meant she wouldn't be barging in on him unexpectedly. He'd been vaguely horny all day, and now, hastened by the alcohol, his dick was growing in his sweatpants. For some guys, drinking inhibited performance. For Bryan, it seemed to accelerate it.

From his secret lockbox, he withdrew the photographs of Jessie. But now he had a few other things to go along with it. His expedition the other day to her house had resulted in some considerable loot. He'd been so shrewd—slipping in through a front window by popping out the screen, then carefully replacing it once he was inside. If Jessie had thought she was secure in that house, she'd had a rude awakening after that. Bryan laughed. And when he'd left he engaged the front door lock so that it would click into place once he closed the door. Brilliant! He knew he shouldn't have made such a mess of things—tossing Jessie's clothes around, pulling things off hangers—but he liked the idea of freaking her out. It got him even harder knowing that she was scared.

Bryan smiled. He pressed a pair of Jessie's blue satin panties to his face.

He knew he wouldn't be content with photos and panties for long, however. He'd been sneaking over to

Jessie's house lately, and spying on her through her windows. But he knew sooner or later—more likely sooner—he would need Jessie herself. Why she had come to occupy nearly his every waking thought, Bryan wasn't sure. It was true she was still hot. It was true that he carried around the feeling of unfinished business with her: she was the only chick he'd ever dated who he hadn't gotten to fuck. But he was smart enough to know his obsession with her these past few weeks was due more to what else was going on his life: the rapid and obvious disintegration of his marriage, his loss of Clare, and his problems at work. Thinking about Jessie got his mind off all of that.

Thinking about Jessie gave him a purpose.

He lay back on his bed, Jessie's panties on his face, the photograph on his chest, and began beating his meat.

That was when the door opened and Heather walked in.

"I come home and the kids are on the warpath and Consuela tells me you're taking a nap—?" she said.

Then she stopped.

She saw the panties, and the photo.

Bryan sat up, looking at her with wide eyes and open mouth.

Heather couldn't speak for a moment. Bryan didn't even try to hide the evidence. It was pointless at this point.

Why hadn't he locked the door?

Maybe, he realized, he'd secretly hoped she'd find him.

Heather looked at him with utter disgust. "You sick

perv," she managed to say, and turned and walked out of the room, slamming the door behind her.

Bryan looked down at the photograph of Jessie.

He had to have her.

Soon.

FIFTY-ONE

Detective Wolfowitz unlocked his door and flipped on his light. He liked coming home to an empty, quiet house. After a day at headquarters, with all that noise and all those phones ringing, this was what he craved: peace and quiet. After his divorce, friends had suggested he get a dog. Or maybe even a cat. A cat wasn't as much work, and didn't mind being home alone all day. But Wolfie thought the idea ludicrous. He didn't want some dog yapping at him or some cat meowing to be fed. At the end of the day, all Wolfie wanted was to be left alone.

He opened his refrigerator and took out a plate of leftovers. He'd fried a couple of cube steaks the night before. He didn't mind eating them cold. He'd cut up an onion and a cucumber. That was all he needed with it. That—and Pabst Blue Ribbon beer.

He popped the top off a beer can and took a sip.

Tomorrow he'd take a ride out to Hickory Dell and have a little conversation with Mr. John Manning, and maybe Ms. Jessica Clarkson, too. He thought this first confrontation ought to be low-key, friendly. He'd arrive without Knotts at his side, maybe even in plainclothes.

That would make it seem less serious. He'd mention casually that one of the detectives, during the search of Manning's house, had found the collection of clippings about the Deetz-Solek murder case. Wolfie would ask innocently how long Manning and Clarkson had known each other. He wanted to see the initial reaction on their faces. Initial, unexpected reactions revealed so much.

He could return later in the day, in a more official capacity, and confront Manning with the information he'd learned from Deetz's cronies, especially Ernie. Wolfie smiled, carrying his dinner plate and can of beer out to the living room. That was when he'd lower the boom.

Maybe he'd even be able to make an arrest before the week was out, depending on what Manning and Clarkson spilled.

But for now, he was just looking forward to sitting in his chair, eating his dinner, and watching a little *Wheel of Fortune*. His stomach rumbled. He was hungry.

Suddenly the lights went out.

"Jesus," Wolfie groaned.

The bulb in the overhead lamp must have blown.

But the kitchen light behind him, he realized, was also out.

He was about to go check the fuse box where there was a sharp, sudden, searing pain in his buttocks. Wolfie yelled out, thrust forward by the pain, dropping his dinner plate and his can of beer. He saw the can fall onto the old brown shag carpet, the golden lager spilling out in a mound of foam.

He reached around to feel his butt. There was something wet and warm. It was hard to see in the dark, but it seemed like blood.

That was when another sharp pain hit him, this time in his thigh.

Wolfie screamed as his knees buckled and he fell to the floor.

Someone was in the room with him. He could hear whoever it was walking around him. The bastard had stabbed him!

"Who are you?" Wolfie shouted.

It was the last thing Detective Wolfowitz ever said. He felt the sting of cold metal at his throat before he felt the pain. And then he couldn't breathe.

FIFTY-TWO

"**H**ow quickly it gets dark these days," the tutor was saying as Jessie walked with her out to her car. "Every year, I'm still never ready for the change of time."

"I know what you mean," Jessie said. "Soon all the leaves will be off the trees."

They stopped in front of the tutor's little powder-blue Prius. A tiny sliver of a moon hung in the sky and a cool breeze had started to blow.

"I wanted to thank you," Jessie said. "You've been just great with Abby. I can tell she likes you very much."

Maxine Peterson was Abby's tutor. Since Mrs. Whitman's death, Jessie had felt better having Abby home-schooled. At least for the time being, she preferred having her at home, where she could see her at all times. She had only told Abby that Mrs. Whitman had passed away, without sharing any of the details. The little girl seemed to suspect something, however. Jessie had noticed in the last couple of weeks Abby had become quieter, more contemplative. There was no more playing with imaginary friends. She seemed sad, and a little distant. A couple of sessions with the school psychologist wouldn't be a bad idea, Jessie figured, and so she'd made an appointment with Dr. Bauer for the following week.

In the meantime, there was Maxine. She was a tall, thin, precise African-American woman with short-cropped gray hair and a soft, calming voice. She taught Abby spelling and reading and some basic arithmetic. Jessie occasionally heard Abby's light, tinkling laughter coming from her room upstairs. That was how she knew Maxine had won her over, and was breaking through her depression.

"She's a delightful child," Maxine told Jessie as she unlocked the door to her car. "And bright, too. I've been teaching children for nearly thirty years and she's one of the smartest. Rare that a child of five can pick up adding and subtracting so quickly, but Abby has done just that."

"I'm glad to hear it."

"By the way," Maxine said, "Abby mentioned Halloween to me today. I didn't quite know what to tell her. Are you thinking of allowing her to go out trick-or-treating?"

Jessie hadn't thought about it. "What made her ask about Halloween?"

"It was in a book we were reading. The little girl in the story was dressed as a princess. Abby said she wanted to dress up just like her."

"Oh." This was a dilemma. "I just don't know. A lot of parents, I'm sure, are wondering about letting their kids go out this year, with what's happened."

Maxine nodded, suppressing a little shiver. "That's

why I just told her she was already as pretty as a princess, and didn't mention Halloween."

"Smart move." Jessie sighed. "I don't like that she can't participate in the holiday. In New York, she always got dressed up and we went to a party in our neighborhood. Maybe I'll just take her to a few houses along Hickory Dell myself. Monica and I can take her the way we used to trick-or-treat. The Gorins and the Pierces and Mr. Thayer."

"There are some children in the new houses through the woods," Maxine said. "Maybe you could drive her over there. The area is very well lit."

"Maybe," Jessie said, smiling.

The tutor got into her car. "I'll see you tomorrow afternoon," she told Jessie.

"Yes, thank you again."

She waved as Maxine backed out of the driveway, the headlights of her Prius slicing bars of light through the darkness.

Jessie was about to turn and walk back up the hill to the house when, in the reddish glow of Maxine's taillights she spotted a silhouette.

The silhouette of a child.

"Hello?" she called.

Her first thought was that it was one of Bryan and Heather's kids. But as soon as the figure took a few steps toward her, still obscured by shadows, Jessie knew this was not Ashton or Piper Pierce.

The child stepped into the soft amber light thrown from Jessie's front porch.

It was a little boy.

Maxine's car was now gone. Monica and Todd

weren't home. Even the Gorins' house across the street was dark.

Jessie stood very much alone, face to face, with this little boy.

He was wearing a white T-shirt and blue shorts, and was barefoot. Even in the dim light, Jessie could see his hands and feet were dirty. The boy was smiling at her. There was something in his big brown eyes that unnerved her.

For several seconds, they just stood staring at each other.

Jessie knew who he was.

"Is your name . . . Aaron?" she managed to say. Her voice, she discovered, was hoarse and dry.

"Yes," he replied.

"You're . . ." Jessie found it difficult to speak, and her heart was thudding. "Abby's friend."

"Yes," the boy said. "Can Abby come out and play?"

"No," Jessie said. "It's dark, and she'll be having her dinner shortly."

Aaron's lower lip pouted slightly. "I never get to see her anymore now that she doesn't come to school."

Jessie lifted her chin as she looked down at the boy. He stood in front of her in the driveway, about five feet away.

"But there's nobody named Aaron in her class," she told him carefully, watching for his reaction. "I checked."

The boy's grin grew wider. "I'm homeschooled, too. But sometimes I go over to the school, because I have friends there." He paused. "Like Abby."

"Oh, is that so? Where do you live?"

He pointed in the direction of the woods.

"In the new houses over there? What's your last name?"

"Smelt," the boy said.

"Aaron Smelt," Jessie said.

The boy smiled.

Something in that sweet little smile disturbed her.

"Well," Jessie said. "You ought to run home. I'm sure your parents are worried about you being out in the dark. You can play with Abby some other time."

"Will you tell her I was here?" Aaron asked. "I don't want her to think that I forgot about her."

"Yes," Jessie said, turning and taking a few steps back up the hill.

She was lying. She didn't want to tell Abby about Aaron. Why she was reluctant to do so, she wasn't sure. But she was. The fact was, she was frightened by the boy. She was trying not to think it, trying not to admit it to herself—but he looked like Emil.

That's crazy, she thought to herself. *What am I thinking?*

Crazy or not, she kept looking over her shoulder until she saw the boy walk away from the house and back down the dark street.

Jessie's nerves were on edge. It was absurd. Why should a little boy scare her so? He was just a kid from one of the new houses on the other side of the woods. His friendship had made Abby happy. Surely his absence was a large part of the reason why Abby had seemed so sad these last couple of weeks. Jessie really ought to tell her daughter that Aaron had come by. It might bring a smile to her face.

But she couldn't. For some reason, she wanted that

boy to stay away from them. She never wanted to see him again. She should have scolded him for enticing Abby out of the house that night and taking her out to the barn. She should have told him she wanted to speak with his mother and to give her his phone number.

She should have, but she didn't.

Because she'd just wanted the boy to go away.

A deep chill had settled within her, and Jessie shuddered.

She hurried up the front steps of her house.

Her hand was on the door to open it when, from out of the shadows on the porch, something moved, causing Jessie to make a little sound in fright.

"Who's there?" she asked.

A hand suddenly reached out of the darkness and grabbed her wrist.

Jessie screamed.

FIFTY-THREE

"I appreciate you helping me tonight, Aunt Paulette," Monica said, hauling a box of baskets out of her Range Rover and into the Sayer's Brook Community Center. "This is one of the biggest classes I've ever taught."

"I'm glad the town is giving you this space to use," the older woman replied, lugging another box herself.

"Giving?" Monica laughed bitterly. "I'm paying a pretty penny to use this room! But what choice do I have? Nobody wants to come out to Hickory Dell since Jessie's au pair was murdered in our backyard!"

"You know, Monica," Aunt Paulette said, setting the box of baskets down on a large table around which were arranged about a hundred chairs, "I wish you didn't keep blaming Jessie for that poor girl's death. She was terribly distraught."

"I don't blame Jessie for the death," Monica replied, unpacking baskets and setting them up on the table. "I just knew that bad things would follow if Jessie came back to town. I wish she had stayed in New York."

"Sweetie," Aunt Paulette said, approaching her niece

with a tentative smile, "I wish you girls could be friends like you used to be."

Monica scowled. "We were never friends."

"Well, I know Jessie could use a friend right now."

"You know, it would be nice if someone—just once!—could be as worried about me as they are for Jessie." Monica picked up an unfinished basket and tossed it against the wall. It exploded like a wicker bomb, ribbons flying everywhere.

"Sweetie, sweetie!" Aunt Paulette attempted to take Monica in her arms, but her niece pushed her away. "I *do* worry about you! I worry whether you're happy, whether you and Todd are getting along—"

"Todd?" Monica snapped her head around to glare at her aunt. "Why do you bring up Todd? What does he have to do with this?"

"I've just noticed how the two of you seem so . . . distant."

"We're not distant," Monica replied curtly, defensively, gathering up the broken bands of wicker.

"Well, I do worry," Aunt Paulette said.

"Stop worrying then." Monica sighed. "Come on. There are still a few more boxes in the car."

They filed back out onto the street. The night was dark, and the streetlamp on this corner was burned out. Monica popped open the back door of the SUV with her remote control, and Aunt Paulette walked around the vehicle to grab a box. But as she did so, she realized there was a man standing behind the car. He scurried away as she approached.

Aunt Paulette stopped in her tracks as if she's been turned to stone.

"What's wrong?" Monica asked, coming up behind her.

"That man," Aunt Paulette said, her words barely above a whisper.

"What man?"

"Didn't you see him?"

"I saw no one." Monica was still in a bad mood. She didn't appreciate her aunt getting her all worked up about Jessie right before a class. How would she be able to concentrate on teaching all these annoying ladies how to thread wicker? "Come on, Aunt Paulette, take one of these boxes, please. We don't have a lot of time."

But the older woman didn't move. "That man," she said dreamily. "You must have seen him."

"There was no man standing here, Aunt Paulette."

"There *was*!" She grabbed Monica's arm. "I saw him! It was the tall, dark man!"

"What the hell are you talking about?"

"I know who he is now!"

"Let go of me!" Monica shrieked. Aunt Paulette's fingers were digging into her wrist.

"It was Emil! It was him! It was Emil!"

"There was no man here, Aunt Paulette." Monica was beyond annoyed. She was pissed. "It's just another one of your crazy visions. Now let go of my arm!"

Aunt Paulette complied.

"Really," Monica said, taking hold of a box and lifting it out of the car, "maybe it's time you should see a shrink. These visions you have . . . they're crazy, Aunt Paulette."

The older woman just stood there, staring off into the dark.

"If you're not going to help me, at least get out of the way," Monica grumbled. She pushed past her aunt, carrying the box toward the community center.

"It was Emil," Aunt Paulette whispered to herself. "But Emil's dead."

She stared off into the dark.

"Maybe that doesn't matter," she said out loud, talking to herself. "Maybe he still has come back!" She looked over at Monica. "I've got to call Jessie. I've got to warn her!"

Monica just rolled her eyes.

FIFTY-FOUR

Jessie looked up into the eyes of the man who held her by the wrist.

It was Bryan Pierce.

"What the hell are you doing here?" she seethed.

"I gotchta talk to you, Jeshaloo-loo," Bryan said, his words slurring together. He reeked of whisky. He wasn't just a little drunk. He was full-blown intoxicated.

"Let go of me," Jessie said in a low voice.

"Please, Jeshaloo, we gotchta talk," he mumbled.

From inside the house, Jessie could hear her phone ringing.

"Let me go, Bryan," she said. "I've got to answer the phone. And Abby is upstairs! Let me go!"

He paid no mind to her pleas. Instead he pulled her in close to him and placed his rank mouth over hers.

"No!" Jessie tried to scream.

She felt his nasty tongue intrude into her mouth. She bit down on it, hard. Bryan let out a yelp, and stepped backward, releasing his grip on her. Jessie quickly bolted into the house, locking the door behind her.

Bryan was banging on the glass. "Jeshaloo, I luff you! I need you! Doncha unnerstand? I luff you! God-damn it, Jeshaloo! I want you!"

Jessie could hear the anger in his voice. Bryan was a dangerous man. He was walking along the front porch, banging on the windows. If he got inside—

Jessie looked around. She had just opened the fireplace flue, in anticipation of chilly autumn evenings. She'd also brought up the andirons and pokers from the basement, looking forward to the first fire of the winter. Jessie grabbed one of the iron pokers now. If Bryan got in here somehow, she'd use it to defend herself.

"Jesheeee!"

He was rattling the doorknob now. Jessie thought about calling the police. But she didn't want to bring their red flashing lights out to Hickory Dell again if she could avoid it. She couldn't bear being asked one more question by that insinuating Detective Wolfowitz.

"Bryan, go home!" she called out to him. "If you don't leave, I'm going to call Heather! Go now before you make this even worse!"

"Fuck Heather!" he shouted. "I want you! And I'm gonna have you!"

Suddenly his fist came smashing through the glass of the front door. Jessie saw his bloody hand reach down to grab the knob. She raised the fireplace poker and began slamming it down onto his fingers. Bryan shouted in pain and pulled his hand back.

For a second there was silence.

Then came a terrible smashing sound. The old wooden rocking chair that had sat on the front porch for decades suddenly came crashing through the window. Glass sprayed everywhere. Jessie saw Bryan's face looking in from the darkness outside.

She raised the poker over her head.

FIFTY-FIVE

"I tell you, Arthur, I saw them kiss!" Gert Gorin was shrieking. "Right there on her front porch!"

Gert had the binoculars pressed up against the picture window again. This was the kind of drama she dreamed of seeing. Usually she'd only caught Bryan skulking in the bushes. But now there he was, with Jessie in his arms, making out for the whole world to see. Gert was in her glory.

Yet it was getting even better.

"Now they're arguing," she reported to her husband, giving him a blow-by-blow of the events taking place across the street, even though Arthur said nothing, just kept his eyes on the television set. "She's pushed him away! She's gone inside and slammed the door on his face! He's banging on the door, wanting to be let in!"

Oh, just *wait* until she phoned Rose O'Connell and told her about this!

"Oh my God, Arthur, now he's really getting angry! I can even hear him! I think he's drunk!"

It just kept getting better and better.

"He's smashing the door down! Oh my God, Arthur, *he's smashing the door down!*"

"Maybe we ought to call the cops," Arthur finally responded, turning away from the television.

"Not yet! Oh my God, not yet! Arthur! Now he's smashing windows!"

Arthur hadn't seen his wife look like this since the last time he'd watched her having an orgasm. And that was a very, very long time ago indeed.

FIFTY-SIX

Jessie steadied her grip on the poker, ready to bring it down on Bryan's head the moment he stepped through the window.

She watched as one leg began to move inside.

But suddenly Bryan stopped. She heard him shout. His leg disappeared from the window. Jessie heard the sounds of a scuffle on the porch.

John Manning was there. He must have seen or heard the commotion from his house and rushed over. Jessie watched as John grabbed hold of Bryan and pushed him backward. Bryan tumbled but—surprisingly for someone so drunk—managed to keep his balance. He came charging back at John like a furious bull.

"Forget it," John said, stopping Bryan's assault by grabbing his shoulders and giving him another shove, this time right down the steps of the front porch.

Bryan lay on the ground, looking up as if dazed.

"You'd better get up," John told him, "and run as fast as your pathetic little legs will take you."

Bryan did as he was told. Within seconds he had disappeared into the darkness.

Inside the house, Jessie dropped the poker and opened

the door. Without exchanging any words, she and John embraced. Wrapped in his arms, Jessie could hear and feel how fast her own heart was beating.

"You should call the police," John told her.

"No," she said. "I can't. It would just bring more scandal."

"That man was going to rape you."

Jessie gently moved out of John's embrace. "Monica is already not speaking to me because I've brought too much scandal since coming back here."

"You didn't bring any scandal!" John insisted. "You're not to blame for what happened to Inga or Mrs. Whitman. And you're certainly not to blame for what just happened here tonight! That man needs to be arrested!"

"I know," Jessie said, but her voice wasn't convincing.

"At the very least, he needs to pay for this damage," John said.

"I'm going to call Heather," Jessie said. "I'm going to tell her what happened, and that I have you as a witness. Can I do that?"

There was only the slightest hesitation coming from John, and Jessie remembered the scene between him and Heather outside his house. But then he said, "Of course you can. And I'm happy to corroborate your account to the police."

"The police can wait. Bryan has two kids. I don't want to hurt them."

John frowned. "Somehow I'm not sure devil spawn *can* be hurt."

Despite everything that had happened, Jessie managed a smile. She knew Ashton and Piper were decidedly unpleasant children. But they were children nonetheless, and having their father arrested for attempted rape would devastate them.

"I've got to check on Abby," Jessie said.

Indeed, when she turned around, her daughter was sitting at the top of the stairs. How much had she seen?

"It's okay, baby," Jessie said, rushing up to embrace her.

"That man broke our door and our window," Abby said.

"It's okay," Jessie told her. "We can get them fixed."

"And he's gone away," John said from the bottom of the stairs. "You can be sure of that."

Abby looked at him but said nothing. Then she moved her round little blue eyes back to her mother.

"Mommy," she said. "Why didn't you tell me that Aaron came by?"

Jessie was caught short, and didn't know how to reply right away. "I guess you saw me from the window, talking with him earlier?"

Abby said nothing.

"I'm sorry, sweetie," Jessie said finally. "I just hadn't had a chance. All of this happened. . . ."

"It's okay, Mommy," Abby said. She stood and walked back to her bedroom.

Jessie watched her. She had the distinct impression Abby hadn't seen her talking with Aaron. She knew that the boy had been here some other way. And that unnerved Jessie even more than the ordeal with Bryan.

FIFTY-SEVEN

This had gone far beyond Gert's wildest hopes.

"I tell you, Arthur," she said, standing between her husband and the television, "that woman is carrying on affairs with *both* Bryan Pierce and John Manning! She made out with both of them on her front porch! And then the two of them fought over her, and Manning won!"

Arthur sighed. "Gert, would you move, please? The bases are loaded!"

Gert's eyes were wild. "I just wonder if *Heather* knows. Because you know, Heather is sleeping with Manning, too. I wonder if it's one of those Bob and Carol and Ted and Alice situations."

Her husband just groaned.

"It was a wicked fight!" Gert exulted.

Watching them had been the most fun she'd had in years.

She hurried off to call Rose O'Connell, much to Arthur's relief.

FIFTY-EIGHT

Bryan was lost. But how could he be lost? This was crazy. Just crazy.

He must have headed the wrong way on Hickory Dell and ended up smack in the middle of the woods. He looked around. The trees were thick, and he was crunching through an ever-deepening carpet of fallen leaves. Bryan had thought he was cutting through the Gorins' backyard; he'd wanted to avoid walking in the street, since he was bleeding from his hand and from the back of his head. But instead of cutting through the yards, he must have wandered into the woods, turned right instead of left.

"Fuck," Bryan said to himself.

He thought he had sobered up a bit. But maybe he hadn't. How else to explain how he'd gotten so god-damn *lost*?

His shoulder ached. He'd probably dislocated it when he'd been thrown down the stairs.

Goddamn Manning. Bryan would make sure he paid for that.

His legs felt unsteady, as if they might buckle at any moment. So Bryan stopped walking and tried to get his

bearings. He looked around. He didn't recognize anything. He looked up. The trees were so thick that he
couldn't see the moon or stars. There was barely enough
moonlight for him to see just a few feet ahead of him.
Up ahead in the trees, he thought he saw a house—
maybe a small shack. But he had no idea where he was.
He'd never been in this part of the woods before.

The night was still.

Terribly still and quiet.

Bryan heard a twig snap.

A squirrel or a possum, he supposed.

He decided to turn around and walk back the way he
came. But which way was that? How far had he walked?
How far was the road?

He couldn't tell. But he began walking, the sound of
crunching leaves unbearably loud in his ears.

After a few moments, Bryan stopped again. He still
had no clue as to where he was, or if he was walking in
the right direction.

He heard leaves crunching from not far away.

Someone was following him.

John Manning. He was sure of it.

"Fuck you, Manning," Bryan shouted, and was aware
that his words were still slurry. But at least he was now
aware that he was slurring. That meant he must be
sobering up.

He resumed walking. Every couple of minutes he
stopped and listened. Whoever it was that was following him was getting closer.

It had to be Manning.

"You want another go at it, Manning? Okay, a fair
fight this time. Not you coming up behind me! Show

yourself, you asshole! And we'll fight this out, like men!"

The sound of leaves crunching ceased.

"Manning?" Bryan asked, eyes squinting into the dark.

Before he even knew what was happening, he felt a blade slice into his gut. He looked down, and saw the shiny metal as it slid back out of his flesh, caught by the light of the elusive moon. A second passed, and then a waterfall of blood gushed from under Bryan's shirt. The pain wasn't that bad. It felt more like having the wind knocked out of him. Already wobbly, Bryan crumpled to the ground. As he did so, he looked up into the eyes of his killer.

"Why?" Bryan managed to gasp, just before the blade swooped down and sliced him across the throat.

Fifty-nine

It began raining slightly before sunrise. It was a torrential downpour that brought a cold dampness seeping through the joints of Jessie's old house, and it was made worse by the fact that the door and window of the front porch were taped over with plastic.

Jessie poured some steaming hot chamomile tea into Aunt Paulette's cup. "You must have been mistaken," she told her calmly.

"I wish I was," the older woman replied. She looked somehow diminished this morning. Her long gray hair hung raggedly at her shoulders, she hadn't applied her usual bright red lipstick, and it was obvious from her eyes that she hadn't slept. "But it was *him*, Jessie. It was Emil."

Jessie sat down opposite her at the kitchen table and took a sip of her own tea. She shivered. "Why didn't you tell me last night?"

"Well, when we got home and I saw what had happened here, I didn't want to upset you further. I figured it could wait until morning." Aunt Paulette looked over at her. "But I stayed awake most of the night, just watching your house."

Jessie smiled sadly. "Dear Aunt Paulette."

If this was true . . . if Emil really *was* still alive as Jessie had long feared . . .

Maybe Monica was right. Maybe Jessie shouldn't have returned to Sayer's Brook. All she'd done was bring anxiety and worry to the lives of her sister and aunt. When Monica had come home last night and seen the damage to Jessie's house, and then learned the reason for it, she'd had a fit. "Jesus fucking H. Christ!" she'd cursed, making Jessie cringe. She knew the curses were directed at her, not at Bryan. To Monica's mind, even Bryan's drunken shenanigans were Jessie's fault.

And now this. Aunt Paulette claiming to have seen Emil last night in town.

"You really think he was real?" Jessie asked.

"I don't know. I wondered if he might have been a ghost." Aunt Paulette locked eyes with her. "I have seen ghosts other times in my life, you know."

"I know." At least, Jessie knew that her aunt had *believed* she'd seen ghosts.

"It seemed possible that he may have been an apparition, because, after all, Monica didn't see him," Aunt Paulette continued. "But the more I thought about it, I think he was a real living human being, because I heard his steps on the street walking away in the dark."

"Ghosts don't make noise when they walk?" Jessie couldn't help a small smile.

"Go ahead, make jokes," Aunt Paulette said, sitting back in her chair. "But I'm worried, sweetie."

Jessie sighed. "I'm sorry, Aunt Paulette. I wasn't joking. I just don't know what to believe. So much has been happening."

"Well, think about it. Was Emil's body ever returned to the United States?"

"I don't know."

"They never informed you of a burial or anything?"

Jessie shook her head. "Why would they? We weren't married. I didn't know any of his family, so whether they were contacted, I couldn't tell you."

"Sweetie, what if the Mexican drug agents were wrong? What if that *wasn't* Emil who died in the shoot-out?"

Jessie ran her fingers through her hair. "Believe me, that thought has crossed my mind many times of the years. But . . . why shouldn't I believe the authorities?" She gave her aunt a look. "And *you* confirmed it for me. You said back then that you couldn't see Emil when you put on your psychic hat. You said that convinced you he was dead."

"It was true that I couldn't see him. But there may have been other reasons for that."

Jessie sighed and stood up from the table. "Aunt Paulette, you have been wonderful to me ever since I came back." She headed over to the sink and began washing out her teacup. "In fact, I don't know what I would have done without you. I love you so much, and so does Abby." She turned around to look at her. "But you frighten me when you talk about these visions . . . this tall, dark man you see out there, and now Emil."

"I don't want to frighten you, but I feel I have to warn you! Should I not have mentioned what I saw last night?"

Jessie sat back down at the table. "No, of course you should have mentioned it."

"If Emil is still alive, and he's come back . . ." Aunt Paulette said, her voice trailing off.

"It would make sense, in a terrifying way," Jessie admitted. "He could have killed both Inga and Mrs. Whitman as a way to terrorize me."

"I've got to tell the police that I saw him."

Jessie nodded. "I suppose you should. I think Detective Wolfowitz will be very interested to hear that."

"You should go back to New York, sweetie. Take Abby and go back—"

"No." Jessie looked at her aunt with hardened eyes. "If this possibly is true—if Emil *has* returned—then I'm not going to let him win. That's what he wants. He wants to terrorize me. Well, I'm not going to let him."

"Oh, but, baby, is it safe?"

"If Emil is really alive, if he's really out to get me, then *nowhere* I go will be safe. I'm not going back to an anonymous life again, hiding out in New York. I'm through with that! I ran from him for too long! Besides, I couldn't be anonymous again even if I wanted to. I've got a name now, because of my book, and soon I'll have another book in the stores. Emil could easily find me wherever I went."

Aunt Paulette reached across the table and placed her wrinkled hand over Jessie's.

"I'm not going to run," Jessie told her. "I'm tired of being scared all the time. I'm tired of crying. Todd is fixing the window and the door today, and tomorrow morning the security people will be here to install the alarm system. Some horrible things have happened, but if it's Emil who's doing them, then I'm not going to let him win. This is my home. Mom wanted me to live here. She told me I was strong enough to face any-thing—and I am! Emil's had me running scared for the last six years." Jessie looked over at her aunt with a conviction in her eyes the older woman had never seen there before. "Well, not anymore. Not anymore!"

The phone was ringing. For a moment, Jessie didn't seem to hear it. Then she stood from her chair and hurried to answer it.

SIXTY

"**Y**ou're writing a book? That's how you explain it? You're writing a book?"

Chief Belinda Walters stood facing John Manning in his parlor. He'd asked her to sit down, but she'd demurred. She'd gotten right to the point, asking him why he kept a dossier on Emil Deetz and the murder of Screech Solek. And why he'd been interviewing some of Deetz's old gang. Manning had replied by saying he was writing a book.

"I don't know why you should seem so surprised," Manning added. "After all, I'm a writer. That's what I do."

"You write about vampires," the chief said.

"I'm making a departure."

"A departure?"

"Yes. Every writer likes to stretch his wings, so to speak. I'm writing a crime thriller. I've had enough of supernatural monsters. There are enough human ones." He grinned. "One of your investigators read my latest work on my computer when your SWAT team descended on my house. Surely he can back me up on that."

Walters nodded. Indeed, the report detailing the search

of Manning's house *did* include a brief summary of what was on his computer. The most recent Word file was the story of a drug dealer. But so far at least there had been no throat slitting or Mexican adventures that would make it seem all that relevant.

"So in all your interviews with Deetz's cronies . . . did you find out where he'd stashed the cash?"

"What cash are you talking about, Chief?"

"Don't bullshit me, Manning."

"I'm not bullshitting you. Here's the deal. I heard about the case while I was in the process of buying this property. Of course, it was only natural that I would, since the woman who'd witnessed the murder had lived next door. The case seemed to me to have the right combination of adventure, melodrama, tragedy, and suspense that I needed for my novel. So I went to the library and did a little research." He smiled, those deep dark eyes of his twinkling. "No crime in that, is there?"

Walters tried to read the man's eyes. He was a cagey one. The little smiles, the half-winks . . . he was trying to be charming. No doubt he'd won over many women this way. But Walters was too old, too shrewd to fall for that.

"No crime in that," the chief agreed. "So you only learned of Solek's murder once you bought this place? You had no idea who Solek or Deetz were before that time?"

"None." Manning's face was a blank slate.

Behind her, Detective Knotts stood glaring at the author. Walters knew she had to keep herself positioned between the two men. If Manning said something to rattle Knotts, the detective might very well throw a punch. Knotts was rather emotional this morning. They all were, given what they'd found a little more than an hour ago.

"Well then, explain this to me, Mr. Manning," Walters said. "What were you doing in Mexico on the day Deetz was shot to death?"

"I haven't been to Mexico in fifteen years." Once again, Manning's face betrayed no emotion.

"That's not what the FBI tells us," Walters said.

At last Manning's eyes widened—not more than a fraction of a millimeter, but it was all Walters needed. She'd seen it. That had been the reaction Wolfie had wanted to see. Manning was cool and collected, but when Walters mentioned the FBI, he had reacted, ever so slightly, and just for an instant. It was enough to tell Walters the guy was hiding something. She knew then that he *had been*, in fact, in Mexico that day—and he most likely knew a hell of a lot more than he was telling them about Emil Deetz.

"I have great respect for our Federal Bureau of Investigation," Manning said, smoothly covering up his reaction, "but in this case, they are wrong. Would you like to check my passport?"

"We would," the chief said, "and we will. Though I'm sure that will tell us nothing."

Manning shrugged. "Border control is very strict."

"Not really," Walters said.

"Tell me, Chief, why isn't Detective Wolfowitz the one to be leading my interrogation? I've gotten rather used to seeing his smiling face at my door."

Walters leveled her eyes at the author. "Detective Wolfowitz was found murdered in his home this morning," she said without emotion.

This time the reaction in Manning's eyes was more

apparent, and he didn't attempt to hide it. Was the man really surprised, or was he just a very good actor?

"I'm—I'm very sorry to hear that," he said.

"His throat was cut," Knotts volunteered, his voice hard and accusatory.

"Then it's the same—or possibly the same—killer," Manning said. "The same who killed the German girl and the schoolteacher."

"Perhaps," Walters said. "Perhaps Detective Wolfowitz was getting too close to something." She paused. "Where were you last night, Mr. Manning, around six or seven o'clock?"

"I was here, writing," he said.

"Anyone who can corroborate that?" The chief gave him a little smile. "Jessie Clarkson, perhaps?"

"Actually, she could. I was at her house last night for a brief period, but it was probably right around six-thirty."

"We're going to be checking with her next," Walters said. "All right, Mr. Manning, that's all for now. Thank you for your time."

She started toward the door. Knotts followed, sending daggers over his shoulder in Manning's direction.

"Chief Walters," Manning said.

Walters stopped, looking back at him. Manning's voice sounded a little bit uneasy.

"I wonder if . . . well, when you see Ms. Clarkson, are you planning on telling her about the files I have on the Solek murder?"

"Why do you want to know?"

"Well, it's just that . . . if you didn't have to tell her right away, I'd rather do it myself."

"Why is that?"

Now Manning seemed distinctly uncomfortable. "It's just that . . . well, we've become friends."

Walters held his gaze, trying to read what was going on in his mind. She wasn't successful. "We'll see," she said, "if it comes up."

She and Knotts headed out the door. The rain was still coming down hard and the sky was nearly black.

SIXTY-ONE

"**O**h my God," Jessie said into the phone. "That's . . . horrible."

Aunt Paulette stood behind her, her hands clasped in front of her chest as Jessie hung up.

"More bad news?"

"It was Mrs. Gorin." Jessie looked at her. "A friend of hers has a police scanner. It seems Detective Wolfowitz has been murdered."

"Dear God!"

"You were right, Aunt Paulette," Jessie said, gripping the counter to steady herself. "It's Emil. He's alive. It must be him doing this."

A rap on the back door startled them. Standing under two big black umbrellas were a man and a woman. Jessie recognized the man as Detective Knotts, Wolfowitz's partner. The woman she didn't know.

She let them inside. Chief Walters introduced herself.

"I just heard about Detective Wolfowitz," Jessie said.

The chief looked surprised. "How did you hear?"

"From Mrs. Gorin, across the street."

Chief Walters gave her a weary smile. "The town crier."

Jessie returned a smile that was equally tepid. "She does seem to know things before anyone else."

"Well, it's true," the chief said, confirming Gert's report. "And like the others, his throat was cut."

"Then it has to be Emil," Jessie said, her voice breaking. Aunt Paulette put her arm around her. Outside a sudden gust of wind and rain slapped against the side of the house.

"What do you mean," Chief Walters asked, "it has to be Emil?"

"My aunt thought she saw him last night in town," Jessie said.

"Emil Deetz?" The chief made a face. "He was shot by police in Mexico."

"It was him," Aunt Paulette said. "The more I think about it, I'm certain."

The chief nodded, taking the information in. "Ms. Drew," she said to Aunt Paulette, "would you give Detective Knotts a full statement to that effect?"

"Certainly."

Knotts took her aside, where they sat on the couch in the living room. Withdrawing his notebook from inside his jacket, the detective began taking notes as Aunt Paulette related the story of seeing a man near Monica's car last night outside the community center. "He was tall and dark and frightening," Aunt Paulette said. "Just the way Emil always seemed to me."

Meanwhile, the chief continued her questioning of Jessie in the kitchen.

"I understand that Mr. Manning was here last night around six-thirty," she said.

Jessie looked at her sharply. "So you're still considering him a suspect?"

"I consider everyone a suspect, Ms. Clarkson. A police officer was murdered last night. A police officer who was on the trail of what is now obviously a serial killer. One of those people he was talking to was Mr. John Manning."

"But John didn't do it. I tell you, the only explanation for any of this is Emil."

"Was Mr. Manning here last night around six-thirty?" the chief repeated deliberately, her fierce blue eyes shining out at Jessie from her round face framed by her helmet of iron-gray hair.

"Yes, he was," Jessie replied.

"How long did he stay?"

"Maybe half an hour, forty minutes."

"What was he doing here?"

Jessie didn't want to go into detail about the incident with Bryan. She had hoped to keep the police out of it, and go directly to Heather. But it was clear that Chief Walters had already spoken with John. He may have told them everything. It wouldn't do any good for Jessie to sidestep the issue now.

"There was a . . . scuffle," she said. "Did John tell you?"

"Why don't you tell me in your words?"

"Bryan Pierce was here."

The chief lifted her eyebrows. "Bryan Pierce. Your neighbor."

"Yes."

"What was he doing here?"

"He was drunk." Jessie sighed. "Look, he has two little kids. I don't want to cause a scandal that will hurt them in any way."

"Please tell me what happened, Ms. Clarkson."

"He came here and got . . . aggressive."

"What do you mean by aggressive?"

"He was . . . trying to force himself on me."

The chief's eyes hardened. "He tried to rape you."

"I don't know if he would have gone that far, but . . ."

"Ms. Clarkson, do I understand you weren't planning to report an attempted rape?"

"I don't want to hurt his kids."

Walters's eyes lifted toward the damage in the other room. "Did Pierce do that?"

"Yes," Jessie said. "I wouldn't let him in after he accosted me on the porch."

"The man needs to be arrested, Ms. Clarkson."

Jessie knew she was right, but she couldn't bear to bring such anguish to his family. "I thought if I just called his wife . . . He has two kids. . . ."

The chief sighed. "I encourage you to press charges. Please think about it. But for now, please go back to explaining John Manning's part in this."

"Well, John came to my rescue. He had heard the sound of shouting and breaking glass, and he rushed over, and took hold of Bryan and pushed him off the porch. He told Bryan to get the hell out of here, and Bryan turned and ran."

Chief Walters nodded, as if this was information she hadn't expected to hear about John Manning. "I see," she said. "And then he stayed for about half an hour, or forty minutes?"

"About that, yes."

"Tell me, Ms. Clarkson. Are you and Mr. Manning lovers?"

Jessie's jaw dropped. "Excuse me, that is none of—"

"I'm investigating a murder. I have to ask questions."

"No, we're not!" Jessie said indignantly. "We are just friends!"

"How long have you known each other?"

"Just since I moved back here. A couple of months."

"And what made you friends?"

"Everything that's been happening. Inga's death. Mrs. Whitman's death. John came by several times to offer his help to me, his support. . . ."

"Would you say he was trying to win you over?"

Jessie felt the anger surge up inside her again. "Win me over? What are you implying? Win me over for what?"

"I don't know. Do you have any idea?"

"He was just trying to be my friend!"

"Why would he want to be your friend?"

Jessie laughed indignantly. "Why wouldn't he want to be?"

"Did you know Mr. Manning is writing a book about Emil Deetz and the murder of Screech Solek?"

The question at first seemed to bounce off of Jessie like a rubber ball. It didn't penetrate her brain. She looked at the chief with uncomprehending eyes for several seconds before it finally seeped in.

"Writing . . . a book?" Jessie asked.

"So he was right," the chief said. "You didn't know."

"That's crazy," Jessie said.

"He told me himself. It explains why he kept a dossier on Deetz. Our detectives found it when they searched his house."

"Well, if he's writing a book about the case, it must be just an idea that came to him in the last few weeks," Jessie said, trying to rationalize the information she had just received.

"Nope. From the looks of the manuscript we read on his computer, he's been working on this project for at least a couple of years. Seems he's known about Emil Deetz and Screech Solek and their drug trade—and *you*—for some time now."

Jessie didn't know what to say. She just stood there, trying to process the information, but found she could not.

"Okay, Chief, I've got the statement," Knotts said, coming up behind her. "I'm going to put out an all-points bulletin to be on the lookout for Deetz. We also need to contact the FBI, since they're the ones who reported to us that he'd been killed in Mexico."

Walters nodded. "Thank you, Ms. Clarkson. Thank you, Ms. Drew. That will be all for now." She headed toward the back door, then turned around again. "I'd suggest a security system be put in place here."

"We've already planned for that," Aunt Paulette said. "They'll be here tomorrow to install it. And as soon as the rain lets up, my nephew-in-law will be here to fix the window and the door."

The chief nodded, then turned to look back at Jessie.

"I really urge you to press charges against Mr. Pierce. He's a danger. If he tried something like that with you, he'll try it with another woman."

Jessie just nodded slowly, still stunned by the news that John was writing a book. A book about Emil.

Was that why he was interested in her? To get information for his book?

SIXTY-TWO

In the police car, the rain assaulting the roof like machine-gun fire, Knotts lifted the phone to call in the report about Emil Deetz.

"Wait one second," the chief told him.

Knotts looked over at her.

"We definitely need to be on the lookout for Deetz, and we need to follow up with the FBI, but let's remember something about Paulette Drew."

"What's that?"

"She's a bit of a fruitcake."

Knott's eyebrows lifted in surprise.

"She's got an ad in some of the alternative-type newspapers calling herself 'Madame Paulette.' She reads tarot cards and predicts fortunes."

Knotts laughed. "I take it you don't believe in all that stuff."

Walters gave him an eye roll. "About ten years ago, I went over to Madame Paulette's cottage with my daughter Emma, kind of as a lark. I'm sure she didn't remember me—it was just a brief visit. But Emma was applying to colleges, and she wanted to ask Madame if she'd get in to any of them. Madame did a lot of hocus pocus with her cards and laying her hands on Emma's forehead. Finally she told Emma that she'd get in to all of the schools she'd applied to except for her top choice, but that in the end, that would be for the best, because her top choice wasn't going to the best place for her. Well, Emma's top choice was Wesleyan, and she was accepted just days after Madame's dire prediction. Four years later, Emma graduated at the top of her class." The chief smirked. "So much for Paulette Drew's reliability as a witness."

"So maybe I ought to wait before calling in the report about Deetz?"

"No, call it in. We can't take that chance. But let's just remember who we're dealing with here."

"You still thinking it's Manning? Wolfie was sure it was Manning."

Belinda Walters sighed, looking out of the watery window in the direction of John Manning's mansion. "I don't know," she said quietly. "So many things just don't add up." She looked back over at Knotts. "But we'll do the math eventually. I promise you that, Knotts. Now, go ahead and call in your report."

SIXTY-THREE

"**Y**ou just say the word, Jessie," Todd was telling her, "and I'll go over to that fucker's house and bash his brains in."

If Todd had disliked Bryan Pierce before, now he loathed him. As he slid a sheet of glass into the wood frame of the window—his father had been a carpenter, so Todd possessed the know-how to do such things—he couldn't get what had happened here last night off his mind. He wished he'd been around, wished he hadn't been kept late in the city, wished it hadn't been that devious, untrustworthy John Manning who'd rushed over to Jessie's defense. In some ways, that was the worst thing of all.

"No," Jessie was saying. "Let's just let the matter drop. I called Heather. I told her everything. Let her deal with it."

"What did Heather say?"

"Not much. She just listened and then said, 'Oh.' "

Todd's eyebrows shot up. "Just, 'Oh'?"

Jessie nodded. "When I told her that I didn't want to get the police involved for her kids' sake, she said,

"Thanks for that, at least.' Then she hung up the phone on me."

"What a bitch."

Todd stood back and made sure the pane of glass was even and sturdy. Satisfied, he moved on to the door.

"I just wish I'd been here," he grumbled. Jessie had brought a bottle of beer out to him on the porch and he took a swig. "I wish I'd been able to take a crack at Bryan myself."

"I'm just glad it's over," Jessie said, wrapping her arms around her torso and hugging herself.

Despite the fact that the rain had let up, fading into a foggy mist, the day was still cold and very, very damp. It seemed winter was coming earlier than ever this year. The torrential downpours had blasted most of the remaining leaves off the branches of the trees, whose gray skeletal arms now stood shrouded by the mist.

"I really appreciate you helping me out, Todd," Jessie said, smiling over at her brother-in-law.

He turned and looked at her. "Well, I couldn't very well just leave you and Abby up here with plastic covering your windows this time of year."

Jessie's smile broadened. "You've been so wonderful right from the moment I moved back home."

Todd felt the emotion in his chest expand. "Jessie, you know I have only ever wanted the best for you. . . ."

Her smile turned a little sassy. "Always? Oh, I think there was a time you were quite fed up with me, like everyone else. And I can't blame you for that."

Todd set down the bottle of beer and took a step toward Jessie. "I was wrong to be impatient with you. I didn't know what you were going through. It's never been your fault, Jessie. Like last night. You've always had assholes making your life difficult. And I can't deny that I wish it was me who'd slugged Bryan, and not that goddamn John Manning. . . ."

"Please," Jessie said, cutting him off. "Don't bring him up."

"Bryan? Or Manning?"

Jessie moved away, standing on the top step of the porch, looking out into the foggy front yard. "Either of them," she said.

Todd was immediately behind her. "Why? Did Manning do something obnoxious too?"

"Not last night. He was terrific last night." Jessie turned to face him. "But the policewoman who came here this morning to tell me about Detective Wolfowitz also told me something about John."

"What did she tell you?"

"He's writing a book about Emil and his crimes! That's why he's been so interested in me . . . and no doubt it's why he bought the property next door!"

"Why, that son of a bitch . . ."

"We had become friends," Jessie said, and Todd was surprised to see tears well in her eyes, tears that she successfully fought back and which never fell down her cheeks. "But he was just trying to get information. That's the only thing I can think now, because otherwise he would have told me right away."

"A friendship can't be built on a lie," Todd told her, and impulsively he took her hands in his. Jessie's eyes flickered up to look directly at him. "You deserve better than that, babe. You really do."

He used to call her babe when they had dated, back in high school.

"I wish you and I had spoken about what happened when we were kids, about why we broke up," Todd said, his voice thick with feeling. "All these years, we've never said anything. . . . I've honored your wish. . . ."

"Oh, Todd," Jessie said. "It was ages ago. We were just teenagers. It doesn't matter. It's all water under the bridge."

"No, no, you need to know," he said, squeezing her hands. "I care about you, Jessie. I always have! I never stopped!"

Without even thinking about it, he embraced her.

"If Monica hadn't become pregnant, you know I wouldn't have left you," he said, his lips near her ear. "You know that, don't you? I only did what I thought I should."

He felt Jessie stiffen in his arms.

"Monica . . . ?" Jessie's voice was very soft. "Pregnant?"

Todd broke the embrace and stepped back to look Jessie in the face. "Yes," he said. "You know, after that night . . . and then, you told Monica that we should be together for the baby's sake. I know you said that I should never, ever mention the subject again, that you never wanted to hear about it again, and I've respected that, but I had to say something. I felt you needed to know that I would never have left you—"

"Monica . . . was *pregnant*?"

Jessie backed away from him, a horrified look on her face.

"Yes," Todd said, confused. "You know, back in high school . . ."

"Then . . . that was why . . . you went with her?"

"Yes," he said. "That's what I'm trying to tell you. . . ."

"You had sex with Monica!"

Todd didn't understand, but then, all at once, it hit him.

Monica had lied to him.

She had never told Jessie that she'd been pregnant.

And if she had lied about that . . . what else might she have lied about?

Todd stood frozen in place, just staring at Jessie.

"I think you ought to go home now," Jessie said at last. "I can get a carpenter to finish the door."

"What?" Todd snapped out of his daze. "Jessie, no, listen, I thought you knew. . . . Monica said she told you. . . ."

"A moment ago, Todd, I said that all this was water under the bridge. And maybe it is. But at the moment, I am just very, very weary of the lies men tell. Of the deceits that have seemed to follow me through life. I'd really like you to go."

"But, please, Jessie, let me explain. . . ."

"I said go!"

He saw the anger in her eyes.

"Okay," he said. "I'm sorry, Jessie. It just happened. And I thought you knew. And I wanted you to know that if it *hadn't* happened . . ."

His words trailed off.

Maybe, in fact, it hadn't.

"Don't say any more, Todd," Jessie said, turning around to head back inside the house. "Please don't say any more."

"I will come back," he promised. "I'll finish this door!"

Jessie just closed the door in his face, the plastic covering the broken glass rustling in the breeze.

Todd stood staring after her for several stunned seconds.

Then he turned, heading back down the steps, ready to confront his wife.

SIXTY-FOUR

"**O**h, no," Monica mumbled to herself, seeing Todd turn around on Jessie's porch and start heading back to their house.

She had been watching him over there, playing Sir Galahad, fixing Jessie's broken window and door. She'd seen their conversation even if she couldn't hear what was being said. She'd seen Todd take her sister's hands, and it had made her blood boil. She'd seen their tender embrace.

And then she'd seen Jessie back away, as if she'd just learned something from Todd that had upset her.

Monica knew it could only be one thing. The way Todd had turned around and headed down the front porch steps only confirmed it.

She grabbed her purse and her car keys and hurried out the door. She was backing out of the driveway as she spotted Todd round the corner of the house. He gestured for her to come back. But she pretended she didn't see him and just sped off down the road.

Monica knew a confrontation was inevitable. But she wasn't quite ready for it yet. She needed time to think of something to say. In her rearview mirror she could see Todd standing at the end of the driveway looking after her, but she just pressed her foot on the gas and got the hell out of Hickory Dell.

SIXTY-FIVE

The sun was dropping low in the sky as Jessie struggled to absorb the information about Monica and Todd. All these years . . . her sister had been deceiving her. She had been pregnant with Todd's child! Jessie wondered what had happened to the child. Part of her didn't want to know. She didn't want to learn anything that might make her feel sorry for her sister . . . like how difficult it must have been for a teenage girl to find out she was pregnant. Had she had an abortion? A miscarriage? Had they given the child away? Any of those scenarios would induce sympathy for Monica, and Jessie didn't want to feel sympathy. Right now she was angry with her sister, and she wanted to stay that way.

She knew it was childish. They'd both been teenagers, for God's sake. Jessie knew she'd forgive Monica eventually. But right now the pain felt fresh and real, as if Jessie was back in high school. She remembered how much it had hurt her when Todd had dumped her for Monica, and now she knew why. All of those old feelings came rushing back at her. She figured she needed to give herself some space to feel her anger and grief and her sense of betrayal.

A soft rapping came from the back door.

Jessie figured it was Todd coming back to apologize again, or maybe even Monica. But as she peered out into the dim light of dusk she could make out the figure of John Manning.

Somebody else she didn't want to see.

She opened the door only a crack.

"May I speak with you?" John asked.

Jessie smiled hard. "Need more information for your book?" she asked.

"So the chief did tell you." He frowned. "That's why I came over. To tell you everything."

"I already know, so don't bother."

"No, you don't know, Jessie. I didn't say anything about this before because I felt awkward. . . . I kept waiting for the right moment to tell you about the book, but so many terrible things kept happening. . . ."

"Yeah, they sure have, haven't they? And won't they make great plot points for your book! Well, here's another twist for you. Emil may still be alive."

John looked at her with those dark eyes of his, eyes that didn't seem all that surprised to hear the news.

"Please," he said, "may I come in?"

"No, you can say what you want right there," she told him, the door still only opened a crack. "And frankly, you only have about a minute more to say it."

"I never expected to get to know you, Jessie, to become your friend. You must believe that my overtures to you were not opportunistic. It was years ago that I got interested in Emil Deetz's crimes. Yes, my book bears some similarities to his story, but I was not attempting to get information from you. I'm writing a novel. It's not fact-based. I never meant to hurt you, Jessie, or for you to get the wrong idea. . . ."

"Look, John, I'm just a little tired of men keeping things from me, or having motivations I'm not certain about, or otherwise not being completely up-front. That's been the story of my life. So I just need a little break. So much has happened since I've returned, and now there's the possibility that Emil may be behind all of this. . . ."

"Why do you think Emil might behind it, Jessie?"

"Your minute's up," she said. "I'm not passing on any more information to you."

"But Jessie, I'm worried about you—"

"Thanks, but I can take care of myself. Talk to Chief Walters if you want to get your next plot twist."

She closed the door on his face. She was getting better at doing that.

All her life she'd let men tell her what to do. She'd lived by men's rules and because of it, too often she'd lived in fear.

Not anymore.

If Emil really had returned, Jessie would stand up to him.

And she'd do so on her own.

SIXTY-SIX

"Four days," Heather told Detective Harry Knotts, her voice level and calm. "Bryan hasn't come home for four days now. Hasn't shown up at work either."

The detective took all of the information down, and gave Heather a sympathetic furrow of his brow. But, in fact, Heather really didn't care if Bryan ever came home. Not after what she'd found hidden in his lockbox—which she'd forced open on day three of his absence.

"Let me ask you something, Mrs. Pierce," Knotts said, lifting his eyes from the paper where he'd been writing furiously. "And I apologize in advance if this sounds too personal, but I'll need to know if I'm going to fill out a missing-persons report."

"Go ahead, ask whatever you need to."

"Have you and your husband been having marital problems?"

She didn't hesitate. "Yes."

"So is it possible that he may have left you without telling you?"

"Absolutely it's possible." Heather leaned back in her chair and crossed her legs. She was wearing a short skirt and hoped Detective Knotts would glance down at her shapely calves, but he didn't. "What *isn't* very likely, however, is that he'd just blow off his job like this. He's already been having problems at the company. He wouldn't want to give them a reason to fire him."

"So he's been having problems at work, too?" Knotts scribbled this new bit of information down in the notepad in front of him.

Heather smiled wryly. "Oh, I think if you probe Bryan's life you'll find all sorts of problems."

"Any in particular you want to share?"

"You could start with Jessie Clarkson."

The detective's eyebrows shot up. "Jessie Clarkson?"

Heather nodded. "I think they were having an affair."

Knotts quickly wrote this down as well. "And why do you think that?"

"I have my reasons."

"And they are?"

Heather smirked. "He keeps nude photographs of Jessie with a pair of panties that must be hers in a locked box in his closet. Pretty good evidence, I think."

The detective didn't look up at her as he continued scribbling in his pad. "I note that your husband's disappearance apparently took place after a disturbance at Ms. Clarkson's home."

"It sure did." Heather sat forward in her chair. "She said she wasn't going to mention that, for the kids' sake, but I guess her word is as worthless as her reputation."

"She didn't report it," Knotts told her. "We learned

about it while we were establishing her whereabouts that night."

Heather's eyes narrowed in wonder. "Why would you need to establish her whereabouts?"

"That much I can't share, Mrs. Pierce."

Heather's mind raced, and then she hit on the answer. "Detective Wolfowitz! That was the night he was killed! You suspect Jessie!"

"We have no official suspects at this time, Mrs. Pierce."

Heather stood up, her eyes wild. "Bryan didn't just up and leave, Detective Knotts. He never came back home after the fight at Jessie's house. She called and told me all about it. And she told me who was there, who punched Bryan down the stairs!" She placed her hands on Knotts's desk and leaned in to look at him closely. "John Manning."

"Yes," Knotts said, looking back at her. He was no longer writing. "A man with whom *you* were having an affair, Mrs. Pierce."

Heather fell silent.

The detective smiled. "I told you some of my questions might get personal. If you want us to investigate your husband's disappearance, we need all the facts."

Heather stood up straight and buttoned her coat. She wasn't going to admit to that. If Bryan was really still alive, then he could use it against her in court. Their marriage was over, one way or another, but if Bryan was still in the land of the living, she wasn't going to make it easier for him to fight her. Heather figured she was already going to have a hard time getting much out of him, since it looked like Bryan would be losing his job.

She suppressed a smile. She'd be better off if he was dead. She'd get a nice fat insurance settlement in that case.

"That's all I have to say, Detective," Heather said, heading out the door. "Good luck in finding my husband."

Sixty-seven

Maxine Peterson told Abby she was doing very well learning her letters. The little girl was sitting cross-legged on the floor of her bedroom and picking wooden alphabet blocks out of a pile when her tutor called for a particular letter. She'd look through the blocks and then hand the correct one up to Maxine, who was sitting in a chair.

"Let's try one more," Maxine said. "How about . . . P?"

Abby studied the pile of blocks. She reached out her hand to hover over one block with a bright red R engraved on its side. But then she thought better of it and grabbed a block with a P. She triumphantly raised it to Maxine's hand.

"Excellent, Abby!" her tutor said. "You are such a smart girl! You're really doing so very, very well."

"Will I be able to go back to regular school soon then?" Abby asked, her round blue eyes looking imploringly up at Maxine.

"Do you *want* to go back to regular school?"

Abby nodded.

Her tutor smiled. "Tired of just playing with old Maxine, are you?"

"I like you very much," Abby said, "and I would miss you." She looked down at the floor sadly. "But I miss my friend."

Maxine's smile turned sad as well. "I'm sure you do, sweetheart. It must be hard not seeing any other children. Maybe sometime your friend could come here and visit. You could play with her here."

"It's not a girl," Abby said. "It's a boy."

"Oh?" Maxine's eyes lit up. "Well, then, *he* can come over and play sometime. I'm sure your mother wouldn't mind."

But Abby's sad expression seemed to suggest otherwise.

"What is your friend's name?" Maxine asked.

"Aaron," Abby told her.

"That's a nice name."

"He's my best friend in the whole world."

"Is he now? Well, then, he must be very nice."

"He is." Abby stood and walked over to the window, where she glanced out, as if she were looking for something. "If I had a brother, he would be just like Aaron."

Maxine smiled. "Well, I'll ask your mother if it'd be all right if Aaron joined us for one of our lessons one of these days. Would you like that?"

Abby turned to face her. "Oh, yes, very much!"

Maxine stood. "We're done for today, sweetheart. I'll see you tomorrow. Pretty soon we'll start building words with the letters we learn."

"I can't wait!" Abby exclaimed.

She turned to stare out the window again.

Maxine lifted her briefcase and headed out of the little girl's room. "Good-bye, Abby," she called.

But Abby seemed not to hear her. She just stood looking out the window.

Maxine descended the stairs.

In the living room she spotted Jessie with her aunt Paulette. The two women were sitting closely together on the couch, and appeared to be deep in conversation. Jessie looked upset, Maxine thought. Paulette's hand was placed on her back. Maxine hated to disturb what appeared to be an intense and personal family moment, but she had to let them know she was done for the day.

"Excuse me, Jessie," the tutor said. "Just wanted to say I'd see you tomorrow."

Jessie lifted very tired eyes to gaze across the room at her. "Okay, Maxine," she said. "Have a good night."

"Thanks, you too."

With what seemed superhuman effort, Jessie summoned a burst of energy and smiled over at Maxine. "Before you go, tell me how you think Abby's doing," she said.

"Oh, she's doing splendidly. You have one very smart daughter."

"I'm so glad to hear that."

"If I might, however, I'd like to suggest that maybe she see some other children. She told me today that she missed her friends from school."

Jessie's fragile smile disappeared. "Well, that was part of the problem. She didn't have any friends."

"She mentioned one boy's name. Aaron."

Maxine noticed the look that Jessie exchanged with her aunt.

"Oh, yes, Aaron," Jessie said.

"She said she missed seeing him, so I suggested he come by and join one of our lessons, if that was okay with you."

Jessie sighed. "Did Abby like the idea?"

"Oh, yes, very much. She seemed very fond of the boy."

"What did she say about him?"

"She said that he was her best friend in the world."

Jessie managed a small smile.

"Well, good night then," Maxine said. "I'll see you tomorrow."

"Yes. Have a good night, Maxine."

The tutor was almost to the door when she stopped and turned around. "Oh, and there was one other thing Abby said about her little friend."

"What was that?" Jessie asked.

"She said that if she had a brother, he would be just like Aaron."

The room was dark, with the shadows of late afternoon gathering, so Maxine couldn't be entirely sure what she saw. But she could have sworn that the expression that suddenly appeared on Jessie's face was no longer one of weariness, but of fear.

SIXTY-EIGHT

"Well, you're going to have to see each other eventually," Paulette said, her voice hard and on the edge of anger. "You're sisters and you live next door to one another."

Paulette had marched over to Monica's house after talking with Jessie. Her niece stood in her sleek, modern kitchen, with all its spun glass and shiny aluminum. The late-morning sun reflected off the polished granite of the countertops. The place was so large and cavernous that their voices echoed.

"No," Monica said firmly. "I can't see her yet."

Paulette took a deep breath and calmed herself. "Where's Todd?" she asked.

"He's left me! Don't you *understand*, Aunt Paulette? Todd has left me because of Jessie!"

The older woman folded her arms across her chest. "Karma's a bitch."

Monica laughed bitterly, and a little crazily. "Just like all the others, you take Jessie's side! Just like Mom, you've always preferred Jessie!"

"Damn it, Monica, I love you both. I just want to bring peace to this family."

"I can't see her," Monica whimpered, covering her face now with her hands.

"Where did Todd go?"

"I don't know," Monica mumbled. "When I came home, he was gone. He'd packed up most of his clothes. He hasn't called me at all."

"Odd that he should do that," Paulette said, her voice edged with sarcasm. "Why should he be angry with you? Hm? Have any idea, Monica?"

"Jessie must have told him something!" Monica poured herself a glass of wine—her second since Paulette had arrived. "She must have told him a lie about me! Something that would make him angry at me!"

"No, I think it was the other way around, Monica," Paulette said. "I think he told *her* the truth, and then her reaction told him everything he needed to know."

Monica took a long sip from her glass. "I don't know what you're talking about."

"I think you do, Monica. You were never pregnant, were you?"

Monica said nothing.

"You lied to Todd that you were in order to win him away from your sister. And then you lied again, telling him that you had told her and that she had asked you never to raise the issue again. That's why Todd acted as if Jessie already knew, and why he seemed so flabbergasted when it appeared that, in fact, she did not."

Monica set her wineglass down and looked Paulette directly in the eyes. "I *was* pregnant," she said forcefully. "I lost the baby."

"Oh, come on, Monica, I was with you when you went to the doctor a few years ago! Have you forgotten that? You asked me to go with you when you were starting your fertility treatments. I saw the reports that came back. I saw that you had never been pregnant— ever! In your entire life!"

Monica covered her ears with her hands.

"And I was there when you told the doctor that he must never share all the details of the report with Todd. I was curious then as to why, but you just said it was too difficult for Todd to talk about. Now I've figured out why you didn't want Todd to see the reports. Oh, yes, I can see your lie very clearly in my mind's eye!"

"Oh, please, spare me your mind's-eye supernatural hocus pocus!"

"I can see it, Monica! Deny it all you want, but I know what you did."

Monica stalked out of the kitchen. Paulette followed, close on her heels.

"Right now, at this very moment, Jessie is down at the police station, answering more questions about Bryan Pierce's disappearance. Ever since she's come back to town, she has faced crises and accusations, one right after another! She needs your support!"

"Goddamn it, Aunt Paulette!" Monica spun on her. "You're right that ever since she's returned, Jessie has faced crises! But they're all of her own making! It's all because of the bad choices she made when she took up with Emil Deetz!"

"Isn't it time you forgave her for that? And maybe in time she could forgive you about Todd."

Monica closed her eyes and turned away from Paulette.

"You think about it, my dear niece," Paulette told her, heading out of the house. "You think about how you want to put things rights—with your sister *and* your husband."

She left Monica standing there in the middle of the living room, the younger woman's eyes closed and her fists clenched tightly at her side.

SIXTY-NINE

"**B**ryan was drunk," Jessie told Chief Walters plainly. "Very drunk and very aggressive and no, he didn't give me any indication that he might be going away or leaving his wife."

She sat stiffly in a chair in front of the chief's desk. Sitting next to her was a calm, mostly silent John Manning. When she'd walked in to Walters's office and seen John already there, she'd given him only a small nod in greeting. They'd both been called down for further questioning about Bryan's disappearance, but so far it had only been Jessie on the receiving end of Walters's questions. She suspected the chief had already questioned John; she was trying to determine if their stories were the same.

Walters appeared to be satisfied, at least for the moment. "Given the recent murders in town," the chief said, "the state's attorney's office in Stamford is investigating Mr. Pierce's disappearance for any connections. I'm trying to gather as much information as I can to share with them. Don't be surprised if you hear from them. I'm certain they'll want to hear what you have to say about this, as well as the three murders."

"Are we still under suspicion for those?" John asked with a sigh.

Chief Walters leveled her steely blue eyes at him. "As far as I'm concerned, Mr. Manning, everyone is under suspicion until definitively proven innocent."

"I defer to your investigative prowess," John said, seeming to enjoy the sarcasm.

"The reason I've asked the two of you here at the same time," Walters said, ignoring the comment, "is to inquire what Ms. Clarkson thinks about you, Mr. Manning, keeping a dossier on Emil Deetz and the murder of Screech Solek."

"Oh, yes, I meant to thank you for your discretion, Chief," John said. More sarcasm.

Jessie felt her cheeks burn. "We've already discussed this," she told Walters.

"No," the chief corrected her. "You reacted with disbelief when I told you. I assume you've confirmed it with Mr. Manning?"

"Yes," Jessie admitted. "I confirmed it."

"And what were your feelings about his literary endeavor?"

"I wasn't pleased."

"Let me ask you another question. Do you believe he's writing a book?"

"Well, that's what he said . . ." Jessie's voice trailed off. Suddenly she wasn't sure what she believed. She could sense John beside her, feel his eyes on her, but she wouldn't look at him. Was the chief insinuating that John might have been gathering information on Emil not because he was writing a book, but because he was in cahoots with him?

"Well?" the chief asked again. "Do you believe that he's writing a book?"

"Yes," Jessie said finally, in a small voice. "I believe him."

The chief wrote something down in a notebook.

"But this is just a side show," Jessie said, sitting forward in her chair. "I might be angry at John for my own reasons, but he didn't kill all those people. What I want to know, Chief, is have you found any trace of Emil?"

Walters dropped her eyes to the desk, not meeting Jessie's gaze. "No," she said. "We haven't."

"Have you even *looked*?"

"I'm not at liberty to share all the details of our investigation, Ms. Clarkson, especially now with the state's attorney involved."

Jessie shook her head. "Emil is the only one who could have done these killings."

"The only one?" Now Walters looked up and found Jessie's eyes. "I've been a police officer for a long time. I've learned that anyone is capable of murder."

"Including yourself?" John asked her.

The chief smiled defiantly. "Under the right circumstances, anyone could commit murder."

"Please keep looking for Emil," Jessie said. "At first when my aunt told me she'd seen him, I was inclined to disbelieve her. But now, with so many dead, all of them with their throats slit, I can only believe that Emil is alive, and he is doing this to terrorize me."

The chief closed a file on her desk. "Thank you for your suggestion, Ms. Clarkson. But for now the next step is in the hands of the state's attorney. I appreciate you both coming in today. That's all for now. You can go."

John stood, but Jessie stayed seated. "Chief," she said. "I wonder if you could answer a question for me now."

Walters lifted an eyebrow in her direction. "If I can."

"Is there a family named Smelt living in town?"

"Smelt?" Walters repeated. "I've never heard the name. Why do you ask?"

"Abby has a little friend by the name of Aaron Smelt. He doesn't go to school, and I'm not sure where he lives. I looked in the phone book and online, but I found no one by that name in Sayer's Brook, or any surrounding town, in fact. I just wondered if you knew anything about the family."

"No," Walters told her. "Never heard the name before."

Jessie sighed. "Well, it was worth a shot."

"All right then," the chief said. "Thank you both for coming in."

Jessie stood, and only then was she aware of how intently John was looking at her. As she filed out of the chief's office, she felt John's eyes on her. She tried to move quickly down the hallway, but suddenly John's hand was on her shoulder. Jessie stopped walking.

"I don't blame you for being angry," John said.

"Good. Because I am."

"Please, Jessie. Would you have coffee with me? Just a few minutes, so we could talk?"

"I have to get back home."

"Fifteen minutes."

Jessie turned and looked up at him. "John, I told you. I need some time—"

"Does the child trouble you somehow?"

"The child?"

"This boy. Abby's friend. The one named Smelt."

Jessie hesitated. "It was just that I was curious about him."

"Have coffee with me," John said. "I think there's something you should know."

SEVENTY

Maxine sat on the back porch watching Abby play on her swings. She'd gotten a call from Jessie saying she'd be a little late getting back from town. Could Maxine stay and watch Abby for just a little longer? She'd pay her overtime. Maxine had told her not to worry about that. She was glad to stay.

It was a lovely autumn day to sit on the porch. There wouldn't be many more days like this with winter waiting just around the corner. The sun was high and warm and felt good on Maxine's face. After she and Abby had finished their lessons, Maxine had told the little girl she could play in the backyard until her mother got home. The tutor settled into the wicker rocking chair and enjoyed an unexpected bit of relaxation in the middle of the day. Watching Abby swing up and down, her little feet pointing out in front of her, her blond pigtails flying in the wind, almost lulled Maxine to sleep.

But then suddenly Abby shouted out in excitement. "My friend! My friend!"

The little girl jumped off the swing, her face lit up with joy. Through the tall yellow grass a small boy came walking. Maxine watched him closely. He was a dark-haired, dark-eyed child whose gaze was fixed on Abby. He wore a dirty T-shirt and a pair of dungarees, and he was barefoot.

"Aaron!" Abby was shouting. "You've come back!"

She ran through the grass to meet him. Maxine stood, watching. She saw Abby take the boy's hand and lead him back toward the swing set.

"Abby!" Maxine called. "Don't leave the yard."

"I won't," she called back. "Maxine, this is my friend Aaron. Can he play on the swings with me?"

"*May* he play on the swings with you," Maxine corrected, smiling.

"May he play?" Abby tried again.

"I don't see why not," Maxine replied. "Hello, Aaron."

"Hello," he called over, lifting his little hand to wave at Maxine.

What an adorable little boy, Maxine thought. She settled back into her rocking chair. Although she recalled Jessie's uneasy expression when she'd heard the boy's name, Maxine thought no one could object to the children playing together when Abby looked so happy. And after all, Maxine reasoned, they were only swinging. Surely no harm could come from that.

SEVENTY-ONE

As they headed out of the front door of the police station, Jessie and John ran straight into Heather Pierce. Her face looked as if she'd been sucking on a lemon.

"Well, well," Heather said, glancing at the two of them. "Fancy meeting the two of you here at police headquarters."

"Hello, Heather," Jessie said.

John remained silent.

"What were you here for?" Heather asked, a mock smile spreading across her face. "The police still questioning you about Bryan's disappearance?"

"I've told them everything I know," Jessie said. "I'm sorry that it had to come to this, Heather. As I told you on the phone, I didn't want to go to the police."

"Bullshit," Heather snarled. "Why don't you admit the truth, Jessie? You were having an affair with Bryan. You came back here and went after him the first moment you could—at that party you threw, in fact. I saw it!"

"That's absurd, Heather."

"Is it?" She suddenly snapped open the purse that hung over her shoulder and whipped out a pair of silk panties, tossing them at Jessie. "Those are yours! Don't deny it! I found them in our room! With naked photos of you!"

"Naked photos?" Jessie was horrified.

"Oh, yes, very naked." Heather now produced an old Polaroid from her purse, flashing it in front of Jessie. "You see, I have evidence!"

"Let me see that!" Jessie exclaimed.

"No!" Heather retorted, holding the photo out of reach like a taunting schoolgirl on the playground.

"If that's me, then it's from a very long time ago. I haven't had hair that long since . . ." Her voice trailed off. "Since college . . ."

The likelihood that the photo was, indeed, her struck Jessie like a body blow.

"Bryan must have taken it when I was asleep," she said, the horror creeping over her. "Give that to me!"

"Nope," Heather said, replacing the Polaroid in her purse. "As I said, evidence."

"Now I really *will* press charges against Bryan!" Jessie declared. "Taking obscene pictures of me without my consent!"

"And the panties?" Heather asked. "How do you explain them? They're *yours*, aren't they? And it doesn't look like *they're* from college."

"Someone broke into my house and went through my drawers."

"Hah! Likely story!"

"I was *not* having an affair with Bryan," Jessie said severely.

"Come on, let's get out of here," John said, putting his arm around Jessie.

Heather saw the gesture, and exploded. "Oh, now I

get it! You're sleeping with John, too!" Her face twisted in rage. "Now I understand everything! Now I understand why you wouldn't see me anymore, John!" She returned her focus to Jessie. "You really wanted revenge on me, didn't you, Jessie Clarkson? You goddamn tramp!"

"Now, that's enough!" John said, stepping in between the two women. "Heather, you're completely out of line."

Heather turned a pair of burning eyes in his direction. "Out of line? I'll tell you who's out of line, Mr. Manning." She jabbed her finger against John's chest. "Maybe when you found out Jessie was sleeping with Bryan, *you* killed him! Just like you killed your wife and that German girl!"

"Let's get out of here," John said, taking Jessie by the arm and hurrying her down the street. "We don't need to listen to the rantings of a crazy woman."

"Crazy, am I?" Heather called after them. "We'll see how crazy I am when I give the state's attorney this evidence!"

John and Jessie hurried down the street.

SEVENTY-TWO

Abby pumped the air with her little legs as hard as she could, struggling to keep up with Aaron on the swing beside her, who seemed to reach the sky each time he flew by.

"How can you get so high?" Abby asked.

"It's easy," Aaron said. "I can show you how."

"Please do!"

"But you won't want to do it," Aaron said, whizzing past her. "Because you're a scaredy cat."

"I'm not a scaredy cat!"

"You were a scaredy cat the night in the barn. You wouldn't jump!"

"That's only because my mother was there. She wouldn't let me!"

Aaron dropped one of his feet to the ground, breaking the momentum of his swinging, and dragged himself to a stop. Abby did the same, stirring up a sudden cloud of dust and soil.

"If you're really brave, Abby, I have lots more special, secret places I can show you," Aaron said, his big round brown eyes shining.

"I can't wait!" Abby exclaimed.

"But you can't be such a scaredy cat this time."

"I won't be!"

Aaron smiled. "Do you promise you will not be scared and follow me wherever I take you?"

"I promise!"

"Good," Aaron said, and he began swinging again. "Because if you're a scaredy cat again, I'll go away and never come back to play with you again."

Abby certainly didn't want that. She had missed Aaron too much to lose him again.

"I won't be scared," she promised, and struggled once more to swing as high as he could.

SEVENTY-THREE

Chief Belinda Walters looked across her desk at the square-shaped face of Patrick Castile, who'd shown up with an air of brisk, emotionless authority from the FBI. The state's attorney's office had phoned her, explaining that the federal agency needed to be brought into the case. Walters was entrusted with bringing the agent up to date.

"So this Heather Pierce has made allegations that Jessie Clarkson was having an affair with her husband?" Castile asked.

Walters nodded, pushing the nude photograph of Jessie across her desk so that Castile could inspect it. She didn't like touching it, so she just edged the Polaroid forward with her fingernails.

"Problem is," the chief told Castile, "it's probably a decade old. Anyone can see that Jessie is a lot younger in that photo. Heather sees what she wants to see, however."

Castile made no expression as he glanced down at the photograph, nor did he pick it up to examine it. "I don't have any interest in the rantings of a scorned wife," he said dismissively. "Bryan Pierce may be alive and well, living in Tahiti or someplace. There's no evidence his disappearance has anything to do with the murders that have been taking place in Sayer's Brook."

"I agree," Walters said. "But the connections are worth investigating."

Castile made no response, so whether he agreed or disagreed, the chief couldn't tell. The FBI agent was a young man, probably not much older than thirty, with a short blond crew cut and drooping shoulders. His questioning of Walters so far had centered around why Jessie had returned to Sayer's Brook, and her connections to Emil Deetz. He had seemed particularly intrigued by Walters's statement that Paulette Drew had claimed to have seen Deetz, and that was the topic he returned to now.

"I'd like to interview this Drew woman," Castile said. "She lives on Hickory Dell as well, behind Ms. Clarkson?"

"Yes," the chief told him. "But let me point out, Mr. Castile, that Paulette Drew is hardly a reliable person. She's a fortune-teller."

"I understand that."

"Frankly, in my view, I think we need to question John Manning further. The dossier he kept on Deetz and the excessive attention he's been showing to Jessie—rather aggressively insinuating himself in her life—is very suspicious, in my opinion."

Castile lifted a thin eyebrow in her direction. "This was the line of investigation pursued by the late Detective Wolfowitz, wasn't it, Chief Walters?"

"Yes," she admitted. "It was."

"A line of investigation you were skeptical of at the time, if the notes I've reviewed are correct."

"I was merely trying to get Wolfie to stay on protocol."

"I find it interesting that you are now championing his theory. Are you doing so out of some sense of loyalty to your fallen comrade?"

Walters frowned. "I don't like the insinuation that I'm not basing my investigation on facts."

"You know as well as I do, Chief, that one has to consider everything. No question is off-limits."

"I never disagreed with Wolfie that Manning was a person of interest in this case. And it just seems the more that happens, the more interesting he becomes. He had a fight with Bryan Pierce, and after that, Pierce disappears."

Castile gave her a rare, small smile. "But there's no evidence yet that Pierce's disappearance is even connected to this case."

"The key word, Mr. Castile, is yet."

The FBI agent's smile faded. "Well, I think I have everything I need for now. But I'm certain we will have many more conversations."

"All right," the chief said.

Castile stood. "Thank you for all your work and your advice, Chief Walters."

She nodded.

She did not like this man.

SEVENTY-FOUR

Jessie and John were sitting in a small coffee shop in town at a table near the back. After the altercation with Heather, they'd walked for a while so that Jessie could cool down. She'd been horrified by the photo of herself that Bryan had taken. She felt violated, sick to her stomach. John had assured her that Chief Walters would never allow the photo to be made public, and that he was certain she would recognize it was an old shot. Jessie shouldn't worry that it would be used against her in any way. If anything, it just made Bryan look worse.

"Thank you, John," Jessie had said. "Your words have helped."

After walking for what seemed to be a mile, they'd come into this café, where a couple of old ladies who had lacquered bouffants and were sitting in a booth up front had seemed to recognize them. The biddies had begun to immediately whisper under the breaths. Neither John nor Jessie had commented on it as they'd found their table in back. They ordered their coffees and sat there drinking them, mostly in silence for the first ten minutes. Jessie had let her mind go numb, still exhausted by the scene with Heather. At last John jarred her back into consciousness.

"Jessie," he said, "I'm not going to write the book."

She said nothing in return, just looked at him.

"I need you to understand that I wasn't using our friendship for the purposes of gaining information," John continued. "I didn't intend to pursue a friendship with you. If anything, the day I first met you, at your picnic, I tried to be cordial but also to keep a certain distance."

Jessie remembered that. She recalled now her ridiculous, childish envy when it had been Inga that John had seemed interested in.

"I'm scrapping everything I've written," John told her. "It's not worth it if it comes between our friendship."

"I can't ask you to do that," Jessie said quietly.

"You're not asking me. I'm telling you it's what I'm doing."

"No," she said. "I can see now that you weren't using me for information. And the book is fiction, as you say. It's not about me."

"My mind is made up, Jessie."

"Look, John. What really concerned me was the possibility that you might somehow have some connection to Emil. . . . That was what I feared deep down. That you were somehow . . . involved with him."

John closed his eyes and rubbed his temples.

"I was scared," Jessie said. "But I believe you, John. You were just writing a book, and you never intended to exploit our friendship. And it's not fair to you to have to stop working on a project just because we've become friends."

John's eyes popped open. "The matter is closed, Jessie. I've already permanently deleted it from my computer."

"Oh, John . . ." Jessie struggled for the right words. "I appreciate the gesture very much. But it seems too much. How could you delete all that work?"

"Easy. I just dragged the file to the trash."

"You must have backups."

"Jessie, I destroyed it all."

"Oh, John . . ."

Those deep dark eyes of his searched her out. "I can't profit off something that might take advantage of the pain of someone that I care about."

Jessie was silent. Finally, very softly, she said, "Thank you, John."

He reached across the table and took her hand in his. "But that wasn't all I wanted to talk to you about, Jessie. I wanted to ask you about the boy."

"You mean Abby's friend."

"Yes."

"What could you possibly know about Aaron?"

"What did you say his last name was?"

"Smelt," Jessie told him. "Aaron Smelt."

She saw the look cross John's face. "Spell it for me," he said.

Jessie complied.

John sat back in his chair. "Jessie . . . does that name mean anything to you?"

"Well," she admitted, "when I was pregnant with Abby, I discovered I was carrying twins. I lost one of the twins in a miscarriage eventually, but I had been planning on naming the boy Aaron."

This seemed to surprise John. "A rather eerie coincidence," he said.

"Yes. I felt tremendous guilt after the miscarriage, because I'd been wishing I wasn't carrying a boy, just a girl. I didn't want a boy who might grow up to be like Emil."

"That's a natural feeling."

"Still . . . when a little boy named Aaron showed up in Abby's life, it freaked me out a little," Jessie admitted.

"But didn't his last name trouble you too?" John asked.

Jessie shook her head. "Why would it?"

"Does 'Smelt' have any relevance to you?"

"No," Jessie told him. "That's why I asked Chief Walters about it."

"Then you didn't know that . . ." John hesitated, then continued. "You didn't know that Smelt was the maiden name of Emil Deetz's mother?"

Jessie's blood instantly ran cold.

"I see from your expression you didn't," John said. "You see, I had done some research on Emil when I was planning the book. I obtained his birth certificate. I remembered the mother's name because I had attempted to track down family . . . cousins and the like. I didn't have any success."

"Emil barely knew his parents," Jessie said. "He was abandoned."

John nodded. He apparently was aware of the facts of Emil's life.

"So Smelt was Aaron's mother's name?" Jessie asked, as if the full force of the news was just hitting her. "That seems too much of a coincidence."

"Did Emil know you were planning on naming his son Aaron?"

Jessie shook her head. "He never even knew that I was pregnant. I hadn't yet told him when . . . when I saw him commit the murder."

"Might he have found out?"

"I suppose . . ." Jessie shuddered. "What are you thinking, John?"

"I'm thinking that maybe your aunt was correct that she saw him. I'm thinking that it might well be true that Emil is alive."

Jessie eyed him cagily. "Why do you think so?"

"I don't know. A gut feeling, maybe."

For a moment, Jessie's doubts resurfaced. *Is there a connection between John and Emil? Why is he suddenly so convinced that Emil is alive?*

John seemed to read her mind. "It's just that . . . well, your aunt's report of seeing someone who looked like Emil, combined with the a boy named Smelt showing up seemingly out of nowhere, has led me to at least consider the possibility that Emil is alive, and that he's back in Sayer's Brook."

"I guess that does make sense," Jessie said.

"And might Emil be trying to torment you in more ways than one . . . the murders . . . and arranging for a boy to spend time with Abby, reminding you of your miscarriage?"

Jessie shuddered again. "I wouldn't put it past him."

"We need to talk with this boy, find out his story," John said. "He could lead us to Emil."

Jessie was aware that he was using the pronoun "us," and she liked it. She took a sip of her coffee, allowing its warmth to calm her nerves. "Perhaps I should tell Chief Walters about this," she said. "About the coincidence of names."

"Eventually," John said. "But she seems disinclined to take the idea of Emil being alive seriously. I suspect . . ." His voice trailed off for a second before he continued. "I suspect the FBI agent, if he contacts us, may be more interested in what we have to say."

"Why do you suspect that?"

"Just a hunch." He smiled and took Jessie's hand in his again. "But for the time being, the next time that boy comes around your house, I'd suggest you pin him down, and find out as much as you can about him."

Jessie agreed.

She was very happy that she and John were friends again.

SEVENTY-FIVE

"I was beginning to worry about you," Mr. Thayer said, stepping aside from his front door so that Todd, carrying a suitcase, could enter.

"I'm sorry," Todd told the old man. "I needed the time away. I kept in touch with the office by phone and by iPad."

"I don't mean that I was worried about business," Thayer said, shutting the door behind him. "I meant on a personal level, Todd. I wish you had come to me before you ran off. I thought we were better friends than that."

Todd frowned. "I'm sorry. Really I am. It's just that . . . I needed some time by myself to think. I went out and stayed at my brother's place in Montauk." He set his suitcase down. "But it's okay that I stay here now for a few nights? Just until my apartment in the city is available?"

"Of course." Mr. Thayer gave him a terribly sad face. "So you're really certain you want to leave Monica?"

"Our marriage has been deteriorating for years," Todd told him. "Now I understand why. It was founded on a lie. Monica was never pregnant—in her entire life. I spoke with our doctor. I asked him directly. He hemmed and hawed, blathering on about doctor-patient confidentiality . . . but that alone told me what I needed to know. I could see from his face that he knew Monica had never been pregnant."

"I'm so sorry, Todd."

Todd looked out the window, down the darkening street toward the home he'd shared with Monica. He spotted Jessie's car as it rattled past Mr. Thayer's house and turned into her driveway.

He pulled away from the window and looked over at Mr. Thayer. "I never stopped loving Jessie," he said. "That's clear to me now. And somehow . . . I need her to know that. If only it wasn't too late to change things."

SEVENTY-SIX

"**I**'m sorry it took me so long, Maxine," Jessie was saying, as she hurried out of her car. "Thank you so much for staying."

Maxine smiled. "Not a problem at all."

"Everything okay with Abby today?" Jessie asked.

The tutor's smiled broadened as she opened her car door. "Oh, yes. After our lessons, she played on the swings. And that little friend came by and joined her."

"Little friend?"

Maxine slid in behind the wheel. "Yes. The one she mentioned. Aaron."

Jessie approached Maxine's car and looked down at her intently. "Did you meet him?"

"Oh, yes. What an adorable little boy."

"What did they do?"

"They just swung on the swings. Then, when it started getting a little dark, I told Abby she ought to go inside and wash up for supper. Aaron waved good-bye and went on his way home."

"Which way did he walk?"

Maxine gestured with her head. "Over there. Through

the woods. I assume he must live in one of those new houses over there."

"Yes," Jessie said, her voice soft.

"I'll see you on Monday, Jessie," Maxine said, starting her car. "Have a lovely weekend."

"Yes, thank you," Jessie said, her voice still far away and distracted. "You too."

As Maxine backed out of the driveway, Jessie hurried into the house.

She found Abby upstairs, in the bathroom. The little girl had just finished washing her face and hands and was brushing her shiny blond hair in front of the mirror.

"Hi, Mommy!" Abby chirped when she spotted her mother's reflection behind her.

"Hello, baby," Jessie said, kissing her daughter on the top of her head. "Did you have a good day with Maxine?"

"I sure did!"

"I understand Aaron came over to play."

In the mirror Jessie saw Abby's blue eyes dart up to her, as if she worried her mother might be angry. But Jessie just gave her a smile.

"I hope you two had fun," she said.

"Oh, we did, Mommy. We played on the swings."

"You know, Abs," Jessie said, stroking the girl's hair, "I was thinking. If Aaron comes over tomorrow, maybe we can have a cookout."

"That would be great, Mommy!"

Jessie smiled, looking up from her daughter to meet her own eyes in the mirror. "I'd like to get know Aaron better," she said. "In fact, I want to learn all there is to know about him."

SEVENTY-SEVEN

Heather could hear the kids arguing from down the hall, but she paid them no mind. The last thing she wanted to deal with tonight was Piper and Ashton's brattiness. She wasn't happy that she would have to deal with them entirely on her own for the next few days—and that included Halloween, much to her regret—since Consuela was off visiting her ailing sister in Rochester, New York. In a burst of generosity, Heather had let her faithful housekeeper-assistant take her car for the six-hour trip. Her Beemer was certainly more reliable than Consuela's old Nissan.

In the interim, Heather could use Bryan's car. His Porsche Panamera had been sitting in the garage ever since he disappeared. Wherever Bryan was, he didn't seem to need wheels.

Heather passed the door to Piper's room. She heard a loud crash from inside, and then her daughter's shrill voice: "You broke the lamp!"

Then her son's: "No, *you* broke it!"

Heather just sighed and continued down the hall.

Before Consuela had left, the kids had squirted dish detergent all over the slick marble floor in the foyer, causing the housekeeper to slip and fall hard on her butt. Piper and Ashton had run away laughing hysterically. Consuela, used to such pranks, had just gotten up and continued on her way, her dignity unruffled. Heather had observed the scene from the living room. She really should punish the brats, but she was too exhausted to deal with it at the moment. She'd get on their case in the morning. Right now all she wanted to do was get to bed.

In her room, Heather undressed, trying to block all unpleasant thoughts from her mind. She wouldn't think about the kids, or Bryan, or John, or that damn Jessie. She would just think of herself tonight. No one had it as hard as she did. She ran this house, raised those incorrigible kids, ran a successful business, and dealt with an unfaithful pervert of a husband. She would have loved a bubble bath this evening, but Heather was too tired even for that. So she slipped into her black satin negligee—which John had once so admired on her—and stood looking at herself in her bathroom mirror. She figured she still had what it took. She'd forget John eventually, and once she was free of Bryan, she could get another man easily.

Heather smiled. Maybe, in fact, she was *already* free of Bryan. Maybe John had taken care of that.

It galled Heather to think that John and Jessie were involved. That was the only explanation for why John had so abruptly ended his and Heather's relationship.

"I could get him back," Heather whispered to herself, lowering her eyes to gaze upon her full breasts in the negligee. "I could definitely get him back."

She giggled a little, then turned and shut the light off in the bathroom.

Her bedroom was dark. Heather had pulled the light-blocking curtains tightly so not even a hint of moon-light might penetrate the room. The only light in the entire place came from the small clock on the bedside table, with the numbers 9:59 glowing green. From down the hall Heather could still hear the muffled voices of her kids. She should really tell them to get to bed, but at the moment she just didn't care. Feeling around on her bureau, Heather found the remote for her iPod, which was docked across the room. She powered it on. Instantly the sounds of Stevie Wonder filled the dark room. *Isn't she lovely. . . . Isn't she wonderful. . . .*

Heather smiled and slipped into bed.

She wondered briefly if Bryan and Jessie had ever had sex right here, in her own bed. The thought re-volted her, but she figured it was unlikely. Despite what she had told Chief Walters, Heather didn't really be-lieve that Jessie and Bryan had been carrying on an af-fair. That photograph wasn't recent. It probably came from their college days, and Bryan, the perv, had prob-ably snapped it while Jessie was asleep. But if Heather could stir up trouble for Jessie, she was only glad to do so. The bitch deserved it after stealing John away from her.

Heather yawned, stretching out in the bed.

Her right arm touched something.

What was that?

The room was so dark that it was difficult to see even a few inches in front of her face. Heather stretched her arm out again across the king-size bed. She felt nothing but air. Maybe she'd imagined it.

But there was a warmth. . . .

And . . . movement.

And . . . breathing!

Someone was in the bed with her.

"Who—?" Heather blurted, reaching up with her left hand to find the lamp.

But she never did. The next thing Heather knew there was someone right beside her, breathing in her ear. The darkness prevented her from seeing a thing, but she certainly felt the cold blade that was suddenly pressed against her throat, and then the warm blood that splattered all over her face and filled up her lungs, leaving her unable to cry out, or even breathe.

SEVENTY-EIGHT

Someone was calling Ashton's name.

The little boy paused in mid-throw—he had an ashtray in his hand, as he was preparing to lob it at his sister's head—and listened.

"Ashton! Ashton!"

Someone was downstairs, calling his name.

"Hey," the boy said, dropping the ashtray. "Whose voice is that?"

"I don't know," Piper said. "But whoever it is, they're calling me."

Ashton frowned. "You mean, they're calling *me*."

"No," his sister insisted. "They're calling *me*. They're saying, 'Piper! Piper!' "

"They're saying, 'Ashton! Ashton!' "

"They are not!"

He was about ready to pick up the ashtray again when the voice resumed.

"Who is it?" Ashton asked, heading out of the room and down the hall.

"I don't know," Piper replied, close on his heels.

It wasn't their mother. As they passed the door to their mother's, they could see it was dark inside, and music was playing. Their mother was apparently sound asleep. The voice wasn't Consuela's either, and it certainly wasn't their father's. It was hard to tell if it was a boy's voice or a girl's voice. But it kept calling to them.

The two children paused at the top of the stairs and looked down.

"Maybe we should wake Mother," Piper suggested.

"No, she'd just get mad," Ashton said.

They listened. The voice was calling them again. It seemed, Ashton thought, to be coming from the kitchen.

"Who's there?" Ashton called down the stairs.

The only answer he heard was, "Ashton! Ashton!"

The voice was becoming more urgent now.

"I'm going down," the boy announced.

"Why are *you* going down?" his sister asked. "They're calling *me*!"

"They are not! They're calling *me*!"

"I'll beat you down there!" Piper shouted.

"Oh no, you won't!"

The two of them began racing down the stairs.

They never saw the wire that was stretched across the staircase halfway down. They barely even felt it. They only knew that suddenly they were airborne, that instead of running down the stairs, they were now plunging down them head first. There was a brief sensation of somersaulting through the air—their feet above their heads—and then came the final thud against the marble floor. The last thing both Ashton and Piper heard was the surprisingly loud snap of their necks.

Ashton's last thought before he died was that his sister was lying on top of him, and he wanted to slug her for that. But at least he had a split second of satisfaction that he'd beaten her down the stairs.

SEVENTY-NINE

"This is what they call Indian summer," Aunt Paulette said, arriving with pumpkin and apple pies.

It was a beautifully warm, sunny day. The leaves might be off the trees, but otherwise it felt like a day in August instead of October. Jessie watched Abby and Aaron play on the swings. The boy had shown up early. How he'd known they'd have a cookout Jessie didn't know. He'd seemed to just intuit that he'd be welcome today, that Jessie would want him to come by. He didn't say much, but smiled a little, obviously pleased, when Jessie asked him to stay for supper. She'd called Aunt Paulette and asked her to bake some pies. Now she was firing up the grill, one eye always on the children on the swings. Their laughter reassured her. Watching the kids play, Jessie had come to the conclusion that there was nothing to fear from Aaron. Whether he was somehow in league with Emil, she was still unsure. But the boy himself was darling.

"Jessie," Aunt Paulette said, setting the pies on the picnic table. "I hope you don't mind, but I've asked Monica to come by as well."

Jessie shot her an angry glance. "I *do* mind, Aunt Paulette. I don't want to get into any heavy discussions with Monica today."

"No heavy discussions," her aunt assured her. "Just let her have a hamburger with us. She's very upset about everything that's happened."

Jessie just grumbled under breath.

"Mommy," Abby called from the swings. "We're hungry!"

"Okay," Jessie called back. "How many burgers can you eat?"

"I can eat a hundred!" Abby said, laughing.

"I can eat two hundred!" Aaron added, his face lit up by a big smile.

Jessie laughed. "I'll make you each two," she said. "And if you want another, I'll throw another patty on the grill."

"He's very cute," Aunt Paulette whispered, drawing close to Jessie.

"Adorable," Jessie agreed.

She looked up. Her sister was coming up the hill, carrying a bowl. Jessie dropped her eyes to the grill. She really wished Aunt Paulette hadn't invited her. She wasn't ready to face Monica just yet. All those years ago, Monica had deliberately stolen Todd from her. Deliberately broken her heart. And she'd done so through trickery. Jessie knew Monica resented so much about her. She was jealous of her relationship with Mom, with the teachers at school. She figured Monica's theft of Todd—and her terrible lie—had been her way of having revenge. And while it all may have been a long time ago, it would still take some time for Jessie to forgive her sister. She didn't want to be hard or cruel. She knew that Monica was going through a rough time now that Todd had left her. But the fact was, Jessie was still hurt by what Monica had done. It would just take time.

"Hello, Jessie," Monica said.

"Hello."

"I made a tossed salad."

"It looks delicious," Aunt Paulette said, taking the salad bowl from Monica and placing it on the picnic table next to the pies. "Are these the last of the fresh tomatoes from the garden?"

"Yes," Monica said. "I picked them this morning."

Jessie thought her sister didn't seem sorry at all. She stood there rather haughtily, smiling, pretending nothing was wrong.

"Who's the boy?" Monica asked.

"That's Aaron," Aunt Paulette informed her. "Oh, Abby! Come over and introduce Aaron to your Aunt Monica."

The children jumped off the swings and ran across the grass. Abby's blond hair was tied in two ponytails on the side of her head, and they flopped like bunny ears as she ran. Aaron's dark eyes were bright and shining. He seemed far more animated than ever before. He was barefoot as always, and his clothes were still slightly soiled and wrinkled. But he seemed a different boy. No longer mysterious or quiet, he was smiling and laughing. When the children reached the adults, they stopped running and looked up at them with bright, happy faces.

"Hello, Aaron," Monica said.

"Hello!" the boy responded enthusiastically.

"Where do you live?" she asked.

"Over there!" he chirped, pointing toward the woods.

"Don't you own any shoes?" Monica asked.

"Nope," Aaron replied.

Jessie overheard, and stepped forward. "Oh, come now, Aaron. You must have shoes at home."

"No," he insisted.

Jessie exchanged a look with Aunt Paulette.

"May I please have three hamburgers?" the boy asked.

"I told you if you eat both of the ones I'm grilling for you, I'll make you another."

"I will eat both of them!"

"All right," Jessie said.

The children ran back to the swings.

"Is the kid really that poor?" Monica asked. "No shoes and his parents don't feed him?"

"He does seem rather neglected," Aunt Paulette observed. "His clothes are quite dirty."

Jessie returned to the grill and flipped the burgers. "Well, if he's hungry," she said, "we're going to make sure he leaves here with a full belly."

The kid did indeed wolf down both of his hamburgers, and asked for a third, which Jessie happily made for him. After that, he had two slices of pie, one pumpkin and one apple. He was smiling and laughing the whole time.

As Abby helped Monica and Aunt Paulette clear off the table and carry the leftovers into the house, Jessie sat down at the picnic table opposite Aaron, who was finishing the last of his pie. "Aaron," she said, "I'd like to see where you live. Will you show me sometime?"

"Sure," he chirped.

Jessie leveled her eyes at him. "That would be okay? Would your parents like to meet me?"

She was testing him, of course, trying to see if he might give away a clue about Emil, if in fact he was somehow in cahoots with him.

"I don't have parents," Aaron said. Suddenly his high spirits evaporated. His smile disappeared; the light in his eyes dimmed. He just sat there at the picnic table, staring at his plate.

"Who do you live with then?" Jessie asked the boy.

Aaron didn't reply. He just looked up at her with his big brown eyes.

"I wish I had a mommy like you," he said.

Jessie's heart melted.

"Mommy!" Abby called. "Can me and Aaron color now?"

Jessie looked up. "You should say, 'Aaron and I.' "

"Okay. Can Aaron and I color?"

Jessie smiled, deciding against correcting her further about using "may" instead of "can"—for the moment, anyway. "Would you like to color, Aaron?" she asked.

"Sure!" the boy answered.

She walked with him up to the house. In the kitchen, Abby had brought out sheets of papers and her box of crayons, setting them on the table. Aaron came into the room and immediately his eyes were drawn to the family picture Abby had rendered at school. He stood in front of the refrigerator staring at the stick figures of Abby's family. His expression was intense.

Jessie stooped down beside him. "Abby drew that of

her family," she told him. "Maybe you can draw a picture of your family now."

"I don't have a family," Aaron said.

"Come on, Aaron," Abby called from the table. "I'll show you how to draw!"

A smile returned to the boy's face and he scampered over to join her.

"Jessie, sweetie," Aunt Paulette said, "you cooked tonight so Monica and I will wash the dishes."

"That's not necessary," Jessie said. She really just wanted Monica to go home.

"No, fair's fair," Monica said, stacking the dishes in the sink and turning on the faucet. Jessie reflected for a moment on the irony of her sister's words, then drifted back toward the table to watch the kids color.

Aaron was working slowly, tentatively, one eye always on Abby's drawing. He seemed as if he had never colored a picture before in his life. He watched as Abby drew, then tried to copy her. He was very intent in his efforts, his little tongue protruding over his upper lip as he concentrated.

Jessie was overcome with sadness. This was what it would have been like if she'd borne both twins. She would have had both a boy and a girl playing around the house. She would have had a *son*—and Abby would have had a friend and a playmate with her at all times. Why had Jessie ever feared that her little boy would be a monster? Her son would not have been like his father. Jessie's little boy would have been just like this Aaron, sweet and innocent. He would have had similar bright brown eyes, and a smile and a laugh that were just as happy.

As she continued to watch the children at the table, Jessie felt as if she might start bawling. The old guilt had returned. How she regretted wishing her baby dead. She had caused that miscarriage herself—she was convinced of that. She'd wished that she might lose the boy but keep the girl. Meeting Aaron was her punishment. It was karma, as Mom would have said. Fate was showing her what she had killed.

Jessie wasn't aware until the last second that Monica had come up behind her.

"Jessie," her sister whispered. "We need to talk."

"Not now, Monica."

"Well, when then?"

Jessie resented being pulled out of her thoughts this way. The last thing she wanted to contemplate at the moment was Monica's treachery. "I don't know," she said. "But not now."

"I can't take any more of this!" Monica suddenly wailed.

Anxious that the children might hear, Jessie strode into the living room. Monica quickly followed.

"Don't you realize what I'm going through?" Monica cried. "My husband has left me! You have to help me get him back!"

Jessie spun around to glare at her. "I have to do *what*?"

"You need to tell him that I told you I was pregnant, and that you *did* ask me never to bring it up again."

"Why would I lie for you?"

"Because I did everything I could not to break your heart further! I didn't tell you that I was pregnant because I figured it would hurt you more. And I fibbed to

Todd that I told you because I didn't want you to find out—I was trying to spare your feelings!"

Jessie couldn't believe what she was hearing. "This is all bullshit, Monica, and you know it. You were never pregnant! You just used that line to snare Todd."

"I was so pregnant!"

Jessie made a face in disgust. "I remember when you were going to fertility treatments a few years ago. You told me then that doctors believed you had a congenital condition preventing you from conceiving!"

"No, no, I never said that—"

"Yes, you did! Look, Monica, please go home. I do not want to deal with this now."

"But Jessie—"

"Please leave, Monica!"

Her sister glared at her for a moment, then stalked out the front door, letting it slam behind her.

Jessie became aware of someone standing behind her. She turned around. There, looking up at her, was Aaron.

"Are you okay?" the little boy inquired, all eyes and concern.

"Yes, Aaron, I'm fine."

"I came in because it seemed you were upset," he said.

Jessie's heart melted again. She stooped down and placed her hand on the boy's cheek. "You are a darling little angel to worry about me, Aaron," she said.

He smiled. "I drew you a picture."

"You did?"

He nodded, taking her hand and bringing her back out to the kitchen. Abby had gone outside with Aunt

Paulette to close up the grill. On the kitchen table sat two drawings. Abby's was a stick figure of a little girl with yellow hair holding the hand of a stick figure of a woman, also with yellow hair. Underneath she had printed: *To Mommy Love Abby.* Aaron's drawing was almost identical, except the smaller stick figure was a boy with black hair. And there was no printing underneath.

"Why, this is lovely, Aaron. Is that you and me?"

He nodded, seeming very pleased with himself. "But I didn't know how to do that part." He pointed to Abby's printing.

"You'll learn how to print soon, I'm sure."

He pouted. "I wanted to sign it like Abby did."

"I tell you what. Your name and Abby's both start with the same letter. A. You see it there?" She pointed to the A. "Just copy that and I'll always know this came from you."

Aaron smiled broadly and quickly got down to work, carefully copying the A on to his own drawing with a crayon.

"Look how high I can go!"

Jessie looked up at the sound of Abby's voice. The little girl had gone back to the swing set for one more ride. Jessie saw Abby swing forward, her little legs pointing out in front of her.

"Be careful," Jessie heard Aunt Paulette call to her.

"Look how high I can go!" the little girl shouted again. "Aaron showed me!"

Jessie's heart leapt into her throat as she watched her daughter swing higher and higher into the sky.

"Be careful, Abby!" Aunt Paulette was calling. "You could fall—"

And in that very instant, she did. Abby flew from the swing and came plummeting to the ground. Jessie watched as if in slow motion. *She'll break her neck. She'll snap her spine.* Abby tumbled through the air and crashed hard against the earth.

"Abby!" Jessie screamed, and bolted out of the kitchen into the yard, leaving Aaron standing at the table with his drawing in his hands.

EIGHTY

Paulette applied a cold compress to Abby's right knee. "Nothing's broken," she assured Jessie, who hovered beside the little girl's bed. "But she'll have quite a bruise."

"Are you sure nothing's broken?" Jessie asked.

"Yes, I'm sure. She can move everything. She was lucky to land mostly on her bottom."

Abby giggled a little.

Jessie sat down on the edge of the bed, stroking her daughter's hair. "How do you feel, sweetie?" Jessie asked.

"Okay now, Mommy," Abby said.

Paulette let out a long sigh of relief. For a moment there, it had been terrifying. Abby had been sprawled on the grass, not breathing. As it turned out, however, she'd just had the wind knocked out of her. Her breath came back to her and the color returned to her face as Jessie lifted her from the ground and carried her into the house. It had been a frightful moment, but it looked as if the worst would be a bruise and a scraped knee.

Yet as terrifying as the moment was, something else

had frightened Paulette even more, and this fear wasn't as easily abated.

As Jessie cooed over Abby, Paulette turned around once more to look at Aaron. The look on the boy's face was still there. He stood in the doorway of Abby's room, watching everything and everyone with eyes that seemed considerably smaller than before, eyes filled with hatred and resentment. Paulette had seen the look on his little face as he stood at the kitchen door watching Jessie run to Abby. It was a look that had transformed his features. It had been a terrible thing to witness, leaving Paulette cold. She shuddered again seeing that the look was still on his face.

As she watched him, Aaron turned and walked away from Abby's room. Paulette followed him into the hall. Aaron was descending the steps.

"Where are you going, Aaron?" she asked.

"Home," he said sullenly.

"Don't you want to say good-bye to Abby?"

"No," he replied, and disappeared down the stairs.

Paulette popped her head back into Abby's room. "Everything okay in here for the moment?" she asked.

"Yes," Jessie replied. "I'm going to read Abby a story. I think she'll nod off."

"A nap would be good for her," Paulette agreed. "Give her more of that Arnica solution on the side of the bed in another half hour. I'm just going to run out for a moment. I'll be back soon."

"Okay, Aunt Paulette."

The older woman hurried down the stairs.

Outside, she caught a glimpse of Aaron as he walked through the grass toward the woods. The sun was dropping lower in the sky, sending long shadows of the bare trees across the yard. The air was getting chillier. But Paulette didn't have time to stop for a sweater. She didn't want to lose sight of Aaron.

Paulette followed at a safe distance. The boy didn't seem to be keeping to any particular path as he headed into the woods. He disappeared into the shadows, but Paulette hurried after him, spotting his small form through some bushes. She hoped to follow him to wherever he was living. Maybe his home would be, as everyone had been surmising, one of those new houses on the other side of the woods. Maybe Paulette would find the boy living there with a foster family, or maybe with some relatives who, from all appearances, were rather neglectful guardians.

Or maybe she'd discover something else: that Aaron was living with Emil Deetz, who'd somehow rooked the kid into spying for him on Jessie.

Paulette struggled to keep the boy in view. She caught a glimpse of the top of his head several yards away and endeavored both to follow him and to stay out of view.

She realized she was frightened. She didn't want him to turn around and see her. Now why should she be frightened of a little boy? It seemed absurd, but it was true that Aaron scared her. That look she'd seen cross his face—it had been chilling.

Paulette moved deeper into the woods. She glanced once over her shoulder. She could no longer see the place where she'd entered.

Looking back in front of her, she realized she couldn't see the boy. She'd lost him.

Paulette stood still, looking around. The shrill calls of crows in the trees filled her ears.

"Damn it," Paulette whispered to herself. Aaron was gone. She tried to find him with her mind, to psychically follow him and maybe pick up his trail that way. But she was unsuccessful. Sometimes her gift worked. Sometimes it didn't.

So much for that. She supposed it had been foolish to even think she could follow the child through woods as thick as these. With a sigh, she turned around and headed back the way she came.

At least, Paulette *thought* it was the way she came.

After walking for several minutes, she realized she was going the wrong way. She tried to tune in, to get a mental picture of where she was. She turned abruptly to the left. Her instincts were telling her to go in that direction, and she trusted her instincts. Her inner voice had rarely failed her.

For some reason, she had an image of Howard. Why should she think of the man she had loved and lost at this moment, out here in the woods?

Because you are about to join him at last. . . .

Whose voice was that?

Paulette stopped in her tracks, realizing her heart was thudding in her chest.

"Get a grip, Paulette," she told herself, shaking off the strange, inexplicable fear. She marched confidently through the fallen leaves, pushing past low-hanging branches and bushes. Just a few yards away, she knew, was Jessie's house.

But the woods only seemed to get thicker.

"This is crazy," Paulette said out loud. She'd known

these woods all her life. But she didn't recognize them. They seemed to extend indefinitely in every direction. And looking up at the darkening sky above her, at the strange gnarled fingers of the bare trees, Paulette thought they were higher than she'd ever remembered. The oaks and maples seemed to stretch for miles up into the air.

Once again she tried to tune in, to psychically find her way out of the woods, but all she saw was Howard—his helicopter exploding and falling to earth in a million colorful starbursts.

She began walking in a different direction, but after about five minutes she was suddenly convinced she was trudging deeper into the woods, and farther away from home. "Concentrate, Paulette!" she told herself forcefully, shutting her eyes and willing her mind to see the way out. But she saw nothing. And when she opened her eyes the sky was even darker.

Paulette strained to see lights through the trees. But there was only darkness. She was lost. It was impossible to believe, but she was lost.

"Howard," she said in a tiny, tremulous voice.

That was when she realized something else. The sounds of the birds in the trees had ceased. Paulette was enveloped in complete and utter silence. The only sound came when she moved, as she crunched through the fallen leaves underfoot. Paulette's heart began to race faster. Terror seemed to surge through her veins in place of blood.

She started to run. The woods weren't infinite, even if they seemed that way right now. She would just keep running until she came to the end. She needed to find her way out of them—whether her side of the woods or the other side—before nightfall. Paulette did not want to still be trudging through these terrible woods when darkness closed in. Because now a new terror had entered her mind.

She wasn't alone.

Someone—something—was watching her.

She knew it instinctively. When she stopped running, she heard the almost imperceptible sound of someone else—some*thing* else—also coming to a halt. Without any sound coming from the trees, Paulette's ears were very attuned to what else she could hear. And she could hear breathing. She was certain it was not her own.

"I've got to get out of here," she said softly.

The boy had led her in. He had known she would follow.

"And now he—or something—wants me dead," she whispered.

Once more, Paulette began to run. She felt it was her only chance. She needed to reach the end of the woods— any end of the woods. She ran, mystified that no matter which way she seemed to go, she saw no lights, no break in the trees.

She stumbled over something, falling forward.

Fortunately, she was able to break her fall with her forearms, and the heavy blanket of newly fallen leaves cushioned the impact. Paulette was quickly back on her feet, looking behind her to see what she had stumbled over.

She gasped.

It was a body.

A dead man.

His face looked like a rotted pumpkin left too long outside in the rain. His dark purple cheeks had caved in and his eyes had sunken deep down into their sockets. The flesh around his mouth had largely decomposed, leaving a jagged, jack-o'-lantern smile. His throat had been cut so savagely that Paulette could see the bone of his neck. Maggots and flies swarmed everywhere, crawling all over his face and through his hair and out of his clothes.

It took several seconds, but Paulette suddenly knew the corpse was Bryan Pierce.

She screamed.

As she ran, she realized she could hear the birds in the trees again. Up ahead, she spotted the lights of Jessie's and Monica's houses. Paulette made a final sprint out of the trees. "Call the police!" she shrieked. "Call the police!"

It was Monica who emerged first, standing outside her house and looking toward the woods with a perplexed expression on her face. "Aunt Paulette?" she asked. "What the hell is going on?"

"Call the police!" she cried as she reached the safety of her niece's house. "I've found Bryan. It's another murder! And tell the police . . . I know who did it!"

EIGHTY-ONE

"**Y**ou mean you're actually putting stock in what that fortune-teller says?" Chief Walters asked Patrick Castile in disbelief, as they stood in the middle of Hickory Dell. The road had been blocked off to public access by police. As the sun rose above the trees, casting an eerie pink glow over everything, a combined force of Sayer's Brook cops and FBI agents were combing the woods for evidence in the murder of Bryan Pierce. There were swarms of men wearing rubber gloves and a dozen barking dogs. Bryan's stinking, water-logged corpse had already been removed late last night and sent to forensics.

Castile looked over at the chief with impenetrable eyes. "I think it's very possible that Emil Deetz is behind all these killings," he replied emotionlessly.

Walters laughed. "But Paulette didn't say it was Emil Deetz who killed Pierce. She said it was the *ghost* of Emil Deetz. She said she'd sensed something *supernatural* out there in the woods. She said she'd somehow *tuned in to* it." The chief rolled her eyes, humming a few bars from the theme music of the old *Twilight Zone* TV series.

The neighborhood was buzzing with people. Gert Gorin, of course, was trying to get past the orange police tape that cordoned off the search area, and had to be constantly told to step back. Mr. Thayer walked up to the scene with Todd Bennett, asked a few questions, then stepped back, shaking his head in dismay. So far no one had emerged from Jessie Clarkson's house, but word had spread through town, and a couple dozen people from nearby streets had begun congregating at the end of Hickory Dell, shouting questions to police, asking if they had any idea where the serial killer might strike next.

Walters had, of course, attempted to contact Heather Pierce. But Heather wasn't home; her car was gone, and no one answered the door when they knocked. They'd tried late last night when Bryan's body had been found, and again this morning. Apparently Heather had taken the kids and gone out of town. At the moment, officers were attempting to track down the Pierces' housekeeper to find out where the family might have gone.

"Look," said Chief Walters, trying to get through to the stubborn FBI agent, "the only evidence, if you can call it that, of Emil Deetz still being alive comes from a very unreliable witness. Your own files indicate that Deetz was killed in a shoot-out in Mexico."

Castile leveled her with another blank look. "There were parts of that report that were classified. If you had been allowed to see the whole report, you'd know that our agents had their doubts about Deetz being killed, as they were never allowed to inspect all the bodies. In the shoot-out, the building caught fire and most of the dead were burned beyond recognition."

"So you're telling me . . . the FBI was never certain of Deetz's death?"

"That's what I'm telling you."

"But something very different was told to us at the time."

"We didn't want panic. We believed we had the situation under control."

Walters felt her anger rising. "My department is pledged to protect this community. We shouldn't have been told that a man who'd killed one of our citizens was dead when he might not have been. And certainly you should have told Jessie Clarkson that Deetz might still be a danger to her."

"I wasn't with the agency then, so I can't say how they might have proceeded differently, but it's possible mistakes were made," Castile said. "But I can tell you that we have been monitoring the situation consistently, and have felt we had it under control. If Deetz had escaped death, we were confident he was not in the United States. A man in Mexico who we believed might have been Deetz was under constant observation."

Walters narrowed her eyes as she studied the implacable face of Castile. "And is that man still under surveillance?"

"He has apparently left Mexico," the FBI agent told her.

"So that's why you think these killings might be the work of Emil Deetz."

"Indeed." Castile looked off toward the woods. "I informed Ms. Clarkson of that fact this morning."

"Well, this changes things," Walters said. "But I'm still not convinced that John Manning isn't somehow involved. I've always suspected he's in league in Deetz."

"Leave Manning to us," Castile said, before moving off to confer with one of his agents.

Walters fumed. The arrogance of the young man infuriated her. How dare he withhold information from local police? Something was very, very wrong here, and Walters knew it. For one thing, her men had searched those woods, every inch of them, after Heather had reported her husband missing. How could they have missed Bryan's body? Unless someone had only recently put the body there . . . someone who had reason to prevent its discovery for as long as possible, so that any physical evidence might decay in the meantime. Someone who'd had a fight with Bryan right before he died, perhaps, and whose DNA might still cling to the corpse?

Emil Deetz might or might not be involved in these murders, but Walters wasn't ready to concede that John Manning was squeaky clean in the matter.

She marched over to his house and up to his gate. She rang the buzzer.

"Yes?" came a voice through the intercom. The chief recognized it as Manning's assistant, Caleb.

"I'd like to speak with Mr. Manning," she said. "It's Belinda Walters."

"Just a moment."

Walters waited. For several minutes there wasn't a response, and she was about to buzz again. But then the gate opened, and John Manning stood there. He was wearing a black satin smoking jacket and sandals.

"Chief Walters," he said.

"Just a couple questions, Mr. Manning."

"Haven't you already asked me everything?"

"You're aware that Bryan Pierce's body was found in the woods last night with his throat cut?"

Manning closed his eyes, then opened them. "Yes. I spoke with Jessie on the phone this morning."

"Well, it's about Jessie that I want to ask you, Mr. Manning. Why did you buy the property next to hers?"

"I think I answered that before. I liked the area."

"Why are you pursuing a friendship with her?"

Manning looked peeved. "I'm not answering that question. In fact, I'm done answering questions for you. I suggest if you have any further things you'd like to know, you take it up with the FBI."

He closed the door on her face.

Walters steamed. *Take it up with the FBI. . . .*

"Leave Manning to us," Castile had said.

What the *hell* was going on here?

EIGHTY-TWO

Jessie was still trying to absorb the information that the FBI agent, Patrick Castile, had given her this morning. "We were never entirely sure that Emil Deetz had been killed in Mexico," he had said.

Castile had some other things as well, things about always having the situation under control and never believing Jessie to be in any jeopardy, but it was that statement that kept ringing through Jessie's mind.

We were never entirely sure that Emil Deetz had been killed in Mexico.

The words unnerved her even more than Aunt Paulette's account of finding Bryan's body in the woods. Her aunt was pacing around the kitchen now, trying to convince Jessie that they were dealing with a ghost. But Jessie thought the foe they faced—the foe the whole town faced—was much more flesh and blood.

"Aunt Paulette," she said, clutching her mug of coffee in both hands as if she were holding on for dear life, "if the FBI says that Emil might not have died in that shoot-out, then that's what we have to fear, not ghosts or avenging spirits."

Jessie was angry that the FBI hadn't informed her of

their doubts about Emil's death. But would she really have wanted them to tell her? By believing Emil was dead, she had found the freedom to get on with her life. She had been able to put her fear and her nightmares behind her.

But now the fear had come back.

Aunt Paulette had stopped pacing and was looking at Jessie intently. "There is something unearthly going on here, Jessie. I feel it. I sense it."

"I know the experience of finding Bryan's body was traumatic for you, but . . ."

Aunt Paulette resumed her pacing. It was clear to Jessie that her aunt hadn't slept all night. Her eyes were ringed with dark circles.

"How do you explain why I got lost in those woods for so long? They were like nowhere I'd ever seen. And the silence . . . the uncanny silence."

"It was getting dark, Aunt Paulette. . . . You just lost your way."

"No!" She spun on Jessie, her eyes wild with emotion. "There is something supernatural about that boy! He led me in there! He got me lost! He wanted me to find Bryan's body! He's possessed by Emil's spirit! That's what I believe."

"There is nothing supernatural about Aaron," Jessie said. "After spending the afternoon with him, I was completely reassured about him. He's a sweet, lonely child."

"He's a ghost!"

Jessie smiled indulgently. "No ghost could eat that many hamburgers and put away so much pie."

"I don't know how to explain it," Aunt Paulette said. "But he's not of this earth. He's . . . undead somehow."

"Aunt Paulette, you know I keep an open mind about your belief in the supernatural, but in this case . . ."

"Jessie, listen to me. Doesn't he look like Emil?"

Jessie dropped her eyes to the table. "He has dark eyes and hair. . . . That's all."

"Even the smile, Jessie." Aunt Paulette leaned on the table with her hands, looking directly into her niece's face. "And his last name, for God's sake!"

"A coincidence," Jessie said quietly, even though she didn't sound very convincing, even to herself.

"Don't you see, Jessie? He's telling us who he is!"

Jessie closed her eyes. No, she didn't want to think this. . . .

"It's Emil," Aunt Paulette said. "It's Emil, come back as a child. His ghost is taunting us. He appeared to me in town as an adult, but he also appears as he looked as a little boy. That way he can insinuate himself with us . . . and with Abby!"

"That's nonsense!" Jessie said, louder than she meant to. She stood up and walked across the room, not wanting to admit to herself how much her aunt's words frightened her. "Aaron's just a lonely little boy who's being neglected by whoever's taking care of him. He's not a ghost! He's not Emil!"

"I'm going to find out who he is," Aunt Paulette said. "I have my ways, Jessie. And I'll use them. Because if I don't . . . you and I and Abby will be the next to have our throats cut!"

EIGHTY-THREE

Chief Walters was back at her desk, going through the pile of papers that had accumulated there, when her cell phone jingled. She saw it was her daughter calling from Philadelphia.

"Emma!" she said happily into the phone.

"Mom, what the *hell* is going on in Sayer's Brook?" Emma's voice sounded worried. "It's all over the news today. Another body found . . ."

The chief sighed. "Yes, sweetie. Bryan Pierce. Do you remember him?"

"Yes," Emma said. "I can't believe it. A serial killer operating in our little town. Mom, please be careful."

"The FBI's taken over," Walters said. "We just mop up the mess from here on in."

"Any suspects?"

"Well . . ." Walters wasn't going to reveal too much. But suddenly she had a question for Emma. "Hey, sweetie, do you remember that fortune-teller we went to see before you got accepted to school?"

"Yeah. Madame Paulette. What's she got to do with it?"

Walters laughed. "Madame Paulette is one of our witnesses, who claims she may have seen the killer. What do you remember about her?"

"Well, I remember she was rather eccentric with her long gray hair and bright red lipstick. . . ."

"Absolutely. Which is why I'm not banking on her reliability. After all, she said you wouldn't get into your top pick of schools. . . ."

"I didn't, Mom."

The chief frowned. "Huh? Yes, you did, honey. You got into Wesleyan."

"Wesleyan wasn't my top pick. I wanted to go to Emerson."

"No, honey, it was—"

"You're remembering this incorrectly, Mom. Madame Paulette was right. I didn't get into my top pick, but that was a good thing, because Wesleyan turned out to be so much better for me than Emerson ever would have."

"Oh," Walters said. "I thought Wesleyan had always been your top choice. . . ."

"No. It just seemed that way, because I ended up liking it so much." Emma laughed. "So maybe you ought to reconsider Madame Paulette's reliability."

"Emma, honey, I have to go. I'll call you later."

"Okay, Mom. Be careful!"

Chief Walters sat at her desk staring straight ahead.

It had been a lucky guess, she told herself about Paulette Drew's prediction of Emma's school. Learning that she'd remembered the incident incorrectly was hardly cause for Walters to reevaluate Drew's position as a witness.

But still . . .

The FBI thought Emil Deetz was behind the killings. Paulette Drew thought it was Deetz's ghost. Wolfie had been convinced that the killer was John Manning—with some kind of assist, knowing or not, from Jessie Clarkson.

Walters's gut told her the right answer might somehow be a combination of all of the above.

EIGHTY-FOUR

"It's my mother's recipe for fried chicken," Manning was saying, as he and Caleb carried in trays of crispy wings, breasts, and drumsticks. "She was from Alabama, so it's got all the best Southern ingredients."

"This is awfully sweet of you," Jessie said.

"I figured you all wouldn't be up to making dinner tonight," John said, giving Jessie a smile. "I've got some whipped potatoes to bring over, too."

"Mr. Manning is a wonderful cook," Caleb said. "I've often told him if he weren't such a successful author, he'd make a terrific chef."

"It smells great!" Abby chirped, as John handed her a drumstick. She began munching on it like a hungry little chipmunk.

"Let's eat out on the picnic table," Jessie suggested. "It's such a lovely afternoon. We can watch the sunset."

She grabbed a pitcher of lemonade and a handful of paper plates and led them all outside. Caleb ran back over to the house and brought over the potatoes, a hunk of butter melting all over them, and they began their feast.

"Thank you so much," Jessie said.

John smiled over at her.

For a few moments, she could push all thoughts of death and fear from her mind. She could forget that someone—something—was out there that wanted to hurt her. She could forget all of Aunt Paulette's crazy suspicions.

"I wish Aaron were here," Abby said. "He'd like this fried chicken."

Jessie thought about the little boy, and wondered where he was. She worried about him, out there by himself, obviously uncared for.

John leaned in toward Jessie. "What have you learned about him?" he asked in a soft voice.

"That he's a scared, lonely little boy," Jessie told him.

John looked at her a little quizzically.

"We have nothing to fear from Aaron," she said firmly.

"Mommy," Abby said, looking up with a face covered with grease, "can I go trick-or-treating with Aaron?"

Halloween was now just a couple of days away. Jessie hadn't told Abby about Bryan's death, but she couldn't allow her to daughter to walk through the neighborhood at night. "I tell you what," she said. "We'll have a Halloween party here. Aaron can come. Will you come, too, John?"

"Sure," he replied. "But how will you let Aaron know? Have you found a way to reach him?"

"Oh, he'll be here," Abby said confidently.

Jessie thought she was right. Aaron would know to come. They didn't have to tell him. He would just come.

And that thought didn't frighten Jessie at all.

EIGHTY-FIVE

From his perch on a log at the entrance to the woods, Aaron watched them. The setting sun cast a red glow on his little face.

He sat there, listening to their laughter. He could smell the food. He was hungry.

Very hungry.

What a happy family they seemed.

He watched them with his dark eyes.

EIGHTY-SIX

The chief's phone rang again. It was Harry Knotts.

"You better get back out here to Hickory Dell," the detective told her.

"What's happened?"

"We finally tracked down the Pierces' housekeeper at her sister's house. She told us that she'd taken Heather's car, and that Heather was home." He paused. "She was right."

"Don't tell me," Walters said. "You went into the house and discovered yet another murder."

"*Three* other murders," Knotts said. "The kids were dead, too."

"Dear God," Walters said. "I'll be right there."

EIGHTY-SEVEN

Gert Gorin pushed her way to the front of the crowd of people trying to get as close as they could to the Pierce house. She'd caught a glimpse of the bodies, draped with sheets, being carried out into the waiting vans. A woman beside her was crying.

"Children!" the woman was saying through her tears. "Now that monster is killing children!"

Gert snorted. She wasn't going to pretend she'd ever liked those two brats. But it was pretty terrible, nonetheless.

It was hard to see what was going on. The police and the FBI were all over the place, but they had turned off all their searchlights, and the moon wasn't cooperating either. It was a cloudy night. It felt like rain. Gert shivered.

"Makes you feel none of us are safe," she said out loud, to no one in particular. "Makes you wonder which one of us is next."

The woman beside her only cried harder.

"If you ask me," Gert said, still loud enough so that everyone around her could hear, "this all started when

Jessie Clarkson came back to town. I hope the FBI is looking into that strange little coincidence."

"That's right," someone in the crowd murmured, and there were other sounds of agreement from the mob.

But not everyone was in assent. "I hardly think you can blame Jessie for any of this," came one voice from behind Gert.

She spun around. It was old Mr. Thayer.

Gert sniffed. "I'm not blaming her. I'm merely pointing out the coincidence."

"That's very unfair to Jessie," Mr. Thayer said, his eyes stern. "She has been horrified by all of this."

"But you can't dismiss the fact that all of the murders have been committed by slitting the victims' throats." Gert folded her arms across her chest and looked defiantly up at Mr. Thayer. "Same modus operandi of Emil Deetz."

Mr. Thayer just shook his head. "Not the children, apparently. Poor little Ashton and Piper died from broken necks, as I've heard. An accident on the stairs."

The crying woman hurried away, unable to bear anymore.

"Still, I hope the FBI is questioning Jessie," Gert said.

"They have been harassing her to no end," Mr. Thayer said.

Gert suddenly felt uneasy. It was that strange sensation she sometimes got, that sixth sense that someone was watching her. Once in a while, peering through her binoculars, she'd see the person she was spying on turn and stare directly back at her. Such moments sent shivers down her spine—to be caught in the act, so to speak. Gert had a similar feeling now, as if someone was watching and listening to her accusations against Jessie.

She looked around. There, a few feet away, standing unobtrusively among the crowd, was that strange, dark-eyed, barefoot little boy.

He was staring at Gert.

She shuddered.

"I'm going home," she said to Mr. Thayer. "And I'm going to lock all my windows and double-bolt my doors. I suggest you do the same."

Gert hurried off down the street into the dark shadows. She was trembling. She couldn't understand why. But she didn't stop trembling until she got back home and heard the reassuring sound of Arthur's baseball game on the television set.

"What are you doing?" her husband asked her.

"Locking all the windows," she told him. "There's a killer loose. I'm not taking any chances."

"Good idea," Arthur said, his eyes still on the game.

Gert thought about taking a peek across the street at Jessie's house with her binoculars. But she decided against it. Tonight, she was leaving well enough alone.

EIGHTY-EIGHT

Inside the Pierce house, as investigators dusted for fingerprints and collected evidence, Chief Walters took Patrick Castile aside.

"Look," she said. "I've put my entire force on the lookout for Emil Deetz. If he's out there, we'll find him."

Castile raised an eyebrow in her direction. "Changed your mind on the likelihood of Deetz being our man, have you, Chief?" he asked.

"I'm open to the possibility," she said.

Castile's arrogance really ticked Walters off. He was a kid. When Walters had started out as a rookie cop, Castile was probably still in nursery school.

"And if I'm willing to keep an open mind," she said, "I'm here to ask you to keep yours open as well."

"Oh, really? What should I be considering, Chief Walters?"

"John Manning."

Castile sighed, and began to say something, but the chief cut him off.

"I'm not saying he's the killer. Maybe he is, maybe he's not. I'm just saying there are questions that just

won't go away and that he's never really given us satis-
factory answers. You were aware that he and Heather
Pierce were having an affair?"

Castile looked at her, but made no reply.

"Manning broke off the affair. Heather made some
scenes. She was harassing him. And she was convinced
he'd killed her husband."

Castile still said nothing.

"It just strikes me as worth investigating why every
murder has had some connection to Manning."

"I'd hardly say there was a connection between
Theresa Whitman and Manning."

"Not that we know of."

"Please, Chief . . ."

"Look, Castile, Manning was the last one to see Pierce
alive, after beating him up. And the victim whose corpse
you just carried out of here on a stretcher sat in my office not long ago and told me she was afraid of him.
Come on. This is basic police work. You've got to find
out where Manning is involved in all of this."

"Look," Castile said, moving close to Walters so he
could speak softly and she could hear. "I've already
told you. We are well aware of John Manning. Leave
him to us." His face hardened. "In fact, Chief, I'd say
your further involvement in this case is no longer
needed. We appreciate all that you and your department have done, but we'll take it from here."

Walters was aghast. "You can't tell me not to be involved when a serial killer is roaming my town."

"I can," he said. "And I am."

He walked away from her.

Chief Walters seethed.

EIGHTY-NINE

Jessie was testing the security alarm system. She'd done so several times already this morning. She would set the alarm and then head outside, locking the new front door—a solid, heavy piece of oak and aluminum. Then she'd take a screwdriver and jimmy the lock—or attempt to open a window—or have Abby walk around inside the house. Each time the alarm sounded, much to Jessie's satisfaction. She'd then hurry back inside and turn the alarm off before the security system notified the police.

"Everything okay up here?"

Jessie looked around. Monica was walking up the hill.

"I keep hearing the alarm going off," she said.

"I'm testing it," Jessie told her.

"Good idea," her sister agreed. "Can't be too safe. The news about Heather and the kids really freaked me out. I'm thinking of staying at a hotel for a while. Do you and Abby want to come?"

"I'm not running away," Jessie said, checking the window locks for probably the twentieth time. "I'm through with that."

There was a heavy silence between the sisters.

"Look, Jessie, I'm sorry about the other day."

Jessie looked over at her.

"Really, I am," Monica continued. "And I hope you'll accept my apology."

"The apology I'm waiting for, Monica, is for the lie you told to me and to Todd all those years ago."

"Jesus *Christ*, Jessie. Why won't you believe me that I was really pregnant?" Monica's face twisted in resentment. "You should be angry at Todd for seducing me that night."

"He didn't seduce you," Jessie said plainly.

Monica smirked. "Oh? Is that what he's told you? Has he been up here to plead his case? He comes to see you but not me."

"No, Todd hasn't been here. I haven't spoken to him. But I know he didn't seduce you. I know that he was in love with me. Whatever happened that night was your doing."

"What happened that night was that he got me pregnant. . . ."

"Bullshit, Monica. You were never pregnant." Jessie laughed derisively. "I'm amazed at how tenaciously you're clinging to that lie."

"I'm not lying!"

"You *are*, Monica! And I guess I understand. It's all you have. Without it, your whole marriage crumbles. Your whole *existence* crumbles! That's why you want me to corroborate your lie. But I won't do it."

Monica's face was bright red. "All I know is that Todd has left me, thanks to you!"

Jessie turned to check the motion detector on the front-porch light. "I hope we can be friends someday,

Monica. I really do. But until you can acknowledge what you did, I don't see that happening."

"You'll be sorry, Jessie! You'll be sorry for breaking up my marriage!"

She turned and stormed back down the hill toward her house.

Jessie sighed. She sat down on the porch steps and put her face in her hands.

Within seconds she felt a light touch on her shoulder. She removed her hands from her face and looked up. Standing beside her, his small hand resting on her shoulder, was Aaron.

"Hello, Aaron," Jessie said, smiling.

"Are you okay?" he asked.

"Oh, I'll be fine. Don't worry about me."

"I don't like seeing you so sad," Aaron told her.

Jessie smiled and wrapped one arm around the boy's waist, pulling him in toward her. "You're a sweet boy, you know that?"

"I like it when you smile," Aaron said.

"Then I'll try to smile more," Jessie replied.

The boy sat beside her on the step. "Where's Abby?"

"She went with her Aunt Paulette for ice cream. She helped me all morning and that was her reward."

"Well, I can help you now."

Jessie tousled his hair. "I'm pretty much finished. I was just testing the security system."

"Is that because you're frightened?"

"Well," Jessie said, careful not to worry the child, "I'm just taking precautions. You know that some very bad things have happened in this neighborhood, don't you?"

"Yes," he said.

"I want you to be careful, Aaron. You shouldn't be walking through the woods alone anymore. When you want to come visit, I want you to call me, and I'll come pick you up."

"So you *are* frightened then."

Jessie sighed. "Well, sometimes I am. But I'm not going to let fear overpower me. That's happened in the past. I won't let that happen again."

"Who are you frightened of?" Aaron wanted to know.

Jessie looked at him. His dark eyes shone out at her. Yes, she could see Emil in the boy's features. Aunt Paulette was right.

"I don't know," Jessie said honestly, in a very soft voice.

"Are you frightened of Mr. Manning?"

"Oh, no. Mr. Manning is a good man, Aaron."

The boy was shaking his head firmly. "He's a very *bad* man."

Jessie frowned, taking one of the boy's hands in hers. "He's not, Aaron. Once you get to know him, you'll like him."

Aaron said nothing, just dropped his eyes to the ground.

"Aaron," Jessie said, still holding the boy's hand, "I wish you'd tell me more about you. Where you live. Your parents . . . or whoever looks after you."

Is it Emil? Do you live with Emil? That was what Jessie was so desperate to know, but too afraid to ask directly.

Aaron seemed to have fallen mute. He just kept staring at the ground.

"Please show me where you live, Aaron," Jessie said.

He looked up at her. "All right," he replied.

They stood. Aaron walked down the steps and turned to Jessie, reaching out his hand and taking hers again. She allowed him to lead her across the grass, over the brook, and into the woods. They spoke no words. The day was bright and the sun flooded the woods through the bare trees. There was no reason for fear. None at all.

But then, just as Aunt Paulette had described, the sounds of birdsong ceased.

It was completely, utterly quiet as they passed through the woods, the only sound the crunching of the leaves under their feet.

They seemed to walk for a very long time. Jessie no longer recognized the woods she had known and played in ever since she was a little girl. They seemed to stretch on forever. But she wasn't frightened. That surprised her. She wasn't the least bit frightened, not as long as she kept holding the hand of the little boy in front of her, who led her deeper and deeper into this place.

He looked back at her once, his face seeming to glow with light. His dark eyes sparkled. He smiled. Jessie smiled back.

She had the weirdest sensation of being outside her body, looking down on herself and Aaron. She kept seeing images of a boy and a woman moving through the woods from someplace high above, as if Jessie were perched at the top of the tree.

Eventually sparks of recognition returned to her

mind. They were near the gorge. Locals called it Suicide Leap—a steep drop of some fifty feet down a
rocky embankment. Mom had always warned Jessie on
their walks through the woods that she should steer
clear of the gorge. It came up on you almost without
warning. The trees grew right to the edge, and then the
land just gave way. Losing one's footing at the top
could mean a terrible tumble all the way down to the
bottom. The drop was too steep to be able to walk
down, and there was very little to break a fall.

For the first time the vaguest tremble of fear pene-
trated through Jessie's cocoon of good feeling. *The
gorge . . . is he taking to me to the gorge?*

Is that what Emil told him to do?

But Aaron turned and headed in another direction.
Up ahead, she spotted an old shack. She thought she
remembered the shack from when she was a child—
but she'd thought that it had been torn down, years ago.
The shack was barely still standing, no more than
seven feet by eight feet, with a broken door and no
windows. The wood was rotted in several places. Aaron
stopped in front of the shack and let Jessie's hand drop.

The birds began to chirp once again in the trees.

"Is this where you live, Aaron?" Jessie asked.

The little boy nodded.

She stooped down, putting her arm around his waist.
"You live here? Where are your parents?"

"I don't know," he said. "I miss them."

She placed her hands on either side of his face and
looked closely at him. "No boy can live here. How do
you eat? How do bathe?"

Aaron had started to cry.

"You're all alone, aren't you?" Jessie asked.

He nodded.

"Your parents . . . abandoned you. . . ."

The boy began to cry harder, falling into an embrace with Jessie. His little arms held tight around her neck.

"What mother . . . could ever abandon . . . her son?"

Jessie's heart broke.

And suddenly she knew the truth.

Somehow—in some strange, mystical, unexplainable way—Aaron was her son. She was his mother. She knew it. She felt it. Somehow he had come back to her. Her son. The son she had forsaken. The son she had wished away. The son she had let die.

"I'm so sorry, Aaron," Jessie said, her voice shattering. "So very, very sorry."

His little body shook with tears as she held him tight.

"You're not alone anymore, baby," Jessie whispered in his ear, as she stroked his hair and felt her own tears falling down her cheeks. "Mommy's here."

NINETY

Paulette stepped on the gas. They had to get home right away.

"Why are you driving so fast, Aunt Paulette?" Abby asked, her seat belt holding her tight in the passenger seat.

"Just because I don't want your mother to worry about us, sweetie," she told the little girl.

In fact, it was Paulette who was worried about Jessie. They'd finished their ice cream cones and were looking in shop windows when suddenly the vision had come to Paulette. Jessie was in danger. She saw her with a dark figure—the tall, dark man had finally arrived! They had to get to her right away!

So she'd grabbed Abby's hand and rushed her back to the car, all the while frantically trying to get Jessie on her cell phone. Her calls repeatedly went to voice mail. So Paulette screeched out of the municipal parking lot and raced across town back toward Hickory Dell, praying she'd get there in time.

But what would she find? What would she be able to do against the dark man—if in fact, the dark man really was the ghost of Emil Deetz?

She turned off Ridge Road onto Hickory Dell, driving past the Pierce house, shuddering at the memory of the carnage that had taken place inside. Bryan Pierce's decomposed face still haunted her. Had the tall, dark man killed all of them? Paulette couldn't figure out why the ghost of Emil Deetz was doing all this. What did Emil have against the Pierces? Against Inga? Against Detective Wolfowitz and Mrs. Whitman? The only answer was that his spirit was trying to randomly terrorize Jessie.

And now Paulette feared he had had come for Jessie herself.

She turned into the driveway and stopped the car. Hurrying around to the passenger side, she opened the door and unbuckled Abby from her seat belt.

"There's Mommy!" the little girl sang out, pointing across the yard.

Indeed, there was Jessie. She was alive, thank God.

She was coming out of the woods.

And she was walking with Aaron, holding his hand.

"Abby, stay here for a minute, in the car, okay?" Paulette said. "I want to talk to your mother for a minute."

"Okay, Aunt Paulette."

She closed the car door gently and made her way across the grass.

"Jessie!" she called.

Jessie didn't reply. She just kept walking toward the house with Aaron.

Paulette hurried over to her. "Jessie!"

Finally her niece turned to look at her. Jessie's eyes seemed somewhat dazed, and they were red from crying. She seemed to look through Paulette rather than actually see her.

"Jessie, are you all right?"

"Yes, I'm all right," she said, in a voice that seemed far away to Paulette.

Aaron stared up at the older woman.

"Jessie," Paulette said, "I've had a vision. . . . Please believe me. I think . . . I think you . . . all of us . . . are in danger."

"That's foolish, Aunt Paulette."

"No, not foolish. It's—"

Paulette moved her eyes from Jessie back to Aaron. She gasped.

The boy's face seemed different. There was a look about him, as if he was full of hatred and malice, as if he was ready to spring at Paulette like a wild dog and tear out her throat with his teeth.

Jessie had seen the exchange. "Why are you afraid of Aaron?" she asked Paulette. "There's no reason to be afraid of him."

The boy's face was back to normal. Sweet, innocent. He offered Paulette a smile.

"Aaron's going to be living with us from now on," Jessie said, as she and the boy began moving again toward the house.

"Jessie, no . . ."

"Oh, yes," Jessie said, not looking back as she walked. "You see, Aunt Paulette, he's one of us. Aaron is my son."

NINETY-ONE

"**Y**our aunt is very worried about you," John told her as they sat on the couch that night, a soft rain tapping behind them on the windows.

Jessie smiled. "I know she is. But she shouldn't be."

"She came by my house and asked me to come speak with you." John sighed as he took Jessie's hands in his. "Are you really certain that letting that boy stay here in the house is a good idea?"

"He belongs here, John." Jessie looked over at the stairs that led up to the rooms where both Aaron and Abby were now sound asleep. "This is his home."

John made a face that showed a lack of understanding. "Paulette said you're convinced that somehow . . ." His voice trailed off for a moment. "That somehow he's your son."

Jessie held his gaze. "I know it must sound crazy."

John gave her a small smile as if to say he wasn't disputing that fact.

"Maybe it *is* crazy," Jessie admitted. "But it's what I believe."

"How is that possible, Jessie? You told me you had a miscarriage."

"I did. A miscarriage I caused by wanting it, wishing for it. You have no idea how much guilt and grief I carried around with me because of that. And I believe I have brought Aaron back the same way—subconsciously wanting it and wishing for it."

"That's impossible, Jessie."

"Is it?" She settled back into the couch, allowing her shoulder to press into his. "Aren't you the author of a book called *The Killing Room*?"

"Yes. Have you read it?"

"I've read enough about it to know the plot. A woman believes very hard that her husband, killed in war, is actually not dead. She manifests him back to life through her grief." Here she made it a point to look up at John. "And through the power of life and death and hope and love."

"Jessie," John said. "That was fiction."

She smiled. "The little boy upstairs isn't fiction. He's very real. I fed him a big dinner tonight, and then I gave him a bath. He had real dirt between his toes. And he peed like any real little boy after drinking three glasses of milk with his Oreo cookies."

"All the more reason to think he might be some kid being used by Emil to get at you," John said, sitting forward suddenly on the couch and turning to look at her hard. He squeezed her hands. "I don't trust that kid."

"He's my son, John."

"You're not thinking clearly, Jessie. Something . . . something's come over you."

"My maternal instinct has come over me," she said. "I recognize my own child."

"Listen to me, Jessie. I believe Emil has come back. It's the only explanation."

She gently extricated her hands from his and stood up from the couch, walking across the room to place another log on the fireplace. The night was so cold and damp.

"The man from the FBI, Patrick Castile, was here to talk to me," she said. "Do you know him?"

John hesitated. "Yes. He came by to see me as well."

"He told me that the FBI has long suspected that Emil wasn't killed in that shoot-out in Mexico."

"That's right, Jessie. That's why you need to be careful."

"Did you know this all along, John? That Emil might not be dead?" She kept her back to him as she nudged the logs with the poker.

"I . . . I had some reasons to think so."

"Really? And you never told me."

"I had no reason to think you were in any danger, Jessie. At least not then. Now I'm worried about it."

She turned to look at him. "I'm not running in terror from Emil anymore."

"I'm not asking you to run, just to be smart and to take precautions. Letting that child live with you . . ."

Jessie smiled. "Oh, John. How could a five-year-old boy hurt me? Don't tell me you're subscribing to Aunt Paulette's crazy theory that he's really Emil, returned as a ghost in the guise of a child?"

"No, of course not. Ghosts don't pee."

"Precisely." She returned to the couch and sat down beside John once again.

He slipped his arm around her, pulling her close.

"But, Jessie," he said. "The FBI is right. . . ." His voice was clearly troubled. "Look, I have to tell you what I know because things are happening . . . and I'm worried about you."

"So you *do* know more than you've told me," she said.

"When I started writing the book," John said, "I went to Mexico looking for Emil. I wanted to find him, to hear the story in his own words. Through the members of his gang that I'd tracked down—and after paying them some money—I determined Emil's whereabouts. I flew to Mexico and located him."

"You—you met Emil?"

"Just once."

Jessie pulled away from him on the couch.

"Please listen to me, Jessie."

"I'm listening," she said coldly. "Go on."

"Emil told me that he'd give me his story if I paid him. I was in the process of trying to raise the cash when the Mexican police raided the house he was staying in, killing everyone inside. But I knew Emil wasn't one of them."

"How did you know that?"

"Because he left a note for me the next day at my hotel, saying he'd still tell me his story if I paid him the money. But by that time the FBI and CIA had arrived and were swarming all over the place. A couple of them interviewed me and made it clear that I was interfering with their investigation. So I got the hell out of there."

"So you knew all along that Emil was alive. . . ."

"The FBI wasn't sure if the note was a forgery, written by another gang member. But yes . . . I had serious suspicions he was alive."

"And you never told me."

"I didn't want to worry you. And the FBI was in touch with me periodically, asking me if I had heard from Emil. They told me to say nothing. And they assured me that they were keeping watch on a person who might be him, and that he had not returned to the United States."

"But now they believe he has. . . ."

John nodded. "And that's why I want you to take all precautions, Jessie. I'm so sorry I didn't tell you everything before."

She looked at him. "Are there any more secrets I should know, John?"

For half a second, Jessie thought she detected a flicker of unease in John's eyes, and a flash of hesitation. But then he said firmly, "No. No more secrets."

Jessie sighed, standing up once more despite John's attempt to embrace her. Did she believe him that there were no more secrets? She wasn't sure.

He's a very bad man, Aaron had said.

Why did John want to separate her from her son— the son she had only just found again after so long?

A very bad man.

"A very bad man," she heard again, only now it was John speaking. "Emil is very bad, very dangerous."

Jessie leveled her eyes at him. "Do you think I don't know that?"

"Of course you do, Jessie. It's just that the idea of

him here, in Sayer's Brook, makes me very uneasy. I remember the cruelty in his eyes when I spoke with him in Mexico. I saw then a man who had no conscience, a sociopath who lived only for himself, and whose motives were greed and revenge."

"Did he say anything about me?"

"Only that you had seen him commit the murder. We didn't speak long. He wasn't going to tell me anything before he got his money."

Jessie shuddered.

"I'm so sorry about this, Jessie. Please. Let me put you and Abby up at a hotel."

"No."

"Or come stay with me. . . ."

"Emil can't harm me anymore, John," she told him. "I won't let him."

"How can you fight off a monster like that?"

Jessie smiled. "Call me crazy, and you probably will, but I feel that the boy upstairs—my son—is here to protect me. That's why he came back. Aaron won't let his father hurt me again."

"You're right. I *do* think that sounds crazy."

"A couple of days ago, I would have agreed that it sounds crazy. I can't explain how I feel, John. But I believe Aaron has come back to protect Abby and me from Emil."

"Fine. But take some other precautions. . . ."

"We have a high-powered, maximum-security system in place."

"I don't think that will keep Emil out if he wants in."

"Look, John, I'm not afraid of Emil anymore. For

too long I've lived in fear of him. But now, you can rest assured that I am indeed strong enough to stand up to anything Emil does." She smiled, looking toward the stairs. "You'll see. Emil will be sorry for everything he ever did to me."

NINETY-TWO

Aaron walked softly through the woods, wearing the clean, sweet-smelling, blue flannel pajamas that Jessie had dressed him in. The only sounds, as usual, were the leaves underfoot. The rain was drenching his hair and the mud was once again soiling his feet.

He reached the shack.

The boy entered, sitting on a broken old chair against one wall. Within seconds, the man entered. Aaron watched him. The man was carrying a sack. He threw the sack behind a pile of old wooden boxes, then stretched out on the floor.

"Sleep," the man said in a weary voice. "I need sleep. . . ."

It wasn't long before the man was snoring on the floor.

Aaron sat there, watching him.

NINETY-THREE

"I can't help you, Aunt Paulette," Monica said. "She won't speak to me."

"She can't allow that boy to sleep in her house! I don't trust him! He's a devil-child! I think he's Emil come back to life!"

Monica poured herself another glass of wine. It was her third in the last half hour. At this rate, she'd have the whole bottle empty soon, and she was absolutely fine with that. The wine made the nights easier to get through.

"You sound like a crazy old woman," she told her aunt, her words slurring slightly. "I've never believed in all your hocus pocus about visions and ghosts. Devil-child! Emil come back to life! Don't make me laugh!"

"It's true, Monica. You must believe me! Jessie's not herself. That child has cast some kind of spell over her."

"Maybe that explains why she's being such a bitch," Monica said, sipping the wine. "She keeps saying I owe her an apology, when it's because of *her* that my husband has left me. . . ."

"Monica, please! Let that go for now. Your sister is in danger! She needs our help!"

Monica gestured at her aunt with the wineglass. "Did you know that Todd is living right down the street? He's staying with Mr. Thayer. I saw him. But he won't speak to me. I've left hundreds of messages. I even went down there. He's put poor Mr. Thayer in a dreadful position. Mr. Thayer was very sympathetic to me when I went down there." She frowned at Aunt Paulette. "It was a nice change to find someone sympathetic to *me* for a change."

"Monica, please . . ."

"But even though Mr. Thayer tried to get Todd to talk with me, he refused. I just don't know what to do anymore, Aunt Paulette."

She chugged back the wine.

"Monica, we need to help Jessie. . . ."

"Jessie can go to hell!" Monica shrieked, and tossed the wineglass across the room. It shattered against the marble floor.

NINETY-FOUR

Outside the window, standing in the rain, peering in through the window, Aaron heard Monica's words.

He turned and trudged up the hill back toward Jessie's house. Halfway there, he paused. He stood in the shadows, watching the scene unfold on Jessie's front porch.

She was saying good night to John Manning. He took Jessie in his arms.

"I've come to care about you a great deal," Manning was saying to Jessie. Aaron could hear his voice clearly from where he stood, floating through the night air and the misty rain. "And I'm worried about you."

"I'm perfectly safe here," Jessie told him. "The security system is quite sophisticated."

"But the boy . . ."

"He's my son, John. I know you don't believe it, and I can't explain it. But he's my son."

"He's *not* your son, Jessie," John said.

Aaron's face darkened.

"Then what is he?" Jessie asked. "A little boy who's lost."

"If that's so, his parents must be looking for him. . . ."

"His mother has already found him."

"Jessie, you should at least talk to Chief Walters about him. . . ."

She put a finger to Manning's mouth.

He fell silent. Then he reached down and kissed Jessie on the lips.

Aaron's mouth twisted downward in anger as he watched.

"We'll talk again in the morning," Manning told Jessie.

"Come by for our Halloween party," she said. "Wait until you see the kids' costumes!"

Manning didn't reply. Aaron watched him as he walked down the steps. His eyes followed the man as he hurried through the rain toward his house.

Jessie went back inside. Aaron heard the lock of the front door, and the soft "beep-beep" indicating that Jessie had just activated the security system. Then the lights in the living room went out, and Aaron could hear Jessie heading upstairs.

NINETY-FIVE

A part of Jessie was just as disbelieving as John was, though she wouldn't admit it. The rational part of her knew that the idea that Aaron was her son made no sense. But rationality didn't matter anymore. She knew he was her son.

Her son who'd come back to her.

And this time, she could not—would not—push him away.

Jessie reached the top of the stairs and smiled.

It was nice, after all these years, to have both her children—her twins—with her. Jessie tiptoed to Abby's room and opened the door. Her daughter was sound asleep. Jessie approached the bed quietly and leaned down, kissing the little girl on the forehead. Then she carefully made her way out of the room so as not to wake her up.

Outside the door to the room next to Abby's, Jessie paused. This had been Inga's room when they had first moved here. But this afternoon Jessie had made it into Aaron's room. She'd put fresh sheets on the bed and hung a photograph of a cowboy on a horse on the wall. The photo had been her father's when he was a little boy. Aaron had smiled when Jessie had shown it to him. She'd promised him that someday she'd take him horseback riding. How Aaron had beamed when she'd told him that.

Of course, people were going to ask questions. Where did he come from? Where was his birth certificate? Had he had all his shots? A part of Jessie—the rational part again—was wondering those same things. *How can he be my son? That's impossible.*

But he was. She pushed the questions aside and opened the door.

In a shaft of moonlight, she saw Aaron fast asleep in the bed. How precious he looked. How angelic. How could John fear him? Jessie had been very happy when John had kissed her. She couldn't deny that she had some feelings for him. But like all the men she'd loved, John had lied to her; he'd kept things from her; he wasn't fully honest with her. Not so with Aaron. Aaron always spoke the truth. It wasn't his fault that he didn't know the answers to all her questions. He'd been lost for so long—abandoned. But not anymore.

Not anymore.

Jessie reached down and kissed him on his forehead. She straightened the blankets around him.

Then she walked to the window, checking that it was locked. It was. No one could get through that window. If they tried, the security system would sound.

She'd keep him safe. She'd keep them all safe.

Looking down once more at her son's sleeping face, Jessie tiptoed out of the room and shut the door.

NINETY-SIX

It was Halloween.

The day was dry and the air felt fresh after the rain. But it was cold. Paulette shivered and pulled her coat tighter around herself as she headed toward the woods.

Chief Walters had seemed to appreciate what Paulette had had to say when she'd gone down to the station first thing this morning. The chief had been very interested when Paulette revealed that Jessie had taken the little boy in to live with her. Paulette had chosen to tell Walters only so much about what she suspected. She told her only that she felt the boy was connected to Emil somehow—that he was going by the last name of Smelt, which seemed a clue. She secured the chief's promise to look in on Jessie, and to check the boy out. After all, he was a lost child, Paulette argued, and his parents must be looking for him. Perhaps the chief should take the boy into protective custody until his parents or guardians could be found. Walters had seemed to agree, much to Paulette's relief. The chief promised she'd go out to the house and look into the matter.

That taken care of, Paulette had returned to Hickory Dell and made her way down to the woods. This was the part of her suspicions that she didn't share with the chief.

That shack Jessie mentioned, Paulette thought to herself, as she stepped over the brook and into the woods. *I know where it is. I can find it.*

Decades ago, she used to meet Howard at the shack. It was their little rendezvous, where they'd go to make out and not be found by Paulette's parents or her sister, Caroline. Paulette never let him get farther than first base, but she did enjoy his kisses. They'd hang out at the shack for hours, listening to Simon and Garfunkel on their transistor radio. Then Howard had gone off to Vietnam and the shack had been torn down.

At least, Paulette thought it had.

The woods seemed alive with sound this morning. Crows whooped from trees. There was the rat-tat-tat noise of woodpeckers and blue jays scolded from above. Occasionally Paulette made out the low hoot of an owl. From branch to branch squirrels leapt and chipmunks scurried alongside her on the path. There were barely any shadows this morning. The sun, nearly overhead, filled in all available space, pouring in easily through the bare trees.

There was no reason for fear on such a day.

Even though it was Halloween.

Paulette tried to push the thought of Halloween out of her mind. It was a happy children's holiday—but she knew its origins. When nightfall came, it was the eve of the day of the dead—the only time, some believed, that the dead could walk again among the living.

Paulette had no idea what she might find at the shack. But she knew she'd be able to sense if something un-

dead dwelled there. She trusted her instincts, her intuition, her powers that much.

She walked, and walked some more.

The shack. Where was it?

Her father—or maybe it had been her grandfather—
had built it, as a place to store hunting equipment. The
woods had been much deeper in those days, stretching
out past the gorge for at least forty miles. Paulette's father had hunted deer in those deeper woods when he
was a young man. Now so much of the woods had been
torn down, replaced with suburban housing developments. All that was left of the once mighty forest was
this smaller stretch that edged Hickory Dell. Paulette
had a memory of the shack being torn down at some
point, her father moving all his equipment back to the
house once the new housing developments started
being built.

But, apparently, her memory was wrong. There was
the shack, some ten yards ahead of her, slumped and
weathered like an old man.

Paulette stopped in her approach, taking a deep
breath. She could still hear the birds in the trees. That
was good.

What might she find inside? Her heart began to race.
All night long, the little sleep she'd been able to
achieve had been torn apart by nightmares of the tall,
dark man. She had tried so hard to see his face. Was it
Emil? Or was it . . . someone else?

She began walking again. She reached the shack's
broken door, hanging limply from rusted hinges. With
a careful touch, Paulette pushed it open.

The place was draped in spiderwebs. Roots had

grown through the old, corroded floorboards, and vines grew up the walls. There were some old wooden boxes scattered about. Paulette stepped inside.

Nothing.

She felt nothing.

Outside the birds chirped wildly in the trees.

"But the boy said he lived here," Paulette whispered to herself.

Why did she sense nothing?

That was when she noticed a couple of books scattered on the floor in the far corner of the shack. Walking over, Paulette bent down and picked one of the books up in her hand.

Sound of a Scream by John Manning.

A dark brown substance had dried over much of the cover.

Paulette knew instantly that these were the books Inga had with her when she was killed, and the brown substance was her blood.

"Dear God," she gasped.

Then she noticed something else. Behind one of the old boxes sat a denim bag. It, too, hadn't been in the shack very long. No mold covered it. And on the floor around the bag Paulette could now make out the muddy footprints of a man's large shoe.

She bent down and pulled open the drawstring of the bag. There were clothes inside. T-shirts mostly. And some papers. With trembling hands, Paulette unfolded the papers and began to read.

"Dear God," she gasped again. "I've got to tell Jessie."

She stood and turned, ready to bolt out of there and run back through the woods.

But then the tall, dark man came through the door. Paulette didn't have time to scream. She barely saw the blade as it swung out at her, whistling through the air before slicing into her flesh.

Howard, she thought. *I'll see Howard. . . .*

The papers in her hand fluttered to the floor of the shack.

NINETY-SEVEN

"**M**onica?"

Todd pushed open the front door and stepped inside the living room. Mr. Thayer was behind him.

"Monica?" he called again.

There was no reply. The house had that heavy feeling of emptiness.

"You see, I told you she wasn't home," Mr. Thayer said. "Her car's not in the driveway."

"Just wanted to make sure," Todd replied, before bounding up the stairs.

"Really, Todd," Mr. Thayer called up after him. "I wish you'd stay and wait for her to get home. The two of you need to talk."

"I have nothing to say to her," Todd called down, as he quickly went through his desk and gathered up the papers he needed. Then he ran into the bedroom and grabbed a couple of sweaters. Eventually he'd move all his stuff out, but for now, this would be enough. Monica wouldn't even know he'd been here.

He felt surprisingly little emotion as he hurried through the house that he and Monica had designed and built. Its sleek marble and glass left him cold. There were no pangs of homesickness, or grief, or loss. Todd was determined to end the marriage as soon as possible. He'd give Monica wherever she wanted—even the house. He just wanted to be free of a marriage that had felt stifling and unnatural for a long time now. A marriage that Todd knew now had been built on a lie told by a teenage girl.

He'd been Monica's prisoner too long.

At the window, Todd paused. Something caught his eye. He could barely make out John Manning's driveway through the trees, but he could see a man walking up toward the gate. It was that FBI investigator, Patrick Castile. He'd been by to interview both Todd and Mr. Thayer about what they might have seen or heard the night of the murders at the Pierce house. They'd had nothing to tell him. They'd seen and heard nothing.

It was a terrible shame about Heather and the kids' deaths. It just made Todd want to put Hickory Dell behind him all the more.

He hurried back down the stairs. "Okay," he said to Mr. Thayer. "I got what I came for. Let's get out of here."

"You sure you won't wait?"

"I told you. I have nothing to say to her."

Mr. Thayer frowned. "Then at least go up and speak to Jessie before you head out of town again. Todd, you can't keep running away from everything."

"I don't think Jessie wants to see me."

Mr. Thayer sighed. "She might welcome the distraction. I just saw Gert Gorin trudging up the hill to Jessie's house."

Todd sighed.

"Just tell her that you're leaving," Mr. Thayer said.

"All right," Todd said, and they headed out of the house.

NINETY-EIGHT

Aaron stood among the trees that divided Jessie's property from John Manning's. He craned his neck, searching for the highest one. Having made his choice, he began to climb.

At the very top of a sweet-smelling pine, Aaron watched. On one side of him, Manning was opening his gate and allowing Patrick Castile inside.

But then he turned, his ears drawn by the sound of voices from the other side.

One of the voices was Jessie's.

His mother's voice.

NINETY-NINE

"I thought you might want to know that the FBI is over talking with John Manning right at this very moment," Gert Gorin was saying, her chin up, her eyes flashing, as she stood on Jessie's front porch. "I just saw that man, Patrick Castile, arrive. It's the third or fourth time he's been by to see Mr. Manning."

Jessie stood in the doorway and sighed. "Why does this information concern me, Mrs. Gorin?"

The neighbor's face contorted in fury. "Because all of these murders only began after you returned to Sayer's Brook! Because an entire family is now dead—a family you and John Manning had conflict with!"

Jessie kept her cool. "Are you accusing me in some way, Mrs. Gorin?"

Gert folded her arms across her chest and twisted her lips into a smile. "I'm only stating facts."

"Well, maybe you can state your facts on your own front porch," Jessie said, attempting to close the door.

"I think I speak for the entire neighborhood—those of us who are left, that is—in saying that we'd be very happy if you just packed up and moved back to New York!"

A new voice was heard in reply. "You don't speak for me," Todd said, walking up the hill.

"Or me," said Mr. Thayer, who was following a few steps behind.

"Why don't you just go home and mind your own business for a change?" Todd was telling Gert. "Just go home and stay there."

"Well!" Gert huffed, marching down the steps of the porch and stalking past the men back down the hill.

"Hello, Todd," Jessie said from the doorway. "Hello, Mr. Thayer."

"Hello, my dear," Mr. Thayer replied.

"Don't listen to that old witch," Todd said.

Jessie gave them a small smile, but didn't invite them in. "I guess she has a point that things did start with my return."

"No one can blame you for anything, Jessie," Todd told her. "For *anything*." He put the stress on the last word.

"Thank you," she said quietly.

"I just came up to tell you that I was going away," Todd said. "Mr. Thayer will have my contact info, if you want to reach me."

Jessie eyed him. "Are you leaving Monica for good?"

"I'll be asking for a divorce."

"I see."

"Jessie, I wish I could tell you how—"

"Please don't, Todd. Too much has happened. I can't hear any more."

"But—"

"I said please don't." Her voice was sharp, sharper than she'd intended.

It was at that moment that she noticed Aaron standing a few feet away, watching them.

"Aaron!" she called. "What are you doing outside? I thought you were up with Abby taking a nap."

"I came out to play," the little boy said.

"Well, you've gotten all dirty again, sweetie. Come inside."

Aaron came bounding up the porch steps, brushing past the two men. When he reached Jessie, allowing her to stroke his hair, he turned around and glared at Todd.

"Sweet little baby," Jessie mumbled. "Come in and let Mommy clean you up."

She closed the door without saying good-bye to Todd or Mr. Thayer.

ONE HUNDRED

"That was odd," Mr. Thayer said.

Todd nodded. "Very odd," he agreed.

They headed off the porch and then back down the hill.

"Why did she refer to herself as 'Mommy'?" Mr. Thayer wondered.

"Very odd," Todd said again.

That was when Monica's car suddenly pulled into the driveway.

ONE HUNDRED AND ONE

•

Chief Belinda Walters sat at her desk, stewing.

She was angry that the feds had taken her department off active investigation of the murders. She was furious that they seemed to be withholding information from her. And she was worried that John Manning, who she still believed knew more about all this than he was saying, would get off scot-free.

But she was also stewing about something else.

Her daughter Emma's comment that Madame Paulette had actually been *right* in her prediction.

Maybe, the chief thought, she'd been too quick to dismiss Paulette Drew's reliability as a witness. Maybe she should at least give what she had to say some consideration.

This morning, Paulette had come into Walters's office. She'd told her about a boy, a strange child who'd been taken in by Jessie Clarkson—a boy that Paulette felt had some connection to Emil Deetz. She was worried, deeply worried, about this boy.

What connection could a little boy have to all these murders? If Emil Deetz was committing them, what part did the kid play?

And where, Walters still wanted to know, did John Manning fit into all of this?

She stood from her desk and walked out into the department. She stopped at the desk of Detective Knotts.

"I'm going out to Hickory Dell," she told him.

"But I thought—"

"I'm still the police chief of this burg. I can take a walk around a neighborhood when there's a report of a lost kid."

Knotts raised his eyebrows. "There's been a report of a lost kid?"

"There's gonna be," Walters said, giving him a small smile before heading out the door.

ONE HUNDRED AND TWO

"**W**hy am I not surprised," Monica snarled, getting out of her car and slamming the door, "to come home and find you walking back from Jessie's when you haven't returned any of my calls or come by to see me?"

"I'm not getting into it with you, Monica," Todd said, attempting to walk past her. "Not now."

She grabbed his arm. "Todd, please!"

He shrugged her hand off violently.

"I'm your wife, Todd!" Monica cried.

"Please, Todd," Mr. Thayer implored. "Talk with her. See what you can work out."

But Todd continued walking down the driveway toward the street without looking back. "There's nothing to be worked out," he said. "I want out of the marriage. End of discussion."

"No!" Monica shrieked.

"I'm sorry, my dear," Mr. Thayer said, passing her, hurrying to catch up with Todd.

Monica stared after them. Her husband was striding down the street now, disappearing from sight.

Walking out of her life for good.

"No!" Monica cried again.

She wanted to run after him. But instead she turned the other way, and ran to her sister's house.

"Jessie!" she screamed, banging on the front door. "Jessie, let me in!"

Jessie opened the door, staring at her with blank eyes.

"Why was Todd here?" Monica demanded to know.

"I have no clue," Jessie told her.

"Were you making plans to meet him later?"

"No."

Even in her fury, Monica detected the unnaturally calm tone of her sister's voice. Standing behind her in the living room was that boy. That strange, dark-eyed boy.

"He's saying the marriage is over," Monica said. "Did you know that?"

The boy came to stand beside Jessie, his little arm gripping her around the waist.

"Monica, I have to go" Jessie said. "I'm getting Aaron's costume ready. We're having a Halloween party. If you like, you can come. . . ."

"Listen, Jessie, my whole life is ruined," Monica told her. "I'm not interested in goddamn Halloween parties! I need you to help me! We're sisters!"

"But I can't help you, Monica."

"Yes, you can. You have to go to Todd. You have to tell him to come back to me!"

Jessie sighed. "You told a terrible lie a long time ago, Monica. That was wrong."

Monica could feel her face burn with rage and hatred. "You bitch! You've always hated me! You always got everything!"

"That's not true, Monica."

Jessie's voice. So calm. So even-toned. As if she were stoned on pot or something. Even in her anger, Monica could sense something was different about her sister.

"I have to go now, Monica," Jessie said. "We're getting ready for our Halloween party. When Aunt Paulette gets back, we're going to bob for apples and string some popcorn." She smiled at her sister sadly. "We might have been a happy family—you and me and Aunt Paulette and Abby and Aaron."

With that, she closed the door on her sister's face.

Monica screamed in frustration, then raced back to her house, where she drank an entire bottle of wine in fifteen minutes, then smashed the bottle and the glass.

ONE HUNDRED AND THREE

Around two o'clock in the afternoon, Chief Walters's car pulled onto Hickory Dell, but instead of proceeding to Jessie Clarkson's house, she pulled over to the curb outside of John Manning's. There was Patrick Castile, walking down the driveway.

"I see you finally decided to check up on Manning," Walters said, getting out of her car.

"I told you we had things under control," Castile said, clearly not happy to see the chief walking toward him.

"Do you? So I can tell the citizens of Sayer's Brook they have no reason to worry letting their kids go out trick-or-treating tonight?"

Castile frowned. "Chief Walters, there is really nothing for you to do here. I'd appreciate you not bothering Mr. Manning again. I've already found out everything I need to know from him."

"What did you talk to him about? Did you ask him to explain his presence in Mexico the night Emil Deetz was supposedly killed?"

"What I spoke with Mr. Manning about is classified information."

"Listen, you young pipsqueak," Walters said, getting up close in Castile's smooth face. "I have my department stationed all over this town tonight. If one more of our citizens gets his or her throat sliced, I'm not going to sit idly by just trusting you guys to track down the killer."

"I have federal agents posted all over town as well."

"I know you do. Too bad we can't coordinate a little. But the federal government doesn't like to share power, does it?"

Castile said nothing.

"I'm not here to talk to Mr. Manning anyway," the chief said. "I'm looking for a lost boy. Heard of him at all?"

"What lost boy?" Castile asked.

"Name's Aaron Smelt," Walters said.

Castile eyed her coldly. "Sorry," he said. "Can't help you there."

"Figured as much," the chief replied, as she walked up the street toward the Clarkson property. Behind her, she heard Castile get into his car and drive away.

God, that creep got under her skin. . . .

Walters knocked first on Monica Bennett's door. When Monica answered, her eyes were red and swollen and her breath reeked of wine.

"What is it *now*?" she asked.

"Just inquiring about a lost boy," the chief said. "A little dark-haired child. Goes by the name Aaron. Have you seen him?"

"Sure have," Monica mumbled. "My sister's got him. Who is he anyway?"

"That's what I want to find out. How long has he been at Jessie's?"

"I don't know and I don't really care." Monica seemed really drunk. "But he's been coming around for a while. Odd little kid."

"Your aunt seemed frightened of him in some way," Walters said.

Monica laughed. "Well, everything frightens Aunt Paulette."

"Is your aunt at her cottage?"

"I suspect she's up at Jessie's. They're having a Halloween party." Monica snorted in drunken derision. "Such a happy little family, them and the two brats."

"So Aaron is up there now?"

Monica nodded. "Well, he was about an hour or so ago. Strange little kid. You should really take him away from Jessie, you know."

"Why is that?"

"Because he doesn't belong there."

"Why do you say that?"

Monica's face darkened. "Jessie always gets whatever wants. She wanted a son, too. A daughter wasn't enough. So she had to get a son, too." She closed her eyes. "Some of us never had any children, but now Jessie has two."

"Are you saying your sister is keeping him there and his parents don't know?"

Monica laughed. "I have no idea who his parents are. Neither does Jessie. But she's keeping him there. Take him away from her, Chief. Show her she can't have everything!"

"I'll go pay them a visit," Walters said.

"Yes, you do that," Monica said, her words slurring, and closed the door.

ONE HUNDRED AND FOUR

"**A**rthur!" Gert Gorin cackled. "Now the police chief is heading up to Jessie's! Maybe they'll finally arrest her!"

As ever, her eyes were pressed against the binoculars that were pressed against the glass of the picture window. Behind her, Arthur had fallen asleep in his chair and was snoring as loud as a freight chain. Still, that didn't stop Gert from giving him a blow-by-blow of what was happening outside.

"First she spoke with that FBI agent in John Manning's driveway. Lord, he had been in there a long time. A couple of hours or more! Wonder what he was asking Manning? Probably really gave him the third degree."

Gert watched as the chief walked up Jessie's front steps and knocked on the door.

"I wonder what the 'third degree' means," Gert mused. "They always say it on police shows."

Arthur snored in response.

"There's some kind of party going on inside Jessie's house," Gert said. "Wish I could see more clearly. Lots of colors. And I can see a lot of movement."

Jessie opened the door and the chief stepped inside the house, closing the door behind her.

"Damn," Gert said, setting the binoculars down. "I was hoping they'd talk on the porch."

She frowned at her sleeping husband.

"Wake up, Arthur!" she commanded. "I need to get the Halloween cupcakes ready."

He shifted in his chair but refused to open his eyes. "What parents in their right minds are going to let their kids trick-or-treat on this street tonight, after all that's happened?" he mumbled.

"Oh, there will be kids," Gert said. "Mark my word on it. And we've got to be ready."

"I'm staying right here in my chair if any kids start ringing the bell," Arthur said, his eyes still defiantly shut.

"I'll pass out the cupcakes," Gert said. "But I need help frosting all of them. I made a hundred. Remember, we give out the best treats in the neighborhood, Arthur. We have a reputation to keep up!"

ONE HUNDRED AND FIVE

Chief Walters couldn't help but smile at the scene she found inside Jessie Clarkson's house.

The place had been strung with orange and black crepe paper. The walls were decorated with images of big smiling cardboard pumpkins. A metal tub sat on the linoleum kitchen floor filled with water and floating, bright red apples. Trays of candies and sweets were everywhere. Jessie was dressed as a friendly witch, in a long blue dress and a blue pointed hat. She had painted red circles on her cheeks.

But it was the two children who really made Walters smile. Little Abby was dressed in a pretty pink dress covered in sparkles, and on her head she wore a cardboard crown spray-painted gold. The little boy—Aaron Smelt, the chief assumed—wore a long white sheet from shoulders to floor, and on his head he wore a plastic pumpkin head. He kept lifting it up to peek out at Jessie with his big brown eyes and flash a toothy grin.

"Would you like some apple cider?" Jessie asked Walters. "We also have lemonade."

"Well, okay, a little cider would be nice," the chief said. "I don't want to interrupt your party too long."

"That's okay," Jessie said, pouring some cider into a paper cup. "We haven't really started yet. We're still waiting for Aunt Paulette to get back. She's been gone all day."

"Really?" Walters asked, accepting the cider from Jessie. "I saw her this morning in town."

"I don't know where she could be," Jessie said.

The kids were laughing as they scooped up fistfuls of M&Ms from a bowl and packed them into their mouths.

"Not so many!" Jessie said, moving the bowl onto the mantel so they couldn't reach. "Don't get filled up before supper! Because afterward, we have chocolate cake with orange frosting!"

"Yummy!" both children called out.

"Now, what can I help you with, Chief Walters?" Jessie asked, turning her attention back to their visitor.

"I just wanted to make sure everything was okay," the chief said.

Jessie smiled. "Yes. And don't worry. I'm not letting the children go outside tonight. That's why we're having the party. Staying in rather than going out."

"Good idea." Walters took a sip of cider. "Tell me about the boy, Jessie. Is this the Smelt child you were curious about?"

Jessie seemed a little uncomfortable. "Yes. I needn't have been concerned. He's a good boy. Nothing to worry about."

"Have you met his parents?"

"He's a good boy, Chief," Jessie said again. "There's nothing to worry about."

Walters looked down at Aaron, who was holding his

pumpkin head up in his hands and staring out solemnly at her.

"Where do you live, Aaron?" the chief asked.

"Here," he said.

"Here?" The chief's eyes flickered back to Jessie. "What does he mean, living here?"

"He was living in an old shack in the woods," Jessie said. "I couldn't let him stay out there, could I?"

"But his mother or father must be wondering where he is," Walters said, studying Jessie's eyes carefully.

Aaron had moved over to Jessie, standing defiantly at her side. "She's my mother," he said, his little hand clinging to Jessie's blue dress.

Walters kept her eyes on Jessie. "Your sister said that I should take him away from you."

Jessie blanched. "Monica said that?"

"She said that his real parents don't know he's here, that you're keeping him here."

"*This* is my mother!" Aaron demanded.

"Sweetie," Jessie said, looking down at him. "Why don't you and Abby go sit on the deck for a minute? We're going to make straw dolls out there in a minute. Why don't you get the straw ready? There's a box of orange twine, too. Set all that out on the table on the deck, and I'll be out in a minute."

Aaron let go of her dress and obeyed, though he kept his eyes on the chief as he walked out. Abby skipped along, her cardboard crown bouncing on her head, held in place by barrettes.

"I know this will sound strange, chief," Jessie said once the children were gone, "but I truly believe that Aaron *does* belong here. He has no place else to go."

"How do you know that?"

Jessie's face tightened. "I just do."

"I think I need to check if there are any missing children reports."

Jessie nodded. "Go ahead. I guarantee there won't be."

The chief gave her a concerned look. "Your aunt said she thinks the boy might be working in cahoots with Emil Deetz."

Jessie laughed, a little bitterly. "I see my entire family has been talking behind my back to you."

"Your aunt was concerned."

"I know she is, but she needn't be." Jessie sighed, then moved toward the door. "If you find someone looking for Aaron, let me know, Chief. In the meantime, it's best to keep him here, don't you think? We can't have him wandering alone outside, can we?"

"I'd like to ask him a few questions, alone," Walters said.

Jessie opened the door. "Not this afternoon, Chief. Come back tomorrow, if you must. Please let him enjoy Halloween for the first time in his life."

Walters took a step toward the door but she wasn't quite ready to leave yet. "How do you know it's the first time in his life he's enjoyed Halloween?"

"I just do."

"You must admit, Jessie, this is all very strange."

Jessie looked out the door into the yard. The sun was beginning to drop toward the bare trees, staining the afternoon sky red. "What's strange is why Aunt Paulette has been gone all day," she said. "If you want to be concerned about something, Chief, then maybe that's where we should be directing our energy."

"Do you think something's happened to her?" Walters asked.

"Well, her car is up at her cottage. But she's not there, though her cell phone is. Yes, I suppose I am getting a little worried about her."

The chief sighed. "I'll have some officers take a look around, before it gets too dark."

Jessie nodded. "I appreciate it."

Walters sighed and stepped out the door. She turned around and looked back at Jessie. "But I am also going to have them look into the boy. If there are any missing-child reports that match his description . . ."

"Then by all means, get in touch with me," Jessie said. "But I'm telling you." Her voice became serious. "You won't find any such reports."

ONE HUNDRED AND SIX

Monica was taking longer to drink her second bottle of wine, but she figured she'd be done with this one, too, by the time the sun had set.

She sat at her bedroom window watching Chief Walters make her way down the hill. She wondered what she and Jessie had talked about. She wished she'd seen the chief escorting her sister to her car in handcuffs.

Down deep, Monica knew she was the one at fault. Not Jessie. Not even Todd. It was her lie that had caused all of this. Her multitude of lies, in fact. Her jealousies. Her resentments.

But she'd never admit that in so many words. Not even to herself.

"Fuck 'em all," she slurred, lifting her glass to her lips.

Her vision was getting blurry. Part of it was the lowering of the sun, and the lengthening of the shadows, and the fact that Monica felt too dizzy to stand up and turn on the light. But most of it, she knew, was the wine.

"Good," she said out loud. "I want to get drunk and just pass out."

She heard a sound. She looked around.

Nothing.

She took another sip of wine. She couldn't believe her marriage was over. She just would not accept the fact. There had to be a way to get Todd back. She'd won him once against all odds. Maybe now she could think of another plan that would get him back.

Another sound.

Monica looked toward the door of her room.

Another sound. Someone on the stairs.

"Todd!" she called out.

But as a figure appeared in the doorway, she could see it wasn't Todd. It was hard to make out just who it was. But it was too small—far too small—to be Todd.

"Hello, Aunt Monica," came a voice.

It was that kid. Aaron.

"What are you doing here?" Monica asked, aware of how slurry her words were.

The boy just stood in the doorway, staring at her.

"How'd you get in here? And don't be calling me Aunt Monica. I'm not your fuckin' aunt."

The boy said nothing. He just kept standing there, staring at Monica in the dim light of dusk.

And suddenly, as Monica attempted to focus on him, his face changed.

Twisted.

Became something else.

Something horrible.

A crazed, evil expression. Eyes that glowed like a demon's.

Monica screamed.

She stood abruptly from her chair, knocking it over.

The boy's face was normal again, looking up at her in wonder.

"Why are you looking at me that way, Aunt Monica?" he asked.

She was backing away. *I imagined what I saw. I'm drunk. And the light's bad. It's getting so dark. . . .*

"If only you hadn't lied to Mommy," Aaron said. "Do you know how unhappy you made her? I don't like it when people make Mommy unhappy."

He began to walk toward her.

"Get out of here," Monica whispered.

"We could have had a happy family reunion today. You and me and Mommy and Abby and Aunt Paulette." He paused. "Daddy, too."

"No," Monica muttered.

"You don't like me, do you, Aunt Paulette?" Aaron asked, getting closer. "You want to keep me away from Mommy, don't you?"

"Get out of here!" Monica screamed.

The boy's face changed again.

This time, so close, she could see it was no illusion.

Monica screamed, running into the bathroom, where a door opened onto a guest room. She ran as fast as she could, sensing that the boy was close behind her. She ran down the hall to Todd's home office and slammed the door behind her, locking it. The boy—that thing!—couldn't get her in here. She was safe.

"You should never have hurt Mommy," came Aaron's voice, suddenly behind her.

Monica spun around. She felt the pain in her abdomen before she looked down and saw the child standing there, grinning up at her like a jack-o'-lantern. She watched in mute horror as he pulled the long razor out of her belly. Monica tried to run, but she was suddenly too weak, or too drunk, or too scared, and she collapsed at Aaron's feet. The boy stood over her, waving the bloody razor in his hand. Then he growled like a dog, baring very sharp teeth, and reached down and sliced open Monica's throat.

ONE HUNDRED AND SEVEN

"Where's Aaron?" Jessie asked, coming out onto the deck.

Abby sat at the table by herself, tying little rolls of straw together with orange twine. She seemed not to hear Jessie's question.

"Abby, I asked where Aaron was," she repeated herself.

"I don't know," said the little girl, seeming mesmerized by the task at hand.

"Aaron?" Jessie called in the yard.

She looked around. It was getting very dark.

"Aaron!" she called again, more loudly this time.

She felt terror rise up in her gut.

ONE HUNDRED AND EIGHT

Gert was sure she'd heard a scream.

She tiptoed up Monica's front porch, noticing the front door was ajar.

"Helloooo?" she called inside.

The sun was sinking below the trees. She really needed to get back to the house. Trick-or-treaters would be arriving soon, and Arthur didn't want to hand out the cupcakes himself. Besides, Gert was scared. She couldn't deny it. If that really was a scream she heard over here, maybe she was better off not knowing where it came from.

But her nosiness—Gert preferred to call it her "intellectual curiosity"—always seemed to win out over her fear.

And here was the Bennetts' door open. . . . What a chance to snoop!

Gert stepped inside.

The house was quiet. Dark and quiet.

"Helloooo?" she called again.

No answer.

She didn't see anything out of the ordinary. She'd hoped maybe to find evidence of all the sexual goings-on that she felt certain were taking place in every house on the street—except for hers, of course, and maybe Mr. Thayer's, although even him she wondered about. What had that Mexican houseman been to Thayer anyway?

Gert paused at the foot of the stairs and looked up into the dark second floor of the house. She supposed this would be as far as she went. Even Gert Gorin's nosiness had its limits.

She turned to leave and noticed a figure in the dark, sitting on the couch. Gert let out a small gasp.

"Who's that?" she asked. "I heard a scream. I came to check. Is that you, Monica?"

But as her eyes adjusted to the dark, she saw it wasn't Monica. It was a child. It was that dark-eyed boy.

"Oh, it's *you*," Gert said, frowning. "What are you doing here?"

The boy sat calmly on the couch, his hands in his lap, his feet not even touching the floor. He didn't reply.

"Why are you always around, little boy?" Gert asked derisively as she headed for the door.

Behind her the boy suddenly spoke.

"You were mean to my mommy," he said.

Gert turned around to tell him that she didn't know his mommy, and that besides, children should mind their own business. But as she did so, she saw his sweet little face change.

Gert didn't have time to scream. Aaron leapt at her, his fangs and claws bared.

He tore out her throat.

ONE HUNDRED AND NINE

As soon as she spotted John walking up the front steps, Jessie bolted out of the house. "Stay with Abby," she said. "I'll be back. I've got to look for Aaron!"

"You'll do no such thing," John said, gently but forcefully easing her back through the door. Behind him, Caleb was lugging a large chocolate cake up the steps. "We're here for the party and that's where you'll stay."

But Jessie was no longer in the mood for parties. "He can't be out there by himself!" Jessie argued. "It's dark out!"

John gripped her by the shoulders. "Aaron has apparently been living on his own out there for months now. He seems to know how to take care of himself."

"He's five years old!"

"Listen to me, Jessie. Sit down!"

She didn't want to obey, but she did. Caleb stepped by with the cake, much to Abby's delight. The two of them moved into the kitchen as John stood lecturing Jessie.

"I had a long conversation with the FBI today. They believe now for certain that Emil has come back. He is definitely out there. They're certain he has committed these killings and that you could be next." He sat down next to her on the couch. "After the party, you and Abby are going to a hotel until Emil is apprehended."

"And leave Aaron all alone? I won't, John. I told him I'd never leave him again."

"Excuse me," Caleb said awkwardly, returning from the kitchen. "I've got to head out. Did you want me to make that hotel reservation, Mr. Manning?"

"Not if it's for me," Jessie said.

John sighed. "Apparently that will be all, Caleb. Thanks for getting the cake."

"Well, have a happy Halloween, both of you," the young assistant said. "And stay safe."

"I'm not hiding out anymore," Jessie said. "I've lived too long in fear. And I'm not leaving Aaron, *especially* if Emil is out there!"

John said nothing more until Caleb had left. Then he turned to Jessie, an angry look on his face.

"What's gotten into you, Jessie?" he asked. "How can you go on believing that boy is your son—a son you *miscarried*?"

"We've been over this, John. I can't explain it. But I know it's so. I know it in my heart and my soul."

"Whether it's true or not, Jessie, you have a daughter to think about. A real, living daughter who's been with you these past five years. And you aren't taking *her* safety into consideration."

"We have a security system installed here—"

"Like that would stop Emil if he has revenge on his mind!"

"Why the urgency tonight? Why the sense that Emil is out there tonight?"

John looked at Jessie with stern eyes. "The FBI has gotten a description of a man they think might be him. A man who was seen on the road beyond the woods, out near the gorge. There's a team of agents right now searching the woods and the area around the gorge."

Jessie shuddered. "Emil . . ." she muttered.

"Let's get out of here right now. Go get Abby and we'll take the cake and all the party favors and get a room at a hotel. We'll have a great party away from all of this."

"I can't."

"Jessie—"

"It's not just Aaron. It's also Aunt Paulette."

John looked at her oddly. "Paulette?"

"She's been gone all day. Her car is here, but she isn't. I've looked everywhere. She's not at her cottage, not anywhere on the grounds."

"Maybe she's with Monica."

"She wasn't earlier."

"We can check with Monica before we leave."

Jessie wrapped her arms around herself. "She would've called me. Something's happened. I fear something has happened to both Aunt Paulette and Aaron."

"Let's call Monica. . . ."

"I've tried. She doesn't pick up. She probably sees it's me and doesn't want to speak to me."

"All right," John said. "Stay here. Keep the doors locked. I'll go down to Monica's and see if she's heard from Paulette. And I'll take a look around. But after that, we're leaving. All right, Jessie?"

She didn't reply.

"All right, Jessie?" he asked again.

Emil . . . he was out there.

You have a daughter to think about.

"All right," Jessie replied.

"Good," John said. "Go pack a bag for each of you. I'll be right back."

He headed off into the night.

Jessie didn't move from the couch. She just sat there, hugging herself.

ONE HUNDRED AND TEN

Aaron scrambled back up his tree. From high above, he saw the figure moving below, making its way through the trees.

It was him.

John Manning.

Aaron leapt. He came down hard on the man's back, knocking him facedown into the leaves. He produced the razor from his sleeve and sliced Manning's neck with such force that the blade got stuck in the spinal cord. With a yank, Aaron pulled the razor free. He stood up, looking down at the twitching, bleeding body at his feet.

That was when he realized the man's hair was blond. It was not John Manning. It was the younger man they called Caleb.

"Stay right where you are!" came a voice.

Aaron looked around. Another man stepped out of the shadows toward him.

Manning this time?

No. It was the one they called Patrick Castile.

"Dear God," Castile said. "It's just a boy."

Aaron leapt.

And Castile's Adam's apple was torn out of his throat.

ONE HUNDRED AND ELEVEN

The sky was awash in reds and golds as the sun set behind the trees. The street was rapidly filling up with trick-or-treaters, nearly all of them teenagers drawn to the dare of being on the "murder street" after dark. Chief Walters had expected this, so she'd posted four cars, with two officers each, on the street. She was there herself as well, her intuition telling her that Hickory Dell was going to be dangerous tonight.

In fact, it was more than intuition: Patrick Castile had admitted that his agents had a report of a man matching Emil Deetz's description being spotted on the other side of the woods, over near the gorge that the locals called Suicide Leap. A massive manhunt had been undertaken, but no trace of him had been found.

Moments ago, Walters had asked Castile if his men had checked the shack in the woods that Paulette Drew had told her about. He'd replied that he was unaware of such a place. His agents had not encountered any shack in the woods. In that superior, monotone voice of his, he seemed to imply that all of Chief Walters's theories and suggestions were irrelevant and absurd.

Damn, he bugged her. Last Walters had seen of Castile, he'd been wandering off in the direction of the trees near John Manning's house. She hoped she wouldn't have to encounter him for the rest of the night.

What was absurd was that the agents hadn't found the shack. How could they not stumble over the place if they'd been all through the woods? The chief remembered the shack from ages ago, when she was a girl and she'd hike through the woods with her friends to Suicide Leap. She and the girls would sit on the edge of the gorge, dangling their feet over the side. It was a risky thing to do—the drop was more than fifty feet—but as a kid, Walters had felt invincible. On the way there and on the way back, they'd always passed the old shack. She was surprised to learn from Paulette that it was still standing. There was no way that the agents could have missed it. In the morning, no matter what Castile was telling her, the chief planned to send some of her own officers out there to check it out.

Walters walked the periphery of the street, keeping an eye on the kids in their Freddy Krueger masks and zombie makeup. She'd positioned a couple of cops in front of the dark, empty Pierce house, so that no over-eager teen tried to get inside and get a picture of himself in the murder house for his Facebook page. Most of the kids just stood in the street talking and snapping photographs, but a good number of devil girls and boys in hockey masks were traipsing up front walks and ringing doorbells. They couldn't get past the gate at John Manning's house, of course, but Walters observed Mr. Thayer handing out what looked like Hershey bars and a harried Arthur Gorin bestowing cupcakes. The chief had to wonder why Gert wasn't doing the honors.

She couldn't imagine Arthur willingly getting out of his chair and leaving his television.

Walters noticed that no one answered the door when the trick-or-treaters rang Monica Bennett's bell. The lights were all off at the house. A few trotted up the hill to Jessie's house, and the chief saw Jessie handing out something, though she was too far away to have a very good view. But then the chief noticed John Manning emerging from the shadows, heading up to Monica's door.

"No one seems to be home," Walters called over to him.

"We're concerned about Paulette," Manning told her. "We were hoping she might be with Monica."

"She still hasn't come back?" Walters asked. "I've told my officers to be on the lookout for her."

"We're really beginning to worry now," Manning replied.

"Hey, Chief Walters!"

She turned. It was Arthur Gorin, yelling from across the street.

"How about finding my wife while you're at it?" Kids were grabbing cupcakes off his tray as he spoke. "She's supposed to be doing this! She went out about an hour ago and hasn't come back!"

The chief's mind began to race. Paulette Drew missing. Now Gert Gorin.

Her intuition had been right.

Hickory Dell would be dangerous tonight.

Walters hurried over to one of her men standing at his cruiser at the far end of the cul-de-sac. "I want you to get all these kids off the street," she ordered.

"Yes, ma'am," he said.

"Immediately!"

Behind her, she could hear John Manning banging on Monica's door.

Something was wrong. Something was very wrong.

ONE HUNDRED AND TWELVE

How long had she been out?

Paulette staggered out of the woods, clutching her stomach. She seemed to have just woken up, and the memory of the last several hours was a blur.

She'd been in the shack.

She'd found the papers.

Then the man came in—

Paulette removed her hand from her stomach and looked down. The moonlight revealed her hand was covered in blood.

"I've got to warn Jessie," she whispered, and began trudging again up the hill.

She remembered now lying on the floor of the shack, pretending to be dead, waiting for the man to leave. When he finally did, she managed to sit up, and used a shirt from his bag to bind her wound, stanching the bleeding—although not completely, as it turned out. Somewhere in the woods she'd fallen, and lost enough blood that she'd passed out. She should have died on the spot, bled to death.

But she'd opened her eyes and seen Howard sitting beside her. He was as young and handsome as she remembered. Behind him, some distance away, his helicopter was smoldering, sending a long black column of smoke into the air.

"Get up, Paulette," Howard told her. "It's not time."

"But I've been waiting for you," she said.

He smiled. "Indeed. So I can wait a little longer myself. Get up. Go home. Jessie and Abby need you."

When she'd awoken, Paulette had tightened the shirt around her. Her wound was deep, but it was clear it hadn't—miraculously—affected any vital organs. If she could keep pressure on it and limit the bleeding, she'd survive until she could get to a doctor.

She had to survive. She had to make it back to the house.

She had to warn Jessie.

She staggered up the hill and made it to the house.

Her niece looked horrified when Paulette walked through the door.

"Aunt Paulette! Thank God!" she shouted. "But you're hurt!"

"I'll be okay," the older woman said with difficulty as she flopped onto the couch. "We just need to stanch the bleeding."

Jessie pulled open her aunt's shirt and affixed a large adhesive bandage across the wound. "I'll call an ambulance," she said.

"Wait, Jessie," Paulette said. "You've got to listen to me first."

Jessie looked at her with wide eyes.

"Emil did this," Paulette said. "I saw him at the shack. I found papers that he'd used to get across the border. He was using a different name, but the photo was definitely him. I was trying to get out of there and warn you when he came in and stabbed me, leaving me for dead. I think he may have been drunk or high. That was why he didn't realize he hadn't finished the job."

"Oh, God, Aunt Paulette," Jessie said, hugging her aunt. "I'm so sorry."

"Listen to me. You've got to take Abby and get out of here."

"That's what I've been telling her," said John Manning, as he came through the door. "We're leaving now for a hotel. I'll take you to the hospital first, Paulette."

From outside they suddenly heard a loudspeaker booming from one of the police cars: "Everyone off the street! Go back to your cars and leave now! Everyone off the street!"

"What's going on?" Jessie asked.

"I don't know, but we're getting out of here," John said. "I've got my car outside. Let's go."

"Why are we going to a hotel?"

They turned. Abby stood in the doorway of the kitchen, still in her princess costume, minus the cardboard crown.

"Sweetie, you go with Mr. Manning," Jessie said, picking her daughter up and handing him to John. "I'll help Aunt Paulette."

As John carried Abby out to the car, Paulette managed to stand by herself. "I think I'm going to be okay," she told Jessie. "I had a guardian angel looking out for me." She smiled weakly. "I'm just so glad that we're getting out of here. I'm so glad that you've agreed to go—"

She turned.

Jessie was gone.

ONE HUNDRED AND THIRTEEN

Jessie ran down the hill toward the woods in the dark. Abby was safe with John. He'd get her out of here. Aunt Paulette, too.

But she couldn't leave Aaron.

He must have gone to the shack.

And Emil was at the shack.

He'd kill Aaron.

Jessie had let her son die once before.

Not again.

ONE HUNDRED AND FOURTEEN

"**I** suspect my wife is drunk," Todd told Chief Walters. "Probably passed out. That's why she's not opening the door."

"I suggest you check on her," the chief replied, then returned to ordering frightened teenagers back to their cars.

Todd sighed. He approached the house. It seemed so dark, so ominous. The chief seemed worried. Gert Gorin and Paulette Drew were missing. Surely nothing had happened to Monica, too. . . .

He was angry at her. He wanted a divorce.

But he didn't want anything bad to happen to Monica.

Todd felt a little shiver of fear as he inserted the key into the lock and opened the door.

"Monica?" he called as he stepped inside.

The room was hung in shadows. Todd flicked the light switch, but no lights came on. Was there a power outage? He stepped inside and looked around.

From outside he could hear the disembodied voice of the policeman ordering everyone off the street. Occasionally a pulsing red police light swept through the room.

"Monica?" Todd called again.

He hoped there wouldn't be a scene. He hoped she wouldn't start crying again, or beg him to stay, or throw her arms around him. He hoped he'd just find her sleeping off too much wine. He'd set the security system and then quietly leave. He'd report to Chief Walters that Monica was fine.

But somehow he sensed that wasn't going to be the case.

Suddenly a terrible, inexplicable grief washed over him. "Monica!" Todd called out.

He was about to go upstairs when he heard something behind him.

Todd turned.

A kid in a Halloween costume had wandered in, standing just inside the front door. Todd could barely make him out standing in the shadows.

"Trick or treat," he said.

"You've got to get out of here," Todd told the kid. "Don't you hear the cops?"

"Trick or treat," the kid said again, stepping out of the shadows and into a shaft of moonlight. Todd saw that he was a small boy, wearing a hideous mask with bulging eyes and long teeth.

"Geez," Todd said. "What the hell are you supposed to be?"

"I'm supposed to be a little boy," the kid said. "But that wasn't how it turned out."

Suddenly he sprang at Todd, knocking him to the ground. Todd had time only to notice the dead, staring eyes of Gert Gorin looking at him from across the floor before the little boy on top of him said in a voice that sounded like a very old man, "You made my mommy cry."

Then he ripped open Todd's throat with his long, sharp teeth.

ONE HUNDRED AND FIFTEEN

Jessie arrived at the shack. It was hunched in the dark shadows of the woods like a wounded bear.

"Aaron?" she called as she peered inside from the doorway.

He sat on the cot wearing his Halloween costume—the pumpkin head and the long white sheet. Jessie's heart leapt in relief. Thank God he was okay.

"Come on, sweetie, we're getting out of here," she said, approaching him. "Come with me, baby. We're going home."

Aaron didn't budge.

"Come on, Aaron," Jessie said.

She stood in front of him.

Something was wrong.

She lifted the pumpkin head off of him.

It wasn't Aaron.

It was Emil—crouched down, hunched over, making Jessie think it was a little boy under that sheet.

But it was no little boy. It was a monster.

After all these years, Emil's terrible black eyes stared up at her once again.

"Happy Halloween, Jessie," Emil said, and grabbed her arm.

ONE HUNDRED AND SIXTEEN

"**W**here the hell is she?" John was shouting as he came up the front steps.

"She must have gone out the back door," Paulette was saying, shuddering and crying. "Dear God, she must have gone looking for Aaron!"

"Damn it!" John was furious. "She's out of her mind!"

Paulette seemed about to faint. She realized she was still losing a lot of blood.

"We need to get you to a doctor," John said, steadying her.

"No, you've got to find Jessie," Paulette replied.

"Hey!" John shouted down into the street. "Detective Knotts! We need your help!"

The policeman hurried up the hill. "What's going on?"

"Get some men into the woods to look for Jessie Clarkson. She's gone off in search of the little boy."

Knotts lifted his radio to call in the request, but John held up his hand.

"And I need you to get this lady to a doctor and the little girl in my car to safety," he added.

"Okay, Mr. Manning," Knotts said, putting an arm around Paulette to help her down the hill.

"Let me get Abby first," Paulette said, and they moved down the porch steps and over to John's car. But even before they'd gotten there Paulette had a sudden premonition of what they would find—or rather, not find.

Abby wouldn't be in the car.

"Abby!" Paulette screamed.

"Hey, Manning!" Knotts called back toward the house. "There's no little girl in the car!"

But now John was gone too.

ONE HUNDRED AND SEVENTEEN

Chief Walters watched as a squad car rushed Paulette Drew to the hospital. A number of policemen were now swarming into the woods, searching for Jessie Clarkson. The chief wondered how many of the residents of Hickory Dell would go missing tonight. Every last one of them?

She suddenly remembered Todd Bennett had gone in to check on his wife. He hadn't come back outside.

She called some of her men to accompany her into the house. Her hand on her gun, Chief Walters ascended the front steps of the Bennett house. She noticed the door was ajar and the house was dark.

Several cops went ahead of her, entering the house with their guns drawn. One of them attempted to turn on the lights but found the switch was not working.

"We need light in here!" Walters ordered.

Powerful flashlights quickly illuminated the room.

The chief couldn't suppress a gasp of horror.

On the floor were the bodies of Todd Bennett and Gert Gorin. Both of them had had their throats savagely ripped open. A couple of policemen hurried up the stairs.

"Another body up here," one of them shouted down after a couple of seconds had passed. "Appears to be Monica Bennett."

"Jesus Christ," Knotts murmured. "How could Deetz do all of this?"

"He's had help," the chief said. "And I suspect from a very unlikely accomplice."

ONE HUNDRED AND EIGHTEEN

"Let me go!" Jessie shouted, trying to yank herself out of Emil's grip.

"I didn't come all the way back here, more than three thousand miles, to let you slip away from me again," Emil said, tightening his hold on her wrist.

"There are cops everywhere! They'll be in the woods any minute!"

"Is that so? Funny how they've been through here a few times but always seem to miss me," Emil said.

"Why did you come back?"

Emil grinned. Jessie noticed he'd lost several teeth. He stunk, too. "I had a little unfinished business with you," he told her.

"What have you done with Aaron?"

Emil spit on the floor. "I don't know who Aaron is, but I *can* tell you that I killed that bitch aunt of yours." He laughed. "She must have crawled out into the woods to die."

"Aunt Paulette didn't die! She made it home and she's safe!"

This angered Emil, who twisted Jessie's wrist, making her cry out in pain. "Well, that's more than you'll be able to say for yourself."

"You've got to tell me what you know about Aaron!" Jessie insisted.

"I don't know who you're talking about!"

"You bastard!" Jessie writhed in his grip. "I've lived in fear of you for too long! Not anymore. Go ahead and kill me, but first you've got to tell me about Aaron!"

"I don't know who the fuck Aaron is!" Emil shouted at her.

"You must! You've been living here with him!"

Emil looked at her oddly. "I haven't been living here with anybody."

"Aaron," Jessie said. "Our son."

"Son?" Emil hooted in laughter. "Oh, I heard you had a kid. But I heard it was a girl. So if you had a son, it wasn't with me, you slut."

"I did! A son . . . a twin . . . with Abby. You have a son, Emil. And he . . . he looks like you."

Emil let her go. "What the hell you talking about?"

"Somehow you found a way to bring him back, to torment me. But it didn't work. Aaron loves me. He might look like you, but he's not *like* you at all. He's good and sweet."

"You're just trying to fuck with my mind," Emil snarled. "I came back to kill you. Simple as that."

He pulled a long razor from his jacket.

"That's not the only reason you came back," came a voice.

Suddenly, from behind Jessie, a figure rushed in. Jessie was violently knocked aside as the figure tackled Emil to the ground.

"Fuck!" Emil shouted. "Manning! We had a deal, man!"

John punched Emil in the face, causing the razor to fly from his hand and rattle across the floor. John grabbed hold of it and while Emil was still dazed, took hold of Jessie and pushed her outside.

"He said you had a deal," Jessie said, her eyes furiously finding him. "A deal for what?"

"Not now," John said. "I've just got to get you to safety."

"I don't trust you," Jessie said, trying to get away from him. "Not if you have a deal with Emil."

John looked down at her with intense eyes, holding on to her sore wrist with even more strength than Emil had. "Looks like you have no choice in the matter," he said. "You're going to have to trust me whether you want to or not."

ONE HUNDRED AND NINETEEN

Mr. Oswald Thayer walked up the hill toward Jessie's house in shock and grief. Todd was dead. Monica, too. So many dead . . . but he was still alive.

Oh, Antonio, he thought. *What has happened to the world?*

Police were swarming all over the place. They were on the street and in Jessie's house, and the chief was calling for backup. An officer had told him to go back to his house and lock the door, but old Mr. Thayer couldn't think straight at the moment.

What has happened to the world?

He wandered into the dark shadows at the far end of the Clarkson estate, allowing his tears to finally come. He'd loved Todd and Monica like the children he'd never had. Even Bryan and Heather he'd once been very fond of, before Bryan had changed and become so consumed by greed and hedonism. Now they were all gone.

And he, well past his eightieth birthday, still lived.

Up ahead, on the grass, heading toward the woods, he spotted two children. It was Abby Clarkson and a little boy. They shouldn't be outside. . . .

"Abby," Mr. Thayer called. "Children!"

They were holding hands. The little boy looked up at Mr. Thayer, although Abby continued staring straight ahead as she walked.

"Children, you must return home," Mr. Thayer said. "It's not safe for you out here tonight. The world has gone mad."

The little boy looked up at him with sweet dark eyes.

"What's your name?" Mr. Thayer asked him.

The boy let go of Abby's hand.

Then he leapt at Mr. Thayer, sinking his long fangs into the old man's neck.

Mr. Thayer died almost instantly.

He wasn't all that regretful. The world had gone mad, after all.

ONE HUNDRED AND TWENTY

As police sirens wailed and flashing red lights filled up the street below, Aaron climbed off the old man's body and took Abby's hand in his once more.

"You're not scared, are you, Abby?" he asked.

"No," said the little girl.

"Good."

They walked into the woods.

"I'm taking you to a very special place," Aaron told her. "You promise you won't be scared?"

"I promise."

"You'll do anything I tell you?"

"Yes, anything," Abby said.

Aaron smiled.

They headed out toward Suicide Leap.

One Hundred and Twenty-one

From the shack, they could hear Emil moaning and coming to. John tightened his hold around Jessie's arm and pulled her along into the woods. She resisted, but he was stronger and pulled her in a thicket of bushes, clamping his free hand over her mouth.

They could hear Emil shouting, "I'll fucking get you for this, Manning!"

Through the bushes, Jessie could see the madman emerge from the shack, rubbing his chin. He ran off into the woods.

For several moments John held her stone-still, his hand still clamped over her mouth. Finally he whispered in her ear, "If I let you go, you must stay right here and make no sound. He'll hear you and come back. I took his blade, but I'm sure he has another."

Jessie nodded.

"The police will be here momentarily," John told her as he released his hand from her mouth. "The chief called for backup and they were going to swarm the woods."

"Where's Abby?"

"Safe. The police have her."

"Aunt Paulette?"

"They took her to the hospital."

Jessie's eyes burned into John's. "Tell me what kind of deal you have with Emil, and how it came to be."

"I have no deal with him. Not anymore. When I met him in Mexico, I promised not to turn him over to the police. That's what he thought anyway. He didn't know that I'd already contacted the FBI and was working with them to find out what Emil knew. If I had any deal, it was with the FBI. As I gathered material for my book, I kept them fully informed. The note he sent me after his supposed death in the shoot-out gave me some very specific details, which I then shared with the FBI."

"What kind of details?"

"He'd buried a huge fortune in cash and jewels on your property. In the note I sent back to him, I told Emil that I'd return to the United States, buy the property and then split the money with him. But what I was really doing was leading the FBI and the CIA to the loot. We found it the day I moved in, buried so far down bloodhounds hadn't been able to locate it. I've been working with the feds all along, Jessie. I couldn't tell you everything because I wasn't allowed to. It was risky for me to tell you as much as I did."

"So he came back not only to kill me," Jessie said, "but to get his share of the money."

"Yes. Apparently he thought I had it waiting for him. Only there is no money. The feds took it long ago."

Jessie glared at him. "Why should I believe you?"

"Why shouldn't you?"

"Because none of this explains Aaron."

"I can't explain Aaron." John looked up through the bushes to make sure Emil hadn't returned. "Except . . . I think, you were right, Jessie. You *did* manifest him. I tracked down some of the paranormal experts I interviewed for my book *The Killing Room*. I described the situation here and they convinced me that it *was* possible. Aaron came back at the same time that Emil did because he wanted to protect you. Your grief and guilt over Aaron kept him alive all this time. His spirit never crossed over. He stayed here, waiting in a way, watching you. As you got stronger and your grief and guilt receded somewhat, he faded into the background. But he was never really gone. And when he sensed you were in danger—that you were being hurt—he came back."

Jessie felt the tears rolling down her cheeks.

"Emil didn't bring Aaron back," John said. "I was wrong about that. He knows nothing about the boy. It was *you* who brought him back, Jessie. And it's you who is going to have to send him away."

"Never," she whispered. "Not again."

"Jessie, Aaron has killed a lot of people."

"No!" she insisted. "It was Emil."

"I spoke with the FBI earlier today. There's been no trace of Emil's DNA at any of these crimes. But what's clear from all of them is that the killer was small. There's always a wound made first in the legs or thigh or abdomen. That brought the victims down, so that the killer could slice their throats."

"That doesn't mean that it was Aaron. . . ."

"He's been killing people he thinks have hurt you, or could keep him from you. . . ."

"That's crazy! Inga never hurt me!"

"Did you have any words with her right before her death?"

Jessie remembered the pique she'd felt, the foolish jealousy, when Inga had gone over to see John. Aaron had been able to sense that. . . .

"But Mrs. Whitman . . . Detective Wolfowitz . . . Ashton and Piper . . ."

"Well, the kids had been rude to you, and besides, anyone connected to Bryan and Heather was going to be fair game if Aaron was trying to defend you. As for Wolfowitz, he'd been hounding you, upsetting you . . . and Mrs. Whitman had insisted that Aaron wasn't real. She blew his cover, in a way."

Jessie was crying. "None of this makes any sense. Aaron wouldn't hurt anyone!"

"What about the night at the barn with Abby? He was trying to kill her."

"No!" Jessie's voice was getting loud. "They were just playing!"

"Look, Jessie, the first thing we've got to do is get away from Emil. Then we deal with Aaron."

"No!" She pulled away from him, getting to her feet. "You're in league with Emil! You have a deal with him! You want me to send Aaron away again and I won't!"

"Jessie, please be quiet!"

"I'm going to the police!" she seethed. "I'm telling them that you're involved with Emil! I don't believe your story! I heard with my own ears that you have a deal with Emil. You're in league with him. I should have known better than to trust any man again. I'm getting out of here!"

"Jessie, no!"

He reached out for her, but she was too fast.

Jessie bolted away into the woods.

ONE HUNDRED AND TWENTY-TWO

Aaron and Abby had reached the gorge.

"Sit here," Aaron told the girl.

Abby obeyed, her little legs dangling over the sheer drop.

"I have something I have to do," Aaron told her. "Wait for me here. Don't move. I'll be right back."

"Yes, Aaron."

The little boy smiled and headed back into the woods.

ONE HUNDRED AND TWENTY-THREE

John dared not call out after Jessie, fearful he'd draw Emil back to them. Instead he just ran forward through the dark, in the direction he thought Jessie had gone.

He stopped running. He heard something. A snap of a twig.

Was it Jessie?

Or Emil?

He stood very still, on alert.

The woods were utterly and completely dark now. Not a sound from the trees. No wind. No night birds. No owls.

Complete darkness and silence.

It was at that moment that John felt the sharp blade penetrate his side. He pulled back immediately, but it was too late. He felt the warm blood collect under his shirt.

Then, burning through the darkness, he saw the yellow eyes of the boy.

"Aaron," he said.

The boy pounced. But John was ready. He deflected the boy off of him and sent him thudding into a tree.

His little body slid to the ground, collapsing into a heap.

But he was quickly on his feet again, snarling, coming at John, his hands now talons and his teeth as long as a wolf's.

"What kind of devil are you?" John cried, before turning and running into the woods.

ONE HUNDRED AND TWENTY-FOUR

"**M**ommy!"

Jessie stopped running. She was breathing hard and fast. The fragrance of the woods filled her nostrils. Old leaves. Moist earth.

And fear. She could smell her own fear. A sweet and sour fragrance, like something rotting.

"Mommy, I'm scared!"

It was Abby. It was definitely Abby's voice coming through the trees.

But John had told her Abby was safe.

John had lied.

Jessie had been right not to trust him.

"Mommeeeeee!"

"Abby!" Jessie called out, turning and running in the direction of her daughter's voice. "I'm coming, baby! Mommy's coming!"

ONE HUNDRED AND TWENTY-FIVE

"**N**ot so fast, Manning! Not so fast!"

Before John could get very far, Emil Deetz burst into view and tackled him to the ground. Rolling through the carpet of dead leaves and moss, John didn't have the strength to fight him off. The pain in his side was agonizing. He was losing a great deal of blood.

"Here's for what you did to me in the shack," Emil snarled, hauling off and punching John in the face, breaking his nose. Blood sprayed everywhere. "I thought we had a fucking deal!"

"You're a fool," John managed to say, although his words were garbled from the blood in his throat. "There is no money. It's gone. I was working with the FBI the whole time. And they'll be here any moment to pick you up. They've surrounded the woods. There's no way you're getting out of here."

Emil sat on John's chest, glaring down at him. "Well, if that's true, you fuckwad, then I still have enough time to finish you off. I don't like traitors. That fucking Screech Solek was a traitor, but you're even more despicable than he was."

He removed a long razor from his shirt and pressed it against John's throat.

"Hello, Daddy."

Emil's eyes darted up.

Aaron stood beside them, looking at the two men with wide, innocent eyes.

"Who the fuck?" Emil blurted out.

"Emil Deetz," John said, struggling for breath, "meet your son."

ONE HUNDRED AND TWENTY-SIX

Jessie pushed her way through a tangle of bushes and branches and found herself on the edge of Suicide Leap.

Abby stood on the opposite side of the gorge, her frail little figure illuminated by the moon. She was crying.

"Abby!" Jessie called. "Don't move, sweetie!"

Abby was perched on the exact spot over the chasm that Jessie's mother always warned her about. *Stay away from that spot, Jessie. It's very steep there. You could fall.* Jessie's eyes looked down into the fifty-foot drop of rocks and ragged earth.

Abby held out her arms to her. "I told Aaron I wouldn't be scared, but I am, Mommy, I am!" she cried.

"Just stay right there, sweetie, and don't move a muscle! Mommy will come get you!"

"Please hurry, Mommy! I feel like I'm going to fall!"

"Hang on, baby!"

And Jessie began a precarious walk around the rim of the gorge.

ONE HUNDRED AND TWENTY-SEVEN

Emil got up off of John, unnerved by the sight of Aaron, although he still held the razor aggressively in front of him. John quickly got to his feet.

"This ain't my son," Emil spit. "I heard that Jessie only had one kid, and it was a girl."

"You never heard about her partial miscarriage?" John asked.

He noticed that Emil was trembling. He shook his head no.

"Well, she had one," John told him, "and this is the boy she lost." He paused, looking over at Aaron. "Only he's not lost anymore."

Aaron smiled.

From the distance came the sound of Jessie's voice, telling Abby she was coming for her. Both men turned in the direction of the sound.

When they turned back, Aaron was gone.

It was just the distraction John needed to sprint off into the woods himself. He was very grateful for the way adrenaline could surge and give someone strength, just at the moment they needed it most.

ONE HUNDRED AND TWENTY-EIGHT

Jessie lost her footing once, sending an avalanche of pebbles and sand cascading down into the gorge. She gasped but kept from crying out. She didn't want to alarm Abby.

"I'm getting closer!" she called to her daughter. "Just stay where you are!"

She looked up to make sure the girl was still there. She was, standing across the chasm, her thin little arms wrapped around her shaking body. Even telling Abby to back up, to get away from the rim of the gorge, was too risky, Jessie thought. The girl was perched right on the edge. To move any which way, especially with the way she was trembling, was to risk danger.

What was she doing there on the edge anyway?

"Don't move, baby!" Jessie shouted. "Just stand perfectly still!"

She took another few steps. She reasoned if she could get back up to the woods, she could move more quickly, and avoid the danger of the edge. Jessie decided to climb upwards a bit. But as she did so, she glanced across at Abby again.

Aaron was now standing behind her.

"Aaron!" Jessie called out. "Aaron, hold on to Abby!"

"Aren't you worried that I'll fall, too, Mommy?" Aaron asked.

Jessie stopped in her tracks, staring over at the children.

"Or is it just Abby you're worried about?" Aaron asked her.

Jessie watched as the boy placed his hands on Abby's shoulders. In that moment, Jessie knew that Aaron intended to push Abby into the gorge.

She spoke quickly. "Of course I'm worried about you, too, Aaron! I want you *both* to be safe. Stand there! Don't move. I'm coming to get you both!"

"Sometimes I think you only care about Abby," Aaron said, his little voice filled with sadness. "You let her live. You let me die."

"No! Aaron, I love you! I'm so, so sorry! I want us all to be a happy family together!"

"Abby," Aaron said to his sister, "we're going to play a game. We're going to jump off the cliff. You're going to go first."

"No, Abby!" Jessie shouted.

"A game?" the little girl asked, her voice seeming strange and faraway.

"Yes," Aaron told her. "A fun game. Last time you were afraid to jump. But this time you won't be, will you?"

"I won't be afraid," Abby said.

"No, Abby, no!" Jessie screamed. She began to run toward them, mindless of the rocks giving away under her feet. "Abby, stay right there! Mommy's coming!"

"Jump, Abby," Aaron said, as a smile spread across his face. "Jump!"

One Hundred and Twenty-nine

Behind Jessie, Emil had snuck up from the woods. He cared little about the drama that was currently unfolding. He had no idea who the boy was. Maybe this Aaron was his son, maybe he wasn't. It didn't matter to Emil. He also didn't care if he pushed the little girl off the cliff. Emil figured she was probably his daughter, but even that didn't faze him. All he cared about was that he had the chance to kill Jessie. He'd shove her over the cliff the moment he saw the boy push Abby. People would believe she had died trying to save her daughter.

He stepped forward from the trees, his hands out in front of him, ready to topple Jessie to her death. Manning might be right and the cops might be here any minute, but Jessie's death would sure make up for all the trouble she'd caused him.

ONE HUNDRED AND THIRTY

Just at the moment that Abby moved a foot to jump into the dark gorge, John burst from the woods and lunged forward, grabbing the little girl and carrying her to safety.

Aaron screamed in rage. His arms held above him, he levitated several feet into the air over the chasm, his scream reverberating against the rocks like the roar of a lion. Then he gently drifted back to earth, where he whimpered on the edge of the cliff like a lost puppy.

One Hundred and Thirty-one

At that very same moment, Emil leapt on Jessie. But instead of pushing her into the gorge, he lost his footing on the broken rocks and they toppled together.

I will not fall, Jessie vowed to herself, grabbing on to whatever she could to stop her slide into the abyss. Her arms found a sharp outcropping of rock that cut into her side as she clung fiercely to it, but it held firm.

"You fucking bitch!" Emil screamed, still on top of her. He tried to break her grip by banging on her shoulders and arms, and force her over the side, but she held tightly. Her body was like glue to the rock.

"You're more trouble than you were ever worth," Emil snarled, pulling out the razor from his shirt and flashing it in the moonlight.

The blade moved toward her throat.

ONE HUNDRED AND THIRTY-TWO

"**M**ommy!" Aaron called.

Emil looked up. "You know, kid, if you're really my son, you've got some pretty amazing abilities there. I don't know how you got 'em, but you and me together could have quite the time. You don't need these pathetic fuckwads. Help me finish them off!"

"Don't listen to him!" Jessie shouted. "You're my son as much as his! You're not all evil the way he is! I love you, Aaron! And I'm sorry!"

Behind Emil, John was about to leap for the razor.

But Aaron leapt first.

ONE HUNDRED AND THIRTY-THREE

Jessie watched. As if in slow motion, Aaron leapt across the gorge, soaring through the air like an eagle. Or an angel. His face looked much older than his five years. He looked like a grown man, Jessie thought, the way Emil might have looked, if he hadn't gone bad.

No, she realized in the split second of time she had, Aaron looked even more different than that. The boy looked ageless, eternal. His eyes were no longer filled with sadness or rage, but resolve. Maybe even a kind of peace.

Without any effort at all, Aaron landed on Emil's back and took him with him as he plummeted over the edge of the gorge.

ONE HUNDRED AND THIRTY-FOUR

"**J**essie!"

John reached her, scooping her in his arms and carrying her away from the cliff.

"Abby! Where's Abby?" she shouted.

"Right here," John told her, as he set her down beside her daughter at the edge of the woods.

"Why are you crying, Mommy?" Abby asked.

"She doesn't remember anything," John said.

"Why are we out here?" Abby asked again.

Jessie embraced her daughter as all around them the woods came alive with flashing red police lights and the barking of dogs.

"Is everyone okay here?" Chief Walters called, running up to them, a dozen men following her carrying powerful flashlights.

"You'll find Emil Deetz at the bottom of the gorge," John told her. "He tried to kill us all, but Jessie saved herself and her daughter."

One of the flashlights was shone down into the darkness. Sure enough, there was Emil's broken body in a pool of blood.

There was no sign of Aaron.

Not that Jessie expected there to be.

EPILOGUE

Jessie watched Abby and her new friends on the swings at the playground off Houston Street. It was good to be back in the city.

Here she could be anonymous. That was good for the author of a bestselling self-help book. It was also good for a woman the FBI publicly thanked for helping to stop a serial killer in his tracks. The media had gone nuts trying to interview her, but Jessie had refused all requests. There was no way she was going to talk about Emil, or anything that had happened.

Of course, the police and the FBI had blamed Emil for all the killings. There was some talk that he might have had a younger—or at least, a shorter—accomplice. But forensics experts determined that the razor found on Emil's body at the bottom of the gorge had been the one used in all of the killings, though the last victims also had their throats ripped out by what appeared to be teeth—evidence that Emil was psychopathic, the FBI had said. Curiously, however, there was no DNA found on any of the victims, something Chief Walters had found very odd. For a while, she kept trying to find out what had happened to the boy Jessie had taken in.

Jessie had just replied that Aaron had gone away; she had no idea where he was. It was the truth. Still, the chief kept insisting that the child had played a role in all of this, even as the FBI declared that Emil Deetz was the sole killer. The evidence against him was overwhelming: the razor, Aunt Paulette's testimony, and Jessie's and John's stories about how Emil had tried to kill them. It seemed clear that Emil was the Sayer's Brook serial killer. And so the case was closed.

And Jessie was pleased about that.

She'd spent the year after the murders in a state of grief. But her grief had pushed her to finish her book, which turned out to be even more successful than her first. Part of that, no doubt, came from the notoriety of the Sayer's Brook murders. But Jessie always refused to go into details of that time. Her sister, her brother-in-law, and her neighbors had been killed. She insisted on a veil of privacy, and the media, by and large, respected that.

Being back in the city helped. There had been no way she could stay in Sayer's Brook. She had thought it was the place where she needed to start over. As it turned out, she'd already been in the place she was supposed to be. It had felt very good to come back to the city.

Mom had told her once that she could do anything if she put her mind to it, so Jessie had set about rebuilding her life, piece by piece. The first step, she realized, was to respectfully bid Mom's house good-bye. A year later, it still hadn't sold, and neither had Monica's house—murder houses often lingered for long periods on the market. So, until the royalties from the book started pouring in, Jessie might have had a hard time of it financially, except that Mr. Thayer had left all his money to her and to Monica and Todd—and whoever survived would inherit the other's share. The money turned out to be a great help just when Jessie needed it most. Dear old Mr. Thayer. He had been so kind to her. But it couldn't replace what Jessie had lost: a sister. But she realized sadly that she had lost Monica many years before all of this.

Meanwhile, Abby was flourishing in her new school, where she'd made friends easily and quickly. There was no longer any need for imaginary friends.

Aunt Paulette had moved to the city with her, and had managed to land a book deal of her own, about how to use the tarot and psychic intuition to help deal with life's problems. It was good to have Aunt Paulette nearby after everything they'd been through.

But for a while, Jessie had kept some distance from John. She believed him now when he said that he had never intended to cause her any hurt by withholding his connection to the FBI and to Emil. But there had just been too many secrets in Jessie's life, and just too many disappointments with men. So for a while, Jessie went solo. She needed the space.

But lately, she'd been e-mailing and talking on the phone with John. He wanted to see her. So she told him he could come to New York. She'd have dinner with him. She had no idea what, if anything, might come of their friendship. But she owed him a great deal; he had saved Abby's life. John had had his own grief as well. Caleb had been a friend of his, as well as an employee. And his nose would never quite be the same after being broken. He sent Jessie a photo, and she thought it made him look rugged. She was looking forward to seeing

John. After all, he was the only one in the world besides herself who had lived through, and remembered, the full story of what had happened that night in the woods and at the gorge.

She thought of Aaron often, though her dreams and visions of him were gone. Jessie slept peacefully through the night now. No more nightmares. But in her waking moments, that little face with its big brown eyes often came to her. She knew that Aaron had done some very bad things. But he'd been just a child—a child who'd lived in some kind of netherworld between life and death, between good and bad, between right and wrong. He hadn't known what he was doing. She was glad that Emil had been given the blame for everything that had happened, because ultimately, he *was* to blame.

As was she. Jessie would have to live with the guilt that because of her rash involvement with Emil Deetz, thirteen people had been killed. People she loved—for all their problems, Jessie had loved Monica. And Todd . . . how Jessie grieved Todd. He had tried to do right by her. And kind old Mr. Thayer and her dear friend Inga. Jessie felt the weight of all their deaths, and carried their memories with her every day, even those who had been cruel to her, like Bryan and Heather and Gert Gorin.

But she had a choice: either to let the grief and the guilt take over her life or find a way to live so that she honored all those who had died. In the past, it had been Jessie's guilt and grief—and fear and doubt—that had kept her a prisoner. It had also kept Aaron from resting in peace, keeping his spirit trapped between this world and the next. Jessie now resolved that grief and guilt and fear and doubt would no longer rule her decisions or color her life. There was nothing to fear, she had discovered, nothing at all. That was the basic point of her book.

And if ever she needed a reminder of that basic truth, all she had to do was look at the little crayon drawing that she'd had framed and hung over her desk.

It was a little stick figure of a boy holding the hand of a stick figure of a woman.

At the bottom of the drawing was printed one letter.

A.

Nail-Biting Suspense from

Kevin O Brien

Disturbed	978-0-7860-2137-6	$7.99US/$9.99CAN
Final Breath	978-0-7860-1777-5	$6.99US/$8.49CAN
Good Intentions	978-1-57566-311-1	$5.99US/$7.99CAN
Killing Spree	978-0-7860-2987-7	$5.99US/$6.99CAN
The Last Victim	978-0-7860-2725-5	$5.99US/$6.99CAN
Left for Dead	978-0-7860-2889-4	$7.99US/$9.99CAN
Make Them Cry	978-0-7860-2084-3	$4.99US/$5.99CAN
Next to Die	978-0-7860-2890-0	$7.99US/$9.99CAN
One Last Scream	978-0-7860-1776-8	$6.99US/$9.99CAN
Only Son	978-1-57566-211-4	$5.99US/$7.99CAN
Terrified	978-0-7860-2138-3	$9.99US/$10.99CAN
Vicious	978-0-7860-2136-9	$7.99US/$9.99CAN
Watch Them Die	978-0-7860-2888-7	$7.99US/$9.99CAN

Available Wherever Books Are Sold!

Visit our website at **www.kensingtonbooks.com**